LITTLE PRETTY THINGS

ALSO BY LORI RADER-DAY

The Black Hour

LITTLE PRETTY THINGS

A NOVEL

LORI RADER-DAY

SEVENTH STREET BOOKS®
AN IMPRINT OF PROMETHEUS BOOKS
59 JOHN GLENN DRIVE • AMHERST, NY 14228
www.seventhstreetbooks.com

Published 2015 by Seventh Street Books®, an imprint of Prometheus Books

Cover image © Media Bakery
Cover design by Nicole Sommer-Lecht

Inquiries should be addressed to
Seventh Street Books
59 John Glenn Drive
Amherst, New York 14228
VOICE: 716–691–0133
FAX: 716–691–0137
WWW.SEVENTHSTREETBOOKS.COM

19 18 17 16 15   5 4 3 2 1

Library of Congress Cataloging-in-Publication Data

Rader-Day, Lori, 1973-
  Little pretty things / Lori Rader-Day.
    pages ; cm
  ISBN 978-1-63388-004-7 (softcover) — ISBN 978-1-63388-005-4 (ebook)
  1. Hotel cleaning personnel—Fiction. 2. Murder—Investigation—Fiction.
I. Title.

PS3618.A3475L58 2015
813'.6—dc23

                                                                      2015001984

Printed in the United States of America

For Jill and the girls,
Jesse and Addison, and Kim
And for Greg, of course

CHAPTER ONE

The walkie-talkie on the front desk hissed, crackled, and finally resolved into Lu's lilting voice: "At what point," she said, "do we worry the guy in two-oh-six is dead?"

The couple across the counter from me glanced at one another. Bargain hunters. We only saw two kinds of people at the Mid-Night Inn—Bargains and Desperates—and these were classic Bargains, here. The two kids, covered in mustard stains from eating home-packed sandwiches, whined that the place didn't have a pool. The mother had already scanned the lobby for any reference to a free continental breakfast. We didn't offer continental breakfast, not even the not-free kind.

I slid their key cards to them, smiling, and flicked the volume knob down on the radio before Lu convinced them they'd prefer to get back in their car and try their luck farther down the road.

"Which room are we in, again?" said the woman.

"Two-oh-four," I said.

"And you said we could go to Taco *Bell*," cried the little girl, five or so. A glittering pink barrette that must have started the day neatly holding back her corn-silk hair now clung by a few strands. She threw herself at her mother's feet and wailed into the carpet. "But they don't even have a Taco *Bell*."

The boy, a few years older, had pressed himself against the glass door to the bar. "Mommy," he hissed. "All these people are drinking *alcohol*."

It was after nine—way past someone's bedtime. The parents and I negotiated by a series of glances between the key cards and each other. They wouldn't get tacos, a free breakfast, or a swim, but the odds seemed better on a dead body in the room next door. "Why don't I get you a room with a little more—privacy?" I took back the cards and pretended to click around on the computer for better options.

7

Under the kids' keening and questions, Lu's low, complaining voice murmured on the radio, and then the door chimed, signaling another visitor.

The Mid-Night Inn had only twelve operational rooms, seven even-numbered upstairs and five odd-numbered down, plus the lobby and bar. In the right light, it had old-school charm. The balcony's wrought-iron railing swirled in a fancy design that snagged our uniform skirts' hems. "Filigree," Billy called it, when he accused us of never sweeping the cobwebs from it. It was a nice touch. We had a single-star rating from some hospitality association, left over, surely, from better days.

Now the Mid-Night was a step above a roadside dive. Technically, it *was* a roadside dive, nestled between the roaring interstate and an overpassing state road out of town that led into the dusty country-side. The motel was a big two-story *U* of rooms, all with exterior doors on a wraparound walkway, all overlooking a slim patch of grass and a couple of struggling crabapple trees. Billy called that the "courtyard," and the eight closed rooms on the other side of the bar that had been left to ruin, "the south wing." At the open end of the courtyard, only a rusty chain-link fence tangled with scrub and brush separated the Mid-Night from the rushing cars below.

In the summer, the Mid-Night's old, blinking neon sign regularly pulled guests off the highway. We got minivan parents who'd misjudged how long they could listen to their kids howl and lone drivers who found they couldn't keep themselves awake until they reached Indianapolis. We often got people who used their expensive, high-tech phones to search for the cheapest overnight stay they could get.

But now in the off season, people could do better and usually did. I could say the Mid-Night was at least a clean place to lay your head. But I was the one who cleaned it, and I knew that wasn't true.

Out of the corner of my eye, I saw the new arrival, a woman in a long coat, hesitate at the door. Her, the Bargains, the dead guy in two-oh-six—this was officially a crowd for a Monday night in the spring, especially since it was just me and Luisa holding down the fort while Billy had his night off. Lu was out pretending to clean up the courtyard while I kept the front desk, and tomorrow morning, we'd flip back to mornings for the rest of the week. I'd get to clean up vending-machine taco-chip crumbs after these cheapskates got back on the road, while she fended off anyone who came looking for a free Danish. Or comment cards. We didn't offer comment cards, either.

I handed over the updated key cards to the Bargains. "You have a nice night," I said. The mother had already decided I was some kind of simpleton. She and her husband each pulled a child along behind them toward the door. I'd put them as far away from the dead guy's room as I could—which located them right over the Mid-Night bar, open 'til two in the morning.

The woman at the door still hadn't decided if she was coming in. She held the door for the family, letting the parade of misery pass back out into the night and watching after them for far too long.

I'd already known there existed a breed of women who made the rest of us notice how far off the mark we were, but they didn't often stumble into the Mid-Night. This woman was their queen. Her clothes draped as if they'd been trained. Her golden hair hung loose and perfectly careless. She was tall and angular, with a chiseled masterpiece of a jaw.

In the middle of the floor lay the sparkling barrette from the little girl's hair. I slipped around the desk and plucked it up, watching the woman all the while. She tucked a strand of hair behind her ear as we both watched the family tramp toward the stairs with their mismatched luggage. The open door let in the smell of green cornfields and wet grass.

I pressed the barrette against my palm and slid it into my pocket.

"Can you pull the door?" I said. "You're letting in bugs."

It was cheap, but all I had. Compared to her, I was shorter, chubbier, mousier. Poorer—that went without saying. I looked down at what I was wearing. Ouch. Her raincoat, as supple as butter and with the belt tied in a casual knot at the back, probably cost more than I made in a month. It wasn't even raining anymore.

She closed the door, a gracious smile cranking up to blind me as she swept across the lobby.

But then she stopped. The smile cut short. "Juliet? Juliet Townsend, is that you?"

A thousand thoughts shoved into my mind at the same time, jamming the works. I couldn't think. I couldn't speak. On the desk, the walkie-talkie hissed and crackled. "Juliet?" Lu's voice, turned to nearly zero, sounded like a bomb going off in the empty lobby. "Jules, I'm serious, pick *up*."

The woman looked at the radio unit on the counter, then me. The smile came back, a few megawatts shy of its original glow. That super-star grin I'd almost received was reserved for customer service. For getting the best room available, and maybe an extra set of towels. This smile—well, this was the surprised-slash-horrified gesture reserved for ex–best friends discovered working below their potential in roadside crap-heaps.

My brain finally jarred loose, throwing out the shard of a memory: a blond ponytail bouncing against thin shoulders, three paces ahead. Nothing holding me back but my aching lungs and burning thighs, and nothing ahead of me but that chiseled jaw, resolutely set toward the finish line.

"Madeleine Bell," I said. The name had always meant the same thing to me. Another loss. Another very near miss.

On the walkie-talkie, Lu's voice transitioned from irate English into furious Spanish. I held up a finger to Maddy Bell and grabbed the handset.

"Please tell me," I said, my teeth clenched, "that Señor Two-oh-Six has requested fresh towels."

Lu said, "There is a *smell* coming out of there—"

"That's far above my pay grade, and yours," I said. "Let Billy handle it tomorrow."

"Fine by me," Lu said. "*You'll* be behind the cart, and *you'll* have to clean up the body."

"I have a guest." I glanced back at Maddy. She'd turned her head, pretending to admire the lobby décor. She probably didn't get a lot of gold-leaf wallpaper and garage-sale geegaws in the places she normally stayed. "And then I'm probably going to need to take my break," I said. I needed a few minutes to die of embarrassment. Just ten minutes to hang myself from shame.

"Roger," Lu said.

Billy insisted we use proper military com lingo when we used the radios, all those over-and-outs, rogers instead of yeses. He'd never been in the military, of course. He only knew what he'd learned from Stallone movies. But when he was out of earshot—which wasn't often, since he lived in room one-oh-one—we took liberties. It was a crummy job. Liberties were what we had, instead of health insurance or bonuses or even a schedule that allowed us to take a second job. Instead of dignity.

I put down the radio and found Maddy watching me. "So you, uh, need directions or something?" Which didn't make any sense. She'd been gone ten years, but surely she remembered the way to her old house. Surely she remembered there were better places to stay forty minutes in either direction.

"A room," she said. "If you have one."

I tapped around the computer's reservation system for time. "How many nights?"

"It's weird, isn't it? Seeing you here?" she said.

"Weird for you," I said. "I'm here a great deal. Just one night, then?"

"One night. Passing through. I didn't think I'd run into anyone."

I looked up. "Hoping you wouldn't, you mean?"

"Maybe I was hoping I *would*. Juliet, really," she said. "How would I have known?"

"I heard you were a big shot in Chicago," I said.

She nodded, slowly, letting my statement hang in the air between us.

"How many guests?" I said. The words almost got stuck in my throat. I'd just spotted the largest diamond I'd ever seen in real life or on television on her left ring finger. Were there any finish lines Maddy Bell wouldn't reach before everyone else? The diamond was cartoonishly big. The palms of both my hands started to itch. I wiped them on my jeans. "How many in the room, I mean?"

"Just me." For a moment the sound of my typing filled the lobby, and then she gasped. "Oh, Jules, I totally forgot. Your dad. I'm so— God, that must have been awful."

Debilitating, actually. And I knew what had reminded her. Here I was, working a dank motel's lobby desk in the same town where she'd left me. No one could have chosen this life. There must be some sad story of ambition thwarted, opportunity denied. And there was. My dad's sudden death—a heart attack, far too young—during my second semester of college had drained my ambition and our family finances. If I'd gone to any other high school in the state, maybe I'd have been the star distance runner and would have been at college on full scholarship. But I'd gone to Midway High in Midway, Indiana, where Maddy Bell's best times still clung to the halls, where Maddy Bell's trophies still gleamed in the cases, ten years on. I knew the records were still up at Midway because all my almost one year of college had prepared me for was a spot as a third-string substitute teacher there. They called once a year or so when all they needed was a warm body, and I went in, gladly. That is, on days when I could tear myself away from the cleaner's cart at the Mid-Night Inn.

"And your mom?" she said.

"She's fine."

"Glad to hear it."

She'd always liked my family better than her own. Maddy had arrived in Midway with ready-made parental tragedy. Her mother rumored to be a suicide, and her dad remarried to a woman Maddy was determined not to like. Her dad had died more recently, quietly and without much fanfare in the local paper. There hadn't been a funeral. "Your dad—"

She waved away the sentiment. She'd never been as close with her dad as I'd been with mine.

"Well, Gretchen comes in for a drink sometimes," I said. I nodded through the glass doors that led to the inn's bar. A look of horror crossed Maddy's face. Her stepmother was apparently not the person she'd hoped to run into. "But not tonight. Not yet, anyway."

I slid a guest-info card across the counter for her and held out a pen. Up close, she nearly glowed. I couldn't look, for fear I would stare. Her perfume wafted over the desk, equal parts spicy and sweet—and warm, somehow, like exotic cookies fresh from the oven. Under the harsh fluorescents, the diamond in her ring caught the light and twinkled.

The door chimes rang again, this time for Lu and the rattling cart. Maddy glanced over her shoulder at the noise, and beamed her supernova smile in Lu's direction. Maddy turned back to hand me her card and pen, and behind her, Lu pulled her long, dark hair into a smoother ponytail and mugged a *la-di-da* hip wiggle. She gave Maddy's clothes a long, lurid look, then glanced down at herself, just as I had. I slipped the pen into my pocket.

"So there are drinks? In there?" Maddy jerked her head in the direction of the dark doors of the bar. "I could sure use one."

"Right through there," I said. "Tell the bartender you're a—tell her I sent you."

"Why don't you join me?"

Lu raised her eyebrows in my direction. We'd be talking about this, whatever my answer.

"I—" I'd meant to take my thirty-minute break to get out of Maddy's rarified, spice-cookie air, to brace myself for the knowledge that I'd be the one to clean her fair locks out of the shower drain in room two-oh-two the next morning.

"Please?" Maddy said. She leaned across the counter, and instead of taking the key card I'd left within her reach, she put her hand on mine. She had the skin of an infant. "We could catch up."

I blinked down at the diamond. Catching up with Maddy was the one thing I'd never been able to do.

CHAPTER TWO

The bar didn't have a real name, but everyone called it "the Mid-Night," too. No one who frequented the place seemed to have a problem keeping them straight. The bar was named for the motel; and the motel was named for the town; and the town, Midway, was named for the fact that it wasn't one place or another. We were halfway to anywhere that mattered, stuck.

The bar was badly lit, badly arranged, badly cleaned. The cleanliness issue Lu and I could take credit for, but the rest of the management decisions were Billy's. He knew what the regulars liked: cheap beer, keep it coming. They didn't care about new linoleum to replace the warped floors or painting over the ancient graffiti in the bathroom stalls. They didn't want the old mirror over the back of the bar re-silvered. They didn't want to see themselves. They lined up at the bar, watched the TV without sound, and drank. A subculture had developed over time from the group of nodding acquaintances, mostly men, who parked on stools side by side and hardly said a word to one another.

That was the scene as I led Maddy through the lobby doors into the dark, hoping to go unnoticed. An undercover mission. We got away with it for a second. A couple of the regulars turned around—there were a few Midway High faces, some hardened regulars my mom's age or older, a couple of people I knew but ignored—but then Maddy's presence was noticed. *Felt.* By the time we'd sat ourselves at a table in the corner and waved over a couple of drinks, three of the guys had dismounted from their barstools to head home. The others stayed to stare and pretend not to.

"I don't even know where to start," Maddy said. "Has it really been since graduation?"

It had been longer. Maybe she didn't remember, or want to remember, that the last time we'd spoken had been weeks before the ceremony meant to send us on our separate ways. Precisely, it had been since the day Maddy had beaten me for the last time. And we hadn't even been running.

Suddenly I remembered Maddy hunched over the edge of a hotel bed, her knuckles white against a shiny, patterned bedspread. The old disgust rose in my throat.

I swallowed around it. "Did you get your invitation to the reunion?" The reunion was why I knew where Maddy lived. Our classmate Shelly Anderson, who was planning the event, worked at the bank, where all deposits of the informational kind had to be made at her window. You always left richer than you came in.

Our beers arrived. The bartender, Yvonne, winked at me.

"Let me get this round, since I'm holding you hostage." Maddy reached inside an inner pocket of the coat and pulled out a bill. "Keep the change," she said to Yvonne.

This round? I took a gulp of my beer, avoiding Yvonne's look. I was sure the bill had been a fifty.

Yvonne stalked away with a sharp glance over her shoulder.

"The reunion," Maddy said with an odd smile. She pivoted her beer bottle on the table but didn't drink. "Right."

"It's a Midway High reunion in here every night of the week," I said, scanning the bar. A few sets of eyes dropped away. "Ten years."

"It seems longer," Maddy said.

To me, it seemed shorter. But maybe that was because I hadn't gone anywhere or done anything. Maybe we all experienced life not by the hour, but by the texture and taste. I hated to think it. If that was how time measured itself, I was still a knobby-kneed kid in an over-sized track team uniform. I hadn't moved on. But neither had most of our high-school class. We saw each other at the grocery store, at Mike's Hardware, at the movie theater. A lot of them went to church together. Some of them had kids in the same class at the elementary school.

We didn't need a reunion. A Saturday in some party room, going-out clothes, and Maddy down from Chicago—

"The reunion wasn't last night, was it? Is that why you're here?"

I'd hoped not to be working the night of the party, so that if anyone stopped by the bar on their way home, I wouldn't have to hear about it. But now I was strangely panicked that I'd missed it.

"Soon. This coming weekend, I think." She frowned at the table. "I doubt I'll stick around for it. I don't have much to report."

I let my beer bottle hit the table a little too hard. Yvonne and the guys at the bar turned in our direction. "Are you kidding me?" I said.

"What?"

"You're probably the only one of us who has anything to show for the last ten years," I said. "Except the ones who are already married or divorced or have four kids or credit-card bills up to their eyeballs. Look at yourself. Look at this place." I knew what I meant to say, even if I hadn't said it well. She didn't belong here, had probably never belonged here.

I'd always thought I didn't belong in Midway, either, that someday I'd get out and make something new of myself. But the truth was that I belonged to my hometown in a way I hadn't been able to shake, and now it felt too late to try.

"You always did think more of me than I did myself," she said.

"It was hard not to look up to you, standing on the lower-medal podium every week." I plucked at the wrapper on my beer. I hadn't meant to say that.

"Maybe I should have thrown a few races." She pushed her bottle away.

"That's hardly what I wanted, Maddy." That was not the truth. Back then, I would have accepted any top placing, however it came to me.

"Well, then," she said. "You should have run faster."

That stung. What did she think I'd been doing all those times I came in second? "I ran as fast as I could for as long as I could," I said.

She looked over my shoulder for a long moment, toward the door. "That's what I was doing, too. I was probably only faster because I was being chased."

By me, she meant. I saw again the blond hair beating against thin shoulders. The back of Maddy's head had been my view of high school, and not just on the track. I was the friend who didn't have a life of her own, the parasite, the loser. The journalism staff had even made some joke about it in our senior yearbook.

In some ways, the ten years felt like ten minutes.

I leaned back in my chair. My break was almost over. I thought ahead to the long night at the front desk, and then the early morning behind the cleaning cart. Maddy had one night back in Midway. I had the rest of my life. And yet, I didn't want to spare even these few minutes on her. "What are you in town for, then?"

"Business," she said.

"What do you do?"

She shrugged. "It's not that interesting."

I felt color rising on my neck. "Do you travel a lot?"

"For work?"

"For any reason," I said.

She smiled a little and leaned forward, waiting for the punch line. "A little."

"You've been to New York? Paris? Tokyo, where?"

She understood me now. The smile slid away. "All those places."

"You've got—I don't even know how many thousands of dollars of diamond on your hand. Is he handsome?"

She blinked at the ring, then nodded.

"After you leave tomorrow, I'll be changing the sheets on your bed. Your job—your *life*—has to be more interesting than mine."

"But you could . . . sorry, no. I'm not going to give you any advice." She checked her watch and seemed surprised by how late it was. An expensive watch, I was sure. "You really shouldn't take any direction from me. Things aren't always as they seem, you know. They weren't then, and they aren't now. Envy blinds you."

I stood up, my chair raking against the floor. I wasn't the one handing out insultingly high tips on cheap beer tabs and pretending things between us were even. "My break is over," I said.

"I didn't mean—that's not—I meant that I'm the one who's envious." She looked up at me with tears in her eyes. Very dramatic. If only she'd had time for the school play back in high school, she might be clutching an Academy Award now, too. "This isn't how I wanted it to be."

"So—"

"I didn't hope to run into you," she said. "I knew I would. I knew you were working here, Jules, and I wanted to see you."

She waited to see how I would take this. "Well, you're seeing me," I said.

"I just—I wanted to make sure I hadn't imagined it all. That I hadn't wasted all my time. So much of it was wasted. Or lost completely." She stood and glanced uneasily at the bar. They'd be watching openly now. A low song on the jukebox kept things civilized. She lowered her voice under the music. "We were friends, weren't we? Really friends, not just competitors? Right? Before all that?"

All that encompassed so much, I couldn't tell if she remembered. *All that* could have meant nothing or anything. Or everything. I felt the pen in my pocket digging into my hip and was thankful for its distraction. "No," I said. "I've had a lot of time to think about it. I don't think we were."

She went still. "Don't say that."

"We were rivals, Maddy. Practices, tournaments—state." She flinched. She remembered. "We just spent a lot of time together, and we were kids. It's not the same thing as being friends."

"It could have been."

"It wasn't. How else do you explain it? As soon as track season was over, we never spoke again. Ten years, Maddy. I've been in the same place. I've been easy to find."

"You don't have to stay here," she said.

"That's not what I'm saying, and you know it. Besides, you—you don't know anything about me."

"I used to," she said. Her jaw was set with the same determination she'd always engaged to stay a half meter ahead of me for an entire two-mile race. "The Juliet Townsend I used to know wanted to run from this place as fast as she could."

"I'm not sure what happened to the Madeleine Bell I used to know," I said. I felt raw, and mean. "You know where they're having it, right? The reunion?"

She started to say something, then thought better of it. She pulled her coat tighter around her. "Let's just say there's a lot about me you don't know, too," she said.

Fair enough. I turned to leave.

"Juliet, wait."

She caught up with me at the door to the lobby and laid a soft hand on my arm. I could see Lu at the desk, leaning her chin on her fist and watching the dark parking lot. For a moment, my life split in two and I was the me I could have been and also the me I'd become.

"It could still be," she said.

"What are you talking about?"

"It could still be the same as being friends. We could—it could be real this time. We could get things right. Chicago's not that far away, and there's the reunion. Maybe I will come back for it, even if they're holding it at the same place—" Her face darkened. "God, what are the odds? But there are some things—I'd like to have a chance to talk to you sometime, really talk. Just think about it, OK?"

Clearly she had no idea how little happened around Midway in a given week. I wouldn't be able to think about anything else. I slipped out from under her hand and opened the door.

I led Maddy through the lobby, Lu watching, and pointed in the direction of her room. Outside, a lean silver car had parked nose to nose with the vending and ice machines. It could only be hers. As soon as Maddy had swept through the lobby, Lu turned on me.

"What the—"

"I don't want to talk about it," I said.

"All this time I thought I was your fanciest friend."

Lu lived in a ranch house overstuffed with her husband, three kids, and mother-in-law. She might have the same terrible job I did, but she'd figured out a few things I hadn't. "You're pretty fancy," I said.

Lu's smile was close-mouthed to hide her crooked teeth. "So why is she here?"

"Business, she said."

"No, I mean here. At the Mid-Night. Did you see her? She could stay anywhere. She could have stayed at—hotels I don't even know downtown, the Luxe even."

I glanced uneasily at Lu. Maddy knew all about the Luxe. But she'd gotten a room here to talk to me. Hadn't she admitted it? But she could have stopped by with her olive branch and still stayed somewhere else. And what had she actually said, in the end?

A pair of headlights grazed over the lobby. The silver car was leaving. Maybe staying somewhere else was the plan she'd had in mind all along.

Why had she come? The car, the diamond, the soft raincoat. The forty-two-dollar tip on an eight-buck bar tab. The room paid for but not used. Maddy Bell certainly wasn't a Bargain.

Which could only mean she was desperate.

CHAPTER THREE

Lu pushed the cart into its closet. I locked the lobby doors behind us and dropped the keys into the slot for Billy.

As we walked out to my car, I scanned the parking lot. Maddy hadn't come back.

"She got a room, didn't she?" Lu said. "Weird."

I wondered why she'd bothered. What had she accomplished? Was putting me in my place worth the price of a room at the Mid-Night? But the Mid-Night was a cheap place to stay, and Maddy could clearly afford to throw money around. "One less room to clean tomorrow," I said, grabbing a brochure that had been tucked under my windshield wiper and throwing it in the backseat.

"At least she didn't bring a guy back," Lu said as we got in. "And then you'd have to clean up? After your friend had freaky sex all over one of the rooms?"

"Lu," I said.

"You don't think she has freaky sex with *some*body? Did you see that ring?"

"Lu, please."

We drove the rest of the way to Lu's place in silence. The Mendoza house was small and plain, on a clean, pleasant street where people invested heavily in flower boxes and kept the paint on their shutters touched up. The house was dark, but Lu's husband had left the porch light on for her.

"Goodnight," I said. "See you bright and early."

She hesitated with her hand on the door. I could already feel how Maddy's visit had changed how Lu thought of me. Lu and I had worked together for a few years now, and we were friends. Really friends—what Maddy had wanted from me. Lu was older than I was by about ten years, and she had a husband who remembered to leave on the porch light. We didn't have a lot in common, but we could talk for hours about what we watched on TV or how we were so glad we didn't live at the Mid-Night the way Billy did. About her three rowdy kids and how coming to work was like a vacation from all their noise. About her parents, back in Mexico, who she missed, or her mother-in-law, who she wished would get her own place. About how she might get her real-estate license someday. About the life she was working toward.

It's not like I hadn't ever told her anything about me. I'd told her plenty.

But now we'd both had a look at Maddy Bell and at the world outside our reach. Her real-estate license must have seemed so small, so far away.

"Yeah," she said, finally opening the door. "See you."

I stopped for gas, counting out the few bills I had on me beforehand. The numbers on the pump turned fast. Inside, I leaned against the counter and chatted with Dickie Buggit, the attendant. We'd gone to Midway High together. Sometimes I had to remind myself that I'd gone out with Dickie Buggit once—oh my God, why? But then there were a lot of guys in town like Dickie and not a lot of guys not like Dickie. Out of all the guys I'd gone out with, gone home with—hardly any—Dickie was the only one I could still be friends with. And by friends, I meant buy gas from. I counted out my change, considered a lottery ticket.

The door chimed.

"Aw, hell," Dickie said under his breath. He reached for the phone, running his finger down a list of numbers taped to the wall.

A woman bundled in two sweaters, a scarf, and house slippers stood blinking in the bright light of the station. Teeny, as everyone called her, walked the streets of Midway as the town ghost—alive, but barely there. For a short, slight wisp of a woman, tiny indeed, she had a large presence, showing up in unlikely places, uninvited and unwanted, mumbling some phrase or another to herself on repeat. She came out to the Mid-Night a lot, but there wasn't much to steal there.

Dickie talked in low tones into the phone. I went to an end-cap to take a look at the audio-book selection: westerns and thrillers marked down, and a few get-rich schemes at full price. I watched Teeny shopping the aisles. She liked color. A handful of gumballs went into her cardigan pocket. She considered and put back a pack of gummy bears.

By the time she made the round trip through the store, her sweater pocket bulged with a stash of bright, round candies.

Dickie hung up and leaned over the counter. "Come on, Teeny," he said. "If you're going to steal, at least be sneaky about it."

She didn't seem to hear him.

"How much are those?" I said. "The candies."

"Five cents apiece, for crying out loud," Dickie said. "Cheapest thing in the store."

The cheapest thing could still be too much. "You called the cops on her?"

"Nah, that place she lives," he said. "She gets loose, they come pick her up. She's going to get hit on the street one of these days."

He made her sound like someone's loose mongrel dog. I glared at him. "Let me pay for some of those." I turned out my pockets, letting whatever change I had fall on the counter.

Dickie shrugged, rang me up.

Teeny was making for the door. I followed her out into the parking lot, looking around for the car or van coming for her. "Hey, Teeny," I said. "Let's wait for your ride, OK?"

She ignored me, shuffling past my car, the pumps, and toward the street.

"Teeny, stop—stay here a second." I came alongside her and reached for her arm. It was thin in the bulky sweater, but she was strong. She ripped her arm away from me. The overfilled pocket swung around, and the candies arced out, pinging against the asphalt around us and rolling in a million directions.

"Sorry, sorry," I said, running to grab a few before she darted for them and Dickie's prediction came true. When I came back, Teeny was kneeling in the lot, gathering the candies to her. She mumbled something under her breath. "I said I was sorry."

I walked the lot, collecting the candies, and brought them back to her, getting mad. What was wrong with her? Why couldn't she snap out of—whatever this was? Why wasn't anyone caring for her, keeping her safe?

The last handful of gumballs returned to the pile, I stood up and watched the street, fuming at myself for getting involved. "I'm going," I said. "It's late."

"The girls," Teeny said.

"What?"

"The girls."

She looked up at me, her eyes wide and concerned. She could have been a hundred years old, or twenty-five, I couldn't tell. She was younger, though, than I'd ever guessed, if I'd ever given any thought to her at all.

"The girls who? Which girls?"

"The girls, the girls." The words were sing-song, but they made sense to her.

"OK, great," I said. "I hope they get rides home, too."

My old car didn't want to start, but at last it did, and I was treated to the gas needle's short trip from empty to not-quite-empty. I drove off with a last glance in the rear-view at Teeny seated in the lot, alone. Some of the candies had been transferred to her mouth. One cheek was distended, full, like a child's.

Where I lived, the porch light was dark.

Which is not to say I couldn't find my way. The whole street was well lit. That was the kind of street it was: houses old but kept up, the grass green and neatly edged. No matter what time I came home, somebody on the block was probably noticing, flicking their curtain back to catch the details. The neighborhood was nicer than Lu's, maybe, the yards a little bigger. But at my house, we'd long ago given up on flower boxes.

My mom was fine, I'd told Maddy.

The first lie I'd told her.

I let myself in the front door, careful to be quiet. My mom slept badly, which meant she could be trying to sleep at any time of the day or night.

She had the time. She didn't work. She didn't cook or clean much. She didn't have friends or make crafts or read. I'd moved back home after my dad's death to get my mom through the cycle of grief. But we hadn't cycled. I was still living in the room I had in high school. The same wall color, the same furniture. I still had trophies from some of my big races on the dresser. My mom still slept in the bed my dad had left that last morning. His clothes were still in the drawers and closet. We were . . . still.

"Juliet, is that you?" my mom called from the kitchen.

Who else could it be? I'd gotten one shoe off, and carried it around the corner. A low-watt light over the stove barely lit the room. She sat at the table in her robe.

What I'd learned from my dad's death was that the Townsends were made of flimsy stuff. One weak heart, one weak mind, and, for baby bear, a weak will.

"Hey, Mom. Thought you'd be in bed."

"I was getting a glass of water."

There was no glass in front of her. I dropped my shoe, kicked off its match, and went to the cupboard. When I set the glass of water in front of her, she reached for it idly, as though it had been there the whole time.

"How was work?"

"The same," I said. That's what I always said. Not just for work, but for everything there was to say. Our lives had been wider, deeper, once. I couldn't help thinking that my parents had had bigger plans for me than this. You couldn't name a little girl Juliet without thinking she would turn out to be something more than a motel housekeeper. At the very least, you might expect a girl named Juliet to turn out to be a little more passionate about life than I had become.

So, the same. It was hard to imagine the past, or the future, being any different. Except tonight had been different.

For some reason, another memory of Maddy came to me—not from tonight, but from that drive back from our failed state track tournament ten years ago. We had a fifteen-person van, and only the four of us—me, Maddy, and our two coaches—inside. It was full daylight, since we'd come back so early. Maddy had wrapped herself in her own embrace against the window, her face puffy from crying.

I blinked the image away. "Actually," I said. "You'll never guess who came in tonight."

"Who?"

"Maddy Bell."

Her eyes brightened. "You're kidding."

I grabbed another glass of water for myself and pulled out a chair at the table.

"That poor girl," she said.

In the dim light, I couldn't see her face. Was she joking? "Why do you say that?"

After a long moment, she finally said, "She always seemed so lost."

I'd seen what lost looked like pretty close-up this evening. Teeny was as lost as they came. But having a real conversation with my mother for the first time in a while gave me a rush of confidence. She wasn't so far gone, at least. "You mean when she was beating me in every race I ever ran?" I said, smiling. "She seemed lost to you then?"

"Well, when your dad used to—" She stood up and went to the sink to dump her glass.

As quickly as the light had come to her eyes, it was gone. The house grew still and silent around us once again.

My dad had come to every race. Sometimes he'd even stop by practice. He'd lean on the fence around the track with our coach, Coach Trenton, who had once been on an actual Olympic team, and the assistant, Coach Fitzgerald. Fitz, he let us call him. My dad had never been an athlete, had never run in his adult life, probably, but he took an interest. He knew all the girls on the team, every year, and congratulated them all for, if not winning, for trying hard. He included Maddy, of course, who never seemed to know what to say to grown-ups. Her dad and stepmom didn't attend races, not even the big ones, not even when she was at her peak, when no one could beat her.

I might have felt bad for her, but after running the second-fastest two miles in the state of Indiana, I'd been too busy checking the finish line for my own family's proud, second-place cheers to see how first place sat on Maddy's shoulders. Afterward, sure, from the lower podium—I'd had plenty of time to study the sharp edge of Maddy's jaw from below. In the first moments post-race, though, with my lungs burning and my dad pulling me off my feet into a sweaty hug, I hadn't spared her a thought.

Coach and Fitz would have been right there, making sure Maddy had all the hugs and high fives she could handle. Still, regrets flooded in, for what I'd said about us not really being friends.

Two things I'd lied about.

I felt the sharp point of the pen in my pocket and remembered the loose knot in the belt of Maddy's raincoat, the easy sway of her clothes. That diamond ring. My palms tingled. "Are you going to bed soon?"

"Thought I'd get some dishes done."

She stood at the empty sink, watching the dark night out the window. Or maybe she could only see the vague reflection of her own face.

"I'm on the cart tomorrow, so . . ." I stood up, stretched. "It's late."

"That'll be fun," she said.

"Um . . . sure. I'll be home by dinner. Maybe we'll take a drive or something afterward."

She didn't say anything.

"OK," I said. "Good night, Mom."

In my room, I tore the pen out of my pocket and threw it. I sat on my bed and rubbed my palms together until they were hot, then tender. They *itched*. I held them flat against the comforter and waited, but it wouldn't stop. I shoved my hands into my pockets. My fingers grazed something—the barrette. I'd forgotten it.

I held it in my palm, then went to the mirror and clipped the bauble into my hair. I let down my ponytail and combed out my hair with my fingers.

I changed into an old T-shirt and sweats and retrieved the pen from where it had landed. I listened for my mom for a second before entering the bathroom and closing the door. In the vanity, a hundred tiny bottles rolled to the back of the bottom drawer and then forward again. The bulk of them pleased me. The scents. The variety of what people left behind from other places they'd been. I chose a lotion, probably a Hyatt or a Radisson brand, better stuff than the Mid-Night offered, and used a dollop to calm the raw skin on my hands. Then I reached behind and under the open drawer and pulled out the old makeup bag I kept there.

The bag was faded black with white polka dots. Something from childhood, maybe. I sat with my back against the closed door, unzipped the bag, and started pulling out the collection. I lined them up on the floor, one piece after another. Nothing valuable: an interesting spiral paperclip; a single earring I thought might be turned into a pendant; a lipstick from a designer brand, but in a color I could never wear. I pulled the glittering barrette out of my hair and added it. My lost and found.

Except that no one ever found these things again. No one ever came looking. Not for the single pink-and-orange-striped baby sock that my hands hadn't been able to resist. Not for the empty cut-glass atomizer that still smelled as fussy as the old woman who'd told me about her trip to visit her grandkids. No one came back for the little pretty things that I couldn't help but want. That I couldn't help but take.

The benefit of the schedule Lu and I split was that I always ended up cleaning the rooms of the guests I'd signed in the day before. I checked in the cheapskates and pensioners, the glassy-eyed parents with yowling kids and sullen teens up until Billy took over the evening shift, and then the next morning I got to see what was left behind. Usually they left me greasy pizza boxes or a sticky, overturned juice bottle, but sometimes they left clues.

Like the jittery guy with a trim beard and a mega-sized gas station coffee, gone by the time I arrived the next day. He'd left a picture post-card of Italy tucked into the bathroom mirror. I'd cleaned the room around it, expecting him to come back—because of course I'd read it and knew that he hadn't meant to leave it. But who means to leave any-thing, even things they don't care about?

I picked it up now and turned it over. I barely needed to read the words—*Pigeon: I promised you something and I mean to deliver. Love, Your Jedi.* Other people led interesting lives. I mean—that was a promise I wanted the guy to keep. That was a promise that I wished I could keep for him.

But most of the things were just things. They had no other life, no other purpose. They were orphans. That lipstick never got used. That private postcard was forgotten. I gave them a home.

I held the card to my cheek until I felt foolish, reminded of Teeny and her gumballs. I packed it all up, adding the pen from the Mid-Night. Maddy had used it.

These things didn't make me happy. They didn't make me sad. Often, when I took them out from their hiding place, they seemed like litter. Why had anyone ever owned them in the first place? Who both-ered with fancy paper clips? Why would anyone allow someone to call her a pigeon? I should throw it out. I should take it all to the motel and put it into the box under the counter, the real lost and found. Or dump it all in the bin in the recessed alcove next to Billy's room. That's what it was. Trash.

But I didn't want to . . . No, I wanted to. I *couldn't.*

The gleam of the perfume bottle or the gold bit on the lipstick tube refused to be thrown away, and once in a while, something small and shiny caught my attention—called out to me, really—until I knew it had to be mine.

Mine. That wasn't the right word. I was the one who was owned. I was the one who was captured—by this little girl's barrette, by this lip-stick I couldn't even wear. And someday I was sure, I would be. I'd be caught.

CHAPTER FOUR

The alarm had me up again the next morning, too early. Always too early. I dragged myself to the kitchen and forced the first cup of coffee out of the ancient coffeemaker. At my seat at the table, my eyes began to open and focus, until I could finally spot the sugar bowl. Beside it, a nest of old mail gathered. Bills, a couple of them second notices. Fliers, a catalogue, a brochure from a senior-care facility. I picked this up. Had one of the nosy neighbors dropped this by? Not that they ever asked how my mother was, but I could feel their judgments.

A red envelope had come loose from the pile. Red for alarm, for dread, for Midway High.

When the envelope first arrived, I'd opened it, noted the expense, and thrown it to the side. But I'd saved it. As much as I didn't want to go, I'd saved it. The invitation was a nice cream card, the time of the event written out in script as though I'd been invited to tea with the queen.

I took the card out and looked again. The Luxe. If Shelly had been a vindictive person, I might have suspected aggression. In any case, the event was too expensive. I got up and threw the invitation and the brochure in the trash.

Maybe I'd have gone, if I'd done something with the last ten years, if I could show up like Maddy, resplendent in her sleek raincoat and diamonds.

Back at the table, I dropped my head onto my arm, remembering the terrible things I'd said. She'd come all that way, and maybe she hadn't tracked me to my stupid job only to make me feel terrible. She'd said it could be real, our friendship. That we could try again. I'd turned her away.

And yet, I wanted . . . something. Not something, but everything. A new job. My own place. My own life. A boyfriend. And more friendships, like the one I'd had in Maddy. I wanted that, even though it had been years since I'd let myself admit it even to myself.

I wanted more.

If only Maddy had actually been staying at the Mid-Night, she might still be there, and I could go make things right.

I could ask Gretchen for a phone number, or maybe that's where Maddy had stayed after leaving the motel.

But Maddy had recoiled at her stepmother's name. "Retching," she used to call her. She wouldn't have gone there.

Then it hit me. The pen. She'd used the pen I'd pocketed to fill out the information card. The info card was standard issue, a formality. It asked for the make, model, and plate number of a guest's car—in case one guest's car nicked another's in the parking lot—as well as a home address and phone number, in case they left anything behind. Anything of value.

The clock on our oven said six-thirty. I had to work the rooms today, not the desk, but maybe if I picked up Lu on time for a change, she wouldn't ask me too many questions when she saw me copying something from one of the guest cards.

I got cleaned up and dressed quickly and, for my mother's sake, quietly. Thinking about fixing things with Maddy made me feel better than I had in a long time. Expectant. Could it be that easy to perk up my prospects? Tracking down a phone number wasn't hiking to the top of Everest or anything. But even as I slipped into my ridiculous maid's uniform, I wondered how much longer I'd have to wear it. As though I'd made some decision about my future.

In the bathroom mirror, I studied myself. The snug black dress bunched a bit over the few pounds I'd gained since giving up running. The white collar could have been whiter. The black-and-white sneakers I wore with my uniform looked silly, childish, but I didn't have anything else. My brown hair hung lank and ignored. I spent a few minutes with the eyeliner, a little mascara. Stuff I didn't usually bother with when I had a date with the toilet brush. I felt Maddy's influence hurrying me. I hoped she'd used a cell-phone number on her card, so I could reach her before she left town.

I pulled out the makeup bag from the hollow place below the bottom drawer and tried the fancy lipstick again. Still a bad color. I wiped it off and went back to my own supplies. A little lip gloss, a few extra strokes of the brush before I put my hair in the standard ponytail. I stood back and gazed at myself.

I had made a decision. Maddy had helped get me into this spot. She could very well help get me out.

"Well, well," Lu said when she got into the car. "Well, *my*."

There was no use arguing that I hadn't put in some effort, but I thought I could detect extra time spent on her part, too. Her hair was shiny and loose, and she'd worn khakis and slip-ons instead of her usual behind-the-desk jeans and tennis shoes. "You going to church after your shift?"

She grinned. "That woman last night—"

"Yeah," I said.

"Where do you even buy clothes like that?"

"Not around here," I said.

"I want that for my kids, you know," she said. "You dress nice, you walk into a room, and people want to know you, be like you. They want to like you, before you even say a word. She has a good job?"

"She must."

"You don't know?" Lu shot me a side glance.

"We only had a little while to catch up last night. But—well, maybe I could do a better job of staying in touch this time."

"So I'm not going to be your fanciest friend."

"In fanciness, you come in a close second," I said. Second place wasn't so bad.

"Well, can you steal that raincoat for me?" Lu said.

"Forget it," I said. "I have dibs."

We pulled into the Mid-Night's parking lot and took my customary spot in the last row. "Hey," Lu said. "Looks like you've got an extra room to clean."

But I'd already seen it. In the shadow of the Mid-Night sat the sleek silver car. It was parked at the end nearest Billy's room, forcing Billy's beater Dodge a spot or two down. Maddy had come back to stay, after all.

Inside, Billy stood at the front desk. He waved us in impatiently.

"You," he said, pointing at me. Billy was the manager, our boss, but he didn't scare either of us. He was scrawny and greasy, with a mustache that looked like he'd been waiting for it to come in since middle school. He also had a series of nervous tics I could barely keep track of and a high, shrill voice with an exaggerated drawl not native to Midway. I did a mean imitation on our walkie-talkies. Billy lived in Mid-Night's room one-oh-one, the end room near the overpass, an honor he never stopped talking about. An honor that included living next door to the niche for the motel's trash bins. We'd never been inside this room, never had to clean it, but Lu and I suspected it smelled a little like dirty hair and cheap cologne, and a lot like garbage. "You," he said again.

"What did I do?"

"Did you tell some Bargains who checked in last night there was a dead body in one of the rooms?" he said, squeakier than normal.

"No," I said, and glanced at Lu. "Is there?"

"I had to comp the room for them, they were so mad."

"That's bullshit, Billy," I said. "They weren't that upset about it last night."

His hand flew to his mustache, and his fingers pulled at the scraggly hairs. Tic number one. "So you did say it."

"It was a misunderstanding," I said. "But they were looking for a way to get their tacos paid for, and you fell right into their hands."

"What does that even mean?"

"See? It's easy to get things mixed up," I said. "Has anyone seen the guy in room two-oh-six yet this morning?"

One of Billy's eyes double-winked at me. Tic number two. "He came and asked for change for the vending machines. Why?"

That, at least, was good news. "He's been in there, do not disturb, for two days. When is he checking out?"

Billy picked up the stack of info cards next to the computer and sorted through the short deck. One, he put to the side. The Bargains, gone and good riddance. I saw the card with Maddy's handwriting flick past.

"Today," he said. "But not yet. Now tell me about the hot ride parked outside my place. We have a celebrity staying with us?"

Lu stepped behind the desk and hip-checked Billy out of the way. "Juliet's friend."

I wished she hadn't said it, but I did feel a glimmer of pride as Billy looked between the two of us, trying to catch us teasing him. "Yeah? Well, thank her for my late night, will you? She and her fella were banging around in there until all hours. That room's going to be a mess."

Lu looked at me sadly. "I hate being right all the time," she said.

I didn't care about that. Maddy's car was still here. I hadn't missed her.

"Oh, and what did you ladies do to my ice machine last night?" Billy said. "It's leaking all over God's creation."

I ignored him and went to the closet to spring the cleaning cart. He and Lu were still arguing over the ice machine as I dragged the cart out of the lobby and over a slim stream trickling all the way from the vending area out across the sidewalk to the parking lot. There'd be no ice within a day, and then we'd have something new for the guests to complain about.

The sun was getting hot. I pushed the cart into the shade of the central stairway, listening to the sound of the cars on the interstate. By ten, when the commuters were where they needed to be and traffic thinned out, everyone else would speed up. It would sound like the Indy 500 out there, the roar of engines bouncing off the walls of the motel.

Inside one of the pockets on the cart, I found the little notepad Lu and I used to keep track of waning supplies or things that needed fixing. Tapping the dull pencil against an empty page, I waited for the right words to occur to me.

When I was done, I tore out the note and tucked it under the windshield wiper of Maddy's car. I hoped she wouldn't ignore it, but she had every right to. I'd tried to hurt her the night before, and when I actually tried at something, I was pretty good at it.

Back to work. In the central breezeway, the light on the vending machine fluttered. Full of corn chips and crumbling pastries, it never saw much action. But it seemed we needed a maintenance visit for the ice machine, anyway. I made a note of it, then popped the lid on the ice chest. Full, for now.

Time passed slowly as I swept crabapple blossoms out of the breezeway and hosed down the sidewalks, one eye always on Maddy's end of the building. Nobody stirred. I took the center stairwell to the second floor and swept the same few feet of balcony for a long time. Nothing.

The door to two-oh-six cracked open.

A pudgy man in a tight, shiny suit emerged. When he saw me, he ducked his bald head and shot past me and down the stairs. "You checking out?" I called. He nodded, his chin to his chest.

Not being able to make eye contact was a bad sign. His room would have to wait. I continued with the broom, sweeping the length of the walkway, always watching for movement near Maddy's room, and then back again, swatting at cobwebs in the eaves of the roof. And then back again, brushing at the detail in the railing. Billy would be pleased with this effort, but there was no sign of Maddy.

Back downstairs, I leaned on the cart, considering all the tasks I could invent to keep myself handy to her room.

"Come in, Juliet," said Lu's voice on the cart's walkie-talkie. "This is Command. You there? Over."

I grabbed the radio. "Uh, yeah, Command. What's up? Over."

"It's ten o'clock. What's the report? Over."

"Checkout is eleven," I said. "You heard Billy. She's . . . tired. Over."

"But weird, right? Did you think she'd sleep in, you know, *here*? Um, over. Lady of Guada*lupe*, I feel like such an idiot when I have to say this over, over, over," Lu said, her accent getting thick. "Over."

"Roger that." I thought for a second. "Do you think I should check on her?" I let up on the button, then had to click it again to finish. "Over."

"Give her the beauty sleep, I guess," Lu said. "Not that she needs it. Over."

And roger the hell out of that. "Help me watch for her, OK?" I said. "I want to say good-bye, at least. Out."

Upstairs I leaned into the balcony for another minute before giving up and going to see what damage had been done to two-oh-six. One swipe of the cart's master key, and the dead guy's disaster lay before me.

Except he wasn't dead, and the room wasn't a disaster.

It did smell, as Lu had noticed. The room had taken on the bouquet of old Chinese food and dirty feet. I propped the door open. In the bathroom, I flipped the switch for the fan and gave the place the once-over. He'd used a lot of towels, but I'd walked into worse. Much worse. I'd encountered bloody towels left behind the door, sheets covered in terrible things. I'd had to clean up spilled beer, used condoms, dirty diapers, and more. People came to motels like the Mid-Night to be someone else for a night, and their new identities rarely wanted to pick up after themselves. Sometimes their new selves wanted to smear things on the walls. We relied on Shinez-All, a potent chemical cleaner in a bright-yellow spray can, for the worst of it. Actually, Lu and I used Shinez-All for everything—nasty things, sticky spills, streaky mirrors, and big spiders.

I toured the dead man's room, looking for any trace of damage or devastation. Even the bathroom was fine. He'd piled all the used linen together in one place on the tile.

I spotted a loose seam on the wallpaper over the sink. I'd have to bring back some clear nail polish from the cart to glue it back down, an old trick I'd picked up.

Other than that, this would be a quick flip. I'd have to vacuum the awful gray-green carpet and wipe the baseboards—for some reason, female guests really cared about baseboard dust—then wipe up any hairs and water drips around the sink, toilet, and tub, and give the mirror a quick Shinez-All polish. Then replace any amenities, as Billy insisted we called the little bottles of freebie shampoo and lotion, and clean up any trash the guest had left. Oh, and corner the toilet paper to a little military point. People made jokes about it, but if we didn't do it? We'd hear about it, and not just from Billy. I could be done in a half hour, and then go see the damage done by the Bargains, and still be available when Maddy woke up.

The framed art over the dresser was hanging askew. I glanced at its sister over the bed. They were the same in every room, ugly, color-drained landscapes of country fields, of dark trees like figures out of a nightmare. Just what you wanted to wake up to in a strange room. If country roads and dirt roads were art, all you had to do was open the front door and gaze at the landscape beyond the parking lot. The problem for Lu and me was that none of the frames were well secured to the wall. They went wonky at the smallest breeze or bump. I nudged them both back into place and surveyed the rest of the room.

Here was a surprise. The guy had wrapped up all his trash into one bag, tied it, and left it by the door. A few bills lay on the dresser, for my trouble. The dead man was a tipper? Hardly anyone was.

I grabbed the trash and took the walkway past Maddy's room to the far stairs.

At the bottom, I thought I heard something. I let the bag drop and hurried around the corner of the building to see the parking lot. The silver car stood where it had been all morning, my note wedged under the windshield wiper.

Back at the stairs, the trash bag lay torn open. I hated to touch whatever the dead guy had been doing with his copious free time and extra towels, but there was no way around it. I knelt to sweep everything back into the bag before it started to blow around in the breeze, tying it into a neat little bundle again.

Behind me, cars rushed past on the highway. People passing Midway, to and fro. They'd be going to work or traveling through, going fast, and who could blame them? I stood up and watched them through the brush in the fence, wrapping my arms around myself. It was spring finally—the time of year that reminded me of childhood, when the windows were thrown open after a long winter. When the new track season started. My youth felt distant, but the clean wind blew in the scent of possibility. I hadn't always been so off course. Something might still happen to change everything.

I thought of Maddy, still asleep upstairs, and pulled my elbows in tighter. Something had to happen to change everything. I picked up the bag of trash and turned, and I knew that something already had.

Maddy.

Maddy, hanging by her neck from the balcony railing.

CHAPTER FIVE

Her face was a color I'd never seen.

No.

I wasn't seeing this.

There was a noise. The noise came from me.

I wasn't seeing this. This wasn't happening.

The noise turned into a strangled sob, then found its way to a scream. I tumbled backward into the scrub and fence, and clung there, the interstate roaring at my back, screaming and screaming until—

No, this couldn't be happening. That couldn't be real. That couldn't be Maddy. That wasn't the belt of her raincoat around her neck—

Then Lu came running around the side of the Mid-Night, and I could see them both: Maddy, hanging limp and gray from the railing above the alcove, like a fish, and Lu, her eyes wide and frantic, and I knew it was happening. It had. It was over, and Maddy was dead.

Billy loped around the corner several paces behind. "What the hell is going on?"

Lu rounded the edge of the building and looked into the alcove to see what I was seeing.

"*Díos*—oh, sweet lady." She ran to me, and pulled me up from the brambles and into her arms. I wasn't sure if the sweet lady was me, or Maddy, or if the Virgin Mary herself had been called upon. I closed my eyes against Lu's shoulder and found I could stop screaming. We clung to one another as Billy hurried around the corner and took a look.

"Oh, hell, are you kidding me? Who's got a—wait, I do." He pulled his phone out of his pocket and fumbled with the buttons. "It's really nine-one-one, right? Oh, *hell*, this is just what I need."

"Shut up, Billy." Lu squeezed me tighter. "Oh, poor, sweet lady."

I wheezed into Lu's nice shirt, my throat and lungs burning.

"This is ridiculous, is what it is," Billy said. "How many years we've been catering to wackos and nut-jobs and not one of them—Hello? Yes, I've got an emergency here—" I peeked out from Lu's hair to see Billy turned from the highway with a finger in his other ear. He gave the address and waited, nodding. "Now I'd like to keep the name of the place out of it. Ma'am, I understand that—"

"Billy, stop being an asshole," Lu yelled.

He snapped his phone closed. "They are going to take our star from us so fast, and then see where you are."

"Billy, shut *up*. That is Juliet's friend. And no one comes for that stupid star, anyway."

"Oh, yeah?" he said. "Then why do they come?"

I leaned my head on Lu's shoulder, waiting to hear what they came up with. It was a good question.

"From now on," Billy said. "They're going to come for the sturdy balcony rail. See if they don't."

Lu shuffled me around the building, grabbing a hand towel from the cleaning cart as we passed it. In the lobby, she forced me into the seat behind the desk and disappeared. When she came back, the towel was wet and wrapped around some ice from the machine. She pressed it to my face. "Oh, poor sweet lady."

A few minutes passed, the only sound my ragged breath. Then sirens, at first distant, then close and wailing. Tires skidding on loose gravel.

"Lu—" I couldn't think of anything to say. I'd had plenty to say the night before, though, hadn't I, and where had that left Maddy? She was the one, the woman we all should *poor lady* for. Poor Maddy. Why had I said those horrible things to her? "Oh, God."

Lu patted my hand, and then went to the windows to see what was happening. "Two fire trucks and two—three cop cars. Four, now. I didn't know we had so many."

What had I said to Maddy? That the true friendship she believed in had been a myth.

Which was a lie.

Because I'd been mad at her? After ten years?

Because she'd suggested she might have thrown a race my way. Because she felt sorry for me. She saw me rotting here behind the Mid-Night's front desk, still fretting over a few long-distance high-school track races from ten years ago, and she pitied me.

But I couldn't let her have even that, could I? I'd stripped her of her compassion until she'd felt naked and exposed. Until she'd felt alone and abandoned enough to—

I remembered all the expectancy and good feeling I'd had all morning. I'd been thinking I'd found the cusp of a new beginning, because Maddy had made me think I could live a larger life, be a different person. And all the while I'd been looking forward to the apology I owed her. The apology that might open up my future, always selfish to the last. But Maddy had needed much more than I'd been willing to give. She'd needed a friend. The real kind.

This was my fault.

"Here they come," Lu said. She came to my side and gave my arm a quick squeeze.

The door chimes sounded. Two of them, dark uniforms, entered. Billy trailed behind, came to the counter, and leaned against it, shaking his head.

"Well, she's dead."

"We know that, *Billy*," Lu said.

"Sergeant Jim Loughton," said the uniformed guy. I looked up, recognized them both. Sometimes we got a patrol out to the Mid-Night, the bar, when somebody had too much to drink, or if a fight broke out. Loughton was big, round-bellied, and looking around in distaste as though he feared touching anything. He took off his cap, revealing salt-and-pepper hair, and gestured to the other cop. "Patrol Officer Howard."

The other cop gave me an awkward wave from her hip. "Hi, Juliet."

I struggled for the right thing to say. There was nothing. "Courtney."

"Weird about Maddy," she said.

I nodded.

Loughton took a second to glance between us, settling his gaze at last on his partner.

"Juliet and I graduated from Midway High together," Courtney said. She took off her cap, too, and tucked it under her arm. Courtney Howard was small—not just for a cop, but for a human—with a cropped barbershop haircut that showed off her sharp cheekbones and sharper eyes. She had a little lisp that was hard to pinpoint, but that made her sound younger than she was. In her uniform, she seemed like a little girl playing dress up.

Loughton cleared his throat with a rumble. "Who checked in the deceased?"

The deceased. I swallowed hard. "I did." My voice was small in the still room.

"When was this?"

I couldn't think. Lu nudged me away from the computer to look it up. "She checked in at nine twenty-six last night," she said.

Loughton gave Courtney a loaded look. She reached for her notepad and flipped it open. "How did she pay?" she said.

"Credit card. Do you need the number?"

"Not yet," Courtney said. "Was she alone?"

They all turned to me. "Yes."

"The hell she was," Billy said.

"She checked in alone," I said. "She said 'just me.' But—"

"But there was a heckuva racket in there last night about two a.m.," Billy said. He ran his hand through his hair five or six times while we all watched. Tic number three. "Her room was right above mine, so I heard it well enough."

I cleared my throat. "What I was going to say was that she left last night—"

"Oh, that's right," Lu said. "We saw her leave right after you came back from the bar."

"Who went to the bar, now?" Courtney said.

Loughton held out his hands, traffic-cop style. "Whoa. One at a time. You," he said, pointing at me. Billy had done the same thing just a few hours ago. I wished it were still then, before I knew what I knew and had seen what I'd seen.

"Maddy checked in, and then she wanted a drink." I thought for a second, and everyone let me. My legs felt shaky. "Except she didn't seem to want the drink, really. We sat in the Mid-Night—the bar—until my break was over, and then I pointed out her room. But Maddy didn't go to her room. We both saw her drive away. This morning—" I remembered finding the silver car parked in the lot and felt again the rising hopes of catching her before it was too late. It was too late. "This morning, her car was here when we came in."

"'We' refers to you and Ms.—" Courtney nodded toward Lu.

"Mendoza," Lu said. "Luisa. Juliet drives me when we have the same shift." Her eyes shifted between Loughton, Courtney, then Billy. "Most days, I mean, she drives me." I could feel her trembling beside me.

Loughton grunted. "And the victim's name?"

"Madeleine Bell," Courtney and I said, together.

"Well," he said, looking between us again. "Now that everyone's properly introduced."

Loughton went out to see to Maddy, leaving Courtney to take our statements. She looked between the three of us, meeting my eyes and looking away. "Ms. Mendoza?"

After a brief negotiation, Billy led them to the doors between the lobby and the bar, unlocked, and flipped the lights for them.

Back at the counter, Billy leaned toward me. "What do you think they want us to say?" he said.

I didn't know. There was a knot in my stomach. "They'll ask questions."

His eye twitched, twitched. "Jesus, what kind of questions?"

"About Maddy, you idiot."

"I don't know anything about her."

"What you—heard, you know. Her and her—"

The guy.

"Oh my God," I said.

"What?" Billy said.

Maddy, hanging from the belt of her own coat, surely a suicide. But what did it mean if she'd had a late-night guest?

"Tell them everything you can about the noises you heard," I said. "Billy, if someone was with her, maybe she didn't kill herself."

He whistled. "What difference does it make? You think they'll let us keep a half star if some bitch gets herself murdered here?"

"Billy, she—"

The bar door opened, and Lu emerged. She seemed stunned.

Courtney stood in the doorway. "Mr. Batts? Billy, was it?"

He smiled wide enough to show the black socket of a missing molar. "Yes, ma'am."

"Ms. Mendoza," Courtney said. "You can go."

"Juliet is my ride."

"Call for another one. We're going to need to talk to Ms. Townsend at length."

They all looked at me.

"Take my car, Lu," I said. "I'll get a ride over to your house later."

"Someone better be cleaning some rooms, is all I want to say."

"Billy, *shut up*," Lu said. "We still have lots of rooms clean and ready—"

"If the premises aren't completely shut down," Courtney said.

"The *premises* is where I live, lady," Billy said. His fingers raked through his hair three, four times. We all waited.

"Well, you must be devastated to have this happen on your doorstep," Courtney said, her lisp menacing in its cuteness. She waved him into the bar. The doors swung closed behind them.

Lu looked at me, shook her head, and pulled me farther from the door. "This is very bad stuff, here."

"Lu, the noises Billy said he heard in her room—you know what that means, right?"

"Oh," she breathed. "Oh, that's why all the bad cop, bad cop. I thought she—"

"So did I."

Lu tilted her head at me. "Don't look so relieved. Your friend got murdered last night."

"I had this bad feeling that she'd—that I'd—" I couldn't bring myself to admit how badly I'd treated Maddy. "I felt bad I hadn't seen the signs, you know?"

She nodded uncertainly. "Instead, we only have a madman stalking the place we work," she said. "That is not a comfort to me."

Or to me. My head swam. I folded my arms on the counter and rested my face in the dark circle they created. I wanted to be at home, in bed, ignoring the alarm clock, or I wanted it to be three days ago, totally unaware that Maddy Bell even remembered my name. Or I wanted it to be three decades from now, when this all might be a dull memory.

But it would never dull. I remembered this roaring ocean of feelings from when my dad had died: confusion, horror. Anger. What was the point of living, really, when it was so easily gone, and left so much disaster behind? My mom standing at my dad's gravesite, head bowed. Then again, just the night before, head bowed over the empty sink. I couldn't quite remember the sound of his voice or his laugh. These things faded, but the pain hadn't.

The bar doors opened, and Billy scuttled into the lobby like a cockroach trying to find the dark. "We're going to go no-vacancy for a few nights, girls," he said, looking at me. I usually scolded him for calling us that, at our age, but I let it go. "Just 'til things die down. I mean. You know what I mean."

"Ms. Mendoza, I believe you were dismissed," Courtney said from the doorway. "Juliet. It's time."

Billy came behind the desk. He nudged me out of the way and clicked through some screens on the computer. With the flick of a wrist, he swiped a room card. Maddy's room. They would have to search it. Billy grabbed under the counter for the switch for the no-vacancy neon we hardly ever had a chance to put into service. I reached into the pocket of my uniform and slid my car keys across the counter to Lu.

Billy held the door for her. "Lock up tight, Juliet," he said, fidgeting with the room key in his hand. "Might be a couple of days." He looked at Courtney. "Or longer." He let the door sail closed behind them.

It was time.

CHAPTER SIX

'd been in the closed bar before, but it had never seemed as ominous. The daylight pouring in from the outside door seemed strange—was it still only the morning? Courtney waved me toward the same table I'd sat at with Maddy the night before. Casual, as though we'd be catching up over coffee. "So, what did you think, when Maddy walked in the front door?"

"I thought, 'We sure are busy for an off-season night.'"

Courtney sat across from me and gave me a long, level stare. "All of this is on the record."

"OK," I said.

"Which means no bullshit."

Courtney and I hadn't been friends at Midway High, or enemies. The hostility seemed earned, though. I searched my memory for what I'd missed. I barely remembered Courtney from high school, couldn't place her among the cliques and groups of girls formed there. Maybe not remembering was the problem. "Sure," I said.

"Were you in touch with Maddy before she arrived last night?"

"I hadn't seen or talked to her since graduation day," I said.

"Your best friend from forever ago arrives unannounced at your workplace one night, and all you can think is how busy you are?" Courtney's sharp cheekbones looked sharper in her disgust.

"I did wonder why she'd stay here instead of at home—at her old home, I mean. But I guess she and her stepmother still don't get along."

"Did you and Maddy get along?"

"I told you, we weren't in touch."

"Not at all?" she said.

I'd seen enough cop shows to know what she was doing. "*Like I said*, not until last night. I heard she lived in Chicago—"

Courtney leaned forward. "Who told you that?"

51

"Shelly. The reunion's coming up." Shelly, our class president, used her bank window as a throne from which to maintain control of her subjects. If I didn't RSVP to the reunion soon, I wouldn't be able to deposit my paycheck without getting a lot of attitude. Of course, with the Mid-Night closed, maybe the greater concern was when I'd ever see a paycheck again.

Courtney fell back against her seat, less rigid through the shoulders. "Shelly. Right. Are you going to the reunion?"

"I wasn't planning to. What about you?"

She reached for a paper coaster on the table and worried it between her fingers. "I don't have much to say to those people."

"Those people?"

"My high-school years don't need to be revisited," she said.

"Your high-school years and mine were the same years."

"Not by a long shot."

"Come on," I said. "It wasn't that bad."

Her glare cut through me. "For you, it wasn't that bad. For Maddy. You were too busy being track superstars to notice anyone else. The rest of us were just blurs."

Now I remembered.

The headline had read something like *And Everyone Else Is a Blur*. It was something dumb Maddy used to say. I'd never given it much thought until she'd said it during an interview with the school paper. In big, black print, it sounded ugly and stuck-up. And people had taken it seriously. Even a few of the other runners had given us a pass after that. Maddy and I laughed it off, but we knew damage had been done. We couldn't really blame the newspaper—nothing in the article had been wrong or misquoted.

But we could blame the student reporter, who'd been waiting for a gotcha, and had constructed one out of nothing. That reporter had come to the interview with a chip on her shoulder. Maybe she had today, too.

"You always read more into that phrase than she meant," I said.

"I report what people have the lack of self-awareness to say in front of me. Then, and now." Courtney pulled out her notebook and flipped it open. "Why weren't you friends with Maddy anymore?"

I looked at the pen's tip on the blank page, then away. "People fall out of touch. Are you still friends with everyone you hung out with in high school?"

"I didn't hang out," she said. "I liked to think of it as doing time. Did you have a fight?"

"When?"

She smiled at me in a way I didn't like. "Back in high school?"

"No."

"Last night, did you have a fight?" she said.

"No."

She waited.

"Not exactly," I said.

"Tell me what happened."

What had happened? We'd compared plans to avoid the reunion, disagreed on how time passed, and then she'd riled me up with her inability to see what separated us. What had always separated us. "She accused me of being jealous of her," I said.

"Were you?"

The only thing Maddy had ever done that I wasn't jealous of was getting killed. "Of course I was. She won every race, ever."

"Except that last one." Courtney looked up from her notes. "Why didn't she run that last race again?"

"She was sick," I said.

"What kind of sick?"

"I don't know. Sick sick." I got up and walked behind the bar. I had always hated everything about this story, and I didn't want to tell it. Afterward, everyone had wanted to know. What happened? What had gone wrong? But by then I'd been shunned long enough because of Maddy's blur comment, and I didn't owe anyone anything. Nobody needed to know. Nobody cared, really, and the few who did just wanted the dirt. But there wasn't any. "You want a Coke or something?"

I aimed the bar's soda gun at a pint glass. I didn't want to remember, but it came anyway—the image of Maddy, curled into a ball on the edge of the hotel bed, the garish bedspread gathered in her fist.

That morning I'd woken to find Maddy already out of the room. She'd gone to stretch her legs or work out the nerves. I thought she might have been with Coach, except he came to our door trying to round us all up for breakfast, or just juice if we wouldn't eat. The Luxe had a nice dining room. Fitz was out, too, so we knew he must have gone looking for her. When she came back, she locked herself in the bathroom and emerged a long while later only after I begged for the toilet. When I came out again, she was pale in her red Midway High uniform, folded over the edge of the mattress. She'd pulled something, she said at first. But it looked to me like cramps. *Cramps.* You're in the state capital for the big show and cramps can stop you?

The melodrama of it still galled me. Both of our big, male coaches bumbling around, trying to make things right. They located maxi pads that truly lived up to the name and ibuprofen, and Coach offered to stretch her out, but nothing could release Maddy from the fetal position. She wouldn't leave the room, and when I tried to leave her side to get dressed to run, she pulled me back down to her and asked me to stay. When Coach went to call her parents and find mine in the stands, Fitz finally whispered if maybe we should take Maddy home. Maddy held tightly to my hand, whimpering into the bedcover. It was my decision: We would both miss the race. "I know you're disappointed," Fitz said. "And your parents will be, and I am, too. Mike's going to be—but it's a small price, isn't it?" But it had never felt like a small price to me.

Now, the whole story was small. I couldn't bear to tell Courtney that it had taken so little to divide us. "Coke?" I repeated.

"No thanks." Courtney turned to watch. "Are you allowed to skim a drink off the bar anytime you like?"

"I'm not a dishonest person, Officer Howard." My hands itched, but I ignored them.

Something flickered behind her eyes. "Of course not. Sorry." She snapped her notebook closed and tapped it on the table. "Can I ask you a question—off the record?"

"You're the record keeper," I said.

She put away the notebook and plucked up the coaster again. It had begun to disintegrate. "Is this what you had in mind?" she said.

I was rinsing my glass in the sink and nearly dropped it. "How do you mean?"

"You know," she said. "Midway, this job. Not that there's anything—"

"Save it," I said. The there's-nothing-wrong-with-hard-work chat I didn't need. Fitz sometimes stopped by for a pep talk, but it always ended the same. Me, here, pulling sheets off the beds abandoned by people who had places to go.

"Maddy seemed like someone with plans, didn't she?" Courtney said. "Even in high school. Like she wasn't just running, but running toward something?"

"That's a far different tone than what I remember from the article you wrote," I said.

She flapped a hand at me. "Yeah, sorry about that. I was just trying to win the Pulitzer Prize. But you seemed driven to me, too. You were leaving the rest of us in the dust. That's how it felt. I always meant to leave, too, you know?" She tossed the coaster to the table and brushed the shredded bits of it from her uniform pants. "When I got that invitation to the reunion last month—I mean, I've been thinking pretty hard about life, ever since. I almost can't remember what it was I planned to be."

I leaned a hip against the bar. "You didn't want to be a cop?"

"My uncle was a cop. He made it sound like something real. Like saving the world, with vacation pay. Striking out for justice, undying gratitude of the community, that sort of thing. Like every day would be a ticker-tape parade." She glanced at me. "He thought I'd be good at it."

"Aren't you?"

She shrugged. "I've barely had a chance to find out. We don't get any decent crime here, just robberies and drunk drivers. Loughton—he's just letting me run with this because he'd rather stay in the car. He'll come out of his seat if we get an arrest, just you watch. And the only parades I've been in were for the Fourth of July, and I was on traffic detail for snotty marching-band kids. A hundred and two in the shade, and me in my synthetic blues."

"Any ticker tape?" I said.

She smiled. "Not for me. What about you? What did you think you'd be doing by now?"

I'd never had a big goal. Some kind of business, maybe. I was organized when I remembered to be. Something with travel? I hadn't even declared a major before I'd had to leave college for good. The truth was that I hadn't been doing all that well in school when my dad had died. I'd had plenty of opportunities to question my own intelligence since dropping out—other people had, too—but it was the memory of failing for the first time that kept me from trying too hard to get back on track. The last time I'd seen my dad, we'd talked about my grades, how I needed to buckle down or get some help, or maybe take a semester off to get my bearing. He wore an old plaid shirt with the sleeves rolled up over his sunburned forearms. He hadn't been to college. *What could you do different?* he'd asked. And I guess that was a question I was still trying to answer. "I thought I'd figure it out, once I got the chance," I said. "Only—"

"Only you never got the chance."

"I never felt like I did," I said.

"First Maddy screwed up your chance at a full-ride somewhere, and then your dad—that's a lot of tough breaks in a row."

I shrugged. The sympathy felt nice, but also heavy for how little Courtney and I knew each other. "Maybe someone else, someone stronger, could have figured it out."

"Maddy, you mean," she said. "It must have been a shock to see her walk in, dressed to the nines. Ms. Mendoza said she had a giant diamond engagement ring." Courtney's voice dropped. "I would have been, like, what have I done with my life? And this—I don't want to use a word I'd regret, you know, but this *woman* gets to have it all? And where am I? You know?"

I stared into the dull shine of the bar sink. "Yeah," I said. The word was barely a whisper. But when I looked up, Courtney's encouraging smile had turned triumphant.

There was a rap on the glass door. Courtney's partner stuck his head in, scowling. "Howard, if you're done interrogating the witnesses, a word?"

"One more thing," she said to him, then shot me a look I couldn't place. "Ms. Townsend, we found the note on Ms. Bell's car. Let me see if I can recall—right: 'I'm sorry—see me before you leave.' Why did you insist on seeing Ms. Bell this morning?"

"I didn't *insist*—"

"What time was that meeting?"

"We never—she was *hanging*—"

"Why are you sorry?"

I swallowed. "I guess I didn't take her visit as well as I could have."

They both stared at me. "Well, then," Courtney said. "You're free to go. However, it would be best if you didn't travel far from Midway until this is sorted."

"Wait." I glanced between them. "What do you mean? Do you mean I'm—I'm a—"

The word wouldn't come to me, and then it did.

Suspect.

"We may have further questions," Courtney said.

But I'd seen the gleam of success in her smile. I'd admitted to feelings I didn't understand, and now I'd need to convince the police that, whatever my reaction to Maddy's return to Midway meant, I hadn't resorted to murder.

CHAPTER SEVEN

After Courtney left with Sergeant Loughton, I went to the other side of the bar, took a stool, and held my head in my hands.

A long moment passed before I had to admit that I looked like a pretty good suspect. Of all the places Maddy might have stayed, she'd chosen the dump where I worked. Ten years with no contact, and she'd made a beeline for me. She'd said she was in the area for work, and now I realized no one had asked me. I had a thousand things to tell Courtney now that she'd left.

Maddy had come to see me, and she'd been killed. Why wouldn't the cops want to know more about that?

For the first time since I'd seen her hanging from the balcony, I felt the punch to my gut—

Maddy Bell was dead.

Maddy, my friend. Memories rushed at me—sleepovers at my house, phone calls that lasted four hours or until my parents forced me to the dinner table or to bed. Riding to track team meets with our knees tucked against the seat ahead of us, hunkered down over each other's dramas. And running. Always running. On training runs or during practice, we kept pace. Maddy's breath was my metronome. We ran as a team, anchored together like conjoined twins, as though we'd never part.

In races, of course, she always had a little more to give than I did, a fault of nature that I hadn't been able to forgive or forget. But it was no one's fault that I had wasted the last ten years. No one's fault but mine.

I stood and went to the bar's exterior door. Outside, the fire trucks were gone, but an ambulance had joined the patrol cars. To take her body, I realized.

A wave of nausea rushed over me. I lay my forehead against the cool glass of the door and took gulping breaths until the brackish taste at the back of my throat was gone. And then I began to cry.

If I'd been asked the day before what my reaction would be to the news of Maddy's death, even this long since I'd seen her, I don't think I would have known how much it would hurt. I had already been living without her.

But Maddy wasn't just the woman I'd been out of touch with for a decade. She wasn't simply the person I'd spent all this time blaming for my own mistakes, or the one I'd begun to pin new hopes to since our reunion the night before. She was the girl who'd been my greatest friend. She was also, and always, the one who'd loved me best. She'd known me better than anyone else ever had, and I was enough.

I would never have a chance to make it right. Doors in every direction had suddenly closed.

I caught my own puffy-eyed image in the door, and stood back. The hem on my uniform had crept north. A crucial button had come undone during the crying, and my hair was falling out of its ponytail. I hadn't been enough—for anyone, and least of all for myself—in a long time.

Outside, the cleaning cart sat in the sun. Someone must have moved it out of the way of the stairs. In all the chaos, I'd never brought it in. I tugged at my uniform skirt, wiped my face, and headed out to retrieve it.

At the cart, I heard a noise. I shaded my eyes and found Loughton, Courtney, and a couple other uniformed officers overhead on the balcony.

Loughton spotted me below. "The key won't work. Where's Batts?"

"I'll make you a new one. Just a minute."

The cart stowed, I took my spot behind the counter and called up the screen on our computer for Maddy's registration.

She was still checked in. I wondered when someone would go into the system and open up that room on the computer. I didn't want to be the one to do it.

It was simple enough to make the card: a few keystrokes and then a swipe with a blank. The card twitched in my shaking hand.

And then I reached for a second blank and swiped it, too.

I slipped the second card into the pocket of my uniform, where it felt heavy and obvious. Trying to breathe normally, I took the center stairs up to the second floor.

Loughton had given up on the dud. They all stood along the walkway with crossed arms.

"Sometimes Billy—when he imprints—he swipes too fast." To my own ears I sounded like someone rushing headlong over the truth. I handed over the card and watched as Loughton and his team pulled their guns and approached the door of two-oh-two. I started to follow them. One of the officers held me back.

Loughton swiped the key. Nothing. He tried again, again. Fast, slow. He fumbled the card in his gloved hands, glancing up at me, tried another angle. "Here, let me," I said, pushing past the uniformed arm keeping me away and into the center of them. I took the card back, turned it, and ran it through at the speed Lu and I had come to understand as the only one that worked without fail.

The light turned green. The lock beeped.

Loughton pocketed the card, nodded. Someone pulled me out of the way, and Courtney and Loughton took up positions on either side of the door. I took a step backward, clutching the rail. None of us knew what might be inside. The murderer. Another body. A blood-soaked nightmare. Anything at all.

Loughton turned the handle just before he would have had to swipe the card again, and he and Courtney jumped into the room, guns swinging into the corners.

"Clear!" Courtney barked.

"Clear!" Loughton agreed.

I couldn't help myself. I peered into the dark room past the shoulders of the cops still at the door, unable to see much of anything except that some of the bed sheets had been pulled to the floor.

Loughton launched himself across the expanse to the bathroom.

"Clear," he bellowed. "Check the closet, Howard."

But Courtney had already raked the room with her eyes and stiffened. "Sir—"

"Don't touch anything, Howard," Loughton said.

"Jim, isn't that—"

I didn't need her to finish. Neither of us could have missed it. Even from as far away as the balcony railing, I could see what had caught Courtney's attention.

On the dresser, bright as a beacon: Maddy's diamond ring.

Before I knew what I was doing, my hand reached toward it. Not pointing, but open-handed and grasping. If I'd been close enough, I might have scooped it up, just to hold it, just to have it against my palm.

I felt Courtney's eyes on me, and dropped my hand.

Downstairs, I sat on the curb. I'd taken the front door keys from the desk to lock up, tight, as instructed, and then put the keys through the drop box in the door. But I'd forgotten to call for a ride. Maybe if I'd had a cell phone like everyone else, I might have called Lu to come back for me. But cell phones cost money, far more than I had to spare.

A team of uniformed guys in rubber gloves picked over Maddy's car. A tow truck sat in the corner of the lot, the motor running. Cops were tramping all around the motel and lot, peering closely at things on the ground and in the weeds against the fence. One of them was on his hands and knees in front of the vending and ice machines. "Do these work?" he called to me. "The ice is almost gone. Looks like someone unplugged it."

"We need to call for service," I called back.

He shrugged.

I felt for the key card in my pocket and rubbed it with my thumb. What good did it do me? Courtney and her friends were going over the room now. It would be a long time before the room didn't have a cop inside it. And once it didn't? There wasn't much for me to do but change the sheets, wipe up the bathroom. Take out the trash.

I thought of Maddy hanging over the trash bin and shuddered.

There might be blood.

I didn't know how to clean up pools of blood. I didn't want to learn.

The sound of a car pulling into the lot drew my attention. Yvonne's Jeep swung into a spot near the bar, and she hopped out, tugging up her jeans and tossing a black waist apron over her shoulder. Yvonne was the kind of woman who made me think I could wear red cowboy boots, too. "Heya."

"Von, didn't they call you?"

"Billy called." She eyed the ambulance. "Sorry about your friend."

I remembered the forty-two-buck tip and was ashamed—of myself instead of Maddy, this time. She was generous. I was the petty, suspicious one. "Thanks."

"You should see what this looks like from the overpass," she said. "I bet you could have seen her from the southbound lanes, even—"

"Yvonne."

"I'm just really surprised somebody didn't run off the *road*—"

"Yvonne, if Billy called you, why are you here?"

"Oh." She was staring hard at something over my shoulder.

The moment had come. The gurney rolled across the uneven ground toward us, the black body bag mercifully strapped down to keep it from bouncing. The matched set of EMTs seemed vaguely familiar, maybe from high school, maybe from the bar. Courtney trailed behind, checking her notes.

"Wow," Yvonne said. "That's some real-life shit, right there."

Courtney looked over at us, then followed Maddy's body into the back of the ambulance. The doors closed and the rig took off across the lot. The flashing lights, which had been rolling the entire time, suddenly cut out. There was no hurry.

We watched the ambulance until it was out of the lot, across the overpass, and out of sight. Yvonne shuffled her boots against the asphalt in a silence I assumed was meant to be respectful. A part of me wished I'd been asked to accompany Maddy to the hospital, to help smooth her passage in whatever way I could. To escort her. Hadn't I been at her wing all those races? Someone else would call Maddy's fiancé. And Gretchen. There was a protocol, but I didn't fit into it.

The other part of me, the larger part, was glad to see the patrol vehicles start to leave.

"Can you give me a ride to Lu's? She's got my car."

"I gotta get the bar ready," Yvonne said.

I watched the toe of her boot draw a line in the dirt.

"Wait," I said. "The inn's closed. At least for a few days."

A smile spread across her face by degrees. "They didn't say a thing about the bar, though, did they? Besides, we can't close tonight. This is going to be the busiest night the Mid-Night's ever seen. I mean, sorry. But it is."

She was right. They'd come in droves. They'd come early, stay late. The guys who'd so much as caught a glimpse of Maddy last night would be back to hold court over those who hadn't. I had no idea what time it was, but had a feeling the not-so-happy hour was almost here.

"I'll give you a ride home after, if you stay and help me serve," she said. "And a cut of the tips."

I thought of my dark room at home. Then: Maddy, hanging by her own belt. Her gray, almost silver face.

I would have no use for my bed tonight. With the Mid-Night Inn closed, I also needed the money.

"Half the tips?" I said.

"Was going to say sixty-forty." She threw her head back and sighed. "Fine. But you have to hustle, all right? No wallowing, just because your friend died."

There was a wink in her voice that made me feel, for the moment, like myself. I let her pull me to my feet. She eyed my uniform, my black canvas sneakers with the white toes. "I don't have anything else with me," I said.

"It's good, actually, cute." Yvonne hooked her arm through mine and led me toward the bar. "And when they show up, go ahead and wallow a little. They'll love it."

CHAPTER EIGHT

We stocked the cooler to capacity. Yvonne gave me her keys to open the lobby and grab some extra chairs from storage. We turned an empty pitcher into a second tip jar. That was Yvonne's idea. "They'll all be wanting you down at their end, see? You make them work for your attention, and I'll keep the beer flowing." She chewed on her lip, thinking. "Maybe we'll send you out to the tables to take orders. Give them all a chance."

I carried her words around like a rock in my gut, but I didn't have time to think about whether or not we should be open, whether or not what we were doing was a good idea. The crowd filed in, filling all the available space, and then called their friends to join them. By six, we were a fire hazard.

Among the crowd I saw people I knew, people I hadn't seen in the Mid-Night in a long time, if ever. Dickie showed up. Teeny, layered in additional layers and smelling of old sweat, skulked around the edges of the room, talking to herself. Yvonne kept an eye on Teeny, pulling the tip jars closer to the center of the bar. I didn't know everyone. Everyone, though, seemed to know me.

"Your friend," one of the regulars said over the noise. He wore a pair of red suspenders over his round belly and a red Mack truck hat. The other guys called him Mack as a matter of shorthand. One of the guys who'd had trouble with Maddy's disruption the night before, Mack seemed shaken at the amount of company he was being forced to keep. He kept turning to give the crowd a raised eyebrow, but stuck tight to his stool. "Mighty pretty gal," he said. "They know what's been done to her?"

"She was murdered," I said.

People turned to listen, creating a small circle around me. "Murdered?" someone said. "Are they sure? I thought—"

65

"Was she robbed?" someone else wanted to know. "Was it a break-in? That happened up in Muncie last year. Some people staying in one of those Regency Stay places—"

"No," I said. "Her jewelry was left behind."

"The girls," Teeny said, barely audible.

The jewelry's reputation had already spread. We'd all watched enough crime-solver TV to know that no one would attack a woman, hang her, and leave the easy pickings of such a bauble. Loughton and Courtney hadn't admitted it, but come on. If there was something I knew about, it was pilfering. Almost anyone would have swiped the ring. Anyone.

"Someone said she come from Chicago," Mack said. "She brought that trouble with her. I used to haul up to Chicago. I once saw a man—"

"What makes you think she brought it on herself?" said a woman from a nearby table. "What kind of thing is that to say?"

"She got killed here," said a loud voice behind me. "Whoever it was, he's probably from here."

The circle, expanded to include half of the room, turned to see who'd dared to say what they all hoped wasn't true. The din dropped a few notches.

I already knew who it was, but I turned anyway. The Mid-Night had certainly turned into a class reunion tonight. "Get you a drink, Beck?" I said.

Tommy Beckwith shot me a look of such force I almost backed up. But I'd had practice. All those years as the tagalong, the chaperone. That hard stare over Maddy's shoulder, when he had hoped I'd be anywhere else but where he was trying to be alone with her. I had learned to withstand it. I'd learned how to plant my feet and lean into it. Maddy's boyfriend didn't scare me anymore.

Then, with clarity so sharp I sucked in a breath, I remembered driving with Maddy to Indianapolis, the jostle of her beat-up car over bad streets.

"Where are we going?" I kept asking. Winter, mittens not keeping my hands warm. Where, where, come on, where. Her coy refusal to say had made me wonder if she was treating me to something special, like my dad taking me for ice cream when I made the honor roll or improved my time on the track. Maddy and I didn't have that kind of relationship, but the idea of a treat occurred to me. The farther we drove into the city, deep into pockets of empty buildings and cracked sidewalks, the more I thought she was tricking me. Trying to scare me. We didn't have that relationship, either. But it occurred to me.

That feeling, that roiling suspicion in my gut. I felt that again now. She was tricking me. She'd tricked me. She wasn't really dead. Where had she gone? Where, where, come on.

Back then, I'd held on to my seat belt, making a plan in case we were lost. She'd been acting strange for a few days, like someone I didn't know. My hands were freezing. I blew hot breath through my mittens, waiting for her to return to herself, to give a sign it would be OK, whatever it was.

When she pulled to the side of a quiet street, I grabbed the door handle.

"That's where we'll run state," she said.

And there it was. The stadium belonged to a university neither of us thought we had any chance of being accepted to or, in my case, paying for. Inside the stadium would be the track, long white stripes on a red circle. The finish line. The launching pad. All of it, the early hours and the late hours and the blisters and shin splints—inside that stadium in just a few months, all of it would come to its natural end. I harbored hopes that we would run one, two, but in the other direction, with Maddy finally seeing what my jaw looked like for a change.

We sat and watched the silent structure for a long moment. And I was satisfied. I felt exactly like my dad had taken me for ice cream, that I'd made the honor roll. That I'd been treated. Maddy and I had shared something special here. We knew who we were. We knew who we were going to be.

In that moment, I knew everything I needed to know about our friendship. Everyone else was a blur.

But then Maddy drove us out of the stadium's shadows and down an even more secluded street. Within a few minutes, we were parking next to long, blank brick wall with a single, opaque glass door.

"What is this place?"

"I need to do something, OK? Will you stay here and wait for me?"

"You can't be serious, Maddy." I looked at the long side of the building, all the good feeling from the stadium dropping away. I couldn't decide where my anxiety was coming from. There was something about the building's empty face that said more than any sign would have. "What is this place? What if you don't come out?"

"You can be so dramatic," she said. "It's just a test, OK? No big deal."

What kind of test. What kind of test. My mouth wouldn't form the words. I knew what kind of test, and why the building was unmarked.

"Are you *pregnant*?" I said.

"No way, shut up." She bit at her nails. "Not a pregnancy test. Another one, OK? You can't tell anyone."

We are *seventeen*, I wanted to say. Surely you can't need any tests. Sex-ed films. All the times we'd whispered behind our hands at girls waddling gut-first past us at school. We were smarter than that. We had better things to do. What were we doing here? We would be running in that stadium in a few months, but only if we did everything right, timed every move perfectly, trained like we'd never trained—and she was getting tested for some sex disease? I wanted to shake her. No, I wanted to shake *Beck*. This was his fault.

I hadn't even known they were having sex. And this was how she told me. It stung. Maddy, rushing past me. Leaving me behind, as ever.

We weren't having the day I thought we were having. We were not having ice cream. We were not sharing something. I was not a part of this.

I sat in the car, the heat roaring but still weak, until Maddy came back. I hurried to unlock her door. She slid into the driver's seat, pale.

"Well?" I finally asked. We might have been halfway home by the time I got up the nerve. We stopped and got tacos—I remembered the bag of tacos keenly now, how neither of us wanted them, how the smell took over the car until I felt sick.

"I won't know for a day or so. They'll call."

"God, what if Gretchen answers the phone?"

She shrugged.

What if it's positive? Why didn't you tell me? I couldn't seem to catch my breath to ask her anything. I felt as though I'd been running hard to catch her.

The drive home was long and silent. When she dropped me off, a part of me wondered if I'd ever see her again, if she hadn't planned the trip as a good-bye of some kind.

It was. Or at least it seemed so for a while. The results must have been something she could live with, because she never mentioned them. She came back to herself after a little while. But I could no longer stand the sight of Beck's hand on her. What disease had he almost given her? How many other girls had he put his dirty hands on? Why hadn't he been the one to take her to that cold, blank building?

Now, Beck was sliding through the crowd away from me. Everyone pulled back to let him through, dark and swift against the current. What had she ever seen in him? Good-looking, in a hard-labor kind of way, sure. But he didn't run or play football or come to school events, or come to school, really, all that often. He was a farmer's kid, who'd driven a tractor long before the rest of us could drive cars. Now he helped run the farm, or that's what I'd heard. Midway was a small place, but in the ten years since graduation, I'd only seen Beck a few dozen times, and never in the Mid-Night. I didn't want to see him. He might have gone out of his way not to see me.

I watched the regulars nod their welcome. They were farmers, some of them. He wedged an elbow in at the bar among them and caught Yvonne's attention.

In his wake, the circle around me dissolved, and the room recovered its roar. Someone put a tragic song on the juke. For the moment, they'd all forgotten about me.

Again I felt that rushing wave of certainty meeting uncertainty. Maddy Bell was dead. How could that be real?

I looked around. It was real and now. Beck, me, all these people.

Maybe we were here for more than gossip and gawking. For more than tip money, in any case, more than an overpriced drink.

They were waiting, watching. Guys like Mack, slumped at the bar. Women from the plant down the street on their third happy-hour whiskey sour. Happy hour was long over. They had kids at home, but here they were. They held out for something that I hadn't thought to give them.

This was not my responsibility, this impromptu wake. No one had invited them here.

Yvonne made a face at me from behind the bar. I searched the room for someone needing service. All the glasses were full, all hands held a bottle. When I glanced back to the bar, Yvonne was handing Beck a beer and jerking her head toward him.

No way. We'd never had a kind word for each other, and we weren't going to start tonight, as some kind of touching scene for the gathered audience.

And then a terrible keening sound cut through the noise and silenced the room. We all turned to the front door.

Our track coach, Coach Trenton, leaned into the room like a puppet with its strings cut. His face hung slack and tortured. Behind him, Fitz, our former assistant coach, wiped his face with his hand.

"We just heard," Fitz said. "The girls, at practice, someone got a text—"

"It's not true, is it, Jules?" Coach said. Only the terrible sobbing music on the jukebox kept the place from falling in on its own silence.

I thought, suddenly, of all the calls I should have made. My mom— oh no. I hadn't softened the blow for anyone.

And then I swung, pendulum-like, toward rage. Why should they be spared? I'd found the body. I'd suffered more than any of these hangers-on. Maddy's gray face would never leave me.

But the truth was that I couldn't have called anyone. I'd never have been able to say the words. And I hadn't wanted to. I was carrying Maddy's death around in my arms like a wriggling newborn, as though I could keep it confined and safe, and—mine. I couldn't put it down. Meanwhile, the news spun away from me, growing monstrous.

"It's true," I said.

Coach seemed to crumple. Fitz held him by the shoulders. "Maybe we could talk, Juliet? Somewhere else?"

"Sure." When I turned to wave off-duty to Yvonne, I saw Beck watching, his fist clenched white around his beer mug.

I'd thought we'd come for a funeral. All of us. We'd all come to be a part of the drama. Some of us had come to sell her memory for a share of the tips.

Except Beck. Out of all of us, he seemed to be the only one who'd come to hold out hope.

Well, too bad. None of us had any. Not anymore.

I led them out into the night. Maddy's car had been towed away. I stared at the empty space and, without a lot of options for where to take them, remembered Yvonne's keys in my pocket and led the coaches back to the front doors and into the lobby. Fitz pulled Coach to the sofa and let him slump to the cushions.

"I can't believe it," Coach moaned.

I tried not to stare. I saw Coach and Fitz whenever I went to Midway High to substitute teach or in town like anyone else, but it had been a while since we'd sought each other out. They seemed older, both of them, but had aged in completely different ways. Fitz had gone big—barrel-chested and muscular, a little on the chubby side. He was the one of them always quickest with a bandage or an ice pack or just a smile. He had a way of touching an elbow or a shoulder, just a small gesture that gave an upset runner a dose of perspective. Coach had gone the other direction. His legs, even now clad in workout gear, were tan and tight as ropes. While Fitz had softened and blurred, Coach looked like a more sharply focused image of himself.

It made sense. Fitz was the former football player never good enough to go pro, but Coach was a former Olympian. His bronze medal had a place of honor in Midway High's trophy case. He'd wanted gold, sure, but had never gone back to the Games. He still trained, though, like someone with his best time trials ahead of him.

"I just can't believe it," Coach said.

I reached for the lights, then realized the spectacle we'd make to anyone in the bar. I turned on a low table lamp instead. In the half light, the coaches looked even more haunted. "It's been an unbelievable kind of day," I said.

"You found the—I mean." Fitz swallowed hard. "You found her? Where? It was really her? You're sure?"

"She was hanging by a belt around the neck," I said. "Off the railing in the back. It was Maddy."

We all lived with it for a moment. In the bar, another sad, twangy song started up.

"What was she even doing here?" Coach had managed to gain some control. He sat with his bony wrists dangling from his knees.

"Business, she said."

"You talked to her?" Fitz said. "When?"

"Well, before."

He shifted in his cross-trainers. "Right. What kind of business?"

"She didn't say." I thought back to our conversation. She hadn't told me what she did. She hadn't told me anything.

"I didn't realize you were still in touch," Coach said.

"We weren't," I said.

"She got away from us all," Coach said. "She couldn't run fast enough or far enough, could she?"

Fitz shook his head.

I felt as though I'd walked into the room late. "Fast enough or far enough from what? What are you talking about?"

"Her dad," Coach said. "If that bastard were still alive, I don't think we'd have to look very far—"

"Come on, Mike," Fitz said. "Not the time."

"Her dad?" I'd met Maddy's dad only once, and he hadn't seemed like anyone to stir such passionate feelings, one way or the other. He worked a lot, was gone a lot. The only time I'd seen him, at Maddy's house the first and last time I'd ever spent the night there, he kept to himself. He wore an ugly cardigan sweater—really ugly, the color of throw-up. And slippers. My dad had never owned a sweater of any type, only flannel or fleece and Carhartts for severe weather; he wore his work boots in the house up to the minute he took them off for bed. To me, Mr. Bell was exotic. He'd gone to college. He worked in an office. Now he and my dad were, at last, in the same place: the nondenominational cemetery on the east side of Midway. "What am I missing?" I said.

"Mike had some idea," Fitz said, "that something—*funny* was going on with Maddy back then. At home."

I looked between them. "Funny how?"

"Did she ever confide in you, Jules?" Coach said. He and Fitz both were nearly twitching from discomfort. They reminded me of the morning Maddy turned up crampy at the state tournament. I would have thought two men who taught and coached pubescent girls for a living had seen a tampon or two in their day. "Anything—not right, with the family?" he said.

My stomach dropped into my shoes. I needed to sit down. "You don't mean—"

But I couldn't finish. A terrible image: Maddy's face pressed into that puke-colored sweater. Then that blank brick wall as I waited for Maddy to come out. I thought I might be sick. Their queasy looks matched how I felt. "No. No, she never said anything like that. How do you—I mean, why did you think so?"

"It was all speculation, or we would have done something." Fitz looked uneasily in Coach's direction. "And it hardly matters now, but we always felt, and not just us—you should have heard what some of the other parents, especially mothers, would say—anyway, we always wondered."

"We *worried*," Coach said. "She just seemed so—sexualized. For such a young girl."

"A couple of mothers did mention how mature—" Fitz gave me a pained, apologetic look, for dragging me into this or for using the word *mother* around me, I wasn't sure which. "But I did have my concerns about that boyfriend."

"Beck?"

"He was a distraction," Fitz said. "That part I'm certain about. Her head wasn't on straight after she took up with him."

"He was possessive," Coach said. "You saw it."

I'd seen it.

An odd look played across Coach's face. "That guy—where is he these days?"

That guy sat on a bar stool less than a hundred feet away. I glanced at the door to the bar, just catching the heel of a boot as someone stepped away. "He, uh, he still lives in the area. I think."

"Well, that's it, then," Coach said. "She got away from him once, but damned if he didn't catch up with her when she came back to town." Coach looked at me, hard.

He couldn't be saying what I thought I was hearing.

"*Beck?*" That was crazy. But I felt again the weight of Beck's gaze, saw Maddy's feet dangling over the trash bin. Everything was crazy. "Do you think he's capable of—" The word still stuck in my throat. "Killing her?"

"Hey," Coach said, throwing up his hands. "I don't know what to think. Who would want to kill Maddy?"

Nobody said anything, but I found myself thinking about our senior year. Maddy won so often and for so long that we'd started to get some guff from the other schools. Not just from the other runners, who liked to trash-talk us at the starting blocks. Sometimes students in the stands had things to say. Sometimes parents. There were adults, we learned, willing to say terrible things as soon as they got you alone. That last year, the closer we got to the state finals, the more people seemed to want to catch us aside and let us know how little they thought of our winning streak. They made accusations of steroids and such, of course. At least that made sense. But we also got called sluts, as though an active sex life might make us faster.

We didn't juice, and we certainly weren't sluts. Now, all this talk of being *sexualized* struck my sense of justice like a gong. Maddy had a boyfriend. A lot of girls did. Even I had managed a date now and then.

But none of that had led, surely, to Maddy's death. Idle threats, ten years on.

"Maybe you should tell the cops about him," Fitz said. "The boyfriend?"

Courtney's triumphant smile came back to me and, with it, a sinking dread.

My mind raced to justify it. If the police had two suspects instead of only one, maybe Courtney and her partner would be more likely to consider all the angles, not just the easy one. If they had two suspects, they'd have to work harder, and they would find the real killer. Right? Since neither of us was the real killer? Well, I wasn't. I didn't really know about Beck. Which was reason enough to tell Courtney about him. His possessiveness, as Coach called it. For the first time since I'd found Maddy's body, I felt a tiny opening. Hope.

"Tell them what?" Coach said. "She dated that kid a decade ago." The opening slammed shut. "But I feel like we need to do something," Coach said, looking at me. "Jules, shouldn't we do something?"

The last of us to see Maddy alive. The first to find her dead.

Me. I was the one who should do something, and fast.

CHAPTER NINE

After a long silence, Coach finally gathered himself and stood to go. He rolled one of his shoulders with a grimace, then glanced my way. "Who knew grief was such a physical thing?" he said.

I took a quick hug from both of them. I'd always believed them to be more demonstrative with Maddy, squeezing her shoulder at practice when Coach needed her full focus or after she'd broken the finish line tape again. But then I'd had my dad there to offer finish-line hugs.

I let them out into the night, imagining a funeral, a place to put all this fumbling for sentiment and solace. I was leaning toward the lamp to turn it off when the door chimed and opened.

"What did those two old ladies want?"

Beck. I glanced down at his black boots. Of course he'd been the one watching us. Who was he to demand anything from me? "Well, they did wonder about your alibi for last night."

"They're a fine pair to be accusing me."

"What's that supposed to mean?" I said.

"They drove Maddy crazy in high school," he said. "She couldn't wait to get away from those guys."

I'd never heard her say anything like that. Even now, even in her death, Beck couldn't share Maddy with anyone. "Maybe she was trying to get away from someone else."

"Me, you mean," he said.

Actually, I'd been thinking of her father. That vomit-colored sweater. But I didn't want to get into it right now. Beck looked like a wind-up toy twisted too hard, one turn away from breaking into pieces. What if Coach and Fitz could see him now? They wouldn't hesitate to talk to the police about him. "Were you still in touch?" I said. "Were you ever, after she went to college?"

That heavy look landed squarely on me again. I waited it out. I knew things about him—maybe that had always been his problem with me. He took a deep breath as I braced myself to withstand whatever he would say. And then he uncoiled, and fell back against the front desk.

"That's the thing I never—" he said. "I never understood it. That stupid race in Indy that she didn't run—"

"*We* didn't run," I said.

"—and then the life seemed to go out of her. Remember?"

His clenched fists were held tight against the thighs of his jeans. I imagined that's what I looked like when I was trying to keep from reaching for something that wasn't mine.

"She wouldn't let me take her to prom," he said. "And she went up to college early to get a head start on classes. Who does that? It was like that race was everything, and when it went on without her—done. Us, high school, Midway, all of it." His voice caught. I looked away. As much as I'd ever hated him, I also hated this new version of him, helpless and ensnared, even this many years later.

I also hated that he'd expressed exactly my own memories. The race, then the end of everything. Except I'd been so busy no longer being Maddy's friend that I hadn't noticed that Maddy had stopped being Maddy. I hadn't known she'd gone off to college early. I hadn't known how hard she'd let Beck down.

The last time I'd seen her before she walked into the Mid-Night Inn was graduation day. By then we hadn't spoken in weeks, not since leaving that hotel room without running the championship race. We were kids—we didn't have it in us to forgive or chuck each other on the shoulder for old time's sake. We'd been friends competing against one another, maybe more literally than most teen girls, but we were still just kids. And then we weren't friends. We weren't enemies. We weren't anything at all. After state, I kept other company, but mostly my own, and when my parents asked me where Maddy was on graduation day, I shrugged and didn't point her out. They would have forced a picture between us. She stood alone, sallow in her Midway High–red cap and gown. Had her parents shown up, at last, to support her? I didn't even know. We'd already gone our separate ways.

And then—there was no better way to say it—she'd lapped me.

Maddy had beaten me so many times. But seeing her last night looking professional and happy and *satisfied* had bothered me more than any second-place finish ever had.

In this contest, I wasn't even coming in second. I wasn't even in the field. I was a spectator.

I had a headache. I hadn't eaten all day. My car was parked miles away in front of someone else's snug, cozy home. I had no income until the motel re-opened, and I had no idea when that would be. My childhood best friend was gone, and the only ray of possibility I'd had all day was the moment when I realized I could turn the cops on the guy standing in front of me. This guy who couldn't talk about his high-school sweetheart without getting choked up. No one had ever felt that way about me. Even in death, Maddy was winning.

We need to do something, Coach had said. And we did. I did. I looked at Beck.

"Tell me." I swallowed hard. "Just tell me you didn't kill her."

That heavy look again. "Don't be stupid," he said.

"I'm about to do something ridiculously stupid," I said. "The question is, do you want to help?"

I locked up the office, tossing Yvonne's keys to her and ignoring the stares as Beck and I passed through the bar.

We took the middle stairs. I couldn't bring myself to take the other way, around the alcove and past the railing from which Maddy had swung.

"Let me get this straight," Beck said at my back. "Why are we doing this again?"

The night was stunning in its blackness. Billy needed to replace about eight light bulbs on the second floor. I felt for my notebook to jot down a reminder but only felt the square of Maddy's room card.

"You and I are suspects," I said. "What more reason do you need?"

"I'm in the clear," he said. "You know why? Because I didn't kill her."

"Neither did I. How airtight is your alibi?"

He snorted. "You've been watching too much prime time."

"You know where I was? I was home, in bed. Alone, before you ask. That's how loser single girls nearly thirty years old who still live with their mothers *roll*." We reached the door to two-oh-two, still crossed by two strips of crime-scene warning tape. "How about you?"

There was just enough light here to see Beck calculating his odds. "I was home in bed, too." His eyes flicked to mine and away. "Alone. And I don't even live with anyone who can say I came home last night."

"Worse news for you," I said. "Billy heard a ruckus from this room last night—a sexual ruckus, if he can be believed to know the difference. Which—anyway, you're far more likely—"

"I got it. I'm a much better killer than you. Great." He turned to the door. "So. How do we do this?" He reached for the handle.

"Don't touch it," I hissed, and slapped his hand away. "Do you not watch TV *at all*? Your job is to keep your fingerprints to yourself. And your DNA—"

"That's awkward," he said.

"I mean spit or, like, skin particles or whatever. There's no reason for you to have been in there and if they can prove you were—at any point—you're getting a lifetime change of address. Stay out here. And don't touch the rail or—"

"I got it, OK? I appreciate your concern for my future defense team. I'll try not to spit. How are you getting in without touching anything?"

"I go into this room every time someone checks out. They've probably already found my fingerprints."

The idea chilled me, but I had to be realistic. I'd cleaned it two days ago. We wore gloves to clean the bathrooms, but I would've touched plenty of things before I'd put them on. The TV remote. We always had to locate it and put it back on the side table. I would have touched the side table, too, cleaning up the water-glass rings everyone left. The trash can, to shake out whatever bits of wrappers and tissues the former occupants had tossed. The door handle, for crying out loud. I would've touched the handle on both sides, without giving it a second thought. I'd only been doing my job.

Last to see her alive, first to find her dead, and my fingerprints decorating the entire crime scene. No wonder Courtney Howard's pie-faced grin still shot through me like an electrical current.

"But how—"

I whipped the key card from my pocket, reached through the tape, and swiped the card at the practiced, perfect speed. The light blinked green, beep-beep, all is well. With one finger, I hooked the door handle.

We watched the door swing inward into the black room.

Why had this seemed like such a good plan?

Sometimes, when a Bargain was checking in to the motel, I caught a whiff of pity. They don't need any evidence at all to believe that I must be stupid to be stuck in this life. I wasn't stupid, or at least I hadn't thought I was, until now.

"Are you going in or not?" Beck whispered.

"Give me a second, OK?" I was not this person. Creeping around in the dark—

I suddenly remembered standing inside Coach and Fitz's dark office, hissing at Maddy to hurry up from the doorway while I watched for anyone to come along. We'd be expelled. We'd never run for Midway again. Her tennis shoes had squeaked dangerously against the floor while I chewed my nails.

Why had we been there? Pranks had been a big team activity that year, getting so out of control at one point that Fitz had to sit us all down and call a truce.

Now I stared at the threshold of this room, trying to grab more of that memory.

"Well, if you're not going in—" Beck reached for the light switch.

I caught his arm. "You have a surprising lack of self-preservation."

He looked at my hand on his arm. I dropped it.

"Wouldn't that be good news for you?" he said. "If I got nailed for this?"

"Believe me, I've already thought of that."

"And?" he said.

"And I really want to know who killed her, OK? Someone killed her, Beck. My best—" My voice strangled in my throat. Apparently Beck wasn't the only one harboring feelings a decade old. When I glanced back at him, his expression was lost in the shadows. "If you get mixed up in this, and you didn't do it—you'd better not have done it, you son of a bitch—we might never know who did."

"Well, what if they think it was you? What if you get sent up for life?"

I wasn't going to let that happen, but I saw his point. "Then at least the two of us will know they got it wrong."

He took a long time to nod, and I felt it, too. We were agreeing to far more than the plan at hand. It felt like we were sweeping away everything we'd ever felt toward one another, and starting over. I turned back to the door, ducking under the yellow tape into the room and using my elbow to swipe at the light switch.

A dim circle of light appeared on the floor, where a lamp from the bedside table had been knocked over. I fumbled for the other switch. A floor lamp across the room showed us the scene.

"Oh," Beck said.

I hadn't gotten a good look over the shoulders of the police earlier, but now I could see the full extent. The place was torn apart. The sheets and blankets had been ripped from the bed, the window shade pulled to the ground, the bedside table ransacked. The dresser, gutted. Its surface was clean, the diamond swept away to an evidence locker.

And of course, the two garage-sale landscapes over the dresser and bed were askew. The nightmare tree and the road to nowhere, both hanging a little off balance, as always.

Disaster, my mind provided. Aftermath. I didn't see any blood, but I watched for it as I picked my way across the room. Blood on my shoes would be tough to explain.

"I was going to ask you if anything was out of place," he said.

In the center of the room, I turned in a full circle. The mattress had been bumped off its box springs. The mirror over the bathroom sink was cracked. The ruckus Billy had heard must have been full-on combat.

"Everything is, but also—"

"What?" Beck said.

"Stay where you are." I couldn't place it, but something nagged at me. Some little piece called out from a place that was more out of place than everything else.

I knelt to look under the bed, then rose and went to the bathroom. Maddy might have only stepped away. Her makeup, lotion, and perfume waited like soldiers on alert.

She'd meant to stay.

The towels were folded as I'd left them the last time I'd turned the room. Only the bathmat was out of place, having slipped off the edge of the tub. Nothing might have happened, except for the ruined mirror.

In it, my reflection was cut diagonally across the neck, folding in on itself along the crease.

I turned my attention to the bottles on the sink, leaning to sniff at them until I'd found the warm cookie scent. It was a small, slim bottle. My palms tingled, then rushed to a fierce burn.

"What are you doing in there?"

"Nothing," I said, but I'd already reached for the bottle and slipped it into my pocket. Against my hip, the perfume was cold. It wasn't the same as stealing from a friend.

"What's taking so long?" Beck hissed.

"Just—be quiet for a second," I said. I reached for the bathmat, realized what I was doing and stopped, then squatted down to take a closer look. The fibers at the tiniest corner of the mat had been crushed into a pattern. A shoe print.

I came back to the room, picking my way around all the sheets. Using my skirt as a barrier against leaving new fingerprints, I pulled open the dresser drawers, one at a time, then closed them.

While Beck fidgeted at the door, I went to the bedside table and peered into the drawer still hanging open. An old phone book, a Bible.

I reached in and felt around the back of the drawer, accidentally lifting the cover on the Bible as I pulled my hand out. A scrap of paper blew out from the pages. I reached back in and plucked it out.

"What you're looking for," it said, with a string of numbers below. A Bible verse, maybe, missing the book name. It had been a long time since I'd been inside a church. Or a Bible.

"Are you almost done?" Beck turned and looked at the courtyard behind him. I added the paper to my pocket.

"Something's not right," I said. "More than just knocked around."

"I don't know how you could tell that. Nothing's where it should be," he said. "I mean, maybe the wallpaper stayed put."

I checked the wallpaper to be sure. There was a dark swipe under one of the framed prints. Something—someone—had been dragged against the wall.

For a long moment, I stared at the swipe. Then the thing worrying me snapped into focus.

"We should go." I crossed the room like a kid jumping from rock to rock across a stream. "Come on."

"What? Why? I thought we were going to—do something."

"I don't want to get caught here. What if someone sees the light on? Or Billy—God, Billy could come up here any minute. Or someone from the bar."

Beck looked at me, then at the wall. "What did you see?"

"What do you mean? Nothing."

"Which is it?" he said. "You don't know what I mean, or you do know what I mean and you saw nothing?"

He stood between me and the cool evening. Over his shoulder, one low star stood out against the hazy, dark horizon. I thought of Maddy again, of course. I was the one who kept her head down, focused, and still lost. Maddy kept her eyes open. I was beginning to understand how well, and how much I would have to pay attention to keep up with her.

As clear as anything, her voice came to me. "Do you think there's a real place, where you go?"

We'd stayed out past my curfew that night, passing a bottle of something terrible from her stepmother's liquor cabinet back and forth, parked in her old car in a cornfield. I was going to get into trouble for being late, and I wasn't sure I'd brought any mints to hide the booze on my breath. But Maddy hadn't wanted to go home or go to my home, or go anywhere. She'd had more than I had, I guess. She didn't seem to mind the taste of whatever we were drinking. "I mean, a real place, where you can touch things, and have a dog, and eat chocolate?"

When you died, she meant.

"Did you ever have a dog?" I'd asked. Supposing that to have a dog in heaven, you'd need to have had one in life. It all made sense in my mind. A lot of things made sense that night.

But I didn't think I'd really answered her question, even then. Now, I knew I hadn't. I understood now what she wanted to know. Did you get a chance to get it right? Or was this it?

I didn't know. I didn't have to wonder, though, if Maddy had been scared to find out.

She'd put up a fight here, a real fight. *Things aren't always what they seem*, she'd said to me in the bar. But this messy room was the opposite of what I'd first believed about her death. She hadn't wanted to die. She'd wanted to live, badly. And she must have known that she wouldn't.

Beck's stare weighed on me.

I turned and went back to the scratch on the wallpaper. Above it hung one of the cornfield landscapes, the one with the dark tree. I pulled the picture off its hook and turned it over. Nothing.

"What are you doing?" Beck looked behind him nervously. "Put that back."

I put it back, then cut carefully back across the sea of torn sheets and blankets to the other side of the room. The frame hung over the bed, almost true, the only thing that might have gone untouched in the room—except it was on the wrong wall.

Lu and I hated these prints. They not only bored us, they defied any cleaning method we'd devised. Bugs somehow got stuck under the glass. The frames grew mysteriously sticky, and even a blast of Shinez-All couldn't take it off.

But we knew exactly where they belonged in each room. These two frames had been swapped in the last two days, since I'd last flipped the room.

That couldn't be a mistake.

The second print was the cornfield cut by a lonely road, the dust kicking up behind an unseen car getting the hell out of there.

I grabbed the frame from the wall and held it up. A white square of paper had been tucked into the back. I lay the frame upside down on the bed and peeled the paper away.

"Oh, what did you do?" Beck said quietly. At first I thought he meant me, but then I knew he didn't.

It was a photo of me and Maddy, Coach, and Fitz after the Southtown regional tournament our senior year. A girl in Southtown black and white stood at the edge of the photo with a grim expression of disappointment. In the center, Coach was picking up his Indiana High School Coach of the Year trophy and medallion. At the moment the photo was taken, he was shaking the hand of an official mostly off camera, and the three of us, me, Maddy, Fitz, are being jostled against him in the chaos of congratulations.

Maddy and I carried our regional trophies against our hips like infants, and Fitz squeezed Maddy's shoulder, gazing upon us like a proud father. But Maddy's face is serious, determined. Her eyes cut to the left of the cameraman, away from the festivities. She was already thinking about the state finals. She was already way ahead of everyone else.

In the photo, I'm living in the moment. My smile is a thousand-watt beauty, all that orthodontia finally paying off, all those chewy vitamins and two vegetables at dinner and access to vaccinations and fluoride in the water radiating from me. I looked like a corn-fed State Fair dairy princess reigning over my subjects.

It was a great photo of a great day. I studied it, letting myself remember. The bus trip home that night had been epic. We sang songs and screamed at passing cars until our throats grew raw. We were strung out on runner's high and winning and youth and the world spinning precisely the way it was meant to. On the bus, Coach passed his

Coach of the Year trophy around, a team win. We ran our fingers over the cool metal of the running figure, over the smooth wood and the etched words of recognition, over Coach's name. Finally the winner, finally after his disappointment at the Olympic Games. He'd worn the medallion from the ceremony, all the way home, a long, dark ride. Fitz commented on the craftsmanship of the medallion, of the sturdy, bright-blue ribbon, while we girls took turns studying the trophy and sending the runner racing for his life, bouncing seat to seat, past the point of hilarity.

"All right, all right, girls," Coach finally said, "Give him back." The round, brassy Coach of the Year medallion hanging heavy around his neck. Maddy had jogged the trophy up the aisle and back into Coach's hands.

That was Southtown, after all the hell some people had put us through, calling us names and telling us we didn't deserve what we'd earned. But that night, we'd garnered our team the two top spots in the state finals, and our leader the state's top coaching honor, and no one could tell us we were anything but champions.

"What?" Beck said. "What is it?"

"It's just—" I held up the photo.

He peered at it, then behind him again. "Let's go."

I put the frame back, then retrieved the photo and held it to myself tenderly.

"You're taking that?" he said.

"She left it for me."

"This is a crime scene, Townsend—"

"She meant for me to find it," I said. "I'm the only one who would have."

He frowned at the photo in my hands. "Shouldn't we—"

There was a creaking sound down behind him. We hurried out and closed the door gently behind us. I led Beck to the center stairwell and down past the office. At the bar's end of the parking lot, several cars remained. A young woman teetering in high heels struggled into the open passenger door of a car with a buckled hood.

I went to the door of the bar and peered in. The crowd had dispersed, but a few of the hardcore regulars were closing it down. I still didn't have a ride home, but now it was too late to call Lu or bother her for my keys. If I fetched my haul from Yvonne's tip jars, I could see who was left sober enough to ask for a ride. But I couldn't bring myself to go in.

Beck's boots kicked gravel as he crossed the lot toward his truck. Something in his movements reminded me of the boy he'd once been—the one who caroused, who skipped out of woodshop and art classes to strut past our advanced English class, winking. The one who wanted Maddy all to himself. Even now, it seemed. Even now, he wanted all the grief there was. I hadn't liked that boy, and I was pretty sure I didn't like the man he'd turned into, either.

For a long moment I watched him walk away. Why had I trusted him?

But I knew why.

Because Maddy had. And she'd trusted me, too. I held the photo of us to my chest and wished again that I'd been better to her on that last night. Maybe everything would have turned out differently.

"Hey," I called to Beck's back. "Give me a ride home, and we'll figure out what to do next."

CHAPTER TEN

The next morning, the phone rang early. I'd been hoping to sleep in, since the Mid-Night was no-vacancy for a while, and then walk to Lu's house to fetch my keys and car. After that, my plans petered down to lying in front of the TV until Billy called us back in. I did a few calculations in my head with the balance of my checkbook. Change of plans. I'd have to get a newspaper for the want ads.

I sat up, reaching first thing for Maddy's photo. Beck had dropped me off the night before without either of us deciding what we'd do next. Well, he had decided. He wanted out of it.

As he drove me home, he kept glancing at the photo in my hands. "It bothers me," he said. He seemed relieved to leave me on the curb in front of my house.

I'd stowed the perfume bottle in my bathroom among my other things, but not in the secret space, where it would've probably spilled. I didn't want to waste a drop. The key card to Maddy's room, too, seemed special. After thinking about it, I slipped the card under a patch of loose wallpaper next to my bed and glued it down with clear nail polish. I imagined the card as a time capsule. Thirty years from now maybe someone else would live here, and they would pull down the flowered paper, horrified that anyone would have such taste, only to find a tiny mystery. Where would I be?

I hated to think that I might still be here, but I had no better plans.

Putting these things away, I was satisfied. But the real prize of the night was the photo. I couldn't put it away. I couldn't get enough of my own glowing skin, my own radiant smile. All these years I'd remembered the disappointment of second place, but Maddy's gift to me was a reminder that second place had come with rewards, too.

"Juliet," my mom said against the crack of my bedroom door, sounding tired. "It's the school."

I threw the covers over the photo. I hadn't had the heart to wake my mother the night before and let her know about Maddy. I couldn't bear to hear what she would say, or wouldn't say.

"Thanks, Mom," I said, waiting until I was sure she was gone before I picked up my bedroom extension. It had been a long time since I'd been called to substitute teach.

"Good morning, Juliet." The clipped voice of the school secretary put me right back in the principal's office. Mrs. Haggerty, stationed at the helm of Midway High as long as anyone remembered, ran the school with an iron fist. Having to see the principal for some indiscretion wasn't much of a punishment if you'd already survived Mrs. Haggerty's displeasure.

She didn't wait for me to greet her. "We could use you in phys ed today," she said. "Coach Fitzgerald called in sick—bereft, I'd say. So sorry to hear about Madeleine, of course. I can't imagine you feel any better about the situation, but he requested you specifically. What do you think?"

The scrap of paper with the numbers from the Mid-Night Bible had fallen from my nightstand. I picked it up, thinking that the last thing I wanted to do today was to stand around a steamy gym while hormone-charged teenagers preened and flirted without breaking a sweat. Fitz got to be bereft, while Coach could barely pull himself upright, and I . . . but I needed the money. My car had nearly reached its last mile. I lived so lean, and yet so many decisions I made in my life came down to this one fact: I needed the money.

I also needed a ride. "I'll be there. Thanks, Mrs. Haggerty."

I tapped the hang-up button and sorted through my options. "What you're looking for," the paper in my hand said. I'd assumed it had something to do with the Bible it had come from, but now I saw it was probably a phone number. I dialed it. The line rang and rang. I didn't know what I expected to happen, but I found myself hoping that Maddy would answer the phone. Maddy, alive, and this would all be a big misunderstanding.

No one picked up. Finally I hung up and dialed instead for what I was really looking for: emergency carpool.

"I'm glad he asked for you," Coach said when he pulled into the driveway. He'd stopped for coffee and picked up one for me, with milk and one sugar, just how I liked it. I sipped at the cup and leaned against the buttery leather seats of his car, feeling cradled and cared for in a way I hadn't in a while. "When one of us is gone, they usually call in that insurance salesman who never finished his master's thesis. We end up sending him out to the track to avoid talking to him. I have magnificent auto, home, and life coverage already, for one thing."

He threw a smile my way.

"No offense, but I'm a little surprised Fitz is the one home today," I said. "You were sort of a mess last night."

Coach's smile slid away, his face going from game to weary in a few seconds. "We all grieve differently. Maddy's . . . death. God, I can barely say that, can you? It was a shock. We were all shocked, of course, but last night, I was under its spell. I just couldn't . . . but Fitz. Fitz is made of tougher stuff than I am, which is how he's always able to take care of everyone else. Always taking care of things. But it wears on him."

I turned to look at the town rushing by, trying to think if Fitz had ever taken care of me. Maddy, sure. But that was small thinking, and I didn't want to be that person anymore. Maybe I'd never needed Fitz's help the way other people did. Maybe a pep talk once in a while was all he thought I needed. But then he'd requested me to cover his classes today, just as my job was in danger. I saw Coach's point.

"You remember," he said. "That day at state—well, with Maddy being so ill and you wanting to run, deserving to run. I don't know what I would have done without Fitz. You know how many times I've had the chance to say that over the years? More than I like to admit."

For a moment, I let myself imagine me and Maddy, years into the future but still the kind of friends Coach and Fitz were. Maybe she and I could have taken over the phys-ed classes when they retired, coming to school in Midway-red tracksuits and whistles on lanyards.

Nothing about this picture made any sense. Maddy had bigger plans, and I'd never finished college. And tracksuits? By the looks of her clothes, Maddy wouldn't have been caught dead—

"Something has been bothering me," I said. "Something you said. Why did you think Maddy's dad—why did you think he was such a creep?" I tried to keep the puke-colored sweater at bay.

"It doesn't matter now," he said. "All this, whatever it was or wasn't, is long over."

I waited, watching his profile.

"Your coffee smells better than mine," he said. "Like cookies."

It was Maddy's perfume he smelled. I'd dabbed a little on my wrists, for good luck—which made no sense, now that I thought about it. I pulled down the sleeves on my fleece. "But—"

He sighed, shook his head at the road. "OK, I understand you're confused, because you didn't notice anything. But remember, you were just a kid. You can't expect yourself to have noticed anything. Let it go. To dwell on it, you're only going to find fault with yourself. It's too late for Maddy. I wish I'd done things differently—but you let me have the regrets, OK?"

I thought of standing in Maddy's room at the Mid-Night, turning in a circle in the wreck she'd created, trying to survive. She'd fought so hard. I couldn't just let that go. I didn't want to. There was something about how torn up that room was, how hard Maddy struggled, that made me want to fight for my life, too. I could never say that, not to Fitz, not to Coach, not to anyone.

She'd done everything, every possible thing, to survive. It felt like an insult not to dig my heels in, at least a little.

Anyway, I had no better prospects. Maddy couldn't get me out of this dead end I'd created for myself, but maybe I still could. How had Courtney put it? This wasn't what I'd had in mind for myself.

"I already regret what I said last night," Coach said. "About doing something. I mean—what can we do? We need to move on. What's done is done, as hard as it is to accept. But that's what we have to do. Promise me, Juliet."

After a long stretch of silence, I realized he was waiting for me to say something, to make an actual promise. I nodded and smiled, but

I didn't mean it. I'd already realized what I could do. I could figure out who killed Maddy. I'd already turned up the photo when Courtney and the whole team of cops hadn't. I could find her killer. And if I did, things would be different. Maddy would save me, after all.

The day's first class was made up of a group of soft freshman girls who insisted they'd been playing rough sports the entire year and were too tired to do anything exerting. The ringleader pulled up her sleeves to show me a bruise she attributed to last week's volleyball game.

Lucky for them, I didn't feel like dealing with nets or locked equipment cabinets.

"You're going to run laps," I said.

"For how long?" asked the bruised girl. Her eyes were the same dark color as the fresh bruise.

"Until I say you're done."

The crowd of them, their ponytails all hanging just so, stared at me. Their shorts were too short, their bra straps visible. When the boys' class marched through on their way outside, the girls shrank into shapes of studied apathy. "I'd rather play volleyball," one of them said.

"We're going to use what you have," I said. "Energy. You're young, and it's eight in the morning. Come on, let's move."

A rough start was soon rewarded. The girls fell into line after a couple of laps, too out of breath to complain. Their smooth cheeks flushed pink.

I counted them off as they rounded the corner, the bruised girl the fastest.

"Are you on the track team?" I yelled as she passed.

"Me?" she turned and ran backwards.

"You should be," I said.

She shrugged, turned back, and kept going. The rest of the girls herded past. Average speed, average effort. And then one last girl, splotched red.

"Are . . . we . . . done?" she gasped.

"You haven't even done a half mile yet," I said. "You're, what, four-teen, fifteen?"

"And fat!" she huffed, smiling.

The other girls looked back, giggled.

"No, you're not," I said. "Anyway, you can still be healthy."

"Not *today*," she panted.

"Every day." I waved her on. "Girls, try not to think about what hurts, or how long you've gone, or how long is this woman going to make us do this. Try not to think. Feel your body—" The herd giggled again, but I noticed the bruiser out front remained quiet. She had fallen into the loping gait of a jungle cat. She had grace as well as speed. If she had stamina, Fitz had better be moving to get her on the team. "Feel the mechanics of your legs, your arms. Reach your arms, left, right. Lift your knees, left, right. Feel how your body is built, how all the pieces move together to do this one thing. You were made to do this."

The bruised girl—a gazelle—ran past again with a look on her face I recognized. She'd hit her stride. She was beyond listening, beyond my voice, every muscle in her body finding its peak level.

After a while, I realized we were being watched. A petite girl with a thick, braided ponytail had wandered into the gym and was leaning against the stairs to the upper deck. She was outfitted in running tights and her shoes, bright and as high-tech as a computer, were probably worth more than my car. "Hey," I called. "You might want to jump into the pack, there."

She pulled headphones out of her ears. "Where's Fitz?"

"I'm Fitz today."

She rolled her eyes. "Typical. Where's Coach, then?"

I noticed the pace of the other girls had slowed to take in the scene. "Keep it up, ladies," I said. To the girl: "What do you need?"

"I have independent study this hour," she said. "Or I'm *supposed* to. I'm in training."

"Well, then, like I said—jump in."

"I don't run *now*." She sneered at the girls as they passed. "It'll throw off my schedule."

These girls. How did Coach and Fitz do this every day? The atti-
tudes. The back talk. The responsibility, and for what? Generations of
Midway girls with quick retorts and complaints, and before that, probably more of the same from the other schools they'd worked for. Coach
and Fitz were better than Midway. I had no idea why they'd chosen to
teach the likes of me, Maddy, these saucy girls.

The girl watched the others for another minute, then stripped off
her jacket and headphones and left them in a pile on the floor.

The middle herd was breaking up into girls trying to keep up with
the pack leader, then girls who could probably keep up their steady, slow
gallop all day, followed by girls who'd decided they hated me, hated life.
The new addition inserted herself into the circuit, bursting through the
middle of a group barely holding their own, then up through the ranks
until she and the gazelle were in step.

I found myself watching their feet—perfectly synchronized, each foot
coming down weightless. After a while, I realized the pace was increasing. I
looked up. The other girls had slowed, but the two leaders were pounding
through the circuit. The entire gym seemed to be holding its breath.

"Come on, ladies," I said to the others, but watching the pair out
front. "Give it your all for your last lap. Just once, put yourself all in.
What are you saving it for? Yearbook pictures aren't today, are they?"

A few of them braked and turned to me, alarmed.

"No—" The pudgy-cheeked girl at the back thudded and panted
toward me, and stopped.

"I didn't say we were done," I said.

"No, the pictures . . . I can't—" She planted her fists on her knees
and coughed until I wondered how fast the nurse could be fetched.

"OK, OK, you can stop," I said. "Point taken."

The two frontrunners pounded around the last turn, each footfall thundering. It was a race to the death. They tied, passing me fast
enough that a breeze whipped across my cheek.

"Hey, Delia," said the gazelle, hands at her hips and hardly out of
breath. The other girl shot her a look and headed for her stuff at the
door. "Are the pictures really today?"

"No . . . I'm trying to say . . . " Delia came up from the ground, her face red and pouring sweat. She had red, curly hair, now plastered to her neck in dark ringlets. "Group pictures are next week . . . *whew* . . . I'm OK." This last addressed to the girls finishing their last lap, none of whom seemed the least bit concerned about their classmate.

"All right, ladies. Go get cleaned up and changed." They turned on their heels, ponytails swinging. A few even found the energy to jog toward the dressing rooms. No whining about running if it came in the service of getting their hair fixed. The gazelle's eyes flicked in my direction as she passed, appraising.

This left the last, red-faced girl. She shifted her weight back and forth, hands on her hips, catching her breath. "You OK?" I said. "I didn't mean to—"

"Don't worry. I just have a free period next, so I usually wait until all the others are done."

I knew who this girl was now. Smart, funny, but wearing her humor as protective armor. She would probably do anything to go unnoticed. The space she took up might as well be a favor she was forced to ask, over and over. So, the tricks, the extra period planned after gym class to avoid the moment when she had to drop her gym clothes and live up to her body being too this or too that. The big persona, because she thought she couldn't be exactly who she was.

Girlhood could be such a piece of crap, if you were just a little bit different. And every one of us was.

"Second hour is pretty early for a free period, isn't it?"

"I guess. It's boring, so I usually get a pass to go do stuff for *Tracks*."

"The—oh, right. The yearbook." *Panther Tracks*, technically, the trail we left behind as Midway High Panthers.

She looked at me, keen. "Did you go to Midway?"

"Many moons ago," I said.

She was nodding. My answer matched how old she thought I must be. I was sorry I'd phrased it that way.

"Hey," I said. "Are there old—I mean past *Tracks* stored anywhere? In the yearbook room, maybe?" A tickle had begun in the center of my palms.

"The library," she said. "They keep a whole set there, I think. Really far back."

"Well, I don't need that far back, just ten years."

She looked me up and down. "Why don't you have your own yearbook? That's weird. Did your house catch on fire?"

"It's not that weird." We stared at each other. Was it? Not everyone at Midway had the extra twenty bucks. Some, like Courtney, must have thought twenty bucks was too much to spend on memories they'd rather not keep. And then some of us would have been happy to shell out a twenty, if only the yearbook staff hadn't been such an insider clique allowed to print anything they wanted about other people.

I felt the hot shame all over again, even though I couldn't really remember precisely what the yearbook had said about me. Something about . . . a third wheel. I felt my own cheeks go pink. "Never mind," I said. "Go get cleaned up."

Delia dragged herself past me to the hall, but only seconds later came running back to the door opening. "Hey, hey," she said. "I don't— hey, they're fighting."

"Who?" I said.

"Mickie and Jessica," she cried. "Come help!"

I ran, following her into the stuffy locker room and into a ring of yelling and jeering girls. On the floor, the independent study and the gazelle were at war. Running shoes kicking, fists of hair pulled. Terrible things were coming out of both their mouths. I blinked at the sight until Delia yelled, "Knock it off, you guys. The teacher's here!"

This seemed enough of a threat to the girls watching, who pulled back to let me closer to the middle of the brawl. I reached into the pile of girls on the floor and came out with the tiny one's arm. She was light, and so I was able to pull her off the other one.

"Slut," the gazelle said, rising from the ground on her own.

"Keep it up, you whore, and I'll knock your teeth in," screeched the girl in my arms, swinging out of my grasp. Her fist struck my face as she shook me off, then she grabbed her things from the floor and let the locker-room door slam on her way out.

"What was that about?" I tried for scolding authority but was shaking too hard. I tested the spot on my lip where the girl had clocked me. Bleeding.

The other girls fell away, grabbing their things. The gazelle, or Jessica, according to those who asked if she was fine, would only shake her head. The bell rang overhead and the girls scattered, leaving me alone with my hand to my fat lip.

CHAPTER ELEVEN

My classes were all girls. Occasionally, Coach brought a class of boys through the gym on their way to and from the tennis courts, giving me a nod or a thumbs-up to make sure it was all going according to plan. Thumbs-up. I turned my cracked lip from him. No other independent studies showed up, no other fights broke out. I force-marched back-to-back classes through laps until a bell rang and a new class failed to emerge from the locker room.

Lunch break, I supposed. I could smell the tater tots from where I sat on the stairs.

I stretched my legs in front of me. White stripes ran down the sides of my tracksuit pants, like a joke. I hadn't been running for months. I patted at my sore mouth. Who was I to prod these kids around the gym? Who was I to take no excuses?

It was just—they had their whole lives ahead of them. They should be racing toward their futures.

I'd already been where they were. I was allowed to lope along, to slow down. It made sense to slow down, didn't it? Since I didn't know where I was going?

But then I did know where I was going.

Past the locker rooms, the hallway led to the weight room, and eventually, to the pool. The air was heavy with chlorine—but hot. Before I'd gone too far, an open doorway roiled with steam. I paused in the opening, taking in the mountain of white towels. I did laundry at the Mid-Night every week, and the piles of sheets always seemed out of line with how many guests we had, but I couldn't imagine keeping up with this amount of work. It ruined your hands. I covered my mouth with the back of my wrist. It probably ruined your lungs, too. Someday we'd all suffer the ill effects of the Shinez-All and bleach.

Far back behind the stacks of clean, folded towels, two of the cleaning staff sat with magazines, smoking. They wore loose, blue uniforms, boxy and unflattering, but I envied how they must be able to move in them. Then one of them, a meaty woman with eyes keen and black, looked up. .

Her name rose like the steam from memory: Cheryl.

For a moment, I could see her dark eyes boring into me, and below them, her mouth pulled in anger.

"Help you?" she barked. She seemed amused, though, not mad.

I shook my head, hurrying down the hall.

I shouldn't have disturbed them. The back halls were their undisputed territory. It felt a little reckless to ignore the unspoken laws, and a little more than indecent to trespass on the domain of a fellow cleaner. I felt scolded.

The back pathway continued past the pool and dumped me out behind some lockers in an academic hallway. Here, it was quiet, the roar of the cafeteria far behind me. A long line of classrooms stretched ahead, and to the left, the library. A thousand memories rushed at me. I took manageable, bite-sized views, grabbing a drink from the water fountain and taking a look at some books on display in the library's broad front window. I caught sight of myself and my puffy lip in the glass. Inside, two girls stood behind the checkout desk. They stopped talking and glanced in my direction, then at each other. It hadn't been long enough since I'd been the object of high-school girl ridicule. I still recognized it.

Outside the administrative offices, I paused to read a few notices on a bulletin board about upcoming Honors Society food drives, and how to buy tickets for prom. Fixing a noncommittal expression on my face, I made my way past the open doorway of the main office and through the lobby toward the long wall of glass cases containing all the honor and recognition my school had ever earned.

Of course I already knew right where to locate my own name. I'd been through the cases plenty of times over the years. Cross-country five thousand meters, track thirty-two hundred meters. County invitational. Tri-county tourney. Southtown Regional. Always the second name, tucked under Maddy's. A matched pair, etched together forever into shining plates and trophy towers, the tops decked out with silver ponytailed girl runners.

The silver had started to tarnish.

As I looked, other names started to leap out. People I knew from school, but also from the Mid-Night. Courtney Howard had received some kind of student journalism award. Yvonne's named showed up on a plaque for something called the Student Business Alliance. All these awards, squeezed together on a shelf, literally under glass like pinned butterflies. Youth caught in mid-wing beat.

Even Coach's youth was represented. Among the brass and glass of lesser awards, his Olympic bronze medal was dull and small, easy to miss. I took a minute to admire it and think of all the hours Coach would have trained, only to miss out on the top prize. If he'd won gold, no one could have missed it.

I checked around for his Coach of the Year trophy or medallion but didn't see them. Again and again, though, on awards chiseled with names I didn't know, I found Coach and Fitz's influence. I'd always considered Maddy and myself the all-stars Coach and Fitz had been waiting for their entire careers, but the truth was that they'd mentored plenty of strong runners. In fact, now that I spent the time to see it, there was a plaque from the state tournament leaning up against the back glass, earned by a track team member before Maddy and I had even joined the team. The wooden plaque was shaped like the state of Indiana, with the expertly carved ripples of the Ohio River at the bottom edge visible through the glass shelf from below. I peered at every angle, trying to catch the name of the student, which was blocked by other trophies. I stood far to the left to read the letters in relief. *Kristina*. Then far to the right, I got a better angle. *Switzer*. I looked again at the fine carving, those ripples, idly rubbing my palms together. Who the hell was Kristina Switzer? How had I never heard of her?

"Well," said a voice behind me. "You've made it to halftime, I see."

Mrs. Haggerty, the school secretary. Her too-red lips twisted into a grimace of a smile. She was a small woman, a cardigan-wearing little bird of a thing who looked like someone's grandmother. But I wasn't falling for that. Mrs. Haggerty held the true seat of power at Midway High. Any punishment dished out by the principal—she'd outlasted or outlived at least five—was nothing next to having Mrs. Haggerty peck at you. If she didn't like me, I wouldn't have been called in to substitute teach. But she did—though I had no idea why, or how to keep it that way. "But I guess that's a bad analogy, given your own athletic interests," she said.

"What? Oh, right. Halftime, er, lunch." I couldn't seem to think of anything to say. "Just looking over the trophy case. It's cool that Coach Trenton keeps his Olympic medal here."

She raised an eyebrow. "If it had been a gold, I imagine he would wear it to parties. I don't think he cares about it. It's his Coach of the Year trinkets he must love, since he never brought them in to add them to the display. Maybe they'll find their way in now, with Madeleine—"

She had the decency to stop herself. "Not too difficult to find your name among the historical records, I assume."

Everything Haggerty ever said sounded like a trap. I felt seventeen again, like I needed to pat my pockets for my hall pass or spit out my gum, fast. "I saw a lot of people I recognized, actually. Courtney Howard. Did you know she's a —"

I didn't want to tell that story, really. Mrs. Haggerty gave me an inscrutable look, until I realized that she might not like me all that much. Maybe she only preferred me, over Maddy. How many times had I sat out in the lobby while Maddy faced Haggerty, then the principal or vice? For being late for school, skipping out of study hall to meet Beck out behind the Future Farmers' tractor barn, or dropping a word-bomb on one of our teachers. Maddy was smart, smart enough to have done well. But she hadn't wanted to, I guess, especially by about halfway through our senior year. She hadn't wanted to be at school, always bringing in ambivalent notes from Gretchen for the days she missed. A headache. Stomachache. *Cramps.* The last semester, when we had first-period phys ed with Fitz, she hardly showed up at all. He must have let a lot slide, or her GPA wouldn't have been high enough to keep her on the team.

Sometimes while I waited outside the admin offices for Maddy to face her reckoning, Beck would wander by or take the seat at the far side of the bench to wait, too. Like rival suitors, we wanted to see which of us would be called upon to console her first, a contest I couldn't remember winning or losing.

Maddy. Beck. For the first time, it occurred to me how much of my high school experience had been rooted in competition. Real competition, but also the kind that hadn't made any sense.

But it hadn't mattered that Beck and I had been in a contest to be the shoulder Maddy would cry on. She always emerged from these run-ins renewed, laughing. She was almost happier with a few detention hours against her. She couldn't be punished. She couldn't be stopped.

"I saw some names I didn't know, though," I said, turning back to the case and the state tournament trophy. Third place, it said. It wasn't as good as Maddy and I would have done, but then we'd both walked away with nothing. The frilly edge of that carved border bothered me. I wanted to run my fingers along it. "Kristina Switzer?"

"Oh, yes," Mrs. Haggerty said. "Your coaches' first love."

"I—" My hands had begun to itch in earnest. I rubbed my palms against the stripes on my hips. "Who?"

"The coaches have their obsessions. They do love a winner. Surely you noticed?" she said. "Madeleine, of course. There's a girl on the team now that has every chance of beating most of the standing records. Oh, yes, even Madeleine's. This might be the year. They're certainly smitten." Her eyes shifted to the trophy case. She pulled out a heavy ring of keys and opened one of the glass doors, then reached inside and turned one of the regional spelling-bee cups a couple of degrees.

I noticed that she'd left me off the list of Coach and Fitz's favorites, but I was too distracted watching her nudge and fuss with the pieces in the case. I crossed my arms and tucked my hands into my armpits to keep from reaching out for something. Not the state tournament prize. Too large. Too special. It would be something small, something carelessly arranged and easily missed. Something that would fit into the makeup bag at the bottom of my vanity.

Then I saw it. A tiny marble tablet, a paperweight with an inscription I couldn't read. It was instant. As soon as I saw it, I wanted it, had to have it, desired it more than any man, any accomplishment. More than a college degree. More than anything.

In that moment, I wanted that little monument more than I wanted my father back. More than my own next breath.

It didn't make any sense. I didn't truly believe my own desire, even as it made my bones hum. The object—I didn't even know what it was—was a magnet, and I was helpless against its draw.

Finally Mrs. Haggerty closed the door and secured the lock.

I took a step back, gulping for breath. With all my concentration, I pried my attention away from the case. "When did she graduate?"

"Kristina? That's an interesting question." Mrs. Haggerty's eyes flicked up and down the hallway. "She went through ceremonies—oh, I'd have to check the year. She was a bit ahead of you."

Neither the question nor the answer seemed particularly interesting or worth protecting to me. But too much curiosity was probably another mark against my character. Would I still be judged against Maddy, or was I being measured against another yardstick now? "What's interesting?"

"Technically," she said, "Kristina Switzer didn't graduate."

"Oh," I said. "Why not?"

"Hard to say," Mrs. Haggerty said. "She drifted away. You don't see that much, not with the promising athletes, not with the ones getting recruiter visits. Like with Madeleine."

Somewhere in my mind, a domino dropped, and I waited for the entire pattern to fall. Finally the last piece knocked over.

"Are you saying—wait. Did you just say that Maddy didn't graduate, either?"

Mrs. Haggerty seemed startled for a moment, then glared. She didn't like me as much as I wanted her to. "I said no such thing—"

"But—"

A girl in bare shoulders trudged by, giving us a long, curious look.

"Miss Whisler," Mrs. Haggerty said. "Where is the rest of that outfit? And I imagine they're waiting for you in chemistry, aren't they?" She turned back to me with her face wiped of any emotion but disdain. A kid without a hall pass and I were getting the same treatment.

"I said no such thing about Madeleine," she said. "I said no such thing about Kristina, either, if it comes down to it. That's confidential information. I thought you must have known about . . . You were thick as thieves, but that's neither here nor there. Consider it an interesting bit of trivia. Better yet, forget all about it." Mrs. Haggerty pulled at the hem of her cardigan. I'd never seen her ruffled before, but she was recovering quickly. She gave me a cool look. "But wouldn't it be strange? If it were true?"

"If it were true—"

"Yes," she said.

"—that two of the best runners at Midway both—" She blinked at me, and I took that as encouragement. "Wouldn't it be strange, if two of the best runners in Midway High history had both dropped out? In their senior years?"

"In their last few weeks of school," she said. "And—" The red lips clamped shut. "Well, that's enough for two poor souls to have in common," she said, giving me a softer look. And then it was over and she was turning to watch another girl hurrying past. "Stop by to sign your tax form before the day is out, Juliet. Miss Nevarez, is that how you want to be perceived? Pull up your pants right this instant."

The wooden plaque of Indiana caught my eye again. Funny how small it seemed, when it was all we'd ever wanted.

I went to look at Coach's Olympic medal again. Less than a handful of metal, dull and aged, with a sun-bleached red, white, and blue ribbon. How small and meaningless everything seemed.

Maddy hadn't run the state race because she was sick. But if she also hadn't crossed the finish line to get her diploma, she must have been—a different kind of sick. Sick in the head. Sick in the heart.

It's not as though I hadn't had experience with both. I leaned against the case, all the bits of glory inside trembling in response.

CHAPTER TWELVE

By the time I walked away from the trophy case, I was overwhelmed by the glare of silver and brass plating. I didn't want to run my fingers over the ripple at the south end of that Indiana-shaped prize. I wanted to smash it.

That third-place plaque dug at me. Who was Kristina Switzer, anyway? Maddy had been faster, better. She would have taken home first.

But now that I'd met the ghost of Kristina, I was forced to consider Maddy a choker. How was I qualified? What had I ever seen to the end? I even cut corners when I cleaned the rooms at the Mid-Night.

In front of the library's windows, I stopped. The two girls at the counter stood close, whispering.

High school.

High school and my friendship with Maddy. The only two things I'd ever finished didn't seem to be finished with me.

Inside, the library was appropriately hushed. The stacks lay open to casual reach. I walked along the outside aisle, running a finger over a few spines. Back in school, I'd only spent time near books when I had to. Running—that was my life. Now I found myself curious. All this abundance, and I'd never taken part in it. A swirl of gold on the edge of one book caught my eye. I pulled the book from its spot and patted the raised, gold letters on the cover. The edges of the pages were gold, too. There was some process by which things were made to shine. It had a name, but I didn't know it. I probably never would. It was frustrating to think of the world as a place full of things I'd never know.

The book back in its place, I made my way around the edge of the room, looking for a way in. Somewhere there was a drawer of cards or a computer that would tell me where to find stuff. Dewey somebody. But I didn't have time to make up for a short education. Lunch would be over soon, and then I'd be urging another group of students around the gym.

The girls behind the desk watched me approach. One of them twirled the end of her long ponytail around her finger.

"Nice track pants," the twirler said. They wore the uniform of teenaged girls as I was beginning to understand it: tiny shirts, bra straps showing, pants so tight they looked wet.

They didn't smile or laugh, but a hint of hilarity peeked out from behind the curtain so that I knew I was the thing that was funny. "Thanks," I said. "If you're in PE class later today, you can admire them every time you complete a lap."

"I have a note," the other one said. She had small, precise teeth that made me think of something feral. A hyena—no, a piranha. I knew expensive orthodontia when I saw it.

"Do you have a broken leg?" I said. "Otherwise, everyone runs."

She scowled. "Did you want something?"

"Where do you keep the yearbooks?"

"Which year?"

"Every year," I said.

They exchanged a look.

I would never have kids. The disdain was just too much. And I'd daydreamed about being a full-time gym teacher? Cleaning up after a wall-thumping sexcapade at the Mid-Night didn't embarrass me as much as being on the other side of this desk, needing the help of these scantily clad children. "What?" I said.

"The librarian keeps them in the back," said ponytail.

"We'd have to bring them out," said piranha. "NBD, but they're kinda heavy."

NBD? "Tell you what," I said. "Bring out the last fifteen years, and I'll give you a break on the laps later. We'll call this an independent study in weight-lifting."

They didn't like the arrangement, but must have seen the bargain for what it was. They had disappeared into the back office before I translated them. No Big Deal.

I set myself up at a study carrel. When I sat down, I was met with the particular scent of old pages and dust. Memories came rushing from all angles. I was seventeen again, anxious to get outside to the track, to go home after practice and make a sandwich out of whatever I could find, and, mouth still full, pick up the phone to see if Maddy was home yet. We'd rehash everything that had happened, as though it hadn't happened to us both.

Had I turned and found Maddy in the next carrel, I wouldn't have been surprised. This place was haunted. Everywhere I turned, there she was.

The girls took a bit longer than they probably needed to but were soon carting out the thick books three at a time, heavy in their skinny arms. On the last trip, the ponytailed girl added a single book to the top of the stack. "One of them's missing."

I nudged the books into a stack and ran my finger along the spines. "You're kidding," I said. My year? What were the odds? I checked again. "That year, out of all the years? It's really gone?"

"Stolen," said ponytail as her friend went back to the desk. "Mrs. Jasper—that's the librarian—was super mad. That's when she started keeping them in the back. She said people couldn't be trusted. 'They'd steal the shirt off your back.' That's what she said."

The piranha girl made an impatient noise to draw her friend back to her.

"Yeah," I said. I'd already been laying plans for how I could slip that same book out of the building. My hands didn't itch this time—they ached. I might have called it a sense memory of holding the book, but I'd hardly had it in my hands the first time. Maddy had flown through the pages before letting me see for myself what they'd said.

Third wheel on the track team bus. That was it.

Now that I remembered what they'd said about me, the insult stung all over again, probably because of its truth. And now more truth: People couldn't be trusted. And given half the chance, I'd have been one of them.

I put a protective hand on the top of the stack. "I'll still take a look at these."

"Let me know when you're done so I can put them away," the girl said, reaching for the end of her ponytail. "Mrs. Jasper—"

"Yep."

When she was gone, I took the top book and cracked it to the table of contents. It had been a while since I'd looked through one of these. Student life. Clubs. Sports. Tombstoned rows of young faces, all shoulders canted to the same angle, all eyes turned toward the same mid-distant focus. All chins pointed toward the finish line.

From the advantage of ten years, everyone looked young, naive, and badly dressed. I found the book for my freshman year and flipped to the pages for my class, jarring my own memory. Maddy Bell's face was wedged between two buck-toothed boys with heavy eyebrows I'd completely forgotten. Even Maddy seemed less familiar. But she was there. I'd almost expected to find her portrait missing, the box where her photo should have been suddenly empty.

My senior yearbook was the only one missing. Stolen. What was so special about the year I graduated? No special anniversary year for the school. No championship team in any sport. No major news events covered in shallow, student-journalism depth. We'd lived through a year like any other year. Classes, homecoming, spring break, track meets, prom. And then graduation, an occasion I was learning had been merely ceremonious to some of us. I couldn't remember much of it, even as the memories pressed at me.

I found the book for the year ahead of me, and turned to the senior class. Then the book for two years ahead, then three. A sea of faces, all young, almost all white. Midway wasn't the middle of anything except nowhere, after all. Finally, in the book from the year before I started at Midway High, five years ahead of my class, there she was, deep in the *S*'s and looking just as she should, a girl with the right haircut, the right clothes.

Kristina Switzer had dark hair and serious dark eyes. Not pretty, exactly, but striking. The kind of face you'd remember. Did I remember it? Like everyone else in the book, she could have been someone I knew, like she might come into the Mid-Night, the bar, once in a while, or maybe she'd waved me ahead of her at a stop sign or blocked my way in the frozen-food aisle of the IGA last week. We'd missed each other at Midway by a year. In my hurry to reach the index in the back of the book, I tore a page.

I checked to see if the library assistants would take the opportunity to scold me, but they'd returned to their own conversation.

In the index, Kristina Switzer's yearbook appearances were limited to two pages, the one with her senior photo and one other. I flipped to that page and found the track team, of course. Again, her face jumped out at me. She seemed older than the other girls, more worldly. In a snapshot, Coach leaned in, his hand gripping Kristina's shoulder for focus. In the team photo, her uniform showed off shapely arms and collarbones as sharp as knives. Her long, black hair fanned over one shoulder. She stood between Fitz and Coach in the back row, the center spot that in most group photos would belong to the tallest member. On the Midway High track team, though, it belonged to the star.

I forgot the book in my hands, the memory rushing at me, whole and full.

Every year, Fitz shuffled the players into position for the impatient photographer while the rest of us waited to see how we stacked up, then preened or fidgeted with the ranking we'd been given. For the photo our senior year, I knew where I'd be situated, and yet I couldn't help hoping that somehow Fitz would realize the special dispensation that needed to be made. Yes, Maddy in the center, of course. But why couldn't I stand next to her, and Fitz on the other side of me, he and Coach like bookends to us both?

But tradition was tradition. Maddy went into the championship slot, and I was put at Fitz's other side. It was an early spring day, all of us cold and exposed in our uniforms. In a minute, we'd go back into the locker room and change into our practice gear, saving the clean uniforms for the first meet. But for the blink of the camera's shutter, we'd ignore the breeze coming off the empty cornfield behind the school. We'd toughen up and gaze fiercely into the lens. This was before sectionals, then regionals, then the big show, as the coaches called it as they urged us around the track. Before the season had even started, so that the yearbook could be done by the time school ended for the summer. At the moment the camera clicked, the future lay ahead of us. We all thought we had a state champ on the team. Maddy.

Standing at Fitz's side, I'd noticed how he turned toward her. Protective. Claiming the prize he already knew she would bring them. That left me with his shoulder, his back. My teeth chattered in the cold.

Now I studied Kristina's team. A few of the girls could have been on the team when Maddy and I joined as freshmen, but none of them stood out to me. I closed the book on Kristina and turned to the yearbook for our junior year again and the track team photo there. Maddy, the coaches, me—and then three rows of girls I should have known.

I didn't.

I closed the book and stared at the date on the spine, now long past. Just like Maddy had said. When you were going as fast as we were, everything and everyone else was only a blur.

And just like Maddy had said more recently, so much time had been wasted. So much lost.

CHAPTER THIRTEEN

In the last period of the day, I met up again with the girls from the library. They'd changed into gym clothes in good faith, so I remembered to give them credit for yearbooks lifted and hauled. The class was made up of seniors already counting down the days until graduation. Complainers all, they didn't want to run but eventually they, too, saved their breath.

When I released them to go change at the end of the day, a few came back still wearing their PE clothes and their hair still in sweaty ponytails. At the final bell, they swung duffels over their shoulders and, instead of heading toward the buses or the parking lot, trudged out the back door of the gym. I ran to use the pay phone in the cafeteria to call Lu for a ride home, then followed them.

Coach leaned on his elbows on the inner fence separating the track from the stands. "Did you wear out my girls?"

"Maybe a little," I said.

"What happened to you?"

I reached for my lip, still tender. Out of the corner of my eye, I saw someone approaching. It was the girl I'd advised to join the team earlier, the gazelle. Back in her street clothes, she seemed less like a track star and more like that bruiser on the locker-room floor with a handful of the other girl's hair in her fist. She was solid, outfitted in sturdy boots and a leather jacket far too warm for the weather. "I might have brought you a present," I said, nodding in her direction.

Coach shaded his eyes and watched the figure coming slowly our way. "How in the world did you do that? Fitzie's had his eye on her all year. He thought she might anchor a relay team."

"Those are thirty-two-hundred-meter legs, in my opinion," I said.

"Well, that's your area of expertise," he said, flashing me a beaming grin. Coach was a sprinter, himself. "In my opinion of your opinion, you might be a fine recruiter. *Well* done."

He hurried off to coax the girl toward the track. I watched after him, his praise leaving me breathless, like a punch in the gut. I didn't like to think how much his words meant to me, how long it had been since someone had noticed I was good at anything. How long it had been since I'd *been* good at anything. Leaning on the fence like this, being here in this place, I missed my dad.

"No chance she wants to be a manager, huh?" someone said. "Isn't she a freshman?"

Behind me on the lowest benches of the stands, the rest of the team tied their shoes and arranged their headbands, cutting secret glances toward Coach and the new recruit.

"It's not you who needs to worry," said one of the other girls. "Right, Mickie?"

"I can beat her," said a girl lying on her side along a bleacher plank higher up. The other girl from the fight. She had a scratch down one cheek and a dark bruise on one of her arms, but she might have been lounging poolside at a spa. "One way or another."

"Juliet," called Coach. "Are you staying for practice?"

I glanced back at the girls. They'd gone quiet. "Until my ride gets here," I said. "What do you need?"

"Get the girls warmed up, will you?"

"I'm warm enough," said one I recognized from the last-hour PE class.

"Stay that way, then," I said. "Let's go, ladies."

They rose in a group. "Have you noticed that all coaches call us 'ladies'?" one of the girls said.

"Except Coach, right? *Girls.*"

"Technically that's what you are, though, right?" I said. They went silent again. I felt the wave of curiosity and suspicion coming off them, but it only urged me on. "If you mean age. I mean, that's the division between being a girl and being, well, a woman." I sounded like an idiot even to myself. They'd called me a *coach.*

"Mickie's eighteen," someone said.

We all gave Mickie another glance. She was gorgeous—slim and lithe as a dancer, her dark hair in that thick braid. I looked around. All the girls were gorgeous. Young, bright-eyed, their skin poured milk, their tiny waists accentuated by the slim-fitting running gear they'd chosen. Little pretty things, all of them. Kids were cuter these days. Or we'd been just as beautiful, and hadn't known it.

"Fine," I said. "Young-women Panthers, let's blow the dust off the track."

Once the girls got moving, they stopped fussing. Coach took his time courting the gazelle—Jessica, I remembered—so I had the chance to check out his pool of talent. Mickie was the star, of course. No one on the track could touch her. She was certainly the girl Mrs. Haggerty had mentioned, the one destined to sweep Maddy's records off the walls of Midway High once and for all.

Beautiful, elegant on her feet, and twice as fast as I had ever hoped to be. I imagined the Midway High trophy case filled with her name, and those with Maddy's and mine shoved to the back and, eventually, into some back-hall storage.

I didn't like her.

The other girls didn't, either. Every start, she bolted ahead. At every finish line, she crossed the white line long before her next competitor. No split-second finishes here. Mickie didn't simply win. She killed. She even outpaced the sprinters. Distance runners weren't supposed to be the stars, but this girl hadn't heard that. By the time I gave them five to go take swigs from their water bottles, the easy camaraderie of the bleachers before practice was gone. While the girls gathered around the pile of their duffels and joked easily together, Mickie stood alone. In this isolation, she reminded me of Maddy. She had the straight back of someone who was used to turning it on everyone else. The price of championship, of winning too often and by too large a gap.

One of the girls had been playing music on her phone, singing along. A new song started, and they all joined in. Even Mickie, taking dainty sips at her water bottle, mouthed a few lines. The lyrics were lost to me until the tune dropped into a rap and an angry voice said something I wasn't sure I'd heard correctly. Something about tying a woman he loved to a bed and setting the house around it on fire.

"Wait, what?" I said, a chill going through me. "Shut that off."

They exchanged confused glances. "What? It's just a song."

"Nothing is ever just a song," I said, not even sure what I meant. I stared at the girl's phone until she silenced it.

Coach was approaching from the gates. "I don't know how you did it, Jules," he said. He waved the girls back onto the track and set his stopwatch. With a single nod of his head, the team shot off the starting line and into a loping, long-distance stride.

"Is she joining the team?"

"We'll see if Jessica's interest survives the night. She's bringing some gear tomorrow." He winked at me. "She's going to try us out. She seems to have a very busy schedule we need to work around."

"Well, I hope you all meet her requirements," I said. I couldn't help admiring Jessica's sense of herself. "She's got some stiff competition."

"Mickie, you mean." We both looked out to find her. It wasn't difficult, as far out front as she was. "She's the real thing, Jules. It's been a long time since—"

He slammed his fist at the chain link. A few of the girls glanced back at the noise. When he leaned on the fence again, one set of knuckles was scraped and bleeding. "I'm just so angry. She deserved more."

"I know," I said. In that instant, my jealous guardianship of Maddy's records was finished. I hoped Mickie stripped them all, and good riddance. Maddy was dead, and Coach, Fitz, and I were the only ones who kept watch. We would see her memory erased from Midway, from history, from everything but our own minds. The whole world would forget or pretend to, in order to spare us the pain of remembering. But I already knew a little about this. The worst tragedy of loss was that the world kept spinning.

I begged off to go meet Lu, hurrying away before I made a fool of myself in front of these self-possessed girls. Or in front of Coach, who was barely keeping himself together for the sake of the team. For my sake. Fitz took care of everyone, he'd said, but that wasn't the entire truth.

As I walked toward the parking lot, I noticed another lone figure at the outer fence. We recognized each other at the same time. Officer Courtney Howard—in her civilian jeans and a sweater, as small as any of the girls on the team—strode toward me.

"What are you doing here?" I said.

"Was going to ask you the same thing." Her eyes scaled the length of my track-pant stripes. At least I wasn't wearing my too-short Mid-Night Inn uniform this time.

"I was called in to substitute teach today," I said. "Phys ed."

"I imagine school was over at three o'clock, like every other day of the year."

Somehow we'd fallen into the well-tread tracks of interrogator and interrogated. "I don't think there's any reason why I'm not allowed to stay and assist the team, is there?" I said. "I mean, I'm not a felon."

"Not yet," she said.

"Get off it, Courtney. You don't really think I killed Maddy. You can't possibly believe that."

She pushed her chin out toward the track and watched the girls circling. "I'm not sure what I believe. But—" Her eyes shifted around, trying to avoid mine. "But I suppose I think it's pretty unlikely that you did it."

"I knew it."

"Unlikely," she said. "Not impossible."

"What's more likely, then? That I conjured her out of thin air after ten years only to hang her—which, how strong would you have to be to pull that off?" An image fluttered out of memory. "Like, like—oh, shit. What about the dead guy? Oh, my God—"

"Dead guy? What are you talking about?" Courtney's attention was all mine.

"He's not really—it's a long story," I said. "The guy staying in room two-oh-six. He checked out that morning. I was taking his trash—oh, that's why he was so neat—"

"I have a lot of questions right now, but I'll jump to the end," Courtney said. "We checked that trash bag. Nothing but a lot of—let's just say he was spending a lot of quality time alone—but no trace of him anywhere near her room or the trash bin, and we're checking his alibi for the time of Maddy's death—"

"How does he have an alibi for being in his room?"

"Her name is Brandi." Courtney looked back toward the girls on the track. "She graduated from Midway last year."

Like Billy said, we catered to weirdos and wackjobs. And apparently a certain clientele who kept themselves too busy making new friends to rack up long-distance charges calling wives and girlfriends back home. It went to show you could never tell about a person. The dead guy had seemed so pudgy and innocent, like an oversized baby, but he'd had a barely legal girl in his room.

And then I shuddered, thinking of the moment when I'd swiped all the guy's trash back into the ripped bag with my bare hands.

"So." She gave me a side glance. "Who else should we be looking at?"

"The fiancé, right?" I said. "I've seen those TV shows. It's always the boyfriend or husband. You'll be looking at him."

"Of course," she scoffed, then looked away from me. "Loughton's interviewing him. He arrived this morning. To see the body."

Maddy's body—on a slab, her lovely skin painted all over with that dead-fish color. The things I knew from those crime shows gave my imagination too much visual detail. I was stuck there until Coach's voice, urging the girls around the track, brought me back to the fence.

"Money," I said.

"What's that?"

"She was—well, it seemed like she was rich. Her clothes and that ring—"

My palms itched at the memory of the diamond.

"So you think someone killed her over her money? And then didn't take her ring?"

"Look, I don't know anything about her life in Chicago. Aren't there millions of people there? One might have wanted to kill her, for reasons you and I know nothing about."

Even as I said it, I knew what Courtney would say. What she had to say.

"She was killed here," she said.

I didn't like that logic at all, since she hadn't just been killed here, in Midway, but at the specific place where I worked. "She said she was here on business," I said, relieved to have this information passed on at last.

The field of girls thundered by on the track. Courtney watched them run away from us. Out in the field, Coach was focusing Mickie, leaning in to get her full attention and giving her shoulder a squeeze.

"What business?" Courtney said.

"She wouldn't say. She only said it was boring. Or, no, that I wouldn't find it interesting. Something like that."

"That's it? That's all she said?"

And here we were, back at interrogation. Courtney hadn't opened up her notepad, but I could hear that we'd gone back on the record. "Honestly, Courtney," I said. "She didn't say anything else. I wish I'd asked more. I wish I'd—I wish I'd done a lot of things differently. That's all she said. But you could call her office, right? Talk to her boss or supervisor. Or if she shared an office or something? They'll know why she was in town."

She leveled me with a look that reminded me of Beck.

Beck. Was he a suspect or was she waiting for me to mention him?

"What about Gretchen?" I blurted.

"What about her?"

"Well." I hadn't thought it out. "Gretchen and Maddy never got along—"

"Gretchen married Maddy's dad, lay in wait for him to die, and then killed his daughter in a fit of delayed ... *dislike*?" she said. "If Gretchen didn't kill Maddy when she was a self-centered brat living in the same house, why bother now?"

Self-centered. Brat? Courtney seemed to know all about it. I might have told her what Coach and Fitz had suggested about Maddy's dad or what I'd learned or not learned from Mrs. Haggerty—except all my ideas and information had already occurred to her or inspired her derision. Maybe I'd stop giving my best ideas away. Maybe I'd beat Courtney at her own job and show her a thing or two. "I was only trying to help," I said sweetly.

"Don't." She pulled herself into an authoritative stance, but without the uniform, she seemed like a bossy little girl who wasn't getting her way. "We don't need you bumbling around with your theories, getting in our way."

"You mean getting into Sergeant Loughton's way?" I said.

Now I felt the full force of her hatred, stronger than anything Beck had ever sent my way.

"You're smart," she said. "I didn't remember you as smart. I hadn't thought of you as anything other than Maddy's shadow, really. Second-place Juliet. Perpetual third-wheel."

I watched the muscles in her face working around the words, knowing I had made a mistake. She hadn't really believed I was a suspect. But every time I opened my mouth, she wanted to believe it more.

That headline about everyone being a blur—Courtney had made that happen. She'd created the opportunity for backlash from our own team, from girls we thought were our friends, from girls who knew exactly what we meant. Maddy had said it. But if Courtney hadn't pulled it out of the story and held it up as evidence—as some defining statement—no one ever would have given it a second thought.

There was the truth and then there was the truth molded into a shapely headline, into the story that would fly.

I was beginning to see the story that would fly the farthest this time, given the right headline. Courtney, always the accomplished storyteller, only had to write it. With enough proof—or whatever looked like proof—she would.

"You're smart. We'll be keeping that in mind," she said.

Courtney stalked off toward the parking lot. I let myself fall against the fence and watched the girls round the track toward the finish line. They were soaked in sweat, pulling loud breaths and running without any thought to form or anything past the next step.

I'd gotten ahead of myself, trying to compete with Courtney. I hadn't bested her. I'd only drawn her attention. Now all those theories and ideas I'd supplied seemed like nothing more than the frantic scurrying of someone trying to avoid blame by assigning it to anyone else. Like nothing more than the desperate clawing of a rat caught in a trap.

CHAPTER FOURTEEN

I had watched the entire team of girls pile into their parents' minivans and SUVs before my own car finally rattled into the lot, Lu small behind the wheel.

"Sorry, sorry," she said as I opened the passenger door. She was unbuckling her belt. "No, you drive. I had to wait for Carlos to get home to stay with the kids."

With the driver's seat adjusted back to the length of my legs, we headed for the exit and toward her side of town. "How was school?" she said, her voice as light as if she were talking to one of her own children, home from the second-grade field trip.

But I knew what she meant. How was I? How was this business with the dead friend coming along?

"Distracting," I said, knowing that I wasn't saying what I meant, either. Working at the school all day should have been distracting, but it hadn't been. Any distance I'd had from my friendship with Maddy was gone. I felt as though I'd spent the day with her.

"How long do you think the Mid-Night will be closed?" she said.

"They haven't said, have they? Maybe Billy's heard."

"But what do you think? Should I—should we get new jobs? We can get by for a little while, you know," she said. "A *little* little while—oh. Of course you know what I mean."

My mother's social-security check wouldn't keep us out of trouble for even a little while. Lu knew that. I'd already wondered how long the check from the school district for today's subbing would take. "I don't know. I might have to look for something else if we don't reopen this week."

A vision of the Luxe in downtown Indianapolis came to me, and me in my grubby Mid-Night uniform, hands and knees, scrubbing the curved stairs leading up to the mezzanine. I'd only been there once, but it had made an impression, and not just because of the drama. But I didn't want to work there. I could barely imagine attending the reunion there.

"That place they're building across the road from the motel," Lu said. "I heard it was an old folks' place. They'll need cleaners, right?"

It was still under construction. "Not for months, though."

"The real problem is I don't want to work anywhere else." Without looking, I could hear the smile in her voice. "Isn't that funny? Working for Billy, that idiot, and all those strange ones who leave us their underwear and dirty stuff and wipe things on the walls. And the long hours sometimes. Now all this. Your friend."

"It's a crappy place, but we've gotten used to the crap."

"We're selling ourselves cheap, huh," she said. "But I don't know what else anyone would pay me to do. Clean houses, maybe. Ride around in one of the little yellow cars with my very own bucket."

We'd both known people who'd worked a cleaning service. Long hours, hardly a break all day. It was no way to live and certainly no way to get ahead. I wouldn't have called cleaning for a service a step down from cleaning at the Mid-Night, but I'd never wanted to resort to it. To me, it seemed like a dead end, like something I would never get away from. A cold finger of dread ran up my spine. Had it only been a day since I'd studied my maid's uniform in the mirror, making plans to ditch it forever? But slipping into a yellow polyester golf shirt every morning to clean up after my wealthier neighbors wasn't what I'd had in mind. At least at the motel, it was strangers you cleaned up after.

"Have you checked the want ads?" I said. "We could stop and get a paper."

"Have you ever looked for a job that way?" Lu made a sound of disgust. The stoplight at the town park snagged us, and I had a chance to glance her way. She looked tired for not having worked that day. "It's no good," she said. "And I'm not sure either of us has the time it takes. But there's not much else to do. Carlos is asking for more hours at work, but he might not get any."

"I could get called in to sub again. If Fitz is really sick—"

"I don't think he is," she said.

"Coach said—"

"No, I mean—isn't that him?" She pointed out the window. Fitz, wearing a Midway High sweatshirt, stood in the park with his hands shoved into his pockets. He watched a pair of young women as they passed. He turned beyond them, as though waiting for someone. "Looks healthy to me," Lu said.

"I guess he'll be back tomorrow, then," I said, but I was watching not Fitz but Teeny, across the street. She stalked the edge of the grass at the curb, looking for all the world like a squirrel about to dart into traffic. And then Fitz was racing to her rescue, holding back traffic to let her cross. Taking care of everyone.

The car behind me laid on the horn. The light had changed.

"Maybe one of the other teachers will wake up with a headache," Lu said brightly as I hit the gas.

"Maybe," I said. "But they could get someone better for science or math. The only thing I can actually teach is phys ed." Something welled up in me. I swallowed hard. "Lu, I might be good at it."

"Don't be so surprised. You're good at lots of things."

Lots of things? The only thing that came to mind was palming something shiny out of the guest rooms without being caught. "I'm putting you in charge of writing my résumé," I said.

I pulled up in front of Lu's house. The porch light was on again, even though it hadn't yet turned dark. I imagined that this was my house and that inside, a pot of something spicy bubbled, waiting for me to put my signature touch on it. That the man inside cared enough about where I was every minute of the day to flick the switch, just in case. I'd always meant to leave town, but sometimes all I wanted was nothing more than the best it had to offer.

"Why don't you come in and stay for dinner?" Lu said.

"Thanks, but I have some things to do."

"Like what? You're unemployed, remember? Come on."

"I want to do some thinking." I'd shared all my ideas about the murder with Courtney and been turned away, but that wouldn't stop me. I couldn't help feeling there was something I could do, if only I thought it through more clearly. "I don't understand why she came all this way just to die. And at the *Mid-Night*."

I'd turned my head, but I could still feel Lu's eyes on me. "It's not your job to figure it out," she said. "Don't do anything stupid."

"Which is more stupid—to try and figure out who did it, or wait until the police decide it was me?"

"But it wasn't you."

Her voice was small. I looked at her. "Jesus, Lu. Say it like you mean it."

"No, I do. I do mean it. Everyone knows it wasn't you. They'll find whoever did this, and then it will be all over. But don't give them a reason to pay attention to you. Keep out of it."

"Yeah," I said, with no intention of staying out of it.

"Yeah?"

"Maybe I'll come over tomorrow," I said. But now Lu's uncertainty had transferred to me, and even I could hear it.

Lu opened the door without looking at me, got out, and crossed the yard. Before she'd reached the porch, the front door swung open and a flurry of brown limbs and pigtails emerged. The kids met her in the yard and drew her inside.

As I drove away, I had to wonder if I agreed with Lu. Would they find who killed Maddy? And if not, could they overlook the convenience of that follow-up story Courtney wanted to write?

Would it ever be over? Would things go back to normal?

I drove down Lu's street and across town toward my house, noticing that the streets seemed narrow and the houses, shabby. The sidewalks were cracked, with little tufts of grass poking through. On my street, the same neighbor's curtain flicked back to check who came and went. I imagined a cleaning-service car pulling up to Mrs. Schneider's house, and me hopping out in a yellow shirt, carrying a bucket up the walk.

In a matter of seconds I would pull into our drive, the same drive, and walk through the same door, and my mother would have slept or not slept, would say or not say the same things she always did. The evening stretched out before me, the same chores, the same shallow conversation, the same everything until there was nothing to do but retire to my childhood bedroom. And then the rote review of my secret treasures, sad little pieces of trash that they were.

The same life. The only thing that had changed was the shame I suddenly felt about who I was. Who I would always be. And the rage rising in my chest, into my throat, until I thought I would have to scream.

At our driveway, I didn't turn in. I held tight to the steering wheel and kept going.

When I drove up the long gravel drive to Maddy's old house, Gretchen already stood framed, arms crossed, in the open doorway. I'd always thought you couldn't surprise someone with one of these mile-long, farmhouse driveways. Since the night Maddy died, Gretchen must have received a number of unwelcome visits. She seemed prepared for whatever bad news I brought.

She shaded her eyes, but I knew she'd have recognized me already. I'd seen her a couple of weeks ago coming into the bar, though we had less than a nodding acquaintance now. Neither of us talked to Maddy anymore. What else did we have in common? That was our unspoken truce.

Gretchen leaned over the porch railing, exposing a wide expanse of cleavage in the loose neck of her nightgown. I opened the car door.

"You didn't bring me a damn casserole, did you?" Her voice was deep and growling. "In my whole life, I've never seen so many dishes cooked with smashed potato chips on top."

"I don't cook much," I said. Maybe I should have brought her something. I knew what Gretchen Beetner-Bell liked best: aged scotch, cigarettes, other women's husbands. But the Mid-Night supplied her with a steady stream of all those. Lu and I kept track of how far from her car the men dropped her off the next morning.

"You know what they say? You don't cook, you don't eat." She winked. "But I have not found that to be the case."

Her laugh was a horse whinny dragged across the gravel under my feet. She dangled a foot over the porch's edge. Her toes were painted a terrible shade of purple, almost gray against her skin. It reminded me of Maddy's dead face above the belt. I forced myself to look away.

"I'm sorry about Maddy," I said.

"Why? Did you do it?"

"No." I thought for a second. "Did you?"

"You're about as subtle as they were, all 'where was I at such-and-such a time,' all 'how do I spend my time all by myself in this big house.' It wasn't *polite*."

"They have to establish who could have done it. Who was, you know, alone and unaccounted for."

"Well, I was pretty well accounted for, sweet pea."

"Will his wife let him say so?"

The laugh again, dredged from deep in her gut. Then the laugh became a cough. "You're a smart one," she said.

Twice in the last hour I'd been called smart, but that's not how I felt.

"I was down at the boats, if you must know," Gretchen said. The casinos, docked down on the Ohio River, skirted strict Indiana gambling laws by docking offshore. They were fantastically popular with the Mid-Night's bar crowd. "Figured I'd try my luck on the slots, but they let me down like everyone else ever has. Not so smart, myself."

"Well, whoever killed Maddy was smart," I said. "So far he's gotten away with it."

Gretchen's face went thoughtful. "Why do you think it's a he?"

"Because you'd have to be strong to—" I struggled to find the most *polite* term.

"To string her up like he done?" Gretchen said.

"Do you think it could be a woman?"

"Well, I don't know," Gretchen said. "But it was the girls that never seemed to get along with Madeleine. Her dad told me I was imagining it, but I was the one who answered the phone. Back then, you know, prank calls just before and after those big races. And she only ever had *boy*friends, not lady friends, not good ones." She glanced at me. "You might as well come on in."

I'd only been over once—Gretchen's comment about Maddy not having any good girlfriends stung—but I remembered the place well enough. It seemed smaller, but it wasn't only that I was bigger. In the ensuing years it had been stuffed from the porch door to as far as the eye could see with mismatched couches, flea-market armchairs, and antique tables and hutches. All of it was crowded together so that none of the drawers could ever open, and the pieces had been stacked with newspapers, magazines, grocery bags, piles of old mail, and collections of strange things that Gretchen seemed to want close at hand, including a bouquet of fly swatters and an array of TV remotes. But who was I to judge someone's collection of anything?

At the foot of one chair lay the morning edition of the *Midway Gazette*. On the front, a teenaged Maddy waved from the top pedestal at some race, and then, smaller, smiled at the camera in a more recent photo.

I reached for the paper and studied it. *Chicago woman found dead at local motel.* Billy would be having a fit. He didn't like people using the word *motel* in relation to the Mid-Night. The words that bothered me were *Chicago woman.* It nagged—was she really? Didn't she still belong to us? Couldn't we claim her this one last time? I studied the recent photo, then the old one. The news was out. It was real.

"Where'd they get the photos?"

"Ones we had here. That one I pulled from an old box. That other one she sent last year for Christmas." She looked over my shoulder. "They cut out the boyfriend. Good riddance."

My heart leapt. Here it was, an open door. The fiancé made for a good suspect, surely. "You didn't like him?"

"You don't think she ever brought him here?" she said. "I never met him, or none of the men she kept with over the years. Her dad never saw a thing wrong with it, but you and I, just us girls, don't believe that for a second. You have a boyfriend, you show him *off.*"

Or you skulk around in the shadows, hoping he'll drop you off all the way to your car door.

"So why 'good riddance'?" I said.

"Well, I guess he did it, right? The police say he has an alibi, but what do they know?" She walked over to a cupboard, wedged a drawer open as far as it would go into the arm of a chair, and pulled out a crumpled envelope. She held it out to me. Inside was the photo of Maddy from the paper. The guy with her was as handsome as she'd promised. He was black, which I hadn't expected. I wondered what the small minds of Midway would have to say about that. He was dressed well, in the style of catalogues that rarely made it into the mailboxes of anyone I'd ever met. Wealthy, of course. The ring had said all we needed to know about his net worth.

In the photo, his eyes were turned on Maddy with such open desire that I was embarrassed. Men had always looked at her that way. Maybe that's what Coach meant when he said she'd been sexualized. Something that was done to her, that she couldn't help.

I looked harder at the photo. Could he have done it? He would have needed a window of almost six hours to be in place. I needed twenty minutes, round-trip. Actually, I hardly needed any time at all, since she'd delivered herself right to my workplace and its sturdy railings. I sighed and handed the photo and envelope back to Gretchen.

"When was the wedding supposed to be?" I said.

"She never told me anything. Not about school or men or work or life." She glanced at me, and I could suddenly see that her eyes were pink-rimmed. "It's not like I didn't try, you know. I tried. Young girl without a mother. Not like I was getting the grand sweepstakes prize when I married her dad and came here." She swept her hand wide at the crowded room. "And then to get Miss Snotnose in the bargain. Oh, I tried with her. But she—well, with Madeleine, I could never win."

Two of us, then. But then I thought of all those Southtown girls and the girls who'd prank-called this house. The girls who'd turned on us the first chance they had, after Courtney's "blur" headline. A lot of us had been pitched against Maddy in one way or another. Had one of them wanted to win so badly as to hold a grudge for ten years?

Hadn't I?

"You know what they're saying?" she asked.

"'They' who?"

"She was going to put me in a home," Gretchen said. "Found some paperwork or application in her stuff. I would have fought like a cat, you understand, if she'd tried that business."

This seemed unlikely to me. Not the cat part. That part I believed. "Her stuff?"

"Her suitcase, from the motel. Mostly just clothes. She always liked the clothes. Some things never change." Her eyes threatened to spill.

The suitcase had been gone by the time I'd been in the room. My palms hummed with the thought of more of her clothes, of more things that had once belonged to her. "Are Maddy's yearbooks still here?" I said.

"It's all here." She waved her hand toward the ceiling. "The Madeleine Bell Museum, of course," Gretchen said. "Memorialized, as she left it. He never let me pack it up. Couldn't get rid of a thing."

I'd forgotten about her dad. He kept falling away, like a chapter in a book I wanted to skip over. That puke-colored sweater was probably around here somewhere. I didn't want to find it. The idea that he'd somehow used Maddy's old room as a shrine to her youth gave my gut a wrench. "Sorry about—Mr.—" The courtesy got stuck in my throat. "Your husband. Was he sick a long time? I mean—did he suffer?"

Her eyes fluttered. "She didn't come for the funeral. Can you imagine?"

A day earlier, I might not have been able to. I forged ahead. "They didn't get along?"

"He . . . had trouble showing affection," she said. "But he sure liked having a winner in the family." She blinked toward the window and the long drive. "But that's one thing I can say in her favor. She loved him." Gretchen glanced at me and saw something on my face she didn't like. "She did. Too much, you ask me. But she wouldn't come here, not even for her daddy's funeral."

I kept forgetting that part, too. "Do you need help with the—uh. The arrangements?"

Gretchen looked bored with me. "He should do that. Vincent."

"The fiancé? I assumed—"

"I'll do my part," Gretchen said. "No one will be able to say I didn't do my part for that girl."

"I meant only that they weren't married yet," I said. "And you're the next of kin."

She went quiet, gazing away from me and letting her hand fall to the neck of her nightgown. "That's true," she said. "I am."

"And of course everything that's here is yours to do with as you wish." I was thinking of that yearbook, but also watching Gretchen's wheels turning. If there was money involved, could she have mustered the strength to kill Maddy? Or hired one of her boyfriends from the bar?

"Not that anyone would want any of that garbage," she said.

"Could I take a look? Maybe there's a memento . . ."

"Help yourself." She picked up a TV remote idly, palming it as she kept watch out the front window. "It's probably all going to the bin. That's to do as I wish, only I wish I'd done it years ago."

CHAPTER FIFTEEN

The second I walked into Maddy's room, I knew I would steal something.

The door creaked as it opened. Beyond lay the bedroom not of a woman gone for ten years, but a teenaged girl who might return any moment and kick me out. The window, covered with only a gauzy curtain, let in a light bright enough to fade the old, yellow wallpaper on the opposite wall. Books and papers were stacked near an outdated computer, the desk chair casually pulled back. The bed was made, but badly. I hoped someone had at some point washed or changed the sheets, but I wouldn't have made any bets. In the closet, her clothes—clothes I'd probably remember—would be hanging there.

The room was a shrine, as Gretchen had promised, but also a showcase. On the far wall, a series of shelves displayed every trophy and award Maddy had ever won. Tourney ribbons in every color, medallions hanging. Trophies up to two feet tall, their silver-plated runners leaping off the pinpoint tops, one foot kicked behind. Some tournaments went to the trouble of making sure that women's awards had silver women runners, silver ponytails flying, but some didn't bother. One of the running figures with no ponytail, dull with age and dust, had come loose from his award and lay at the feet of the others. On his side like that, he looked miserable and embarrassed, reminding me not of a triumphant runner hitting the finish-line tape, but Maddy, fetal on the edge of that hotel-room bed so long ago.

I turned and surveyed the room. If nothing had been moved since Maddy had gone to college, the yearbooks had to be here. But the only books stacked in the low, small case under the trophy display were old textbooks. When I opened the bedside dresser drawer, dust kicked up, making me sneeze. It was empty.

I went to the window and hooked one of the sheers to the side. The long drive curved into view and then out again, behind a stand of trees between the house and the road. Wind blew the tops of the trees in a synchronized dance. I knew it would rain later, because the leaves were tipped upside down, showing their white bellies. I knew this, as well as I knew that Maddy had bought a yearbook, even when I hadn't. Even when she would abandon everything inside of it within the year.

I knew she'd bought the yearbook, because of the scene.

She'd wrangled her copy away from the yearbook staff that morning, long before most of the senior class had heard they were in the building. We huddled over it in the cafeteria before homeroom, trying to keep it to ourselves.

We already knew that spring sports got the short shrift so the yearbook made its print deadline. But our senior pictures, alongside quotes or song lyrics we'd chosen, would be on full display. Our last yearbook, our last chance to put our mark on this place. But our senior pictures were old by then, taken almost a year ahead. Our hair was different. Our senior quotes seemed distant, chosen by someone else. Our favorite song lyrics made us laugh. We didn't even remember liking that song.

"Wait," I said, when Maddy flipped through the page with my photo too fast: "What idiot thing did I say?"

Too late. She tore through the class pages and clubs to the sports, the skinny-legged junior-varsity teams giving way to varsity football and wrestling. The boys, with their thin chests thrown out. Then basketball. Then cheerleaders. Maddy ripped the page, turning it.

"Slow down," I pleaded. I wanted to take the pages one spread at a time, really give the cheerleaders a sneer, and take a two-student poll between us on who in our class looked better since their class pictures were taken and who looked worse.

The track team turned into view. I held out my hand to stop the pages, but I shouldn't have bothered. This is what Maddy was racing to see: more skinny legs, pale, and some of us clutching our elbows against the cool breeze that day. Maddy stood in the back row, her neck stretched long. I stood at Fitz's elbow, hunched and miserable.

She made a noise and let the book fall into my hands.

"What?" I studied the pages hungrily. They'd included another photo of her, something staged, where Coach had her by the shoulder, giving her a pre-run pep talk. She looked amazing, bright-eyed and fierce. I'd have given anything to be in her place. What was she complaining about? She was the star, forever, the one no one would ever forget. A split second behind her in every race, I was an afterthought, only appearing in the team picture. The book trembling in my grip, I couldn't help but hope that I would yet show them, that somehow I would pull out a win over Maddy at state, only a couple of weeks away. What if I trained harder? What if I put myself on a strict diet and cut a few pounds before sectionals? Lighter, swifter. I imagined holding my own against Maddy, imagined the sharp cut of her chin turning toward me as I passed her. I would never see it, but maybe someone would take a photo as I broke the finish tape before her. Just once.

And then I turned to my senior picture and read the silly captions the yearbook staff had added for each of us.

Third wheel on the track team bus.

"So what?" I said. "So stupid, anyway. It should be a bicycle, not the team bus. Buses have a lot more wheels than three." Maddy stiffened and wrenched the book away to see for herself. By then, she was the one trembling, pale with anger. "What the hell?" she said. She tore to her own photo, holding the open book away from me. Her lips moved as she read, and then she quietly shut the book and threw it across the room. It landed flat, and sounded like a gunshot. A couple of girls screamed, their chairs scraping and knocking over. Chaos reigned until a teacher or the vice principal or someone came to see what the fuss was, and Maddy got pulled in for a chat, the retrieved book under her arm.

"You're not buying one of them," she called to me as she was led away. "No way. Promise me."

And I promised. I was ashamed of what the book said for myself, and for whatever Maddy had seen when she turned to her own photo. I was ashamed, maybe for the first time, of how people viewed me. Third wheel, tagalong. I wasn't even a person to them. I didn't matter.

The promise was an easy one to keep. Maddy was the only one who mattered to me. I hadn't needed to remember anyone else. And then the state tournament went on without us, and I didn't want to remember her, either.

Now I held my wrist to my nose and smelled the spice-cookie perfume. I wanted to remember now. I wanted to remember more than anything.

I searched under the bed, inside the closet I hadn't wanted to open, in any drawer or cubby that presented itself. Everything I touched or moved riled up dust until I had a low burn in the back of my throat. No yearbook. Nothing personal, really—just the trophies and ribbons and accolades that should have been packaged up and stored away a decade ago. I went to the award display again, noticing that for all the dust in the room, the awards had collected an even thicker layer. There was a thin umbilical of web draped between two silver ponytails. The little silver runner separated from his trophy lay on his side, stretching toward me.

She hadn't cared about them enough to take them.

I checked the inscriptions. Her highest placings were here, all the big races I could think to look for. After all that time put in, all those laps run, all those mornings when we'd rather have been sleeping in instead of dozing on a bumpy school bus to the next tournament. All those jeers from people who didn't know the first thing about us. All those times she'd showed them what she, what *we*, were made of. And she'd left the trophies behind. Just like Beck had said. For whatever reason, she'd been done with this life.

Looking at the trophies, I suffered all over again. I wanted them. I wanted them all. My hands began to tingle.

"Did you find what you were looking for?"

I jumped.

Gretchen stood in the door, her hip thrown out against the jamb.

"You were right," I said. "It looks . . . the same."

"It's a big house. I guess we had room for a museum," she said, looking around. "Should have packed it up and sent it to her at her fancy place in Chicago, just to have it gone."

"Did she take anything when she came last? Maybe any books?" My hands were pins and needles. I could barely pay attention to what I was saying.

Gretchen's eyes sharpened. "When she came last? When do you think that was? She never came here again, not after she left for her snooty school. He was always wanting to visit her there. Even promised not to bring me, if you can believe that. Promised her not to bring his wife, to leave me here, alone. What do you think of that?"

I thought Gretchen had every right to want to pitch everything in the room into a bin and set it alight. I thought that perhaps Courtney had heard this story, because the telling of it certainly inspired me to think of Maddy as a brat. I thought that Gretchen had plenty of things to do with nights she might be left alone. And I thought that maybe I'd broken into a sweat. "What about that night? Did she come here?"

"What night? The night she was killed?" Gretchen scoffed herself into a laugh and then laughed herself into a cough. After a long while, after I had tracked a drop of sweat running down the full length of my back, she took up again, her voice shredded and hoarse. "You think she'd come here, after all this time? To see me? And do what? Call me Mommy?" Another ragged breath. "You done here?"

Gretchen turned to lead me downstairs. In the split second before she looked back again to see if I was coming, my hand shot out and enclosed the little silver runner with no trophy to call his own. His cool metal body was sweet relief to my palm. I had no pockets, so I carried him under the hem of my fleece all the way down the stairs and through the jumble sale of Gretchen's living room, out the door and to the car. And when I drove away, I held him under my thigh so that I could wave to Gretchen, standing alone in the doorway just as I'd found her.

The silver man poked into my leg. I regretted him. I would take him back.

But I didn't. I couldn't. I kept driving. I wanted him. I wanted him more than anything I'd wanted in a long time. I wanted him the way I must have back in school, when he could have been mine the traditional way. Which trophy had he come from? Which race was it that Maddy pulled ahead and took him away from me?

It didn't matter anymore. She was gone, and he was mine.

But I still hadn't landed a copy of the yearbook. Halfway back to town, I realized who would have a copy at hand. Shelly Anderson probably had all four yearbooks lined on a shelf in a special, archival air-quality room. I looked at the clock and sped up. The bank would still be open if I hurried.

When I pulled into a spot out front, Shelly was leaving the bank with a couple of people I didn't know, laughing and calling back to them. I slid the silver runner under my car seat, watching her approach.

Shelly hadn't changed a bit. She was who she was going to be, it seemed. Sturdy in stature, sturdy in nature. Hair and face and hands thick and purposeful. Someone you couldn't trust with a secret. You could trust her to deposit your paycheck with precision—while she took note of the balance. Shelly never let on, but working in the hometown bank, she knew things that no one liked other people to know. When a bill was late. When, despite your best efforts to balance your meager allotment in life, the water bill cleared two days too early and the whole program collapsed. Shelly, Midway born and raised, would never be a powerful woman the way Maddy had been. She wouldn't turn heads here, let alone in Chicago. But she did well on the information exchange. That was real power. We were all a little afraid of her.

I slipped out of my fleece and dropped it on the passenger seat, then opened the car door and got out. When Shelly saw me, the smile fell from her face, replaced by a long blink, as though she'd caught a prayer passing by on a breeze.

"Oh, Juliet. You poor thing. It's a shame," she said. "People coming in today couldn't believe it. Such a remarkable person as Maddy was, they just couldn't."

I imagined the lingering customers at Shelly's window, the theories and half-remembered facts that must have been slipped across her counter today, keep the change. Everyone having his or her say. "Remarkable"? To Shelly, anyone might be remarked upon, especially if life had taken a sour turn for them.

"I can't believe it, either." I couldn't. The news felt ridiculous to me all over again, as though I were watching a day-long cop-show marathon, or having one of those busy dreams where you woke up exhausted. And before I could say or think anything else, I was. Exhausted. All the anger I felt toward the gossips left me and I sat, hard, on the curb.

"Are you OK?" Shelly rushed to me and knelt down, looking around in real fear. Tomorrow I would be a charming story of grief for the first fifty customers, but for now I was causing a scene and keeping her from getting home.

"Sorry . . . I don't know," I said. "I just needed to sit down."

"Do you want me to get you anything?"

"I'm fine," I said. I'd scraped my palms on the sidewalk, but maybe that would shut them up for a while. "Really. Things just caught up with me for a second."

Shelly stood up and took a step away, glancing down the street one way and then the other. Then, in a flash of understanding, I knew that I wasn't simply keeping her after work. I was forcing her to fraternize with a suspect. Not that Shelly Anderson didn't want the dirt. But she didn't want to be seen digging in it.

"Look, Shelly, I get it. But I need a favor."

She had started to edge away.

"Can I borrow our senior-class yearbook for a couple of days?" I said. "I swear I'll get it back to you."

Her curiosity got the better of her. She stopped, considered. "What for?"

"It's . . . hard to explain. I'm trying to make myself remember some things from senior year. An exercise in mourning, I guess."

She sniffed. "If only there had been a chance for you to buy a full year of memories for only twenty dollars."

"Were you on the yearbook staff?" My voice came out sharp. A few of my questions could be settled by someone from that year's *Tracks* staff.

"I would have been, if I'd had time," she said. "I helped out here and there, but senior year was like a full-time job for me, you know. Class president is a lot of work, in case you haven't noticed or, you know, RSVP'd to our reunion."

"Shelly, I might be in jail by then."

That got her attention. She looked at me shrewdly. "People were saying today, 'Juliet Townsend' but I kept telling them no way could Juliet do something like that."

No way I could do it. Not *would*. I might—but it was a matter of skill, of ability. I wouldn't be capable of pulling together a murder, not the way Shelly could plan a reunion.

"I didn't, of course not, Shelly. But it looks like not everyone knows my limits as well as you do. Courtney Howard, for one."

"Courtney, good lord," Shelly said, reaching a hand to help me up. "But I suppose she's in a position to have her opinions listened to. At long last."

I dusted the palms of my hands lightly on my track pants. They burned, but in a real, physical way I didn't mind. "And her opinion of me is well known."

Shelly blinked at me. Maybe she didn't know what Courtney thought of me. Or maybe I'd read her wrong again, and her opinion of me had always been just as low. "Is that why you don't borrow Courtney's copy of the yearbook?"

I laughed. "Right." Courtney was the last person in my class I'd have expected to own a yearbook, not to mention the last person I'd be asking for favors. "But seriously, can I borrow yours? I'll take special care of it. I only want to take a look at a couple of pages."

Shelly suddenly went still. "Are you—wait. Have you been reading too many Agatha Christie novels? You think her death had something to do with *high school*? Juliet, really? Where is your dignity?"

In the Midway County morgue. No, I knew just where it was: Back ten years ago in a room in the Luxe, when I held out for running the state tournament longer than any best friend should have.

I was about to say so when someone raced past us. We turned to watch a tall man give the bank doors a violent yank. The doors rattled in place, locked. He raised his hands to peer in, then pounded on the glass until I thought it would shatter.

"Hey," Shelly bellowed.

The man turned, but instead of running away, he lunged out of the building's shadows toward us. He was tall, dark-skinned. I knew who he was at once. "Is there anyone left inside?" he said. "I need to talk to someone in that bank."

"The bank is closed, sir," Shelly said, her voice insulted for the door's sake. "You can set your watch for it to open tomorrow at eight."

"I could be in jail by then," he said.

Shelly looked my way. "My," she said. "But that jail is getting very crowded."

CHAPTER SIXTEEN

Maddy's fiancé blinked between us.

I stood back. In the flesh, he was tall, imposing. The affectionate gaze from the photo Gretchen had showed me was gone. Instead, his eyes tore me apart, a look sharper than any Beck had ever attempted. If this guy had tried to get me to leave him alone with Maddy, I would have done it. Shelly pulled her purse close to her body.

The name came to me. "Vincent."

His features couldn't decide between relief and suspicion. "Yes, how did you—wait. Are you Juliet?"

We stared at each other in stunned silence while Shelly took another long look up and down the street.

He knew my name. Had she told him about me? Had I still been special to her? I wanted it to be true and not true at the same time. More likely that she'd taken her yearbook with her and had shown off a few track team pictures one lazy afternoon. Or maybe one of her trophies made it to Chicago after all, and she'd mentioned how tight a race she'd run. Against whom? Just some girl named Juliet.

"She told you—" I started.

"Or are you Kristina?" he said.

I stared at him. "Who—"

"Oh, you're that guy," Shelly brayed, grabbing my arm and pulling me closer to her. I was the suspect a few minutes ago, but now that we had a better one, I was her bodyguard. "Oh, no, no, this is too much," she said. "It is locked up tight, and you can forget about it until this is all sorted out."

"The ring," Vincent breathed.

"What about the ring?" I shook Shelly off and turned on her. "Why would you have the ring?"

143

"Well, I don't have it, but the bank—"

"Why is it here?" I said.

"It's evidence in an ongoing investigation," Shelly said. "The authorities felt the ring would be best kept in the vault, where it would not fall into the very hands that strangled that poor woman."

"She was strangled—by hand?" I felt my own hand at my throat and dropped it. "But the belt—"

"That was just a cover," Shelly said, a little too brightly. "Her murderer looked her in the eye and strangled her until she was dead. And then hung her up like a—"

Vincent made a noise that convinced Shelly not to give any additional visuals. "That's what I heard, anyway, and you'll just have to wait until they know it wasn't by your hands that she died before you get the ring back."

"That ring belongs to Maddy," Vincent said. Shelly backed up. "Not to some hick town or any of its dough-faced inhabitants." I glanced to see how Shelly was taking this. Her face was indeed doughy, now that he mentioned it. "If I find out that you had that ring on your greasy finger, I'll never let you forget where you went wrong. None of you." He gestured wildly up the street. "This shit hole has always had too much of a hold on her. And now it's finally taken her from me. If I could think of someone to sue, I would sue—"

"A lawyer," Shelly said to me.

"—and the—the—*devil* who did this, he'd better hope the cops get to him first."

Shelly shot me a mock impressed look. "I'll bring the yearbook to the bank tomorrow if you want to stop by," she said and turned on her heel. "Stay out of jail, now. Juliet, I mean. *You*, sir, can check yourself in anytime you like."

I watched her down the street and around the corner, then tried a glance in Vincent's direction. Staying out of jail suddenly didn't seem like the biggest problem I had.

He stood with his fists clenched against his thighs. Maybe he'd done it, but his anger seemed real. His hands could have strangled a woman easily—or maybe they only ached for revenge or action, the same way mine did for whatever shiny piece of crap I couldn't help wanting.

My grabbing had come from the same kind of loss. The first time I nabbed something pretty that didn't belong to me, my dad had already died. I'd already been through the funeral, but I was still angry. As I packed up the last of my things in my dorm room, knowing that I would never come back, I took a lipstick case of my roommate's I'd always admired. It was gold and carved like something from a museum. She must have known I'd taken it, but I didn't care. I was *owed*.

My first crime. My hands hadn't itched that time.

But the time after that, they tingled, urging me on until I took the thing, until I owned something that I hadn't only a minute before. There was magic in that, power. This thing—shiny, silver, gold, pink, beaded, flowered, whatever it was. Some little pretty thing that was someone else's. With the flick of a wrist, it became *mine*.

Now, I looked Vincent over. He was extraordinarily good-looking. Maddy hadn't evaded that question, of all the things I'd asked her.

My thoughts drifted away and then snapped back.

"I heard you had an alibi," I said.

"I heard you didn't," he said, his eyes flat. The fists, the heaving breath. I shouldn't have worried about Shelly leaving me alone with a possible killer. I should have worried she'd left me alone with someone who thought I'd done it.

"Not really," I said. "But if Maddy told you about me, maybe you already know that I wouldn't hurt her. At least—I wouldn't hurt her any more than I already did."

"You know, that's one thing she could never explain to me," he said. "She talked about you. She showed me all the old pictures and stuff, told me all the old stories. But she never called. Even when I suggested we invite you up for the weekend. She wouldn't come here, but I thought, maybe . . ." He closed his eyes and sighed.

A weekend in Chicago. This was a shining mirage I'd hardly dared imagine. I swallowed hard. "What did she say?"

When he opened his eyes, they scared me again. They were bottomless, black. Empty.

"Never the right time," he said. "Work or that thing we promised to do or that event we got tickets for. The opera, that show, a wine tasting, a—goddamned sailing lesson." He scuffed the heel of his shoe against the curb. "You see what she did? She kept us so busy with events and lessons and seminars and ribbon cuttings that we never got around to getting married or coming down here for me to meet her family. This place ruled her, but she didn't want to bring me here. What am I supposed to take from that?"

"Maybe she was protecting you from this place."

Vincent turned on me. "What's that mean?"

I'd said it without thinking. "I'm not sure. Only—well, she came back and ended up dead. Maybe she was protecting you."

"You don't think I did it, then."

I didn't know. So far I hadn't met anyone in my life I thought might be capable of murder. Maybe no one I knew was. Maybe whatever Maddy had been mixed up in had nothing to do with Vincent or me or the motel or Midway. Maybe she'd chosen the area to conduct her business—what I wouldn't give to go back and ask her for more details—because it was a place that was already ruined. A place that was already lost to her.

"What was she here for?" I said.

"No clue," he said. "You know what they're saying, right?"

His fists had clenched again. He radiated raw anger that anyone would say she'd had a lover in her room.

"She told me she was here for business," I said. "What does she do for a living?"

He took long enough to answer that I began to wonder if her work had been scandalous or seedy in some way. Lu and I sometimes ran into people near the motel who weren't guests, weren't likely to be coming from the bar. Strays, we called them. They were women, mostly, often quite young-looking. But they were there on business, too, we figured. Where they came from, we had no idea.

"Nothing," Vincent said at last, his rage gone. "I guess that's the honest answer."

"What do you mean?"

"She lost her job a couple of years ago. Two or three. Oh, man, longer ago than that, I guess. She didn't bounce back from that."

"She didn't work."

"She wanted to take some time, maybe go back to school."

"Which school? To study what?"

He looked over at my eagerness, confused. "A master's degree in something, but she never did," he said. "She toyed with law school a lot. She had some causes that really fired her up." He seemed to fade away. "When she got going about things—tough stuff, like child brides, abused kids—well, you know how she was."

I didn't want to argue the point, or think about where Maddy's interest in abused kids came from. "So she finished college? The first time, I mean?"

"Of course she did."

"What was her degree in? Did you ever see the diploma?"

"No, but who keeps their diplomas lying around?" he said. The black eyes landed heavily on me. "What's going on? What is this about?"

If Mrs. Haggerty's slip could be trusted, Maddy had never started college, let alone finished, but Beck had said she'd left for college early. What if, instead of arriving to college early and eager, she'd dropped out of high school and out of Midway and out of life, struck out on her own and not looked back?

She could have talked about going back to school every day of her life and not done it, knowing that she'd have to start way back at the beginning.

The important thing was that she hadn't had a job. Whatever business she'd been in town to conduct couldn't have been professional. It had to have been personal.

Beck.

I hated to think it, but there it was. If she'd not gone to see Gretchen and she'd only stopped by to talk to me on her way to another appointment, there was really only one person left. And only one kind of unfinished business I could think of.

"What's this about?" Vincent said again.

"Truthfully, I'm not sure." I felt sick, remembering my hand on Beck's arm. Had I touched a murderer? Had I taken a murderer back to the scene of the crime? Had I taken pains to keep a *murderer* from leaving any damning evidence? "Did she mention anyone from here by name? Was she in touch with anyone?"

"Just you," he said.

So many myths to dispel, I couldn't begin. "Other than me."

"There were some teachers she didn't care for. She wouldn't say why."

I looked at him. Was it worth explaining that far more teachers had never cared for Maddy? "Wait," I said. "You said Kristina. Who's Kristina?"

"Some friend of hers. Her name came up once in a while."

"From here?"

"I assumed. I mean, yeah, because she knew her from the track team."

The rippled edge of that Indiana-shaped trophy came back to me. Kristina. In the end, she'd done what Maddy never had. She'd run state and come home with a prize. But how had Maddy even known her? "She never mentioned someone named Tom? Tommy? Beck?"

"Who's that?" In a flash he was fired up again, spit flying and fists tight. "If he did this—"

"If he did this, then the police can deal with it," I said. "But you're a much better suspect. Running around after your investments was probably not the best way to spend the day. You're supposed to be a man in mourning."

"I'm a lawyer. We don't mourn—" At this, his face started to crumple. He conquered it, composed himself. "We don't mourn the same way as other people. Besides, it wasn't just the ring I was after. They said her effects were here. I thought something in her pockets, or in her purse, her phone, would give me some idea how she spent her . . . last day."

I didn't remember her carrying a purse or a phone.

For a second, I was strangely protective of Maddy. No—of Maddy's death. Maddy's murder felt like something that had happened only to me. Vincent, shutting off his pain. Gretchen, her eyes lighting up at the idea of being next of kin. Lu, telling me to stay away from it all. Billy, flipping on the no-vacancy sign as though he couldn't get out of there fast enough. Maddy's death hadn't just happened near me, but somewhere deep in my bones. Somewhere under my feet, and now I couldn't stand on such uneven ground.

There was no point in keeping all the grief to myself. I was the one trying to save an eighteen-year-old girl who hadn't been eighteen years old in a long time. If anyone had a right to this, it was Vincent. Gretchen. Even Billy, listening downstairs.

Billy.

Billy was the one who knew how Maddy had spent some of her last hours.

"I'm sorry, Vincent," I said. "I need to go. Will you hold the funeral in Chicago? Or here?"

He stared through me. "Oh, God, I don't think I can do this."

I knew I couldn't do it, either. But I knew who could. I felt eyes watching us up and down the street, felt the nods and exchanged looks as I led Vincent to my car for a scrap of paper. I couldn't find anything but a brochure tossed on the floor of the backseat, something I'd picked up somewhere, and tore a big corner off the back. A pen, finally, in the glove compartment. Handing the phone number over, I hesitated, then reached for Vincent's shoulder to squeeze, the least I could do, and so was in place to catch him as he fell toward me and landed upon me. I held on, straining under his bulk and the additional weight of the things he believed about my friendship with Maddy. It didn't seem important at the moment to clear anything up. It didn't seem important, petty really, to point out that it looked like we all grieved the same way, after all.

CHAPTER SEVENTEEN

At the entrance to the Mid-Night's parking lot, I braked and let my car shudder and buck under me as I gazed over the dark, empty expanse. Billy's rusted beater took up a space as always—except it wasn't as always. This time of night, the bar should have been lit up and hopping. Either the police had come to put Yvonne's side business on ice, or everyone who'd wanted a good look had already been to visit.

I took the spot next to Billy's but couldn't go around the alcove end of the building. I went around to the breezeway instead, past the vending machines. The courtyard was blacker than I'd ever seen it, all the rooms and overhead lights dark. I felt my way around the walk to his door and knocked hard. I rubbed at my cold arms, then pounded at the door again. Nothing.

The night was quiet except for the whir of cars racing past on the interstate. I stepped back and peered up at the door of Maddy's room. It was still barricaded by crime-scene tape.

I folded my arms around myself and walked toward the office. I'd had to arrive at the Mid-Night early, in the dark of winter many times, and I'd had to leave late, but this was different. The empty lot and the shadowy courtyard gave me a sour-stomach feeling.

My foot hit a patch of something and slid. I fell on my butt, scraping my palms against the pavement. I held my hands aloft. In the dim light, they were slick and wet.

Not blood. Please. Anything but blood.

I smelled my hands, then wiped them gently on my pants, looking around until I traced the puddle under me to the underside of the ice machine.

Back around the corner, the office was dark except for the "No Vacancy" neon. No Billy, no sign of anyone.

I went back to my car, then instead of getting inside, kept going. I didn't want to be there or to go where I was going, but I couldn't stop myself.

I passed under the stairs and edged up to the corner of the building and the alcove. Here, the interstate roared with cars racing by. People had places to be, futures full of promise to get started. I braced myself and turned the corner to face the garbage bin and the railing above.

Some punishing part of my brain expected Maddy to be hanging there still. I let out the breath I'd been holding.

And then something whistled near my ear, flicking my ponytail. I swatted at it—June bugs were a terrible Indiana affliction—just as one arm then the other were nipped by mosquitos. But then the mosquitos weren't mosquitos, but something rough against my skin and tightening across my chest.

I couldn't think what was happening but then grabbed enough air to make some noise. I fell, tangled, my arms tight to my sides and only stopped screaming to gather more air. I couldn't breathe. A rope. A pair of boots appeared next to my head. I clawed at the ground, my scream now hoarse. "Sure, sure, you scream your head off," said a man's voice.

A figure stood over me, backlit by the bare bulb over the garbage bin. I located a shadow on the ground, in time to catch the shadow raise his arm and run his fingers through his hair.

One, two, three times.

"Billy?" My voice was strange. I coughed. The rope. A thousand thoughts came at once. The rope. Maddy. *Billy.* "Jesus, Billy, please—"

"Jules? Is that you? What the hell are you doing tiptoeing around here?" In a split second, he wasn't the murderer stringing up another victim, but just Billy, gazing stupidly at me. Even in the dark, I knew one of his eyes would be wink-wink-winking at me.

"Billy, untie me this second—" I coughed and hacked, struggling at the rope.

Billy loosened it and untangled me. I sat on my knees, choking until I caught my breath, then punched at Billy's nearby knee. "What the hell, Billy? Who's tiptoeing? I knocked on your door about fifty times." My voice still wasn't right. "What are you doing with that rope?"

"I'm on guard, like," he said. "They've been after the railings, like I told you they would be."

"Who? Who's been after the—you mean suicides? Really? Did you catch anyone trying to do it?" My heart was still thudding. I pawed at a spot on my arm that the rope had burned. It had broken the skin. The blood was staining the sleeve of my shirt. After a minute, I stood up and dusted myself off, feeling like a fool, even if I was a slightly smaller fool than the one in front me. In the bare light, I could see a furtive look on his face.

"Well, no," he said. "Not suicides, anyways. Some kids, probably, poking around. Some asshole came out and was taking flash pictures, if you can believe that." He gestured at the highway. The cars zipping by serving as the insulted audience. "That's not the kind of thing we need happening here."

"A couple of photos surely won't ruin this *murder* we have going on," I said. "Look, Billy, I need to ask—what did you hear that night?"

"Well, I don't know." He turned his face into the shadows, where I couldn't see his eye going crazy. Or any expression at all. "I don't know if that's something to talk about in polite company."

What was with everyone being polite all of a sudden? It wasn't polite to hang people from banisters, but here we were. "Go ahead and be rude, Billy. I want to hear the awful, messy, impolite truth."

"They were giving each other what-for up there." He looked embarrassed. "Real loud."

"Like . . . passionate sounds?" I tried not to imagine any passionate sounds that Billy might know of—or make. I felt my neck and cheeks going hot and was glad of the dark. We worked side by side in a cheap motel, but we'd never talked this directly about what must go on in the occupied rooms. "Like, moaning and, um, stuff?"

"Well, no, not exactly. More like . . . rough stuff." He turned away from me again. "I thought we had some more of them dominatrix types."

A group of them had passed through on their way to a convention once, and Billy hadn't been the same since. They'd actually been very neat, cleaning up after themselves, but apparently they'd made a great deal of noise.

"It sounded like rough stuff," I repeated. "It sounded like someone was getting hurt?"

"I think that's what they're into—"

"Not the dominatrix night. The night Maddy was killed. It sounded like someone was slapping someone else around? Like someone was getting hurt?"

"That's not what I thought—"

"Because you would have called for help, right?" I said. "You would have stopped him?"

"I've been running this place for a long time, Jules," Billy said. "You hear a lot of things. You don't know where the line is, sometimes."

"Like, screaming?" Billy made sure his face was turned into the shadows again. I swallowed hard. "We didn't check in any black leather that night. All you had to do was check the cards. One minivan of Bargains, the dead—the guy who stayed in all night, and Maddy. Nice car, single occupant. You could have checked. You could have knocked on the door and asked if everything was all right."

"Hell, Juliet, I don't know," Billy said, pleading. "Who knows what they'll do when the time comes? None of us knows how much of a chickenshit we are until we have the chance to show it."

He could have said *hero*. He could have said that none of us knew to what heights we might rise if we were given the opportunity.

"Billy, I think we know how much of a coward you could be," I said. "It's your greatest natural talent."

"No reason to get nasty with me, little lady. I didn't have anything to do with your friend getting herself—"

"No," I snapped. He stepped back from me. "She didn't *get herself* anything. Someone did this to her, and if you had the chance to help her and you didn't, well, I hope you don't believe in heaven and hell, because you've made your choice."

"Well, I made that choice a long time ago, didn't I, when I moved into this place." His fingers raced through his hair, three, four times until I thought he would pull out a handful. He'd never said a bad word about the Mid-Night. I didn't know how to ask why he thought worse of his low-rent palace tonight. "You're making the mistake of thinking you know everything about me, Juliet, but you don't. You see my eye twitching and m-m-my—my—" The stutter only came out in dire situations. "*P-problems*, and you think you know all about it. I guess you go around thinking you know it all. You're smarter than the rest of us, aren't you? I got news for you—"

Billy stopped and turned his head. I'd heard it, too. In a moment in between cars on the highway, somewhere along the back of the motel's south wing and its empty rooms, a branch had snapped.

He held a finger up to his mouth, as though I needed a reminder, and crept away, his rope over his arm like a lasso. A Bugs Bunny cartoon. I was in a Bugs Bunny cartoon.

Or a horror movie.

I clung to the corner of the building and braced myself for a chance to run. Like Billy so gallantly had put it: We didn't know how chicken-shit we could be until we got the chance. I'd had too many chances already for one week.

Billy's dark figure melted into the shadows. I waited, all senses tuned to hear anything I could under the highway noise and my own blood pounding in my ears. Waiting in the dark reminded me of lying in bed at night as a kid, knowing something was under the bed or in the closet.

As a child I had a reoccurring dream of getting separated from my parents in a busy crowd. A mall, an amusement park. Even places I knew in real life stretched into vast seas of strangers and confusion in my sleep. My school, the IGA, the park. In my nightmares, any place I went with my family was a place I could lose them. Come daylight, I didn't worry about such things—but of course daylight is when it happened. The dark didn't seem as frightening, once you grew up, once you realized how many ways there were to lose someone.

Billy had been gone a long time when I started to wonder if he'd left me to fend for myself. I slid around the corner into the courtyard and looked around, trying to see anything or anyone, then worked myself around to the breezeway. I could one-up Billy in cowardice. I could slip through to the parking lot here and drive away. Never come back. I had never had more reason to walk away from the Mid-Night Inn.

But I couldn't.

Maddy's death should have made me want to run, but this was where she was. Here and the high school, but the best I could hope for there was a dumpy blue uniform and late nights with the industrial laundry machines.

I could work here for the rest of my life. What choice did I have? Maddy would be here, reminding me, making me wonder what kind of coward I was. I would have to see this to the end. And there might not be an end.

I kept going, following the perimeter of the motel until I was around the end of the south wing and could see the far end of the empty parking lot.

But then a strange sound came from behind me. A yelp. A wounded-bird cry, half swallowed.

I turned and was flooded by a bright light. Through my fingers, I could see the dark outline of someone on the other side of a flashlight and the glint of a gun. A gun, pointed in my direction.

"Let me see your hands," a woman's voice said.

"Courtney? Oh, God, OK, oh, good. I didn't know—"

"Put your hands up, I said."

I did as I was told. She approached, the light filling my vision until I couldn't see anything but shine. She nudged my arms higher, and then patted at my hips. "You're still wearing those ridiculous jogging pants?"

"Busy day," I said.

"Making the rounds, I heard. Except I don't know if you're doing Nancy Drew or worse."

"Where's Billy?"

The light dropped away from my eyes at last, showing me Billy's prone body at our feet. He waved. "Thanks for your concern, Jules," he said. "You know, ten minutes later."

"Shut it, Twitches," Courtney barked. "From what I heard a few minutes ago, you're probably a few wait-and-hope-for-the-bests shy of karma helping you out of a bind. Your story sounded a little different back when I was the one asking you questions. Why are you here?" Courtney said.

Billy heaved himself to his feet and dusted off his jeans. His rope had been transferred to Courtney's arm.

"Keep telling you people, I live here."

"Not you," Courtney said. "You. What are you doing here, Juliet? And don't say you work here. We shut down the bar after last night's shenanigans."

It was a decent question, considering she didn't know that I had to be here, that I couldn't not be here until this thing was finished. Like the dark things under the bed and in the closet behind a door not pulled tight, Maddy—not a ghost, but my memories of her—peered at me from every place I looked. But I couldn't tell Courtney Howard that. She'd only write it down. Write it down and make me feel bad for it later.

"I don't know," I said, finally.

The flashlight lit up my shoes. Courtney gave me a chance to think of something else to say, but I didn't. I didn't try. Every time I said something, I could only feel myself slipping deeper into the story she wanted to tell. Maybe the best approach was to say nothing at all.

"Trespassing at a known crime scene," she said, her voice telling me I only had myself to blame.

"I work—" I started, and then let my mouth snap shut.

"It's late," she said, lowering the gun at last. "Maybe you two had a date? I did hear some talk of moaning. Rough stuff. That what you're into?" The flashlight flicked over my face, and I flinched away.

I waited for Billy to say something he'd regret, but he was keeping a low profile. Smarter than he seemed. He knew this was about me more than it was about him, the motel, the murder, or Maddy. Where was Courtney's police partner? I wasn't the only one here for suspicious reasons. But I said nothing. Two roads appeared, and neither of them seemed to go anywhere I wanted to visit.

"Let me give you a ride home, Juliet," Courtney said.

"My car is—"

"You can get it later. Right now I want to see that you get home and tucked in for the night. You must be tired of those stripes on your pants. Let's get you home to your bunny slippers and maybe some cocoa before your head's in bed."

Billy and I exchanged a quick, silent glance. *Heads in beds* was the motto of hotel management everywhere, code for filling rooms, filling beds, making quotas, making money. And a head in a bed meant a guest asleep—a satisfied customer who wouldn't be at the front desk at 1:30 a.m., asking when the music in the bar went off, a rested guest who got back on the road bright and early without complaints or special requests. Heads in beds was everything. And now I was the overtired traveler who needed to be put away before I became trouble.

Courtney had hit one thing square. I was exhausted. I did need to go home. I remembered the silver running man hiding out in my car and skipped the argument over who would get me home. I let Courtney lead me around the corner into the courtyard. She shined her flashlight up over the closed-off rooms.

"Wait, what about Billy?" I said.

He was still lying low, waiting for Courtney to leave before he moved a muscle. Courtney said, "You want to take him home with you?"

"No, I want him to open the office so I can clean up my arm."

She pointed the flashlight at my arm. A dribble of blood ran down my forearm and across my elbow. There were bits of dried leaves stuck to the trail. The flashlight hit my face again. "You didn't come here to do anything untoward to yourself, did you?"

"It's a cut from the rope, Courtney," I said. "Just get the keys."

Billy came jingling. He got the lights while I borrowed the keys and opened up the supply closet. A wave of familiar scents washed over me. In a pocket in the cart, we kept a first-aid kit, almost empty. I found a bandage and retreated to the front counter to perform surgery. My skin felt hot. I could have used some ice. Billy shuffled his feet under Courtney's watch. I had the bandage in place and was throwing out my handful of trash when I saw another shadow flit past the window.

Courtney turned to see what I was looking at. "What?"

"Nothing," I said. "Must have been—"

I stopped. I'd seen what I'd seen, but it made no sense.

"Probably one of them cats you feed," Billy huffed. He'd forbidden us from feeding animals that showed up. But not all the strays were cats.

I hurried to the door and pushed it wide. "Jessica?" I called into the parking lot. "Billy, turn on the lights."

"It's probably nothing," he said, but finally reached for the panel under the desk. The Mid-Night's front walk and parking lot flooded with light. The girl had been slinking away under the cover of blackness, but now she blinked away from the glare.

"Who is it?" Courtney said at my shoulder. "Miss? Can you come back here, please?"

"What's a young girl like that doing out here this t-time of night?" Billy said from behind the counter, his fingers going to his hair, once, twice, three times. He cycled through a few more tics before sliding his hands into his pockets to still them. "This used to be a nice place."

In measured steps and her head down, the girl made her way back. "What?" she said. "It's a free country, isn't it?" The lights on the side of the motel created deep sinkholes where her eyes should have been.

"This particular patch of country is private property, shut down by the police," Courtney said. "Can you tell me why you're here?"

Jessica shrugged, her face still tilted toward the sidewalk. "Just wanted to see, you know," she said. "See where that woman died."

It sounded like a lie, and not even a good one.

Courtney turned to me. "You know this one?"

"Midway," I said. "She's a strong runner."

Jessica glanced up, and that's when I noticed something wasn't right. "Hey," I said.

Courtney was way ahead of me. She pulled out her baton flashlight and lit Jessica's face from below. The deep hollows of her eyes weren't shadows. She was growing one hell of a black eye. She ducked her head away from the light, but we'd had a good look.

"Jesus," Courtney said. "What happened to your face, kid?"

Behind me, I heard Billy make a noise. He came to the door and looked over my shoulder.

Jessica shook her head.

Courtney put away the flashlight and was silent for a moment, looking off into the parking lot. "Look," she said. "If there's something going on with your parents—"

"It was a—a man," Jessica said. "Tall, big. He—grabbed me."

"Are you hurt? Besides the eye?" I asked.

"Did you get a look at him?" Courtney said.

Jessica held up her hands. "No, no—look, forget it. He was nobody—"

"How tall? Was he white, black, what?" Courtney's voice was rising, excited. I saw what she was thinking. Maybe Maddy's killer had made another attempt, and this time left a witness.

"No, no," Jessica pleaded. She glanced at me. "OK, he was tall, like—just tall. And, uh, maybe not white?"

"Think hard," Courtney said sternly. "Not white? Black? Hispanic maybe?"

Jessica nodded slowly.

"Hispanic?"

"Yes. Maybe. Not black. Maybe—I don't know. It was so fast." The tears came finally. This time when she hid her face, we let her.

Courtney called for backup. While she went to look the place over, we hurried behind the desk and into the laundry room, kicking the piles of dirty sheets to the side. Billy didn't have a word to say, which went to show how rattled he was, or how much he feared losing that stupid star.

In the end, Jessica wouldn't admit to any other injuries or give much more of a statement. She also wouldn't take a ride home from Courtney. Her car wasn't too far away, she kept saying, so finally Courtney talked her into accepting a ride to the car, and offered her the passenger seat.

Then she offered me the back door, where the criminals sat.

"Come on," I said, but got in, and let her guide my head under the roof, allowed her to close the door behind me, and didn't bother with further complaints when she set the lights rolling. We dropped Jessica off at her car, which was indeed across the road, in the dusty lot of the construction site there. We waited for her to get in, start the car, and drive away. Courtney gave the site a long look, then started off toward my house.

"You're making it very hard for me not to think of you as a suspect," she said after a few minutes. She caught my eye in the rear-view mirror, her face cross-hatched by the wire divider between us.

"Didn't realize you were trying to fight your feelings. I'm touched."

"What were you really doing out there?"

I watched the town pass in the dark. All the good people were already inside their cozy homes, the occasional flickering blue lights of a TV through a window the only visible life. Only degenerates like me, rolling past in cop cars, left awake to see how pretty it all was.

At least she hadn't started the siren.

"It seems to me that this person who attacked Jessica is a much better topic—"

"What were you doing there?" Courtney insisted.

"I wanted to ask Billy what he'd heard."

"Kinky."

I glared at her in the mirror and looked away. "Actually, I just wondered if Billy even knew what that sounded like. I don't think he's ever had a girlfriend. I mean, I'm sure there's someone somewhere who would date Billy, but I've never seen her. And he doesn't seem to go out or anything. He doesn't even hang out at the Mid-Night."

"The bar," we both said in unison.

"You're saying you think Billy Batts, a grown man, wouldn't know what sex sounds like?"

"He probably watches porn, anyway. And of course he lives in a cheap motel. I don't know why I came. It was a dumb idea."

Courtney sat up straighter in her seat. "It wasn't a dumb idea," she said. "You got him to admit it, didn't you? That he wondered, even while the noise was going on, if someone was getting hurt? He never said that to us. Asshole."

The car cruised through my neighborhood. "Is that what you think it was? Just sex?" I was thinking of Beck. It couldn't have been anyone else. No one else in town would have held any interest for Maddy.

Courtney was looking at me in the mirror.

"What?" I said.

"Was going to tell you something. Not sure if I can trust you."

"Frankly, Courtney, I'm not exactly keeping a lot of company right now. There's no one to tell."

"All those teenaged girls at school . . . What about your coworker?"

I recalled the waver in Lu's voice when she said she didn't suspect me. "Not sure when I'll be seeing her."

"Swear it. Swear you're trustworthy."

"Come *on*. Do you want to pinkie swear or what? I didn't miss this part, this, this—girl-versus-girl crap," I said. "You wouldn't trust me, no matter what I said, and I'm not sure I can trust you, either. That's how it's always been. That's probably how it will always be. So what do you want to do about that?"

Courtney turned the patrol car into my street, and I was gratified to see the curtains at Mrs. Schneider's house pulled tight.

"If I hear about this from any other source—"

"Courtney, I give up. Don't tell me and do us both a favor."

"Fine. It's this: Maddy hadn't been participating in any . . . sexual activities. Not the night she died."

The car stopped in front of my house. Dark, of course. I hoped that meant my mother would also miss my arrival by police escort.

"They can tell that?"

She turned off the lights. "They can tell lots of things. She hadn't had any drugs or alcohol, either, which is bad news for you, since you claimed she had a beer with you."

"I said she bought a beer. I also said she didn't drink it. She wasn't pregnant, was she?" Sometimes the happy-hour ladies stopped drinking inexplicably, and their friends went to town on them about being knocked up. The thought of it—Maddy a mother?—gave me a deep, terrible feeling not entirely from the fact that she wouldn't get the chance now. The palms of my hands hummed with the slightest tickle.

"You're missing what I'm saying. She wasn't raped, and she wasn't having sex in that room. At least not—well, you know."

At least not the kind of polite sex we nice Midwestern girls would know about. "Yeah," I said, so she wouldn't continue. I already had too many disturbing images in my head tonight. "I heard she was strangled first, before the belt."

Courtney turned in her seat. "Who—"

"Shelly."

"Damn, she's fast. Look, I'm sorry about making you leave your car tonight. If you want, I can come pick you up tomorrow and take you out to it."

This was as near an offer of friendship as I'd ever received from Courtney Howard, beyond that day at the Mid-Night. But that was the day Maddy died, and Courtney had tricked me into admitting that I harbored something like ill will toward the best friend I'd ever had. I hesitated, and then imagined the patrol car rolling up to my house again, only this time in the daylight. "No, thanks," I said. "I'll take care of it."

She got out of the car and shut her door. For a moment I sat in the back of the police car, waiting for Courtney to come around and let me out. I didn't believe in premonitions or in ghosts, but they were both living in this backseat with me. And so was guilt. Guilt and frustration and fear. And death. It was all here, soaked into the faux-leather seats from those who had come before me, a scent radiating out and onto my skin, a cloying smell that I'd never wash off, never get out of my nostrils. The car was small, tight.

When the door opened, I leapt from the car and hurried up the walk, home again at last.

CHAPTER EIGHTEEN

"**H**ey, Coach!"

I looked up from the stopwatch I'd been using to time the gazelle's laps. But the voice didn't mean my Coach, *the* Coach, Coach Trenton, or even Fitz, who had called in sick to the school a second day. The voice meant me. Jessica ran past me with her mouth twisted into a wide grin, her newly blackened eye puffy but hidden behind thick makeup. She'd been claiming allergies to the other girls.

"What?" I said.

"Where are those *sweat*pants?"

"They were sweaty from yesterday," I called back, checking the time again. I couldn't believe how fast she could do a circuit, not even out of breath and now taunting me from boredom. Daring me to say anything about her attack, to ask her again if she was OK, to mention how she seemed to be protecting her left side. Was she running this fast with a cracked rib? The independent study, Mickie, didn't show, and that was a good thing. I had no idea what would have happened. The news had been in the paper and on the radio that morning—another attack, unknown assailant, male, possibly Hispanic.

"Oh, did you run home?" she said. "Because I'm pretty sure I didn't see you doing laps here yesterday, either."

"And they were running pants," I said. "You should try keeping this pace in your big combat boots and shredded jeans and see how much breath you have left to chat."

The other girls snickered. Probably at my expense, not Jessica's, but I didn't care because they'd stopped complaining. They didn't have the lungs to complain anymore, even at their age. Not at this speed. The redhead brought up the rear again, huffing and pink-faced, silent. Jessica lapped her without a glance. Delia. I hadn't remembered that name, but I'd heard one of the other girls using it. Delia was the sort of girl whose name was often forgotten. I felt ashamed for not trying harder. "Come on, Delia. You've got this."

She rolled her eyes in my direction, and we both knew she didn't have anything and would have even less if she answered me.

"So Fitz is pretty sick, I guess," Jessica mused from the across the gym, loping on long legs.

"I guess." It was Fitz who'd called that morning, actually, and he hadn't sounded sick. He hadn't looked sick, either, when he'd come to the house to pick me up and take me to my car so I wouldn't have to ask Coach for a ride again. This was Fitz's idea. Coach had done taxi service for me cheerfully the day before, but there were limits to what I would ask of either of them right now. *Bereft*, Mrs. Haggerty had called it. Fitz definitely seemed that way. He also seemed to understand that by calling in sick, he was calling dibs on grief.

"I'm sorry to ask again," he'd said, big, tan hands on the wheel. Fitz didn't have a roadster like Coach. He drove an old trash heap of a truck, even though I assumed his teaching salary could do better. "I just have some things I need to see to, plus seeing the girls right now is too … distressing, I guess. Are you doing all right? Are you sleeping?"

His call had woken me up, but I didn't say that. I didn't want to sound like I was complaining, because I needed the money.

I needed the money. How long would my life always come down to this one single sentence? Surely not forever, but then here was Fitz in his junker truck, and my mother, barely scraping by with my help. Billy and his cheap rent for living in a place he compared to hell. Lu, thinking she'd have to find another job because a single week with no check from the Mid-Night made that much difference to her family's survival. I'd always thought I'd outgrow this hand-to-mouth life eventually, but what made me special? What made me different from those around me? This might be it. This might be the best I could do.

"I'm fine," I told him. "As fine as I guess any of us are."

"Are you scared?"

I started to say no, then yes. I hadn't slept the night before, thinking about Jessica's attack and Maddy's death. Together, what did they mean?

What came out: "You're the first person to ask me that." And I had been scared, and not just in the moment I'd found her body, and not just when Billy had hog-tied me behind the motel or when Courtney's gun gleamed in the dark or Jessica's shiner was revealed. Since Maddy had died, I'd been living with a sort of low-grade electric buzz inside me. In my nerves, in my blood. I felt tender, bruised but all over, and I thought I might have to live with it. It wasn't going away. I told him about Jessica's black eye.

"So I guess whoever it is, he's not done," I said.

He was silent a long time. "That place," he said. "You're not going there again, are you?"

We traversed the same drive I'd done with Courtney the night before, in reverse. This time, though, I had a front seat and my dignity. The AC was hitting me square in the face. I leaned over and nudged it toward Fitz. "Do you think I have a reason to be scared? I guess I thought—"

I thought Maddy's death was somehow Maddy's fault. I was as bad as everyone else. I raised my wrist to my face, but then remembered I'd decided against wearing Maddy's perfume for a while. "But now . . . Is that where we are? It could be anyone, and they could do it again?"

"Until we know more about this, I want you to be careful," he said. "Watch what you say and who you say it to, OK? Just . . . let the cops do their jobs, Juliet. They have something to go on, now. Be patient, but in the meantime, be . . ."

He couldn't think of the word, and neither could I. *Quiet? Low-key? Paralyzed?* In any case, this was the opposite of what I'd been.

We were pulling into the lot of the Mid-Night, my dusty car the only sign of human activity, when I realized what Fitz had done. He'd found a way to keep me safe and busy, and away from Maddy's murder. By calling in sick every morning when he wasn't sick, he'd smuggled me into the safest place he could conceive of.

At my car, he wished me a good day and waited to leave until my engine revved to life. Taking care of everyone else.

I had to think that's what it was. The only other reason I could think for Fitz making sure I was inside Midway High all day, every day, was to keep me handy for my arrest.

"Hey," someone yelled, bringing me back to the present. I stood amid girls, girls everywhere, collapsed on the floor or stretching and talking. Jessica holding her side—cracked rib from last night, for sure. "Hey," she said. "I *said*, 'What kind of sick is he?'"

"Did I tell you ladies to stop running?"

"We ran them all," one of the other girls whined. "All the laps there are. I literally can't run another lap."

I looked around. Even Delia had finished. "Yeah, OK," I said. "I must have lost count. Hit the showers."

They thundered off, except Delia, who slid to the floor and made a poor show of stretching out her legs. And Jessica, who positioned herself in between me and the door.

"What?" I said.

"What kind of sick?"

"Why is it your business?" I said.

"Because I'm getting the hard sell about joining this track team from him and that other one, Trenton, and I want to know before I commit—is he mental? Does he miss practices a lot? Are they worth my time?"

I'd never seen girls like this. How had they been raised? By fan clubs instead of families?

"If you're not into competition and camaraderie, then give it a pass, Jessica. Coach and Fitz are great guys, and you could learn a lot from them." She looked unconvinced. "Look, you're good. You're really good. If you join the team, you'll probably medal in a lot of races, win sectionals, and place in regionals, and, maybe, run in state. To some people it's a big deal." I tried very hard to keep my face neutral. "And you're only a freshman, so you're going to get lots of chances to win it all. But if you think you're doing anyone but yourself a favor by joining, then don't. They don't need someone who's going to make them feel bad for enjoying what they enjoy. They just need an anchor for their relay team.

Maybe someone who can do the thirty-two hundred without losing wind resistance from her flapping mouth."

A twitch of her lips had grown to a full grin by the time I stopped talking. "I guess to some people it's a big deal," she said.

"To some people," I said.

"You ran with that woman, didn't you? The one who was killed?" Delia looked up.

"Yeah," I said, leaving the word open, a question. "And?"

"And she was on this team, with Coach and Fitz? She was good?"

Was. I didn't like how easily people who didn't know Maddy pushed her into the past. "She . . . was good," I said. "She was really good."

Jessica kicked at the gym floor, making a challenging little squeak. She wanted to know that she was better yet than Maddy, that her time on the team would be worth it, even if she died young someday. But I wasn't sure if she knew that's what she wanted to know. She was only fifteen or so, anyway. What had I known about myself then? Nothing at all.

"She was really good, Jessica. And we all loved her, me, Coach, and Fitz." We stared at each other until I knew what I wanted to say. "He's heartsick," I said. "That's the kind of sick he is."

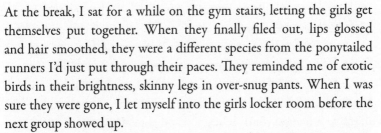

At the break, I sat for a while on the gym stairs, letting the girls get themselves put together. When they finally filed out, lips glossed and hair smoothed, they were a different species from the ponytailed runners I'd just put through their paces. They reminded me of exotic birds in their brightness, skinny legs in over-snug pants. When I was sure they were gone, I let myself into the girls locker room before the next group showed up.

Ten years, but it smelled the same. Steamy, sweaty, like the air inside was holding tight just this side of a rain forest, but with a side of bleach disinfectant. I admired the scent professionally. If Lu and I had been in charge of keeping this space, the smell would have teetered into mildew.

A set of dark offices lined one wall. They were empty, being used for storage, since all the phys-ed classes were covered by men at the moment. What if . . . I pressed my face to the window in the door, imagining the photo Maddy had left for me framed on the wall, and some of my trophies on a shelf over the desk.

One glance through the glass, though, and I caught the trail of a fleeting memory. Me, standing in the boys' locker room. Maddy, scrounging around in the dark in Coach and Fitz's office.

We'd been pulling some prank. But no, that wasn't right. Prank season had been called off before sectionals—"We're getting serious, here, and if you're not, it's time to pack it in," Fitz told us—but this night in the boys' locker room was after we knew Maddy and I would run at state. Coach Trenton's Coach of the Year trophy leaned against the wall in the corner, getting ready to join other awards in the lobby trophy case. And then I'd turned to watch the doors, nervous.

Rooting around in a teacher's office, illegally inside the school after hours. More than expulsion, we gambled everything we'd been working for. My dad would have been so disappointed, if we'd been caught.

Except . . .

I couldn't quite remember what this place wanted to tell me.

I looked around the locker room, feeling daintily at my sore lip. Maybe they'd slapped a new coat of paint on the old lockers, but otherwise it was the same: the same fluorescent lights, the same wall of mirrors, the same rolling plastic bin of wet towels. In the open shower room, the same blue tiles.

I was turning to go when the door from the pool opened and another bin banged and clattered in. Behind it came chubby, pock-marked arms, and then blue shirtsleeves, and then the janitor, Cheryl, her short, dark hair plastered into a black cap against her head. "Sorry," she said. "I figured you'd all be good and gone. Let me grab my towels, and I'll be out of the way."

The shower room suddenly felt strangely crowded. I took a step backward, but the feeling grabbed at me. Me, her, one of those empty bins—we were falling into place in my mind. That night of sneaking into Coach and Fitz's office snapped back to me, whole.

We *had* been caught.

No wonder the sight of this woman in the back hallway or here in the shower room made me shrink away. That night in the dark locker room, while I'd stood shaking in dread and hissing for Maddy to hurry up, the janitor had wheeled in one of her bins. Startled, mad, she'd hustled us out of the office and the locker room, and down the hall and across the lobby, scolding us like a grandmother and chasing us out into the night.

"I'm sure sorry about your friend," she said now.

I looked at her more closely than I ever had. She was younger than I remembered, but had lived hard. Those scars. They must have been burns from an occasional run-in with the school's industrial washer and drier. I was shamed by how well she kept these wet, sweaty rooms. I vowed to work harder, any place I ended up. I glanced at her arms and away again, hoping I wouldn't end up here.

"Thank you," I said. I let a long moment pass, trying to grab at that memory. Here we were again. "You remember us," I said. "I mean, you remember me from—"

She waved her hand at me, pushing the empty tub over the rough tile to sit next to the full bin. The racket was tremendous. "Kids'll be kids sometimes," she said when the cart stopped moving. "Ain't the kids that are the problem, you ask me. She wasn't any trouble, was she? Spirited. But she didn't deserve what's happened to her."

"No."

"They don't get a break, the girls. I've seen it." She pulled the full bin toward her, tucking in a towel that had been left dangling over the side. "I heard another girl got hurt over there at that mo-tel. Just a little girl."

"A student here," I agreed.

"That should help find the one that done it, then."

I swallowed hard. "I hope."

Cheryl sang a little tune under her breath, flipping the wet edge of towels into the bin. "Hey, how old's that little one now?"

Her scars were lighter than the rest of her skin. I stared at them for a long moment, then found her eyes. "The student?"

"Nah, I meant—never mind." She spun her bin away, clucking her tongue and murmuring to herself.

"Cheryl—"

"*Shirl*," she said, and she started the full bin bouncing thunderously toward the pool door.

"I'm sorry," I called over the noise. "Shirl. I'm grateful that you didn't tell anyone about us in the boys' locker room that night. You know what would have happened to us?"

She stopped and stretched to open the door. "I've had to ignore a lot worse."

"We'd have been expelled, wouldn't have been allowed to run the state tournament."

She mused at the room around us. "Seems like I heard you didn't do that anyway."

And then Maddy hadn't finished school, and I had, but I hadn't done a second of growing up since. So what had we gained, breaking into the school that night?

"Shirl," I whispered, my words hissing against the tile. "Which little one?"

CHAPTER NINETEEN

When the last class of girls headed toward the locker room, I bolted out a side exit and to my car. I put the keys in the ignition but couldn't think of where I wanted to be. Out at the track, Coach was straightening a set of hurdles. He probably could have used my help today with Fitz gone again.

I rested my head on the steering wheel for a while. When I looked up, a straggling line of girls tramped from the school out to practice. Their duffels, as big as body bags, bumped against their legs.

Body bags. Now that I'd seen one up close, this was my point of reference. I pounded the steering wheel with my fist. Then again.

Again, and again until I could feel the pain. I cradled my hand to my chest and listened to my own ragged breath.

Maddy's little one, of course. That was what Shirl thought I'd known and hadn't wanted to tell me.

One of Shirl's jobs had always been to clean out gym lockers at the end of each semester, when everyone popped off their padlock and cleaned out their hair bands and dirty socks. Girls were creatures of habit. We used the same lockers semester after semester and left things in between, sometimes on purpose and sometimes not.

Ten years ago, when a used pregnancy test turned up in the back of one of the girls' lockers, Shirl tossed it but took note and watched. The test had come from Maddy's locker.

"It was a plus sign," Shirl told me, giving me a look. "You know what the plus sign means, right?"

I didn't want to believe it. "Could it have been someone else's test?"

Shirl leveled me with a look of pity. It could have been. But it wasn't. She'd never said a word to anyone. When Maddy hadn't run state, Shirl had all the confirmation she needed. But she didn't know then or now what I knew, what I understood at last.

On the morning of the state tournament she'd worked for four years to run—and probably win—Maddy had miscarried a baby.

Now, sitting in my car cradling my sore hand, I believed it. I felt for that thin girl sitting on the edge of the hotel bed, clutching at her gut. Seventeen, scared. She'd gotten dressed in the bathroom. Why had I not noticed how strange that was, for a girl who got dressed in front of other girls for gym and at meets every day of the week?

Maybe I hadn't wanted to notice. I only wanted to run, while my best friend convulsed in pain a few feet away.

Of course she hadn't said anything, and I wondered why she hadn't confided in me. I would have been shocked. I was shocked now. I would have been pissed, too. Well, I'd already been mad, but at least I could have been mad about the right thing. My surprise might have eaten away at some of the anger, and I could have ... helped, or insisted she get help.

We could have stayed friends. I wouldn't have left her to face the aftermath of a miscarriage alone. I wouldn't have considered leaving her in that room to run state, not for a second.

At least I hoped I wouldn't have.

I knew a couple of things, though. I knew I wouldn't leave her now. And I knew that Beck deserved a piece of my mind.

I turned the key in the ignition and pointed the car toward Beck's end of the county.

He'd never been good for her. At best, he could have been a waste of her time, but instead he'd ruined everything she hoped for. Now I could see how she'd so easily let state go, how she'd finished with school before school was technically finished with her. How she might have gone off on her own instead of to college, and started a new life where she didn't have to answer old questions or be compared to old ideas of herself. So much made sense. So much and nothing.

Beck must have made her promise not to tell me. Well, he'd run out of luck keeping his secret. I had to tell Courtney. This was relevant. This was motive.

Unless . . .

Unless he hadn't known.

This lightened my foot on the gas pedal as I passed around the edge of town.

In any case, my anger seemed to me ridiculous, pointless. What would I say to him, even if he had known?

My pride was at stake, that was all. She hadn't told me. She hadn't even told me she'd had sex. All those phone calls, and late nights staying at my house, the subject came up all the time. I was innocent and stupid on the topic, and she was pregnant.

And when Maddy told me not to leave her alone with Beck, was that some joke they shared?

Maybe that was the part that stung the most. Always behind, always left in the dust. But then she'd left him behind, too, hadn't she?

At a stop sign, I let the car idle and looked around. The cornfields were green, but low. They went on forever, like the framed prints in each Mid-Night room. No markers, no houses, just long, dusty roads. The car driving off the edge of the print was mine.

I had to think about where I was going. I'd been to Beck's house once, long ago, when Maddy had dragged me along to a party there. But the party had not been what we'd expected. Instead of other people from Midway High, most of the guests had been Beck's friends from around town, mostly older guys who worked at some plant in Lafayette. Maddy and I got tired of how they stared at us and left, back to my house. We always went back to my house, never hers.

Never to hers.

That terrible puke-green sweater.

It sideswiped me. I fumbled with the gearshift, then my seat belt, and the door, and barely made it to the weeds at the side of the road. I threw up until I was empty, and then stayed in position, dry grass and dirt caught in my fists.

I missed the sound of the approaching truck until it was upon me.

Beck leaned out the window. "You praying?"

I wiped my mouth with the back of my hand. "Shut up."

He got out of the truck and came around. "What? Ah, man. You

OK?" He looked around the way Shelly had, as though whatever afflicted me might attach itself to him.

I found my feet. The scratches on my palms from the day before were raw again. I dusted the gravel from them gently. "I'm fine."

"Uh, huh." He glanced toward the puddle I'd left on the side of the road. "A little late in the day for morning sickness, isn't it?"

I opened my mouth to say something sharp. Nothing came out.

If Maddy had been pregnant by her own father—well, I couldn't say that. And if she'd been pregnant by Beck but never told him, was it my place to fill him in? And if he'd known all along . . .

"What?" he said. He already seemed like a different person than the one I'd always hated.

Standing alone with him on the side of a gravel road, I couldn't decide which way to go. The countryside seemed so vast and empty.

"What are you doing all the way out here, anyway?"

"Driving."

"Driving to see me?" he said.

"Why would I be coming to see you?"

"Thought maybe something had happened. You know, with Maddy's, uh, case, or whatever."

He'd hear about it sooner or later. Midway was like that. "The fiancé showed up," I said. "Vincent. I ran into him downtown. And he wigged out over Maddy's ring being kept at the bank."

"Why does he care about Maddy's ring?" he said.

"Maddy's ring probably doubled the bank's net holdings. You should see—"

"I mean, why does he care about Maddy's ring and not Maddy's *death*?"

"That's not fair," I said, remembering Vincent's weight on my shoulder. "He definitely cares about her death."

"Meaning?"

I sighed. "Meaning he got enraged talking about it, and then really sad, and then sort of, overwhelmed, I guess, at having to put together a funeral service."

"He went from enraged to sad to overwhelmed right there on the street? So he's manic, is what you're saying," Beck said. "He can't control himself. This is our guy."

I didn't like the eagerness in his voice. As much as I would have liked to have the killer turn out to be someone from far away, I wasn't sure Vincent was our guy.

Our guy, as though Beck and I were in this together. I wished I'd never taken Beck to Maddy's room.

When I didn't say anything, Beck went still. "You still think I did it."

"I didn't say that."

"You don't have to. The way you're looking at me—" He kicked at the gravel, sending rocks and dust flying into the corn. "But why should anything be different now? You're not the only one who lost her, you know. I mean, neither of us had her, but we both—*had* her, as much as anyone ever did. I don't exclude you from that, so why should you exclude me from this?"

"This . . . what?"

"From—" He waved his hands up and above his head, as though directing the fields around us to rise up. "From this, from tracking down whatever festering disease did this to Maddy, to us, to this town."

"I'm not excluding you from anything," I said. But I remembered all the times he'd wanted me to leave the two of them alone, and Maddy had made me promise not to. Maybe I was keeping him out, from habit. Or maybe I hadn't excluded him from the list of suspects yet, not entirely. Either way, I wouldn't be telling him or Vincent about the terrible green sweater anytime soon.

I realized I'd put my sore hand on my stomach, thinking again of Maddy clutching her own belly. I dropped it. "I have to go."

"Where?"

I couldn't think. Not the Mid-Night. It was closed—really closed, and I'd been escorted off the premises enough for one week. Not the school, where all the fresh-faced youth was starting to get on my nerves. Track practice was probably over by now, anyway, and I'd missed Shelly at the bank. "Home," I said. But I knew I wouldn't go there yet. I still hadn't told my mother about Maddy. I didn't have the guts. "I don't know," I said. I had nowhere to go. "I don't—Maddy was pregnant."

It was outside my mouth, like words in a cartoon balloon, before I knew I was going to say it.

His face jumped from concern for me, to confusion, to something I didn't recognize, and finally, to sadness. "That's terrible," he said. "I can't believe—did she tell you? Or, oh . . . the fiancé, I suppose. Wow, just when you think the news can't get worse."

A gentle wind made the cornstalks in the field rustle. "I didn't mean when she was killed."

Our eyes met. "When?" he said, his voice small. "When was she pregnant?"

It was too late to pull back. The truth was the only way forward. "At state," I said. "She miscarried. That's why we didn't run."

His expression morphed again, this time to solid rock. "That's not true."

"I'm sorry. I know what this must mean to you—"

"I doubt it." He took a step backward, looking around the countryside as though he had just woken up there. "You couldn't."

"So she didn't tell you," I said.

"She most certainly didn't." He looked as though he might need to throw up, too. "You're sure?"

Was I sure? I thought it through. Shirl's discovery of the positive pregnancy test. Everything I'd learned about Maddy's last year in school. That morning in our room at the Luxe, Maddy's thin shoulders hunched over the edge of the bed. "It all fits," I said.

"Well, excuse me for saying so, but it doesn't fit for me," he said, and he kicked gravel toward the field again. "Maybe it might have, if Maddy and I had ever slept together."

"Oh," I said.

"*Yeah*, oh," he said. "Oh, my girlfriend who I loved and worshipped and followed around and devoted myself to was cheating on me. God, this shouldn't sting at all, should it? We were—what? Seventeen. I should have been cheating on her, too—who the hell cares, right? We were kids! What the—"

He turned to the side of his truck and leaned on it with both hands. "Who?" he said. "Who was it?"

The news could get worse, but I couldn't tell him. "I don't know."

"Who else did she see?"

"No one," I said, relieved to be able to tell a little bit of truth. "She hardly had time to see you, remember? School, track, homework."

"And you were always there," he said to the bed of his truck. "How in the world did you think I managed to knock her up when you were always there?"

The sting had been taken out of this one long ago. "Just so we're clear, she begged me not to leave, no matter how rude you were to me," I said. "You were incredibly rude, by the way."

"I wanted to make out with my girlfriend," he said. "I wanted to—well, you know what I wanted, and so did she, and that's why she kept you there, isn't it? You were the chastity belt. And the whole time—oh, God, this should not suck this bad." He reared back and kicked the side of the truck. It left a dent. "I'm an adult now. I can go to the Mid-Night and take just about any woman home any night of the week. Who cares if my high-school girlfriend was a tramp the whole time she was putting me off?" He kicked his truck again. A bigger dent.

"Stop it," I said, checking the road. Deserted. I should have kept my mouth shut. "We don't know enough—"

"She was pregnant and I never laid a hand on her," he said. He backed up and eyed the dent. "I think there are a couple of words I can use if I feel like it."

"It's just high school, right?" I said. "It's all in the past."

The problem with that: there would be no answers, no putting anything to rest. I felt scared for his next girlfriend, for the next woman he took home. For myself, alone with so much anger. The kind of anger I'd never seen in person. I remembered the swipe in the wallpaper in Maddy's room at the Mid-Night.

"I'm sorry," I said, and retreated to my car.

My hand shook at the door handle. I wanted to say I didn't think he'd done it. But the last two days had taught me a few things about how much I trusted, how much I assumed. Fitz was right. I had to be more careful.

I slid into my car. Beck stood by as I brought the rattling engine to life and pulled a U-turn back to town. He didn't move, not until I was out of sight of his truck, not until I was gone.

At Lu's house, the porch light was out. I rang the bell and waited for what seemed a long time before the door opened. Lu peered out. "Hey," she said, drawing the word out. She wore a sweatshirt too big for her with the sleeves rolled up. For some strange reason, tears stung my eyes. I remembered the way she'd cradled me away from the sight of Maddy, calling me gentle names. I supposed most people expected these things from their mothers, but if one source of comfort was closed off, at least I had Lu.

"Hey," I said. "I've missed you."

"I've missed you, too. It's weird, isn't it? Not having the Mid-Night to go to."

It was weird, too, that I still stood on her porch, dusk at my back. "Can you, uh, talk?"

"Sure." She opened the door and slipped outside. She sat on the top step and patted the spot next to her. "The kids—better to hear ourselves," she said. "Carlos is in a mood, anyway."

"Did he have to take on extra hours?"

She glanced up and down the street. "He asked for them. I don't know, Juliet. I might have to go on one of the services for a while, clean some rich lady's home or something. My own house is too clean now, you know? I see a piece of lint, and I have to stop and pick it up, and I look at it, try to decide where it came from. And the kids are screaming at me, and Mamá is here all the time, watching game shows with the TV yelling, and now Carlos—" She flicked her hand at the closed door. "He doesn't want me to go back there, even if it opens tomorrow."

I could see why. Until this thing was solved, who was to say the Mid-Night was safe? And if it never got solved, better to be in a group of cleaners in a little yellow car than to be the single cleaner going in and out of dead people's motel rooms. "He's just worried about you," I said.

"He's worried about . . . a lot of things."

"Like what?"

"Oh," she said, letting her eyes wander from me down the block again. "Nothing."

We sat in silence for a few minutes.

"Nothing?"

She hung her head. "Maybe his job. The things on the news—it's not good for us right now. He keeps saying the immigration people will come, this and that."

"But," I said. "But you're legal. Aren't you?"

Her look was sharp. "Yes, of course, and Carlos and the kids and Mamá. You don't know what it's like, and it's not just us we have to think about. Carlos's uncle Lester just came over, and his cousins—"

"What do they have to do with Maddy? Or me?"

Lu rubbed a spot on her elbow, trying not to look at me.

"Lu?"

"Just—everything," she said, sighing. "The police have been in the neighborhood all day. Coming to the doors, questions, questions."

I couldn't think what she was talking about. "Today? Oh—" The attack the night before, the possibly Hispanic male. "Oh, no."

"Yeah, it's bad," she said. "Someone says 'brown skin' and we spend the day saying 'yes, officer, no, officer.'"

"I didn't even think—"

"You're lucky that way," Lu said. "How many questions did you answer today? How many times did they come sit at your kitchen table and ask you everything. So much everything, I think why they didn't ask the color of my underwear today. How many times did they come to your house?"

Once, and only to drive me home. But then I did tend to run into Courtney everywhere I went these days.

"Do you mean Courtney? I mean Officer Howard? She came here?"

"That one, the other one, some new ones I never saw before. Carlos says he can't take all this. This, this terror—what's the word, what they're doing?"

I thought for a second. "Terrorizing."

"Because it happened at the Mid-Night, they think Carlos—" She pulled her knees up to her chest and curled around them. "I wish things could go back."

"Me too." At the same time I said it, though, I realized I meant it only by half. If I could have saved Maddy, I would have gone back. But if I couldn't, I knew I would do anything not to have to live it again. I took a quick look at Lu. I never wanted to go back to the Mid-Night, and not just because Maddy had died there. Because I wanted more. I deserved more, and so did Lu—

The door opened behind us, a string of Spanish trailing off into silence.

Lu said a few words to the dark figure there, and the door closed again.

"Was that Carlos?" He was usually friendly, always taking the time to say hello.

"He's—"

"In a mood, yeah, you said." But I knew which mood, now—the same one that seemed to be infecting most of the town. Wherever I went, people started to edge away. "I guess the invitation to come over anytime is withdrawn."

"You have to understand, Jules," Lu said. "He's scared. He's scared because I'm scared, and the kids—they know something is wrong. It has to go back at some point, right?"

"I don't see how things are ever going back, Lu," I said. "Maybe we should start wishing for something else. Something new."

"Easy for you to say," she said. "White girl scrubbing the toilets. Give me a break."

I froze. "I cleaned as many toilets as you did."

She rolled her eyes. "You could be in an office—"

"Cleaning an office."

"Or in the bank, maybe," she said.

I could picture Shelly's face if I asked after jobs at the bank. "You think I haven't imagined a different life? Same as you?"

"You say the same, but you don't know. I walk in, and all anyone can think is what the brown girl might steal." She gave me a pointed look. I'd never stolen anything from her, but maybe I hadn't been as careful as I could have been around the shampoo bottles and the lotions. Or the lost-and-found box. "You get to walk into a room, any room, and be who you are."

"You seem to think that's someone worth being," I said.

"Stop feeling sorry for yourself," she mumbled. "Why are you being like this?"

"Being like ... what? Sad that a friend died? Sad that another friend is leaving me on the porch?" She flinched. I stood up. "I'm sorry you're getting bothered by the cops. It's not fair—but none of this is my fault. I expected you to understand. You *saw*—" My voice twisted into strangeness. "You saw her. Of all people, I thought—"

I'd expected something from her that she didn't have to give. She sat with her arms clutched around her knees. To keep from trembling, maybe. To keep from saying other things she hadn't been able to tell me, or didn't want to tell me. She was right. We weren't the same. We didn't have the same experience of the Mid-Night or of the town. As much as we'd talked about what we wanted from this life, had we ever talked about what we'd gotten, what we might have to settle for?

The Lu who'd *sweet-lady*'d me away from Maddy's body was gone. This was someone else, someone I didn't know. She'd seen Maddy swinging from the balcony and thought—what?—just a white woman on the wrong end of something, none of her business? A good excuse as any to cower on the steps and not look in my direction. As long as she didn't see me, none of this was hers. None of this touched her.

I stumbled through the yard toward my car. I might have looked back if Lu had made even a small sound or movement. But she didn't. I drove away, watching to see if she would change her mind and stop me.

Now.

Or now.

Or before I turned at the next block and could no longer see the small form huddled under the darkened porch light.

"Now," I said under my breath. Then she was gone.

CHAPTER TWENTY

On my street, our house was a beacon, lit from within and without. I parked the car and stared, looking over my shoulder to see if the neighbors were at their windows, wondering. Down the block, a patrol car had taken up residence in front of Mrs. Schneider's house.

I hurried out of the car and up the walk. The front door was open. "Mom?"

I heard the TV, the microwave. Finally. Finally we'd reached the upswing of my mother's psychosis, and every electronic appliance in the house hummed with her manic energy.

"Mom?"

"There you are, Juliet, my God." My mother appeared in the kitchen doorway, one hand to her throat. "Why didn't you tell me?"

"Tell you." I heard a chair scraping the floor behind her, and then Courtney stood there, uniformed and watching. "Oh," I said. "I mean—I didn't know how."

"Well, it turns out it's very easy," my mom said. The hand at her throat fluttered. "Officer Howard here assumed I knew."

Courtney had always been one for breaking news. "Well, you didn't. She doesn't read the paper," I said, giving Courtney a hard look. The police had been visiting Lu's house, so I supposed it was my turn. "What are you doing here? Did something happen?"

Courtney tilted her head, reminding me of the tiny sparrows that fought over spilled pizza crusts near the Mid-Night's bin. "Actually, I thought you were the one with something to say."

Vincent. God, this town. "Maddy's fiancé made it to town. But I guess you know that."

"That poor man," my mom said. Behind her, the microwave dinged, and she didn't notice.

We both looked at her, then each other.

"Thank you for talking with me, Mrs. Townsend," Courtney said. "Sorry to bring you such awful news."

Mom nodded and turned back to the kitchen.

"Is there somewhere we can talk?" Courtney rolled her eyes in my mother's direction. "Without disturbing anyone."

I'd led her halfway down the hall to my room before I realized I could have put us on the front porch, as Lu had done to me. In a lucky move, I'd left the running man from Maddy's room in the car.

I opened the door, suddenly seeing the room through the eyes of a visitor. It was a child's room. I lived in a child's room, slept in a child's bed. I still had clips from high school up on a bulletin board on the closet door, and some of my biggest trophies still stood on the dresser. I had blamed Maddy for my inertia, but she hadn't decorated my room.

"It's been a while since I had a guest," I said, trying not to think how long ago I'd cleaned the place. "Maddy. Maddy was probably the last person here, senior year."

Courtney's sparrow eyes took it all in. She walked to the bulletin board and peered at it.

The photo Maddy had left me lay on my bed. I pulled the comforter up over it. Courtney turned around in time to see me tucking the cover around the pillow. I sat down on the edge of the bed.

"It might be time for a change of season in here," she said. "Maybe a—" She waved her hand. "Facelift?"

She had alighted on the kindest possible thing to say. I was on notice. "You know all about the thing with Vincent, right?"

"I would never take a storytelling opportunity from you," she said. "Is this the bathroom?"

She'd opened the door and helped herself to the light switch before I could answer. "Nice lighting," she said, leaning into the mirror, then rooting through the bottles in the mess on my vanity. "What kind of scent do you wear?"

"What? I don't wear anything... much."

Her fingers landed on the spice cookie perfume bottle just once, and then moved on. I tried not to imagine the mechanics by which her knee might nudge the bottom drawer and reveal the bits of shiny trash hidden there.

Not stolen, exactly. Nothing prosecutable. I thought.

"The car smelled sweet after you got out the other night—cinnamon, maybe. Is it shampoo?"

"Maybe. Look, Courtney, what do you want?"

She finally turned her attention away from the bottles and came to lean in the doorway. Her gold badge gleamed.

My palms, dormant for most of the day, began to hum.

I ran them across my jeans to remind them of their recent interaction with the gravel road. I looked up. Had she heard about that already, too?

"What I really want is to solve this murder and get promoted," she said. "Or use it to leverage a spot on a unit in Indianapolis or Chicago. Anywhere that isn't here. That's what I *want*. What would I settle for tonight?" Her eyes were bright with ambition, but as soon as I saw it, she seemed to realize what she was saying. The raw desire dropped away. "I'd settle for even a tiny shred of information that I don't already have about Maddy's murder."

I had talked to the fiancé, and I bet she hadn't. Loughton would be keeping some of the low-hanging fruit to himself. My dumb luck—some might say bad luck—had given me more access to a suspect than her job had. Courtney was indifferent now, hanging out in my bedroom as though we'd always done so, but I couldn't think of another reason for her to be here. I felt the old buzz of competition. She was here because I had better information, maybe better ideas. "Has her purse turned up yet?" I said, and I enjoyed Courtney's expression traveling between raging curiosity and nonchalance. An ambitious woman who thought ambition was dirty. Maybe she would have done better not to have any, as I had done.

But of course I carried my own dirty desires around with me, too. We all did. What Maddy hadn't wanted people to know about her. What I didn't want anyone to know about me or my family. The filth was inside, invisible.

"Her phone did," Courtney said. "Crushed, in the bin, and wiped."

The phone rang. We both turned to look, and then my mother called my name from down the hall.

"Probably the school—er, Fitz, I mean. To see if I can sub."

"By all means," she said. "Lean times with the Mid-Night closed."

When I picked up the phone, the caller drew an indignant breath and unleashed a tirade of noise. Shelly. I held the phone away from my ear and checked to see if Courtney was getting what she'd come for.

"How am I supposed to pull this off?" Shelly cried. "The reunion and now a *funeral*? Why did you give him my number? How am I going to explain this to—well, anyone? Juliet, really, how? Surely there's someone more—more *appropriate*."

"You met him," I said. "And he's a mess. I just thought—well, Shelly, who's more appropriate than you to help him pull it together? You're the only one of us with this kind of organizational skill."

She sniffed. "I know what blowing smoke up someone's skirt sounds like, Juliet."

"I'm not, I swear. He seemed so lost, and Gretchen can't be trusted to do it well, and you're so good at this kind of thing," I said. "It's not flattery if it's true."

Courtney made a noise behind me. I whipped around, my heart racing, sure she'd be elbow deep into the bottom drawer of the vanity or spraying herself with Maddy's perfume, but she was still in the doorway. She raised her eyebrows at me.

"Fine," Shelly said. "I'll help a possible *murderer* bury his *strangled* wife, but you have to work it out in trade."

My hands, at least, had stopped itching. "What then?"

"I help him, and you help me—with the reunion," she said. "People think it comes together by magic, but it does not."

I turned to Courtney, who was watching me as though I were her favorite TV channel. "When is it again?"

She sighed. "Saturday, Juliet. This Saturday. And thanks to you, it just became a memorial service, too."

Right after I hung up the phone with Shelly, it rang again. "You're so popular," Courtney said, crossing her arms and settling in.

This time it was Fitz. "I hate to ask for another day, Jules—"

"It's OK, I could use—I mean, I'm really enjoying it," I said. "I'm just having them run. Was there anything else you wanted them to do?"

"You got them to run? They always complain when I make them do that."

"Oh, they complain," I said. "I recruited a new thirty-two-hun-dred-meter runner for you. Jessica somebody?"

Fitz was silent for a moment. "That's incredible," he said. "What did Mike say?"

I blushed a bit. Coach had said I had a good instinct, and I must have lit up like a twelve-year-old at the praise. All the girls ended up with a crush on one of the coaches, but I thought mine should have dis-sipated by now. "He was impressed. He said you'd had an eye on her."

"Well, of course," he said. "Who wouldn't—"

"I'm sorry if I overstepped."

"Not at all, not at all," he said. "I was just thinking about the rest of the team, how she might fit in. Mickie runs the thirty-two hundred, but since when is it a problem to have two teammates challenging one another? You know that better than ... anyway, maybe some drills for the girls tomorrow. There will be more whining for you to put up with, but you seem to have the talent for getting them to do what you want."

He sounded tired. *Heartsick*, I'd said, but what if he really was sick, the kind of sick you couldn't see and didn't easily recover from? Or recover at all. I thought of my dad, and the call that robbed him from me forever. We hadn't seen that coming. Coach and Fitz were about the same age that my dad would have been. I was keenly aware of Courtney watching me. I wouldn't cry. I wouldn't. "So do you, Fitz," I said. "You have that talent, too."

He cleared his throat. "Mike's got it, enough for both of us. I'm excited to work with Jessica, if she comes through. Whatever you said to convince her, let's get that on a recruitment brochure right away. T-shirts, even."

When I hung up the phone, Courtney said, "Jeesh, the longer we hang out, the more the track team seems like a cult."

Was I allowed to tell an armed officer to shove it? "We just lost someone we care about. Also, I've found when you *hang out* with someone a lot, you start to indulge in a little hero worship." Coach, especially, drew our adoration. We were protective of him and his missed chance at the Olympics. Sort of like Maddy had just missed state, now that I thought about it. They might have had a lot to talk about, afterward, if you could compare losing out on a gold medal for a bronze—not too shabby—with what Maddy had gone through.

"Hero worship, huh? I'm flattered," Courtney said. She flicked at the door to my closet and glanced in. "But what I've noticed is more of the self-worship variety."

"Maybe that's because running that far and that fast makes you feel like a god," I said, reaching past her and closing the door.

She looked at me in surprise. "I didn't know that."

"You couldn't know that," I said. "The newspaper staff not being that active a sport."

"So Maddy thought she was a god? A goddess?" Courtney said. I could tell her mind was racing to fit this newfound knowledge into the map of what we knew. "Maybe someone didn't like being reminded he or she was merely human in her worship-worthy presence?"

"That wasn't who she was."

"Well, look who's back in the fan club," Courtney said. "How touching."

Maddy had been through more loss than Courtney had ever known, it seemed to me. More loss than anyone had ever or would ever give her credit for.

I'd been too honest with Courtney. She had no idea what I meant. She'd never known the feeling of running twelve to fourteen miles, of walking off the track knowing you'd given everything you had. Knowing you were made of better stuff than most people. Knowing you were a hands-down bad-ass, even if it was the basketball players who got all the attention. Maybe she'd never had something like that, that sense of belonging to something, the solid feeling under our feet of having something to reach for and having someone to help you. It wasn't worship. It was only love. We had loved each other and Coach and Fitz, who held the team together like a family.

Like a regular family, which Maddy had not had, and I'd had, but lost.

I pictured my mom sitting in the bright kitchen with the microwave pinging at her every two minutes.

I went to my bedroom door and opened it. Courtney shrugged, slid off the doorjamb, and strolled across the room and past me into the hall. She dawdled at a photo on the wall—me in severe braces—before she would let me escort her to the front door.

"Thanks for the hospitality," she said. "But before I go, I have to ask you a few questions."

"What have you been doing this whole time?"

"Warming up?" she said, grinning. "Oh, right, no. I've been prying. OK, what I need to ask you about is what you know about Billy's side business."

"Billy hardly works his regular business," I said. "What side business do you suspect him of?"

"Why is half the motel closed up?"

"Uh—I guess because we never get enough people to make it worth keeping the whole place up," I said. We had used the no-vacancy sign before, but the owners had decided to keep the south wing closed up rather than to renovate. That was what Billy had said, anyway. "What's going on?"

"What kind of clientele do you get down at the Mid-Night most nights? Think outside the minivans."

She was moving fast enough, my head swam. "The minivans are Bargains—I mean, the coupon-cutters. They're cheap. Or they're really tired, sometimes both."

"What about people who would rather stay somewhere nondescript with a shocking lack of security cameras?"

"We had those dominatrix people a few years back," I said. "Do you mean . . ."

The pudgy, shamed face of the dead guy from two-oh-six flashed from my memory. His alibi: a young woman.

"Now you're catching up," she said happily. "Remember that round fellow who checked out that morning? His alibi was a prostitute barely out of high school?"

I stared at her. "What do you mean?" She couldn't mean what I thought she was saying. Billy? I remembered wondering if Billy would even know what sex sounded like. "You can't mean—"

"Billy is right this minute going to jail," she said. "For turning the Mid-Night into a turnstile for hookers and the men who want to use and abuse them."

"Billy Batts." I ran my hand through my hair three or four times rapidly. I tried out my version of his weedy drawl. "'Come in, Juliet, room one-oh-niner needs more toilet paper. Over.' *Billy?*"

Courtney's smile faded quickly. "Young girls. Young," she said. "Have you ever seen anyone around the Mid-Night who didn't belong there?"

Who belonged at the Mid-Night? The bar made it impossible to keep track of all the people who came and went, and most of them had better places they could have been. But then the girls started to take shape: young women getting into and out of cars, young women getting dropped off in the back parking lot, young women asking for change for the vending machines. The strays, too young for the bar. I mean, Teeny was always showing up, too. Surely she had no part in this. But *the girls*, as Teeny had so eloquently put it.

Lu and I had seen hundreds of women hurried into rooms over the years. We joked about it. But it wasn't funny.

"How young?" I said.

"I'm pretty sure when the news breaks, we're going to find that one or two of them still attend Midway High," she said. "The men, of course, don't. I can't wait to find out which assholes they turn out to be."

She opened the front door. In the porch light like a star on stage, Coach Trenton stood with his hand raised to the bell.

"Really popular," Courtney said.

"I don't think your bell works," he said. His eyes flicked over Courtney's uniform and then back to me. He took a step backward. "I hope I'm not interrupting."

"Officer Howard was just leaving," I said.

"If there's going to be a worship service, I could stay," she said.

I opened the screen door, let her walk past, and gestured Coach inside.

At the bottom of the steps, Courtney turned. "I wanted to ask you about—"

"Good night," I said, and shut the door.

"That young lady has been getting around town," Coach said.

"She's been to see you, too?"

"Quite a few of the teachers," he said. "Asking about Maddy, as much as we remembered. Very thorough. I suppose you have to be, or justice will never be served."

"Do you think justice will be served?"

In the kitchen, the microwave dinged. Coach winced a bit into the glare of the kitchen. His face, always thin, seemed drawn, tired. "I don't know, Juliet. I hope so. It's crazy right now, everyone looking at everyone else askance. All the parents are up in arms, did I tell you?" He threw his hands up. "I've no idea how they expect their girls to be ready for their first meet if this keeps up."

"If what keeps up?"

"All the extra chaperoning, for one thing," he said. "There are too many stage parents in the stands right now. It's distracting."

The microwave chimed again. Coach glanced toward the kitchen, then back at me. I must have looked as startled as I felt. "I didn't mean anything against your dad, Juliet, of course. He was an active part of our community, and of course you were hyper-focused. I didn't have to worry about you. But Mickie is easily influenced."

"Mickie's parents are coming to practices?"

"The mother. She's a flirt, so it's me she trying to distract."

A hot blush burned its way up my neck.

"The worst part, though, is Fitz falling off the face of the planet," he said. "Have you heard from him at all?"

"You haven't?"

"Messages. A text, once." He drew his phone out of his pocket and studied it, frowning. "But when I text back or try to get him on the phone, nothing. He's been odd since this Maddy thing."

This Maddy thing. This murder that had rent our town, taken my old best friend, and ruined the best friendship I'd had since. The microwaved dinged again.

He looked up from his phone. "I'm sorry," he said. "That's not what I meant to say. We're all sad about Maddy. We're all going to be sad about Maddy for a long time. Not even when—I'm saying *when*—they find who did it. We're not going to be able to hang it up, are we? She meant too much to us to let it go so easily."

The tears I'd been choking back all day threatened. I wanted to tell Coach everything—the pregnancy test, the miscarriage, the puke-green sweater. My stomach hurt from holding in all the things I'd learned. But I couldn't bear to. Now that she was gone, what reason was there to bring up all that old stuff?

"I heard from Fitz just a little while ago," I said. "He wants me to take his classes again tomorrow. I don't mind."

"Well, at least he's talking to someone," he said. "And of course no one minds you being there, Jules. You're a natural." The microwaved dinged again. "What is that noise?"

"I have a theory that Fitz is keeping me safe by putting me at the school," I said.

It sounded pathetic even as I said it, and Coach's twitch of a smile made me feel worse. Poor fatherless girl. Soft-headed, lonely wreck. "That's possible," he said. "But I've known that lug for too many years to think this is good for him. Something's wrong. More than Maddy and, anyway, we need to stick together right now. We're a team, right?" He brightened. "And a damn good one, all those years."

Now I wondered which years he meant. The Maddy years or the Kristina years? But I didn't want to ask, and hear how petty I'd sound.

"Strange that it's taken Maddy's death to bring us back together," he said, looking fondly at the portrait of me in my team kit. "Look at you," he cooed. "It's good to see that girl in Midway's halls again."

"It's a little weird, though," I admitted. "Things are the same and not. Our trophies in the case could be from yesterday or a thousand years ago, either one. But you probably know what I mean. Your Olympic medal's right there in the front."

He waved his hand. "That was an actual thousand years ago."

"I thought your Coach of the Year stuff might be there," I said. "Or maybe I didn't look hard enough."

"I keep those pieces privately," he said. "Frankly, they mean more to me than any Olympic medal."

I'd forgotten that Mrs. Haggerty had said as much. But—I had seen the trophy in his dark office that night we'd slipped in after hours. "Oh, you kept them at home," I said. I'd never been inside his home, but based on his car, I imagined a clean, streamlined bachelor pad. "But an Olympic medal—"

"Not the Olympic medal I was capable of," he said. "In any case, the Coach of the Year trophy got damaged early on and I never had it fixed. The medallion has survived the years, though. Quality materials—not one of those cheapie ones with the tear-away ribbons. That's my gold, Juliet. And you girls made it possible. Maybe I'll wear it to—" The microwaved sang out again. "Is that something trying to get our attention?"

"I'll get it," I said, and led him back to the door. My mother wouldn't be up to two visitors in one day.

He was a gentleman, at least, and took the hint. I watched him to his car, waiting for the wave I knew he would throw as he got inside his little roadster. We needed to stick together, the few of us left.

In the kitchen, my mother stood at the sink. I opened the microwave and took out the plate of old macaroni and cheese, long gone cold again. "It's late, Mom."

"Just wanted to do these dishes."

I peered over her shoulder. There were actually dishes to clean. "Did Courtney have dinner here?"

"Oh, no. Just a snack. She's a nice girl. I don't remember you ever bringing her home before."

I scraped the mac and cheese into the trash and added the plate to the sink. "I didn't bring her over this time," I said. "Which—maybe it's for the best if you didn't let anyone in when I'm not here, at least for a while."

She flicked on the water and squirted dish soap into the sink. "I'm not a child, Juliet."

The soap foam rose. Where did she think the dish soap came from? And whatever she'd fed Courtney? And basically every cent that had kept a roof over our heads and food in our kitchen for the last few years? Like Shelly had said: people thought some things happened by magic.

"I didn't call you a child," I said. What did she think of the word *invalid*? But I didn't want to get into it.

I went to the refrigerator. We were almost out of everything: milk, butter, cheese, eggs. In the drawers at the bottom, there were a few wrinkled carrots that had fallen out of the bag, a shrunken head of lettuce. In the cabinets, we had a few more boxes of generic macaroni, some canned beans.

"Are you hungry?" she asked.

"No." When would Midway High send me the check from the past two days? Not soon enough. Not soon enough to fix years of neglect and avoidance, of hand-to-mouth, of sometimes nothing in the hand to put to the mouth.

"Maddy was special to me, too," she said.

She didn't need to say it. Maddy's death had woken her from her stupor. I should have been relieved, even happy to see my mother again. But I couldn't reach out for her, couldn't comfort her, and I noticed she still hadn't tried to comfort me. How many times since Dad had died had I wished someone would offer?

I turned toward my room, feeling small and mean for thinking it, but thinking it just the same: She cared about Maddy enough to come back to me. But she hadn't cared about me enough not to leave in the first place.

CHAPTER TWENTY-ONE

The next morning, Jessica, Delia, and their peers showed up in the gym in their tiny shorts and high ponytails, and watched as I demonstrated how I wanted them to run the sprints: out to the free-throw line painted on the court floor, and back, then to half-court and back, and finally all the way to the other side of the gym and back. "Where is Fitz?" Delia asked. She didn't sound concerned for his health, but her own.

They were talking in the ranks about the motel. It had been all over the news last night and this morning, with more updates promised. The combination of young women and sex was too much to ignore. A few names were going around, but I had no idea where they'd come from.

"Come on, ladies," I said. "Enough gossip until I've seen some speed."

I ran them through a warm-up and then they broke into teams of four and ran in relays. One of the teams was lopsided with only three members, so I took a turn. I was catching my breath on the sidelines when I heard giggling and looked around to see what the comedy was. Jessica was loping across the gym in a stagey jog, as slow as she'd ever moved in my presence. She clowned all the way to the other side of the gym and back, running in place at the finish line before her teammate slapped her shoulder to tag in for her.

A few of the girls shot me side-eye looks to see what I would do. I stretched, and then did another round of sprints. As I shot back across the gym on my last distance, still pretty fast for not having run in a long time, Jessica started her next set, again exaggerating her stride without getting anywhere very quickly.

I did a U-turn and pulled her aside. "You're almost going backward," I said. "Is this some kind of pantomime or something?"

She glanced back at the other girls. They'd all stopped to watch.

"All right, gawkers," I said. "Laps, until I say you're done."

The moans rose up, but they quickly assembled a pace.

"So what's up?" I said to Jessica. "Is your rib hurting you? Did your first practice with the team wear you out? Are you just tired?"

She shifted her weight to one foot, and pulled the other up behind her, stretching. Her black eye was fading to a smudge of purple and green. She hadn't tried to cover it up today. No one had believed the story about allergies, anyway. "Tired, definitely."

"OK," I said. "Why the circus act then?"

"What's the big deal? No one's ever goofed on you before, Super Teacher?"

I would accept sarcasm, if it came dressed up in such a way. "You know I'm not a real teacher, right? I'm just trying to do for you what someone did for me."

She'd been stretching the other leg, and set her foot down hard. "What's that?" Her eyes were like shutters. Defiance—*snap*—something else just there—*snap*—and it was gone.

"Introduce you to long-distance running. Look, you don't have to join the team. Trophies aren't everything." I thought of the sad silver running man still hiding in my car. The perfume bottle. The stupid barrette and all the crap stuffed into my secret compartment. What were they, if not trophies? The most ridiculous trophies ever collected. "You could probably get a scholarship to school, but maybe you're all set."

"Let's say I have all the funds I'll ever need, and I don't care much for buses and sing-alongs or standing on a podium. What then? Why bother?"

What had I told Courtney the night before? Long distance turned you into a god? My file was probably getting pretty thick over at the Midway Police Department. I needed to stop saying idiotic things, and also stop doing them. I needed to put all the shiny trash under my bathroom sink out in the bin and get my life together. I needed . . . a run.

"Running quiets the voice in your head," I said, more to myself than to her. "People who do the short distances don't know it. It's a secret, so don't tell them."

She snorted.

"That voice that tells you you're not good enough, pretty enough, smart enough. That you don't know anything. That you'll never amount to anything," I said. "That you'll never have the things you want, will never stop wanting what you don't have. The voice that points out how you compare to everyone else."

The girls thundered all around us. Jessica took a step in to hear the terrible things the voice would say.

"It says all the other girls don't think about the things you do," I said. I felt my cheeks burn. My mind raced to Vincent, his skin against mine as he cried on my shoulder. Had he smelled Maddy's perfume on me that day? And then, for some reason, Beck came to mind. Beck, kicking at the gravel on the side of the road, saying—what was it?— that I had always treated him badly. "That voice that says other girls are the enemy."

Jessica looked away. "I know what the enemy looks like, OK? Anyway, they already have a long-distance runner."

"You can have more than one, believe me. One of you will win more often," I said. "But you don't have to be in *real* competition. There's enough air for everyone. You'll push each other to be better than you would have been."

She didn't believe me. Who could blame her? It had taken me ten years to learn that lesson.

"Look," she said, and she seemed much older than she could possibly be. "I appreciate what you're trying to do. But I don't need saving. Not quite yet, anyway." She stepped into the path of the lap runners. Within a few minutes, she had passed them all, and led them the rest of the way.

At lunch, the memory of where yesterday's tater tots ended up was strong. I eyed the snack cake rack. Was it bad form for the gym teacher to have doughnuts for lunch? I finally decided on a leafy salad. In line, the bowl slid around on the tray as I dug for my money. A hand shot out and caught the bowl just before disaster struck. At the end of a freckled arm: Delia.

"Is that really the only thing skinny girls eat?" she said. "I'm doomed."

The salad had turned less appealing since I'd picked it up. "I've only recently given up fried foods. Yesterday, actually."

She brightened, then blinked at me expectantly. "Did you mean what you said? To Jessica? About the voice?"

"Which part?"

"I didn't hear it all—but the thing about, you know." She looked around and leaned in. "About 'not good enough, not smart enough.' I mean, I hoped I wasn't the only one." She put the salad back on my tray and stuck her finger into her pudding cup, pulled it out, and licked it. "But most of them—poking themselves in the mirror, moaning they're so fat, when they're anything but. They just want you to tell them they're wrong, that they're really perfect. Same with grades. 'Oh, I can't believe I got an A-minus, wow I hardly studied at all.'"

"It doesn't seem fair. It will never seem fair, by the way."

Delia's finger stopped on the way to her mouth. "Thank you. Thank you for not pretending it's all fine."

My turn at the register came, then I waited for Delia to pay. "That's not your lunch, is it? I mean, that's not really going to last you the rest of the day."

"I had something already," she said. Her face had gone pink. "I just really like pudding."

Everything I could think to say sounded condescending. "I almost got a honeybun for lunch, so don't take advice from me. Of any kind. Seriously, career, life. No advice coming from me."

She smiled and rolled her eyes out toward the sea of tables, loud with students and silverware and chairs scooting across the floor. "Want to sit with me?"

I'd meant to escape back to the gym, or maybe even brave the faculty lounge, but I couldn't think of a way to refuse her. What if she sat by herself every day? Of course, sitting with me wouldn't up her credibility with the other students.

She led me down a long aisle between tables until we came upon a group of girls from the first-period PE class. My team.

"Hey, Coach," some of them said, and they slid over to make room. Delia took a spot across the table.

"Hey, Dill," one of the girls said. It took me a minute to locate the source of the nickname. I'd been worried she might have to sit by herself, but it was really her pity for me that had brought me here.

"Ladies," I said. Our little thing. I refused to call them girls now, no matter how old they were, at least not aloud. "What's good today?"

"Not a thing," Jessica said.

"The French fries," another girl said, and gave Jessica a look. "What's your problem?"

Jessica glanced my way. "Not a thing."

"We're used to it with Mickie, but shit."

The girls tried to hide their smiles and sidelong looks at me. Mickie sat at the head of the table, stirring a serving of corn with her fork. "Shut it," she said.

They seemed willing to take orders. A few of them picked up their trays and left, and everyone scooted down to fill the void. The shift left me sitting alone, so I slid down, too.

"You guys hear that motel by the highway was a front for a prostitution ring?" Mickie said.

The chatter grew loud and obnoxious. The girls simultaneously couldn't stand to hear a word and wanted to know every detail. One of them had stayed there, which elicited a great deal of discussion. Delia looked uncomfortable and pinker than when I made her run.

"I know someone who's spent a great deal of time there," Mickie continued, looking at me.

"I cleaned the toilets, Mickie," I said. "It wasn't a front." The girls all leaned in to hear me. "Not exactly. It was a real motel, but the—look, I don't know anything about what was happening there."

Mickie was smirking at Jessica now. "You must have cleaned up a lot of—"

"So this voice," Delia said around a mouthful of pudding. "You hear it for real?"

"Not in a schizophrenic way," I said, grateful for the change of topic. "Less a voice and more like my own voice, my own thoughts. If you don't know what I mean, count yourself lucky."

"No, I have the voice," Delia said. "'You shouldn't eat that, Delia. You shouldn't wear that, Delia. Nobody likes you, Delia.'"

"We love you, Delia," said one of the girls.

"You shouldn't be so hard on yourself, Delia," I said.

"It never says that," she said. "But is it true? What you said about running making it go away? You're not just trying to get me to lose weight, are you?"

"You're fine the way you are," I said, poking at my salad. "Even if the voice never says so. Even if no one ever says so. You're great."

"You don't even know me."

"That's the point, Dill," Jessica said. "Coach Feelgood over here wants to make sure you understand what a special snowflake you are."

I pushed my tray away. "Enough. If you don't want me to sit here, that's fine. I'm nearly thirty years old, so I don't go in for teenage bullsh—attitude anymore. I'll see you on the track later." I threw a leg back over the bench.

"Not me," Jessica said. "I won't be there."

Words sprang to mind that I couldn't say. Sometimes the sprinters flamed out, but distance runners were usually tough. We were in it for the long haul, for the guts, for the miles. What a little daisy this girl was. I'd lasted four years. One race shy of four years.

Mickie looked up from her corn. "You're quitting already?" she said. "What a loser." She started to laugh, a low, sneaky sound that gathered speed and force and hysteria until she looked insane. "You lasted one day? One *day*?"

The other girls, thrown off by the terrible laughter, waffled between smiling and looking concerned for first Mickie and then Jessica. Then Mickie again.

"One day was enough," Jessica said. "I'm not going to be a horse in someone's stable."

Mickie bent over her tray, coughing and crying with laughter. A few of the other girls grabbed their trays and got up. Around us, the other students had started looking our way. I didn't slide down to fill the empty spots this time, and neither did Delia, who quietly finished her pudding, then said, "I found an extra copy of your yearbook. You had pretty goofy hair."

"We all had goofy hair. Your hair is going to look goofy a lot sooner than you think."

Mickie hiccoughed. "I'm not a horse," she said. Tears ran in beautiful rivulets down her face. "I'm a *thoroughbred*."

Jessica stared at her for a long moment, then stood and walked down the table to her. I braced myself for another fight, and so did the other girls, including Mickie, who stuck out her chin but didn't move.

"Come on," Jessica said, tugging at Mickie's sleeve. After a moment's hesitation, they went off, leaving their trays behind.

"That's weird," Delia said. "I didn't think they liked each other."

I knew they didn't. But I was starting to remember how easily you could hold two opposing feelings at the same time. You could love someone and still keep secrets from them. You could despise someone and still trust them. But I didn't remember as much as I wanted to remember. "The yearbook," I said. "Where is it?"

Delia let me into the student-activities room and hit the light. The tables were covered in computers, a long line of them, back to back. When Delia bumped a chair getting to a cabinet in the back of the room, one of the screens glowed to life.

"You guys do the newspaper, too?"

"Same room, different students." She stood on her tiptoes to pull the book from the top shelf. "A few kids do both, but you have to be pretty far ahead on, like, your math classes and stuff."

She held the book out. It was red faux leather, with a fat panther paw print raised on the cover. A normal yearbook, even a nice one. And yet somehow I'd come to think of the thing as some magical—no, *evil* object. But it was just a book. Delia held it out, the sleeve of her shirt pulling up to reveal a set of raw-looking scratches on her wrist. She saw me noticing, put the book on the table, and pulled down her sleeve. The class-change bell buzzed overhead.

"Just leave it here when you're done, OK?" she said. "I'll get killed—I mean. I'll get in trouble."

"Delia—"

"Just put it back on the shelf and close the door when you're done," she said, not meeting my eyes. "I'll be late."

She hurried out the door. I sat at one of the computers, stunned. Whatever I'd just seen, I knew the voice in Delia's head had said some awful things.

The longer I was at Midway High, the more I wanted to leave and never come back. Everywhere I turned, there was another girl to worry about. How did teachers do this, day in and out? How did *parents*?

I had another class starting in a few minutes, too. I shook myself back into focus and flipped through the yearbook quickly to the index. No surprise that my name only had two page entries. In my individual picture, my ten-years-younger self grinned like a jack-o'-lantern. The braces had come off, and I hadn't stopped smiling that year. I looked happy. I *was* happy then; the picture had been taken at the beginning of the year, not the end.

The other index entry led me to the track team pages. The main photo was the one I remembered, Coach bent over in Maddy's face, giving her a pep talk with a side of shoulder squeeze. The next largest photo was the team portrait with Maddy in the star position between the coaches and Fitz's back turned ever so slightly toward me. My smile here wasn't as bright. It was cold that day. There was a small photo of Maddy hitting the tape. I'd been cropped out. My foot kicked into the frame.

That was all. Because of the timing of the yearbook delivery, the season never got fully reported. No team stats, no personal bests. With only the photos and a couple of quick captions to go by, anyone could see that Maddy was the star. No wonder she hadn't wanted me to buy the book. My foot was in more of the photos than my face. I would have fretted over that shoe for the rest of the year. Longer.

Maddy had a few more entries in the index than I did. I flipped between the pages until I found her in the spring homecoming court. I'd forgotten about that. In the photo with the other princesses, she was hunched over, like carrion sitting on a wire.

The last index entry made up for it, though. Near the back, in a series of pages of photos taken over the course of the year, a sort of highlights reel, there was a nearly full-page photo of Maddy. She was running, mid-stride—stretched into flight, athletic and angelic at once, her ponytail jouncing behind her in the wind. In black and white, she gleamed, just like one of those silver girls on the trophies we both took home.

The difference a split second makes. We only had room for one goddess, and maybe the shoelaces coming in right behind her.

I got up and threw the book up into the shelf, never more glad that I'd not wasted the twenty bucks. Maddy had saved me that reality for ten years. Forever, if I hadn't gotten in my own way and insisted on seeing how little I'd meant to everyone at Midway High. Running hadn't made me a god. It had made me a ghost. I hit the lights and slammed the door behind me on the way out.

CHAPTER TWENTY-TWO

The rest of the day, groups of shoes pounded the gym floor. One direction, then the other.

At one point, I looked up to find Coach bringing his boys through. "Time for the showers, isn't it, Juliet?"

The girls didn't wait for me to agree. They pivoted from whichever position on the floor they held and jogged toward the lockers. The clock over the door revealed that I'd let the last period class go too long, almost too late for them to get ready to catch their buses home. I was no longer their coach.

Coach walked over. "I heard from Fitz, if that's been worrying you. He's fine, or at least he says he is. He says he's helping with the service."

"Service?" I said. "Oh." Maybe Shelly wouldn't have to do all the work. Fitz would get it right. "Better him than me," I said. "I went to see Gretchen, and it was weird. Maddy's room was weird. Everything was the same, the trophies and ribbons and stuff all still where she left them."

Coach looked at me. "All of it? Like a shrine? That would be . . . upsetting, I think."

"But she's not the same," I said. "I mean . . . she wasn't who I thought she was. And I certainly didn't know who she was when she died. It's not fair to bury her as an eighteen-year-old girl, is it?"

"I'm not sure what you mean," he said, giving me a closer look. "Are you OK?"

"I've spent too much time here," I said, "I'm not even sure this is good for me right now. But I need the—anyway, Fitz is being so generous."

"Is that what it is?" he said. "I suppose I'm glad one of us is the beneficiary of his kindness right now. I feel a little let down, myself. Any hope you can stay and help put down the revolution?"

"Revolution?"

"That Jessica creature didn't work out," he said. "These girls don't like to be told what to do. I hate to sound a thousand years old, but I miss girls like Maddy, you. You just wanted to run. You didn't need to be told why."

Now that I'd seen the payoff of all the time and effort—the yearbook stung, I couldn't help that—I wanted to know why, myself. "Her loss," I said, not sure I believed it.

"Yes, but she's taking my star with her."

"Mickie?" I remembered Jessica taking Mickie's arm at the lunch table. "You said Mickie was easily swayed. You were just worried about the wrong influence. I'm so sorry. I haven't gotten anything right here, have I?"

He gave me a gentle pat high on my back. It wasn't the same as getting one of his bracing shoulder grips at the finish line like Maddy used to get, but it was something. "You always got it right, Juliet. It wasn't your fault it didn't work out the way we all wanted it to."

I nodded, and he dropped his hand and walked away.

The bell rang. Beyond the gym doors I heard the scatter of students rushing for escape. I followed closely behind, and was halfway to my car when I thought to wonder what the outcome that we'd all wanted had been.

Maddy winning? I had wanted something else. Even if she'd won, nothing about my life would have been any different. Same dead father. Same helpless mother. Same dead-end job. I had to admit: I still wanted something else.

A group of students gathered at the exit. I nudged through them and outside. Clouds rolled darkly overhead, and a few fat raindrops had begun to fall.

Out in the lot, a police car was parked in one of the aisles, askance. My broken car sat nearby, ugly and pathetic. Courtney leaned up against it, writing in her notebook. Her partner, the big guy whose name I'd forgotten, sat back in the passenger seat of the patrol car.

As I got closer, I realized Courtney wasn't writing in her notebook. She had a ticket book out and was making good on it.

"What, Courtney?" I said. "What could I have possibly done now?"

"Your tags are out of date," she said. "You'll have the ticket, a fine—oh, and your insurance rate is not going to like this at all. Or is that out of date, too? Open up and let me see your proof of insurance."

The group of students at the door had gotten deeper, peering doubtfully out at the weather.

"My tags can't be out of date," I said, but I didn't know. I unlocked the passenger side door and popped the glove box. On my back, I felt the rain pick up. The wind turned shear, blowing at the hem of my T-shirt. Courtney looked over my shoulder into the car while I dug out the paperwork—a registration that was indeed out of date, and an insurance card that wouldn't have been any help to me, either. "Dammit."

"Thought so."

Tags for my junk heap were cheap, but I didn't have even that. Forget the fine or a renewal for the insurance policy. I checked the date on the card again. It was so out of date, I'd be lucky if they agreed to insure me at all after this.

Courtney ripped the ticket out of her book and held it out. It waved dramatically in the sharp wind. "I'll make you a deal. Everything you know in exchange for this ticket never touching your hand. I can't do anything about the insurance, but I can make this go away. No fine. You can probably get your tags renewed before the end of the work day if you hurry."

I calculated the damage. "What is it you think I know, Courtney?"

"Where's the ring?"

"It's . . . in the bank," I said. "At least that's what Shelly said."

"When did Shelly tell you this?"

I tilted my head back and let drops of rain hit my face. It had only been three days since Maddy had been killed. "The day the fiancé showed up," I said. "Was that yesterday? Two days ago."

"Well, there's a problem with that ring. It's a fake."

My arms were cold. I folded them around me. "I don't understand."

"We don't either. Explain it for us. Where's the real ring?"

I glanced back at the students at the door. A few had gotten bored and left, but some of the girls, duffle bags against their legs, remained. "You think I have the ring? Would I still be scrounging babysitting fees from Midway High if I had a giant diamond ring to pawn?"

"Is that what you did?" she barked. "We can find it, so it's better for you to tell the truth."

"If you can find it, then find it, hot shot." I didn't feel desperate anymore. I felt flayed. What could she do to me? I didn't have the ring. I hadn't killed Maddy. "She had it on her finger that night she showed up at the Mid-Night, and then—you were there when it was sitting on the dresser, remember? I got you the key and—"

"Your prints are all over that room."

"I cleaned that room the day before she checked in," I said. "My prints are all over every room there. Except Billy's."

"Billy, who has lots to say now that he's facing a few felonies," she said. "He said he might have seen you heading up to that room later that night. A room that is strangely missing a piece of evidence."

I swallowed. "You guys took the ring that day. Maybe you're the one who swapped it for a fake."

"Nice try." She went to the patrol car and grabbed something through the window. "Is this the ring Maddy was wearing the night she arrived at the motel?"

Even inside the plastic evidence bag, the ring sparkled like a star brought to earth. "I thought you said—is it not the same ring? It looks the same to me." I'd never owned a decent piece of jewelry in my life. I studied the ring in the bag. There was something obscene about it, now that I knew it wasn't real.

"What did you do with the stolen evidence?"

Stolen. My hands burned at the word, and yet I couldn't exactly disavow it. "She left that photo for me. No one else would have ever found it—"

"Photo? What photo?" Courtney glanced over her shoulder at her partner. Loughton, I finally remembered. He got out of the car and came toward me.

"I was talking about the perfume," Courtney said. "The perfume bottle I found in your bathroom, the same one missing from the crime scene. We have photos of our own, you know. But a photo left behind by the deceased is even more interesting."

"Did you take a photo of the bathmat?" I said.

Courtney's eyes shifted to Loughton and back to me, coolly, but I'd already seen the hunger there. "Of course we did. Stop telling us how to do our jobs."

Loughton held up handcuffs. "Miss?"

"What?" My voice cracked. "Do we really have to do this?"

Time stretched out as Loughton opened the cuffs. This was happening, and at the same time couldn't be. Ten years I'd been lifting and swiping, hoarding bits and bobs that didn't matter to anyone else. What I took wasn't treasure; I only made it so in the taking. And so I'd forgotten that what I was doing was still stealing.

Loughton waggled his finger at me to turn around. I was sick, shaking. I took a step to turn and nearly fell. Loughton grabbed me and shook me back to my feet, then pulled my wrists together behind my back. Back at the open door to the school, a few gawkers were holding out to watch. Faces might have been pressed to each window in the side of the school. Rain pelted my bare arms. This was happening.

"Do we have to do this?" Courtney said, opening the back door for me. "No, but we're going to. Take me to that photo. Oh, and you have the right to remain silent, by the way."

CHAPTER TWENTY-THREE

Riding in the cruiser was much less comfortable this time. That burned-in stench of fear and anger wasn't as evident, maybe because I was adding to it. I slid down in the seat and ducked my head. When we passed Mrs. Schneider's pulled-back curtain, though, I peered around Courtney's head. Patrol cars filled our driveway and the street out front, alongside a gathering of neighbors and onlookers who'd come to watch.

My mother stood on the porch, rubbing her arms. Outside our home for probably the first time in more than a year. I couldn't stand how thin and scared she looked.

Loughton pulled me from the car. I let my hair hang down, hiding my face. Loughton led me to her, but I looked at my feet.

"They had a warrant," she said.

"It's OK, Mom."

She hugged me, awkwardly. Loughton gestured her inside and pushed me ahead of him through the door.

Inside was chaos. Drawers and couch cushions were pulled out. The bookcase was empty, the contents rifled through and set aside. While we stood in the doorway, something in the kitchen crashed to the floor. "My bad," a voice called out.

Everywhere I looked, someone in a blue uniform was taking a closer look at another corner of our lives. My mother seemed to be taking the invasion stoically, but I shook with rage.

Additional officers emerged from the hallway, carrying a handful of my things in a series of plastic bags. They offered them to Loughton, who nodded in Courtney's direction.

She took them, held them to the light so that I could see my old friends: the lipstick in the color I could never wear, the barrette, the spiral paper clip, the baby sock. The old lady's empty atomizer. Maddy's perfume. They'd put each item in its own bag. This was museum-quality care and presentation.

Courtney studied each offering as the room grew still around us. I saw the barrette through her eyes: confusing. The baby sock: inexplicable. "Tell me about this," she said.

I wavered on remaining silent. "Which one?"

"Not any one thing," she said. Her voice was quiet and more respectful than it had ever been. "All of it. Explain it to me."

"I don't know if I can," I said. "I don't understand it myself. It's out of my control, or at least it feels that way."

"And these were things you took from the rooms?"

My mother gasped.

"Absolutely not," I said, looking first at my mother. "Well, not exactly. Most of it was left behind. Maybe I could have worked harder to get some of it back to the rightful owners, but I never took anything until—"

"Until the perfume bottle. When were you in her room?"

I returned my attention to the floor. "The night after I found her. I didn't touch anything. The bottle, but not—I wanted to understand what happened to her. I don't know, I thought I might be the only one who'd be able to figure out what happened."

"And the perfume just happened to be a crucial clue to your investigation," Courtney said.

"Well, no," I said. "I just wanted it. It's vanilla. The scent she wore, and the same one I wore that night in your patrol car. Vanilla, like cookies. I just—wanted it."

Courtney looked around the room at Loughton and the others. "Where's the photo?"

"Inside the pillow on my bed," I said. "There's a cover, with a zipper." Someone marched off to collect it.

"Grab her shoes," she called after him. Courtney's eyes found mine. "Were you lovers?"

"What? No. Friends."

She shrugged. "Had to ask."

The cop who'd gone back to the room returned and held out the photo, sealed in its own baggie. Courtney took it, spent a long, silent moment studying it. "Surprised this didn't make *Tracks*," she said, handing it off and waving it away.

That she knew it hadn't caught me by surprise. "You got a yearbook?"

"You didn't?"

"Maddy told me not to."

"Maddy told you not to buy your own senior yearbook." Courtney clucked her tongue. "Now I'm starting to wonder if you weren't master and pet."

"*Friends*," I said.

Another officer came up the hallway with my old running shoes, a pair of scuffed high heels, a pair of boots, and some slippers. We could hear others tramping around the back of the house, then the door to the other bedroom open. Next to me, my mom stiffened.

"What does that photo mean to you? What do you see?"

How to explain my conflicted feelings, to explain that every time I looked at the photo now, it was like a prism, showing a different view of my life and everything I'd done right or wrong? One day I am forgiven. One day I am forgotten. One morning I see nothing but my triumphant smile. Another morning I see the dark pall over Maddy's face, and I remember all over again what was taken from her, and then from me. "I was jealous of her," I said. "In that photo, I'm happy, though. Do you see? I only remember how petty I was when our season ended short. I only remember the envy. But that photo shows that I wasn't only jealous. I wasn't only petty. I was other things, too. Look at everything going on around me. All that Southtown business and the jeering, people calling us terrible names, and then Coach and Fitz picking their favorite again and again, right in front of my face. Look at them—they're already planning her celebration party, her ascension. And I'm still happy."

"Why didn't you tell me about all this when I said I wanted to know everything?" Courtney said.

"Everything about her *death*," I said. "I don't know anything about her death that you don't." My hands were growing numb behind my back. "Everything I know is about her life."

Courtney brought out her phone and thumbed at it a bit. Then she held her hand out toward the guy with the shoes. "Those," she said, pointing at the running shoes. "Turn them over."

We all studied the worn down treads. "That's it? That's what you run in?"

"I don't run anymore," I said.

She eyed the black canvas sneakers with white toes I wore. "Kick one of those up for me."

My heart rose in my throat. They were matching the print mashed into the bathmat, I was sure of it, and I'd worn these shoes into the room. I turned my heel up, and we all studied that worn pattern.

I put my foot down. Courtney and I stared at each other for a long moment, then she nodded to Loughton, and he moved to take off the cuffs. I rubbed at my wrists. Courtney's gleaming badge raised no tingle of desire in my hands whatsoever.

"The killer has better shoes than you," she said.

Not surprised. I hung my head, waiting.

"You might not know this," she said. "But a death like this is always about the life that preceded it."

She sounded as though she'd found this out the hard way.

"OK," she said. "We're not going to arrest you—yet—on the evidence tampering. Tell me there's nothing else back there I need to worry about."

"No, nothing. No giant diamond ring, either, you noticed."

"Point taken. No charges, no ticket," she said. She seemed to notice the officer still holding my shoes. "But I have one demand."

I braced myself.

"We go running tomorrow."

Everyone in the room turned to look at her.

"I told you I don't run anymore," I said.

"Great, then maybe I can keep up. One run, tomorrow, and I'll do what I can to keep all this tamped down."

My mother and I both turned to look out the window. The neighbors had umbrellas.

"A misunderstanding," Loughton said. He waved the officers from the hallway out the door. Within minutes they'd decamped the group inside and dispersed the onlookers outside. One by one, the patrol cars shut down their lights and rolled away, the last idling with Loughton in the passenger seat.

"I'll meet you here," Courtney said. "Six too early?"

Not for someone who might keep me from jail. I shook my head.

"Great," she said.

I found that I couldn't let it go. "'A death like this'?"

"The unquiet kind," she said. "I'll have one of the guys bring your car back to you." She nodded toward my mother. "Ma'am, sorry for the disruption."

When the door closed behind Courtney, neither of us moved. Behind me, the house was in shambles. My mother had taken so many years to crawl out of her waking coma. What would this do to her? Finally I looked her way.

"Now I know," she said, thoughtfully, "why you never invited that little bitch over."

CHAPTER TWENTY-FOUR

The next morning, I waited on the front step in old, faded running pants and a baggy T-shirt I'd pulled from my dad's dresser.

I missed the photo already, yearned for the pile of stolen trash they'd removed from my vanity. It was all gone, something I'd recently wished for. But not actually gone. It was out there, tagged with my name. Every time I thought of Courtney holding up each bag, in turn, I felt sick again. I was sick—that was the only explanation, and why Courtney's voice had gone soft and gentle. I was sick and now everyone would know it.

When the car pulled into our drive, I sighed and stood, then realized the car wasn't Courtney's.

Vincent unfolded himself from the driver's seat and closed the door. "Good morning," he said, crossing the yard. "You heard about the ring?"

"I was accused of taking it," I said. I wondered how much longer I could say something like that and have people believe me.

"You didn't, though."

I remembered his panic at having it stowed at the bank. The bank, where jewelry appraisers could probably be called upon at a moment's notice. Had he given her a fake diamond engagement ring to begin with? "How do you know?"

He stopped a few feet away and glanced up and down the street. "I've been thinking about it," he said. "A few weeks ago, Maddy wasn't wearing her ring. It's hard not to notice when it's gone, you know? She said she was having it cleaned. When I noticed her wearing it again, it was—different. It was shiny and—too shiny. The stone. It wasn't right. I thought it was from a good polishing, but now—now, I don't know."

"You think she had the stone replaced with a fake? Why would she do that?"

"I'm not sure," he said.

For a moment, I caught that feeling again, that Maddy was really gone, that everything she had been would never be reconciled with the girl I'd known. Or thought I'd known. None of it would ever match up. All that was left of her were her trophies. Trophies and questions.

"If she replaced the diamond, where is it?" I said.

"Or the money from selling it." Vincent's eyes had gone glassy and far away. "God, didn't she know that I would have given her anything she needed or wanted? No questions."

"Is there unexplained extra money in her bank account? Stocks?" I didn't know how any of this worked. My bank account was flat, but I supposed rich people had more than a passbook savings that scraped bottom every month.

"She didn't have any extra, ever," he said. "She didn't work, remember?"

"Wait, no money at all?"

"I supported us," he said. "Our apartment, the bills, whatever she wanted for clothes and entertainment. My finance guy takes care of it all."

I couldn't imagine how such a thing worked. "So how did she go to the grocery or go shopping? You gave her an allowance?"

He gave me a sharp look. "She wanted for nothing, I promise you."

"But it was all yours," I said. "Oh, God. She was a trophy."

"What? She was not—she was never a trophy."

I stood back and glared. "Don't you see? She would have hated that. She needed something of her own."

"Maddy had plenty of her own. Her charities, her good works, her—" His shoulders dropped. "I never meant to . . . it never was supposed to be that way. She wanted to go to law school. She wanted to work for reproductive rights and for abused girls. She wanted to prosecute rapists. These news stories—last year there was a little girl abducted and drowned in the Chicago River—" He made a terrible sound in his throat. "Any one of those stories could set her off. She had such . . . fire."

His face was lit up with her memory. I looked away. My hands had begun to itch, and I was afraid of what it was they wanted me to steal. There was nothing of Maddy's that I hadn't wanted for my own.

But I didn't envy what her life had become. That ring, sure, that coat. But the fire, as Vincent called it. I didn't envy that, and he had no idea where the spark had come from.

A car door slammed. Courtney approached, strangely feminine in form-fitting running pants and a windbreaker. She had good shoes—better shoes than I'd ever had.

She wore a prim little pack at her hip.

"You don't have a gun in there, do you?" I said.

"Funny." She narrowed her eyes at Vincent. "You're not ready to run," she said.

"What?" he said, visibly startled, and eyeing the pack that did or didn't have a gun in it. "Oh. No, I don't run. That was Maddy's . . . I—I'll just talk to you later, Juliet."

Courtney and I watched him to his car.

"You sure can chase a guy off," I said.

"Girl's got to have a hobby," she said, shrugging. She gave me a long, empty moment to fill with what I'd been talking to Vincent about, and when I didn't jump to fill it, she did. "Well, then. Here's the deal: Let's forget about Maddy's death for a little while, OK? I want to hear about her life, as you put it. I wouldn't mind feeling like a god before we're done, here, either."

We started off slow down the block. The first strides were stiff, filled with little aches and pains. My knees. My ankles. My thighs chimed in with complaints from the sprints I'd done with the classes the day before. I looked over at Courtney, whose gait was short and bouncing. Her breath was shallow. I slowed down a bit. "Don't forget to breathe," I said. "Deep, slow. Stretch out and let the pace choose you."

"Pretty sure the pace that would choose me is back on my couch," she said.

"This was your idea, not mine."

"Tell me about her," she said.

"You have to breathe, or I'm not talking to you."

I waited her out, and at last she found the right posture, the right kick, the right landing. She glanced at me, appraisingly, the same way

Jessica had the day I'd helped her find more breath, more distance, more speed.

The girls would be assembling in the gym in a few hours, and I wouldn't be there. I wondered if Fitz had made it back from whatever ailed him, or if they'd had to call in someone else more long term. Someone to try and find the source of Jessica's attitude or Delia's secrets. Girls. I had never understood them, and having been one had never helped.

"I can tell you about her then, or I can tell you all the ways she's confused me since," I said.

"Start from the beginning."

There was no beginning. We'd been friends for so long, I couldn't remember the first time we'd met. But I tried: the year she showed up in junior high with a dead mother, a hated stepmother, an arrogance, and the best collection of lip gloss any of us had ever seen. The day we both stayed after school to see what the cross-country team was about. Seasons of meets, the giggling on the bus, the first time in our sophomore year when we'd beaten all the seniors on the track team and they'd shaving-creamed our lockers to full capacity. The overnights at my house. I left out the overnight at her house, the vomit-green sweater. When I got to senior year, I jumped around, skipping the problems with Beck and the trip we'd made to the stadium and the clinic just behind it.

When I got to the story of the state meet, Courtney stopped and leaned on her knees, gasping. "I thought you didn't run anymore," she gulped. "You're killing me."

I looked up. We'd come as far as the park. "We can rest for a few minutes," I said.

Courtney staggered to a nearby bench and sprawled across it. "Tell me about that morning at the state tournament, and slow down for once in your life. Tell me the details."

The truth of that morning lay heavy in my gut. I wanted to tell someone. I needed to. No one else knew how much Maddy had survived, only to be cut down. It wasn't fair to her. It wasn't fair to me. I didn't want to carry it around anymore.

I started with waking up to find her gone.

"Where was she?"

"Let me tell it, Courtney."

The assumption that she'd gone to warm up, to stretch. Normal. Coach at our door, looking to gather us all up for breakfast, even though neither of us would have eaten much. And then, with her return, the dawning realization that things weren't normal. Maddy changing in the bathroom, then sitting on the edge of the hotel bed, clutching herself. I saw her now so much more clearly: a little girl, skinny arms, legs scrawny in running shorts. A little girl hunched around her secret and her pain. A little girl holding on to my hand, not letting go. She must have been so scared.

I turned deeper into the park and took a shaking breath. She must have felt so alone.

Courtney sat up. "Wait. What?"

I hadn't gained control over my voice yet.

"Are you saying what I think you're saying?" She hopped up and started pacing. "Do you even know what you're saying?"

She'd called me smart not a week ago, but now I wasn't bright enough to understand my own story.

"You tell me," I said.

She paced, then took to the bench, hopping up on the back and tapping her feet on the seat. "That boyfriend—"

"It wasn't him," I said. "He said they never—you know."

"And you believed him?" she said.

"You didn't see his face."

"This was ten years ago. He's had a lot of time to prepare that reaction." Courtney's feet jittered in place some more. "It all hinges on where she was that morning."

"You're not a reporter for the school newspaper anymore," I said. "What's the point of any of this?"

"This isn't a story, Juliet. It's motive," she said.

"You think a miscarriage she had ten years ago holds the key to her murder," I said. I had left out one thing, the one thing that would

shut down this runaway train—the awful green sweater. I knew who'd
gotten Maddy pregnant, and he'd died long before she had.

Courtney turned her attention to me. "Miscarriage," she said.
"Probably not the key. But I think her abortion might be."

For a moment, I couldn't find my next breath. The park around me disappeared, and I was in a stuffy hotel room, willing a girl quickly becoming
a former friend to stand up and get it together for the sake of both our
futures. And then past that, past that to sitting in a cold car watching the
side of a long, ominous brick wall, waiting for the single, unmarked door
in it to open. So I could forget this place, and get back to my normal life.

Not a pregnancy test. The other one, she'd said. But later—she
might have had to come back for more tests, later, and she'd left me
home. Or she could have been lying.

Things had been happening to Maddy that I didn't understand,
would never understand.

I went to the bench and sat down heavily.

Courtney was watching me. "Your poker face needs work. OK,
let's try again. Start from the beginning. Tell me about Maddy. I have
the feeling a few mileposts may have changed."

The walk back to my neighborhood was slow and silent. I'd told
Courtney everything, even the part about not graduating. Then the
green sweater, watching her face grow ashen. I knew what I was saying
this time, no question.

Courtney opened her mouth to speak, but said nothing.

"I know," I said.

"I can't imagine—"

"I know." Our feet scuffed at the sidewalk. "But now you see why
all that stuff in the past doesn't matter."

"It all matters," Courtney said. "Everything she ever did, everyone
she ever knew. It's all relevant because murder victims usually know
their killers."

"You know what?" I stopped, forcing her to look at me. "I think you have a bias. You want it to be someone here. How else will you get that promotion or a chance to go to the big city?"

She sniffed at me. "That's fair. I probably do have a bias. I had one about you for a pretty long time." She narrowed her eyes over my shoulder. "Are all those cars at your house?"

I turned. At first I thought Courtney's coworkers had come back for another tour through our underwear drawers, that Courtney had pulled me away from home so they could get my mother alone. I wasn't sure what I was seeing until the cars began to snap into focus, one by one. In the driveway and along the front of our house sat Fitz's truck, Gretchen's junker, another car, a newer model I didn't recognize, and another car I almost did. A parking lot, but in front of my house. "Oh, no."

I took off running.

At first I heard Courtney behind me, forgetting her rhythm and new stride, then huffing and gasping. Then she was gone, and everything was a blur. I was full tilt winning this race, no trophies ahead of me, no prizes, no ribbons. Only the hard, cold fact of all these people in my house. What had happened in the short time I'd been gone? My mom—

My old dorm room flashed through my memory. That's where I'd taken the call. That's where it had all ended. If something happened to my mom now, I would never forget this run, this taste of bile in the back of my throat. I would never forgive Courtney, or Maddy, or anyone.

Up the steps to the door, I fumbled the handle, rattling the door in its frame and stumbling into the room. I took an awkward step, rolling my left ankle and landing on the floor at the feet of my dad's old chair and Fitz's cross-trainers.

He leapt up, and so did my mother, Gretchen, Shelly, Vincent, all of them in one room suddenly lunging for me and making surprised and then concerned noises that might have been words if any one of them were speaking above the others. I was so relieved to see my mother that I felt tears spring to my eyes. Fitz pulled me up and helped me hop to the chair while the others gathered around and my mother's voice finally won out. Of all people.

"Juliet, what in the world?"

"I thought—" I wasn't sure what I'd thought. I'd been away for an hour and come home to find my empty, silent home overrun. I looked around at them. I still didn't know what I thought. "What's going on?"

"It was your idea," Shelly said, returning to the spot she'd left on the couch. Gretchen perched on the arm of my chair, and leaned in to pat at me maternally. I got an eyeful of her bosom, and so did Vincent. He turned and retreated to the other side of the room.

Courtney opened the door. Her shoe managed to find a corner of the floor mat there, and she tripped into the room, too. Everyone turned to look. She waved them away and leaned on her knees, coughing into the floor.

"Were you being chased?" Vincent said. He went to the window and peered out.

"My idea," I said. "My idea was to—really? You're planning Maddy's funeral? Here?"

"Your mom was generous enough to invite us," Fitz said.

"We thought it would be quiet here," Shelly said. She had a pad of paper in front of her, the top page filled with notes. "We've made a lot of progress, but we still have a lot to get done. Is there any more coffee, Mrs. Townsend?" She got up and led the way. Gretchen jumped up with her empty mug and followed along. Vincent hesitated, then hurried after them.

Courtney's coughs were gaining strength. "Mom," I called. "Can you bring some water for Officer Howard?"

"And an ice pack for Juliet's ankle, I think, Joan," Fitz added. He knelt in front of me and took my leg gently up on his knee. My ankle was tender and growing fat.

"Is it—going OK?" I said.

"Looks like you've got a sprain," Fitz said. "Oh, you mean the— yes, I suppose. As well as you can expect. Some people have more ideas about things than they should, given their tenuous relationship with Maddy."

"Shelly's good at getting things done," I said.

Fitz smiled at me. "Your mom is, too."

Gretchen came into the room with a glass of water. She took in the scene of my ankle, hissing through her teeth. "Seen that before, haven'tcha, Coach?"

She would have known what to call him, if she'd ever come to a single one of Maddy's meets. Fitz and I glanced at each other.

Courtney gulped at her water, keeping an eye on Gretchen as she returned to the kitchen, brushing past my mother, who brought out a plastic bag filled with ice and wrapped in a dish towel. "Ouch, Juliet, and just when you'd taken up running again." She handed the pack off to Fitz. He pulled a cushion off the back of the couch and transferred my foot to it. The pack, even through the cloth, was harsh on my hot skin.

"I'll get you some juice," she said, turning back to the kitchen.

Fitz rearranged the pillow, higher, and the ice.

"Do you have medical training?" Courtney said.

Fitz didn't look up. "First aid, a bit. It helps out on the track to have someone who's ready with the bandages."

"You seem pretty—familiar." She glanced at Fitz's hand on my leg. "With the protocol, I mean."

"Juliet's an old pro at rolling an ankle. She'll be back in no time."

"What about Coach Trenton?"

Fitz stood up. "What about him?"

"Does he have the same first-aid training?"

"Sure. But Mike's better suited to motivating the girls," Fitz said. "I'm just the hired hand. The fetch-and-carry."

"Don't be ridiculous, Fitz," I said. "You're the heart of the team."

Fitz ducked his head. "Sweet of you to say, Jules, but Mike—well, maybe he was always the brains, then." He looked down at my ankle and reached to shift the pack again, but stopped. From the kitchen came the sound of the laugh Gretchen reserved for the Mid-Night. Her coffee either had a bit of the Irish, or she'd taken a new shine to the man who would now never be her stepson-in-law. Probably because she still thought of herself as next of kin, with the windfall of Maddy's estate coming. "I guess I'd take heart over brains, if it came down to it."

Courtney had spotted a photo of me from my track days across the room and made a beeline for it. "So you don't make your decisions together? I guess I thought you'd been a team for a long time."

I reached out and patted Fitz's arm. He gave me a distracted squeeze back. "More than thirty years."

"Remind me. Where did you coach before you came to Midway?"

"Small town up north, Minnesota. A high school."

"A couple of seasons. I remember now. And before that?"

Fitz gave me an uneasy glance. "A college in Washington state."

"Also a couple of seasons," Courtney said. She picked the frame off the table. "And before that—another school. A girls' school. You've been at Midway High a long time. It seems to have worked out for you better than the other places you've taught. Can I say 'taught,' or is 'coached' more accurate?"

Fitz drew himself tall. "We always have teaching appointments— we've both taught physical education, personal training, health, sex ed—"

Courtney turned on her heel. "What's that?"

A light blush gained on Fitz's neck. "Any health topic, really."

"Could have sworn you said—"

"Sometimes we teach human sexuality courses," Fitz said. "Not at Midway, but . . . we have."

"Is it uncomfortable teaching, uh, what are we calling it? Human sexuality. Is it uncomfortable teaching human sexuality to young women?"

I couldn't see how it could be more uncomfortable than this conversation. "Courtney, lighten up," I said, at the same time Fitz answered.

"Yes," he said.

Courtney shrugged, set down her glass. She got out her phone and thumbed through messages. "Sorry. The job. You should know that Juliet coached me today. Taught me a few things."

A few things about running as well as a few things about Maddy. I couldn't look at Fitz. He'd be heartbroken when he found out about Maddy's pregnancy. He might even be angry that an appointment at some shady, blank building had been what kept us from running the race of all our lives.

And then it occurred to me.

He already knew.

I'd been a kid at the time, but Fitz was a grown-up, someone who'd taught human physiology. Maybe he and Coach had known the whole time what Maddy was going through. The panic over tampons and maxi pads. The resignation that neither of us would race.

"You knew," I said. "Didn't you?"

Fitz looked between Courtney and me, his features traveling the distance from confusion to stricken. "Knew what?"

"You knew Maddy was—that she was—" I lowered my voice. "What was happening that morning at state. You would have recognized it, even if I didn't."

He eyed Courtney.

"Oh, I know all about it," she said, waving her phone and then returning to it. "Don't worry about me."

Fitz paced toward the door, paused to look outside so that I wondered if he would simply leave. He grated his palms against one another and stalked back. "I wasn't sure at first," he said. "Mike said—but I knew that boyfriend was no good for her."

Courtney waved her phone again, at me.

"The boyfriend claims they never . . . slept together." I struggled to believe I was using these words, having this conversation. This was still Fitz. Fitz was almost a parent to me, to Maddy. He may have taught sex ed at some snowbound private school for girls, but I'd certainly never had this conversation with him. The closest we'd ever come to talking about sex was the night Maddy was killed, and he and Coach had suggested Maddy's dad had molested her.

I'd been hiding that fact for so long, I'd forgotten the source. I blinked at him, not wanting to repeat Coach's accusation to him. I didn't want to say the words, not again.

"We trust what the boyfriend says?" Fitz said, turning to Courtney. "Of course they slept together—you should have seen how possessive he was, how he hung around all the time. It was all Mike could do to get her to run. Who else could it have been—"

A shutter came down on Fitz's face. He remembered the conversation now: *sexualized*, but not by an age-appropriate boyfriend. By her own father.

In the kitchen, Gretchen's laugh was a bray. He turned toward it, and then away. "Tell your mother," he said, backing toward the door. "That I—whatever they want. Whatever they decide is fine by me."

Courtney stood up and followed behind, but the screen door smacked closed in her face. "What was that?" she said to me.

"That was Fitz remembering he'd left the iron on." I sat back to await my juice. We hadn't had juice in the house in a long time.

CHAPTER TWENTY-FIVE

I received juice. And a Danish. And fresh strawberries, cut into bite-size chunks. Courtney declined to stay and helped herself to the door instead, thumbing at her phone and distracted in her farewell. The other guests left shortly afterward with a few *tut-tut*s over my ankle from Gretchen. Vincent hesitated near the door, then finally let himself out. I held the plate on my elevated leg as my mother stood over me, fussing with the ice pack. This was more doting than I'd seen since my childhood, more fresh food than had been stocked in our house in weeks.

"Did Shelly bring all this?" I was already calculating how ashamed I needed to feel at the state of our home and lives. I couldn't believe I'd been roped into helping with that reunion, but I still had no plans to attend. What could I say to anyone I saw there? And now half the town had been inside our home-sweet-hovel.

Except that the place seemed tidy, even clean, especially after the ransacking Courtney's fellows had given it the day before.

I glanced over at a section of baseboard trim peeking from behind the couch. Clean.

My mother seemed to be handling all this fine. Better than fine. Nothing in the kitchen was billowing smoke or beeping incessantly. And this plate on my leg: it was a marvel, and the fork sitting on the edge of it gleamed.

"I got the food," my mother said. "I remembered there was a place out there where they'd trade you doughnuts for dollars."

I felt a strange smile on my face. Where had the dollars come from? I put the plate aside. "I need to take a shower."

"But your ankle—why don't you just relax for a while? Did you want coffee?"

She disappeared into the kitchen to cater to my next whim.

The change was too immediate, too startling. I didn't like it. She moved too fast, too much. She'd been out while I slept, and invited people into our house without even mentioning it. Spending money from mysterious sources. If it turned out that someone like Fitz or Coach had palmed her some cash, I would be obligated to die of embarrassment.

I picked at a fat strawberry on the plate and popped it into my mouth. Delicious. What was she up to?

The worst part: I had nowhere else to go. The Mid-Night remained closed. The high school, too stuffed with memory. Lu's door, closed to me. I shoved a forkful of Danish into my mouth, and chewed on it and on everything that had happened that morning.

A strawberry seed had got stuck between my teeth. I used the tip of my tongue to worry at it distractedly. Across the room, the photo of me in my track uniform had been turned at a new angle.

What had Courtney said? Murder victims usually know their killers.

And the murder had happened here.

That was simple math, one-plus-one stuff, surely. Someone Maddy knew in town had killed her. Well, everyone Maddy knew in town, I knew.

I sat up. How simple could the math be?

I counted them off on my fingers. Beck. Gretchen. Me. Coach. Fitz. My mother.

My mother chose that moment to bring me a mug of steaming coffee, made with cream—real cream, even—and a little sugar. Just the way I liked, but I hadn't realized she knew that.

She went back to the kitchen, where I could hear her puttering and humming under her breath.

Shelly, I continued. Courtney. Girls from our track team and from other track teams—none I could put a name to. Yvonne, but just that night with the too-big tip. And Vincent, who couldn't be left out.

But that list was unrealistic—too short, too close to home. Who else did Maddy know?

Are you Juliet? Or are you Kristina?

I nearly spilled my mug.

I knew who Kristina was now. Kristina Switzer, the name etched into that state-tournament trophy in the Midway High brag case like a slap in the face. What I didn't know: how had Vincent known who Kristina was, and how had Maddy?

Kristina had just made the short list of suspects. Only Vincent could tell me how she'd gotten there.

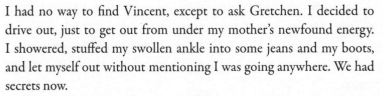

I had no way to find Vincent, except to ask Gretchen. I decided to drive out, just to get out from under my mother's newfound energy. I showered, stuffed my swollen ankle into some jeans and my boots, and let myself out without mentioning I was going anywhere. We had secrets now.

The car gagged and coughed. When at last my engine turned over, I drove not out to Gretchen's—I wasn't sure my car had enough gas to get there and back, actually—but to the other side of town where Yvonne lived. She owed me my tips from that night at the Mid-Night, and I needed the money.

I needed the money.

I swept wet hair off my neck and shook my head. Always. Always, this is who I would have to be.

At Yvonne's, the door was propped open. "Von?"

"Hey, Julie Bean," her voice called back. "You're out and about early today." She came and unlocked the screen, held it wide for me. A wad of pink gum rolled around in her mouth. Her feet were bare, with nails the color of some exotic bird. A small, shaggy dog came running from the back of the house, panting and dancing. "Never mind him," she said, scooting the dog back from me with her foot.

Inside, it smelled of cigarettes and bacon. A large TV lit up one corner of the dark living room. The sound had been set so low, it was nearly muted. For some reason I thought of all I'd missed by leaving college when I did, of never living with another woman my age or having any roommates other than my mother. I stood looking down at the dog, not knowing how to start. Always, the girl gone begging. I chickened out. "Have you heard anything about the Mid-Night opening again?"

"I think we've got the bar cracked open in a day or so," she said. "But that business with Billy—I don't know when they'll open the motel. I mean, surely they will, right?"

None of us had met the owners. They lived on the East Coast and only dealt with Billy. He threw in their existence whenever it supported a point he wanted to make, but he normally liked to forget anyone else had a say in what went on there. They'd have to have a say now.

"Maybe you or Lu can be the new manager," Yvonne said. "That would be wild."

"Not me," I said. "Maybe Lu wants to run it, but I don't."

"And then you'd work for Lu? Can't think of a way for that to ruin things."

"Things are pretty much ruined, Von."

"Yeah." She waved me toward a lumpy couch. I sat, and the little dog hopped up on my lap. I'd never been around a dog, any dog. I patted the top of its head, hoping it would leave me alone. The dog seemed to enjoy the patting and settled in for more. "Buster," Yvonne said. "Down."

Buster's tail thumped, but he didn't get down. He curled up in a ball, his warm little body snuggled against my thigh.

"Never should have taken on someone else's dog," Yvonne muttered.

"I thought people adopted strays all the time."

"He's not a stray. His owner comes over most weekends—whatever, right?—except now I have a full-time dog and his owner's only *part*-time."

This conversation seemed so far afield of where I needed to go, I didn't know how to get back. My palms hadn't itched in days, but now they were sweating. I rubbed them against my jeans. That money was mine. We had a deal—and yet I couldn't bring myself to say the words. I didn't like owing people money, or having someone pay my way, even for a moment. But I couldn't seem to form the words to ask for what was mine. It was still asking.

I hadn't minded stealing as much as I did asking for what was coming to me.

But I cared that everyone would know about the stealing more than anything else. Courtney knew. My mother. All those cops. It would be around town in no time. I didn't have a reputation to keep sacred, but I'd killed any chance of finding another job in town.

I finally thought of something to say. "Do you know someone named Kristina Switzer? She went to Midway."

"The runner. Would have figured you two knew each other."

"Missed her by a year," I said. "Were you friends?"

"Those girls were never friends with anyone but each other," she said.

I reached for Buster and ran my fingers through his fur. I wished I could have said she was wrong. "But you know her?"

"Everybody knew—" She looked up, frowning. "Why do you want to know about her?"

"Maddy might have been in town to see her."

The pink gob of gum made another appearance as her eyes shifted back and forth across me a few times. "I doubt it. She's dead."

I must have squeezed Buster. He yipped and leapt away from me, resettling at the other end of the couch with a disappointed look in my direction.

"Sorry, I—what? How did she die?" Maddy's gray face rose from memory, but now her skin had the sheen of silver plating.

"Suicide. Went crazy, swallowed some kind of poison. That's what I heard, anyway, just gossip from the bar—oh, dang! I owe you your tips. Hang on." She hopped up, disappeared, her bare feet slapping the floor. I fell back, shuddering with relief.

I turned to the TV in time to see what looked like the Mid-Night on a news promo and then a weather map and a paunchy white guy swinging his arm this way and that.

Then Yvonne's heel-heavy steps came back. She placed a fat roll of bills, rubber-banded, in my hand. It was heavy. I clutched the money, then realized how wild-eyed I must have looked. I stuffed the bills into my jeans pocket and held a hand on the bulge to reassure myself it stayed there.

"It's about three hundred," she said, too kindly. She'd noticed that starved, fearful look of the mouse scrambling for crumbs. "Maybe the motel will open up this weekend and we can do it again. Maybe after the *funeral*."

My stomach gave a lurch. Now that I had my money, I couldn't think of anything to say, or how to get myself to the door. Then Yvonne's phone, lying on the floor next to her chair, starting buzzing and singing.

"I'll let you—"

"Just a second." She raised a finger to hold me where I sat. But the conversation didn't end in a second, or a minute. After a few minutes of listening to Yvonne getting digs in at her part-time boyfriend, I pantomimed an escape and stood. My ankle stung, tight in its boot.

"I'm in the *middle of something*," Yvonne said into the phone, following me up and toward the door. Buster leapt up and clattered after us, yipping at top volume. "I'm not always in the middle of something, but right now I am. *Buster*. Well, it's none of your business who's here."

I thought I knew why the part-time guy had left a full-time watchdog. "I'll just—" More hand signals passed between us, with Yvonne's still insisting I stay, traffic-cop style. Yvonne turned her back to me and hissed into the phone. "I guess you'll just need to hang out here more often yourself if that's a concern of yours."

On the TV, I thought I saw the Mid-Night again. Had something happened? I leaned in to take in the screen, and my ankle announced itself. Teetering, I grabbed for the nearest surface, and put my hand down on a nearby bookshelf. My fingers grazed a set of keys.

I grasped them. No itch. Not even a tickle in my hands.

And yet the keys found the inside of my pocket before I knew what I'd done, and why. When Yvonne finally waved me out the door, without even noticing what was happening on the TV behind her, I was eager to leave. I held the keys and the roll of cash to my hip, giddy and afraid of each, of both, of everything.

CHAPTER TWENTY-SIX

The keys bulged in one pocket, the money in the other.

I drove to a gas station, putting a few bucks in the tank while I fretted over how I could replace the keys without admitting that I'd stolen them.

At home, my mother's door was shut tight. She must have gone back in for a nap after so much company that morning. I slipped by as quietly as possible, then prowled back and forth in my room, not sure what I would do next. I didn't want the keys. I could just throw them out.

She'd have to replace them. Her car key. Her house key. She'd have to change locks. She would drive herself crazy wondering what she'd done with them.

I could drop them outside the bar, as though she'd done it the last time she'd been there.

Maybe. I paced some more. The idea had flaws.

My pacing slowed. I didn't like the plan, but something inside me wanted to go with it anyway. The Mid-Night. As much as I never wanted to see that place again, I wanted to see that place again. Von's keys would open the bar, maybe even the office. But not the rooms.

And I wanted to see that room.

What had I done with the extra key card? I thought back to that night, the next morning. I hadn't put it with the perfume or with the things Courtney's team had found. I'd put it somewhere special, not knowing that I'd been saving it for myself.

I knelt by the bed and pried up the edge of the loose wallpaper. The card was there, of course, tucked into the baseboard. There was a possibility it wouldn't work, that the magnetic strip would have been damaged in its hiding place, or that the system would have checked Maddy out automatically after a day or so. Or—so many things.

I heard a noise. At the front of the house, the door opened, then closed.

A raw fear gripped me. So many people had been inside this house in the last two days and, with the math I'd done, one of them was likely a killer.

What had Maddy heard in her last minutes? She wouldn't have known—she couldn't have—that each noise she heard was the last. The last knock on the door, the last footfall, the lamp crashing off the bedside table, the last chance to draw attention and rescue. She wouldn't have known that the simple click of a door closing could be the end of her life.

My eyes swept the room for a weapon. I grabbed the largest of my trophies from the dresser and crept into the hallway, wielding it over my head.

At the end of the hall, I paused and listened. My blood was pounding in my ears so that I couldn't locate a footstep or a breath.

Pressed against the wall, I wasn't sure I could do what I needed to do. Maddy. I had to keep reminding myself how hard she fought.

I took a step and leaned around the corner into view and pivoted directly into my mother.

We both recoiled, screaming.

"Juliet, what on *earth*?"

"I thought—" I didn't know what I'd thought. That Maddy's killer had come for me? How likely was that? I lowered the trophy. But then I'd thought she was still asleep, in her room. The parameters we'd been living by were breached. "I guess I'm a little punchy," I said.

"No one blames you." She took in the trophy. "Your life changed this week."

This conversation alone provided the evidence. Not to mention that my mother had just arrived from some sort of errand. She wore an old jacket. A raincoat, but thankfully with no belt.

"Where were you?"

She slipped out of the coat and opened the closet door. "My expertise as a widow has finally been put to use."

The trophy slid from my fingers to the floor with a thump. "What?"

"Arrangements for Maddy." She hung up the coat and closed the door. "Gretchen isn't any help, and that young man . . . well, he's paying for everything, but he shouldn't be bothered with decisions. And Fitz didn't show up. With how quickly this has had to come together, you'd think—but we all do what we can, I suppose. I know that better than anyone. Thank goodness for Shelly—oh, and before I forget, she sent that home for you."

She gestured to a thick envelope lying on the couch. I'd forgotten to tell Shelly I didn't need the copy of our yearbook.

"She told me to tell you—six sharp. *Sharp*. She made me say it back to her, just like that."

"Six . . . oh, no," I said, fighting a rushing dread. "What day is today?"

"Sweetheart, it's Saturday," she said. "Six sharp tonight."

Crap. I had no idea how I would be able to face Shelly and the rest of them. I didn't have the right clothes, the right makeup. I didn't have a date. Too late I realized they'd all be married. Paired up to dance, all of them laughing, talking about their jobs without shame. I didn't even have a shameful job anymore. I was freelancing in shame, unpaid. They'd have kids, houses, minivans, vacation snapshots, bills paid. And I had nothing.

I reached for the trophy at my feet. The silver runner at the top was tarnished, dusty. Second place, regionals. It had all mattered so much, once.

I had pulled into Gretchen's long driveway before I realized I couldn't remember why I'd come. Then I turned a corner in the drive and saw a passel of police cruisers parked all around the house. A cop held up his hand and gestured me forward and to roll down the window. It didn't roll down, so I cracked the door.

"Whoa," he said, hand to his gun. "What's your business here?"

"I'm a . . . friend. What's happened?"

"Not at liberty. How do you know the homeowner?"

I was grateful he hadn't said "the deceased."

"Everyone knows everyone here, Gary," Courtney said, walking up behind the other officer. It was true. I hadn't known his name until now, but I'd seen Gary policing the parking lot of the Mid-Night before. Sometimes he policed the bar, too, with a beer in front of him.

Gary wandered off. I got out and looked around. "Is Gretchen OK?" I asked Courtney.

"Shaken up. He didn't tell you? A break-in—or at least she says so. I can't tell that anything is missing in that place."

"Crowded, isn't it?"

"You've been to visit recently?"

I tried not to hear the accusation. I could feel the keys in my pocket as I nodded, the blush creeping up my cheeks. I'd finally done it. I'd stolen from a friend, a friend who was alive and would suffer the loss of what I'd taken. "After Maddy, I came to see if I could do anything."

"Did you? Do anything?"

"I took a look in Maddy's room," I said. She would have heard this already, I decided. There was no chance Gretchen hadn't mentioned it. "Seemed dusty, but otherwise exactly as she left it years ago."

Courtney nodded, and I was grateful for being able to tell the truth. Part of the truth. I suddenly remembered the running man loose from his trophy from Maddy's room. But I'd lost track of him. Courtney and I stared up at the house while I retraced the silver man's path from this house to my lap, then to the floor of the car, under my seat.

It was still there. With a shiver, I realized it had been there the whole time—including the night a cop had returned my car to the house after the handcuff incident.

I leaned back against the door with a thud. "What—um, what does Gretchen say is missing?"

Courtney looked back at the house. "Something from Maddy's room, but she can't say what it was. It's a bust. But the window was left open, so someone was here."

"The window in Maddy's room?" I stood up straight. Someone had really broken in, but looking for what? "That was sealed tight when I was here."

"Probably just some kids messing around. Maybe they saw the news and figured out how to make a terrible situation even worse. People are like that. We'll check into it."

It seemed to me they were still checking on quite a few things. "Anything on the diamond yet?"

Courtney made a face and glanced all around before she turned her back on the house and said in a low voice, "Funny you should ask."

"Not funny, really," I said. "I have nothing else to occupy my time, you know. Until the Mid-Night opens."

"Have you looked for a different job?" she said. "I mean, just in case? And what about the reunion?"

"What about it?"

"Maybe you could use it to . . . network?" she said.

I glared at her.

"OK, fine. You're not—bringing a date or anything, right?"

We were in competition again. "And where do you I think I'd get one of those?" I said.

"Good, OK."

Had I agreed to be Courtney's plus-one? For the briefest moment, I imagined walking in on Vincent's muscular arm. "Funny I should ask?"

"Right, the diamond. We can't seem to track down any jeweler who will admit they purchased or brokered a purchase of Maddy's diamond. We found the guy who cut the fake for her, but he says he handed her back the original gem, too." Courtney looked at me pointedly.

"So she sold it on her own. Maybe she was in town to drop it off—"

"Do you know anyone here with two cents to rub together? And, besides, no one's come forward to say they had a meeting scheduled with her."

"Would they come forward? If they were buying a diamond that shouldn't have been for sale?"

"Didn't say I thought she was selling it." Courtney chewed at her pinkie nail and looked over her shoulder at the house. She didn't understand how unlikely it was that Maddy would have come here at all, let alone put the diamond in Gretchen's care. But I saw why she was attached to that story. Something was stolen, but no one could say what—except I knew at least one thing missing from the house, because I'd taken it.

"Did something happen today?" I said, suddenly eager to get away from the subject of Maddy's room. "I saw the motel on the news, I think."

"Billy's arraignment was today," she said. "He's probably not going to miss a beat, you know? We hardly have a thing on him, and that very young witness changed her story yesterday. Convicted, he'd have to register as a sex offender, but he's probably going to walk. Slap on the wrist at best. That was my big bust."

"What about the girls?"

"There's always plenty of them," she said. "He'll have no trouble—"

"No, I mean—will they get some help or something?"

Courtney looked at her shoes. "We don't know who they are. But if they came forward, no, help is probably not what they would get."

"Would they get a slap on the wrist?"

"Now *they* would probably get public humiliation," she said. "As if the guys who paid them didn't exist at all. Double standards are the *best*. Hey, speaking of public humiliation, what are you wearing to this thing?"

"What—oh, the reunion." I hadn't thought about it. "My uniform from the Mid-Night."

"That will turn some heads."

"No sense in pretending to be something I'm not," I said. Except I wasn't a housekeeper anymore, either. I looked at the clock on the dash. I needed to get going. I had yet to do Shelly's bidding for the reunion and would need to get cleaned up. It was a lot to ask of someone who didn't want to attend the event at all. "I'll wear a dress, a regular one. It's black. I'll probably have to wear it to the funeral, too." It was the dress I'd worn to my father's, in any case.

"That's lucky, since the funeral is right before the reunion."

I waited for the punch line. Shelly had said . . . but she was joking, surely.

Courtney looked at me shrewdly. "You haven't heard? I thought with your mom involved, you'd know all about it. Hey, are you OK?"

The scene around us receded into the background. Courtney grabbed me, opened the door of my car, and let me fall into the seat. I held my head in my hands. "Right before? Like . . . at the hotel?"

"A memorial service. She's being cremated—hey, Gary, can you see if there's a bottle of water in one of the rigs?" She squatted down beside me and after a short silence, a bottle of water appeared in my narrowed vision. I took it and held it against my face. Courtney grabbed it, opened it, and put it back in my hands. "The committee you put together decided this was the best way to get mourners to the service. What with her not, you know, living here anymore."

With her not being a person people liked. I gulped at the water until my vision cleared.

"I didn't mean for Shelly to turn the reunion into a funeral," I said.

Courtney smirked toward the house. Her compatriots were spilling from the front door and down the porch stairs. "I'm actually looking forward to the reunion now," she said. "The speeches will be tremendous."

They would want me to speak. I gulped at the water, then let the empty bottle drop to the floor. Courtney watched the bottle roll under the seat. I retrieved it before she offered, before she reached for the bottle and found the thing missing from Gretchen's house. "Who?" I said. "Who's giving speeches?"

"Only everyone who might have killed her," Courtney said.

CHAPTER TWENTY-SEVEN

At the Mid-Night, I parked across the road at the construction site and walked in, keeping to the edge of the lot. There were no news crews or anyone at all. They'd moved Billy's clunker out to the back of the lot and set up crime-scene tape across the front of the building. The place looked totally abandoned now.

I felt bad for Billy despite everything, and I didn't want to. I didn't need to.

I stopped. Shadows from the high sun on the face of the Mid-Night played with my eyes. Someone might be there by the stairs, or in that dark spot near the vending machines. The sun was high overhead. A brisk wind rose, raking over the tall grass at the edge of the parking lot and lifting my hair. I hugged my elbows and imagined the women who'd been employed here secretly. The strays.

So many girls never had the chance to find out who they really were before other people started telling them. Maddy was among them, and I didn't mean just that Maddy had died too young. It all started long before that belt, that railing. *Sexualized*, Coach and Fitz had called it. I had my own memories: boys grabbing at me on the bus, jeering faces over Southtown High sweatshirts, men the age of my father calling out from cars as I ran. The more I catalogued my own experience, the more panicked I felt to understand it, to stop it. God, when did it *end*? The girls at Midway High, showing off their bodies, taunting each other, calling each other names. Giving the worst of it to each other.

At last I made my way to the nearest stairs and up and around the end of the building. I paused at the section of railing where Maddy had been hanged, then slipped around to the courtyard side of the walkway. Here, the shadows were deeper. At the door to two-oh-two, the crime-scene tape had been removed. I pulled out the card and swiped, and the light flashed green. At the moment I used my forearm to push down the handle, I heard something under the wind.

Before I could look, I was grasped from behind, plucked off my feet, and shoved into the black room, a hand over my mouth cutting off my scream. I kicked and raged, scratching and swinging with every ounce of fight I had. There might yet be something to knock down in this room. Not here. Not yet. Not me.

The door closed behind us, leaving us in almost total darkness. "Quiet," a man's voice said. "It's me."

I froze. I recognized the voice but couldn't place it. The killer. The killer was someone I knew. I raced through the math again, but I couldn't make anything add up through my own panic.

"I'm going to let you go now, OK? No screaming. It's just me."

He let me slide out of his arms to my own feet and held me upright when my knees threatened to buckle. I ripped myself out of reach and turned, listening as someone fumbled at the wall switch. A shallow pool of light from the fallen lamp lit his anxious face.

"What the—Vincent, what the hell?" I slapped at him until he grabbed my hands. I had backed him up to the wall. Now his shoulder bumped the other light switch. In the new glare, we blinked at each other.

"I didn't know it was you, not at first."

I was shaking. "Who were you hoping it was?"

"Someone I could beat to a bloody pulp." He showed me a place on his arm where I'd gotten in a good gouge. A welt rose the length of the scratch. "Guess I played that wrong."

"No kidding. Jumping out at me after everything that's—don't let that blood drip in here." Always giving advice to possible murderers. "Why are you here?"

He was staring past me to the room. A strangled sound escaped him. He pushed past me, rushing from one vision of horror to the next, from the toppled furniture and torn sheets, to the bathroom's cracked mirror and back. The groan in his throat turned into a pathetic cattle low.

"What—" he said. "What happened here?"

I watched him carefully, but he seemed legitimately confused by the wrecked room. "She fought for her life."

"Can you believe what I thought? When I heard she'd been killed at some cheap—" He turned from me.

"It's OK," I said. "It is really cheap." I kicked at the matted gray-green carpet, which had certainly supplied the color of Maddy's dad's sweater in my memory.

"I thought she'd been with some guy," he said. "And you know what? I wanted to kill him. Really kill him, not just a thing you say. Actually take his neck in my bare hands and crush it."

His eyes were sunk in shadow, but I felt held in place by them. I glanced toward the door.

"And then," he said, "I wanted to kill *her*."

I believed him. I believed him not because I'd decided he was capable of such a thing, but because I felt, deep, the same inclination. I wanted to kill her, too. For doing this to me, for sweeping in after so many years and giving me hope. She'd taken both of us with her, again, and at the same time, here I was, alone.

There were patches of dark dust on the surfaces of the TV knobs and dresser handles where the police had checked for fingerprints. This room would have to be cleaned someday soon.

No one else would be here to do it.

I couldn't let anyone else do it.

"You wanted to kill her but she was already dead," I said. "And that seemed like the worst part. You couldn't even tell her how bad you felt that she was gone." Vincent's gaze was heavy. "My dad. I really wanted to tell him how sad I was. About his death." I managed a smile, but it was false. I let it slide away. There were things I was angry about that would never be resolved, and now Maddy was another one of them.

"And then." Vincent's voice was a nail pried from old wood. "And then I wanted to kill myself."

And then? Would he continue? Did he not know that there was a lower point, yet, when you had accepted your own fate but found your-self too weak to go through with it? The point at which you understood you had made not a single ripple in the pond, and neither would your loss.

Vincent's head dropped. He grabbed at his ears, as though to block anything anyone would say. I thought I knew why he'd agreed to the slapdash memorial service. It hurt less to let it pass him by, to let someone else push him through the motions.

I went to him and, after an awkward moment, placed my hand on his arm. He reached for it, and pulled me against him. This time he didn't topple on me but held me against his chest. We stood in silence for a long moment. The air had changed around us, or was it only that I couldn't breathe from how tight he held on?

The palms of my hands began to hum.

The wind pushed against the door, time and the rest of the world hoping to intercede. To interrupt. To put a stop to this, whatever this was or could be. I could almost feel the shudder of the building in the wind, the beginnings of a quake that wanted to swallow me up for entertaining ideas. Vincent's breath was shallow.

I stood on my toes and caught the edge of his mouth with mine, flicking my tongue at his lips. The groan returned, and I felt an answering hum of blood rushing not just through my palms, but throughout my body.

Vincent slid his hands down my back, my ass, my legs, then rubbed them up my body again, taking me up against him. Our mouths tore at each other until he dropped his face to my neck. He bit at the thin fabric of my shirt, moaning against my skin. I scratched my fingers across his back, luxuriating. It had been a long time since a man had held on to me with desire.

And then the moan in Vincent's throat caught. "Maddy," he sobbed against my neck.

We both froze.

I dropped my arms, and he let me step away.

"I'm—I'm so—"

"No," I said. "Don't."

"I don't know what I was thinking."

"Probably the same thing I was," I said. "Nothing much." But that wasn't the truth. We'd both been thinking of Maddy. Vincent, seeking comfort. Me, keeping track. Me, taking and taking.

The Mid-Night shuddered again. This time, Vincent looked at me. "What was that?"

"The wind—"

A fist thundered against the door.

We looked at one another. He held a finger to his lips.

"Police," boomed a dry voice. "Open up or we'll break it down."

I rushed to the door and swung it open. Loughton stood with his hand to his gun, and behind him, a line of other officers, Gary, smirking. Below in the courtyard stood two figures.

Beck shook his head. "Wow," he said.

"Of course," Courtney called. "Why wouldn't you be in there? Who's in there with you, I wonder?"

"No one," I said.

Loughton shifted against the doorway. "Sir?" he said.

Vincent hesitated, finally appearing, squinting into the sun.

"Mr. Beckwith here happened to witness your assault and made us aware of the situation," Loughton said. He eyeballed me, then Vincent and grinned. "One of many possible situations, I should say."

"Are there any charges?" Courtney called.

In a low voice so that even I could barely hear him, Loughton said, "Any charges, there, Miss?"

I shook my head.

"No charges up here, Howard," he said. "Any charges down there?"

Courtney's laugh was a bark. "God no. I'm sick of them both. Get them out."

I led the way around the end of the second floor to the far stairs and hurried down them. Vincent and Loughton lagged behind, but Beck cut through the center breezeway and caught me at the edge of the parking lot, grabbing my elbow as I tried to pass. "What kind of friend are you, anyway?"

"Not yours." I shook him off.

"Nobody ever made that mistake," he said. "But this—" He waved his arm to the stairwell, where Vincent and Loughton descended.

"Careful, there, Beck," I said. "You're caring an awful lot about things that are none of your business. What are you doing here, anyway?"

He blinked at me, and reared back a step at the sight of Vincent. "Keeping an eye on things—"

"On me, you mean."

Vincent came up to me and tried to pull me aside. "I just want to say—"

"Please don't," I said, flinging off his hand. I was tired of men touching me and talking to me right now. "Vincent, Beck. Beck, Vincent. You two have so much in common."

They sized each other up. Beck looked away first. "Not as much as you might think," he said.

"You're the guy?" Vincent said. "If I find out you laid a hand on her—"

"You didn't cover that during pillow talk, Jules?" Beck said.

"Leave her alone. That—that was my fault," Vincent said, wincing. He held up his arm. The welt where I'd scratched him was garish. Blood dripped in a trickle through the fine dark hairs on his forearm. "Does this need stitches?"

"I would know, with all of my medical-school training," I said. They stood staring down at me. "I don't know. Wait here. I can get you something for it."

I left them, jogging across the lot to the vending area. I let myself in with Yvonne's keys and then tried a few of them on the cart closet before finding the right one. I grabbed a clean hand towel and a bandage.

Back outside, I lifted the lid on the ice machine. Empty. I'd forgotten the leak.

A lone ice chip sat at the bottom of the bin, defiant. I let the bin lid fall closed, and started back out. The trickle of water out to the lot had long ago dried up. At the edge of the curb, I stopped and shaded my eyes.

Courtney and Loughton conferred at their car. Vincent and Beck formed an uneasy pair, both determined to stick it out to say whatever they wanted to say to me.

I turned back to the machine and lifted the lid again.

My hand shook on the handle. Time slowed, stopped. I imagined the thing I was supposed to do. Then the thing I knew I would do.

I reached into the depths of the ice bin and plucked out Maddy's diamond, loose and heavy and worth more than her life. Worth far more than mine. I held it in my hand and then I closed my fist around it.

CHAPTER TWENTY-EIGHT

The diamond in my pocket, I went back to the office and ran the towel under cool water. The bar would have ice. I felt for Yvonne's keys, but at the door to the bar, I stopped. I could see the table where we'd had our last drink. That last chance to be with her, and I'd left it lying there. And now I had the sum of her life in my pocket. It was possible no one would ever be punished for what had happened to her. For any of it.

And now Billy would go free, too, and, in his wake, leave the Mid-Night tainted, our jobs lost, and all those strays without anywhere to turn.

If only the police had turned up something definitive in Billy's room. And then I realized: Billy's room would have its own freezer.

Here was a last chance I couldn't leave on the table. I grabbed the front-desk keys from the drop box at the door and slipped out the front door and through the breezeway to the courtyard.

My hands shook as I let myself in, looking all the while over my shoulder for one of them to come after me.

Inside, I closed the door behind me and stood in the dark, waiting for the stench of unwashed man and old pizza boxes to waft over me. But the room was just a room. I hit the lights. The room was configured differently than a guest room, with a narrow galley kitchen up front and the bed and TV hidden behind a screen. He'd removed the country cornfield prints from the wall and redecorated with a series of beer-logo mirrors and neon signs. The room smelled a little dusty and close, but not like the dumpster bin.

I hurried, taking in as much as I could without touching anything, then throwing out the rules. I opened drawers and rifled through whatever was there, hoping I would know what I was looking for when I saw it. In the bathroom, I checked below the bottom vanity drawer—it was a good hiding space—and for any loose wallpaper. I stood on the toilet and pushed at the ceiling tiles. Nothing.

Back in the kitchen, I tried all the drawers and cabinets, but found only canned goods and boxed pasta. The mini-fridge held only squares of orange cheese and a few cans of soda, and the tiny tray of ice in the freezer was almost empty. I scammed what ice I could from the tray and went to the sink.

An old office phone sat on the counter. On the wall above it, a phone number had been written in pen. I filled the tray and put it back in the freezer, then returned to the counter. The phone number seemed familiar. *What you're looking for*. I picked up the phone and dialed, only to hear an auto message. The number was disconnected.

I checked the wall, the drawers again, then the cabinets above, pulling everything out. There, behind the boxed pasta, was a handwritten list of numbers, long strings of them with a single letter afterward. Some of the numbers had been crossed out, but a handful remained. The bottom number looked freshest. I hesitated using Billy's phone, and then realized that using Billy's phone might be the only way anyone might pick up. I dialed it.

"Thought you were in *jail*," a young woman's voice said. "I thought we were out of *business*. Which room?"

My thoughts raced. I channeled Billy's stuttering, stringy, hillbilly voice. "One-oh-n-niner." And then I hung up. Room one-oh-nine was the room just next to the vending machines. I had no idea what I'd just done—maybe nothing. My Billy impression was fine for fun with Lu on the walkie-talkies, but did it hold up for people awaiting his calls?

Someone pounded on the door. "Police," came Courtney's tired voice. "Again."

I opened the door. She stood with her arms crossed.

"How many rooms am I going to have to pull you from?" she said. "What are you doing?"

I brandished the homemade ice pack. "Getting Vincent some ice for his arm."

"So romantic, getting it on in the motel where his girlfriend was murdered," she said, batting her eyes at me. "You're such an easy date. And an easy suspect, really, when you think about all the motive you keep giving me."

"Nothing happened. And anyway, it ... wasn't planned," I said, wondering how much I was giving away. "I didn't know he would be here."

"You just can't leave this place alone," Courtney said wearily. She looked around. "What's the draw?"

The Mid-Night had not drawn me. Maddy had. But I couldn't say that. And I was not sure it would be the whole truth, no matter what I said. "Come on," I said.

The parking lot was empty except for Billy's car and Loughton, steadfast in the passenger seat of the police car. "We sent your suitors along home," Courtney said.

"Can you get your partner to move your cruiser behind the bar for a little while?" I said. "I want to try an experiment. Call it a sting if that makes you happier."

She looked at me oddly but went to talk to Loughton. I shook the ice cubes from the towel and returned it to the laundry room, where piles of sheets and towels still lay tangled on the floor.

On the way out, I left the lobby lights on and flicked the neon sign back to *vacancy*. The Mid-Night was open for business.

Back outside, both Loughton and the cruiser had been tucked away. I led Courtney to the door of one-oh-nine. I battled both sets of keys out of my pockets around the money and the diamond. Courtney raised her eyebrows. "You always seem to have the key," she said. "Have you noticed that?"

I flipped the switches for the room's lights, gestured Courtney past me, and closed the door. The remote was where it was supposed to be. I found a baseball game on the TV and turned it up a bit.

"What are we doing?" She seemed as uncertain as I'd ever seen her.

"I'm showing you the draw." I flung my arms wide.

"I don't get it."

"No one knows where we are," I said. "Except maybe your partner out there, no one knows and no one cares." I turned to the window, pulled the curtains tight, and set the air-conditioning to cool. It rattled to life, knocked about, and evened out.

She looked uneasy now. "Hiding out here didn't work out so well for Maddy."

"Just listen for a second," I said. "It only takes fifteen minutes to turn over a room, but Billy thinks it takes longer. Probably should take us longer. I mean, if you were the next person staying in the room, you'd want it to take longer."

"So you sit up in one of these nasty rooms and—what?—watch your soaps?"

"Lu does, even though she won't admit it," I said. "I usually just sit for a while. Sometimes I keep a book in the cart to pass the time." And sometimes I sat and stared at the framed prints of dark trees and a car driving off the landscape into the unknown, wondering what it would be like to take that trip. When hiding out in a dank motel room was your escape, your fantasies could be simple, even stupid, because none of it would ever happen.

"What do you read?" Courtney said.

I looked away. "It's silly."

"Lots of people I know don't read at all," she said. "I read a little, crime, mystery. They kill off a lot of women, have you noticed? Always beautiful, never ugly. I would be scared to walk around if I was at all good-looking."

I stared hard at the baseball game, trying not to see Maddy's silver face, turned ugly in death. "I got the reading list from some English courses at one of the universities," I said. "The books come from the library." There was something about wanting something so badly that was hard to admit, as though I were opening up my chest to show her my beating heart. As though I'd pulled out the silver running man stolen from Maddy's room to show her what raw ambition looked like. But she'd already seen the grubby little trophies I'd hidden away. I felt at my jeans pocket for the roll of cash and the diamond I'd tucked inside it. Things were going to change. And because of that, I didn't mind telling her how it had once been. "At least, I used to get the books from the library, until I dumped Shinez-All on one and couldn't afford the fine."

There. Now Courtney had all she needed for whatever headline she wanted to write for my life. I wanted so badly to be someone I wasn't and yet a fifteen-dollar library fine could cut all that determination off at the knees.

Courtney opened her mouth to speak, but then a small knock came at the door. I held up my hand to stop her, glancing at the alarm clock next to the bed. That was pretty fast service. Faster than you could get pizza delivered, you could have what you were looking for.

That is, if what you were looking for was a girl.

I moved toward the door. Courtney followed, flipping the cover open on her gun. I shook my head at her.

The knock came again, a little more insistent.

I reached for the door and pulled.

A little pretty girl.

The gazelle stood at the door, ripped jeans in place, the combat boots replaced by cheap stiletto heels. Her eyes, heavily made up to cover the last of her bruise, shuttered—*click*—to disaffected.

"You guys got any change for the machines?" she said.

I was shaking, recognizing at last what I hadn't wanted to believe. Jessica hadn't been here to sightsee that night we'd discovered her. She was just another stray. "Cut the crap, Jessica," I said.

She hitched a thumb toward the vending area. "I was really hoping for a Yoo-hoo?"

Courtney looked her up and down. "Is that trade jargon?"

I went to the phone and dialed the number I'd called from Billy's room. Jessica's phone began to buzz in her pocket. She rolled her eyes. "Fine," she said. "You Sherlocked the shit out of that one. What do you want?"

"Not what you came to give," I said, hanging up. "Come have a seat."

She hesitated, then wobbled on her heels to the bed and sat on the very corner. "Was that you on the phone?" she said. "Nice. I should have known he'd still be locked up. Who would bail him out?"

"If you don't want to join him there, you might want to tell Officer Howard here everything you know about this operation," I said. "There's an answering service that only works if you call from the motel, I know that much. They dispatch you to the room—" I waved my arm magician-like across the scene. "—we don't need the details after your arrival, but maybe if you tell us enough, Officer Howard can find a way to look the other way when you teeter out of here in those shoes."

Courtney was mouthing something to me over the girl's head. *How old is she?* She managed to clear the horrified expression off her face in time for Jessica to turn in her direction.

"The rooms," Courtney said. "The closed-off rooms as your head-quarters. The dispatch system—anything you can tell me about that guy, I want to hear. I just have to—where are your *parents*?"

Jessica shrugged. "My mom thinks I'm out with friends. I get a call, I go out. NBD."

Courtney looked at me. "No big deal," I said, stuck on the idea of the south wing of the motel serving Billy's sideline. Now I knew how the dirty laundry had always seemed to outpace the number of guests checked in. "It's kind of a big deal, Jessica." I tried to recall my pity for the girls who'd turned to Billy, of all people. "Why in the world would you do this? You have your whole life ahead of you."

Jessica glared at the baseball game. I leaned over and hit the power button. "The more clarity we have here tonight, the faster you get home to bed, alone."

"My whole life ahead of me," she said. "Yeah. My whole, awesome life which won't be worth living if I just let it happen. My parents," she said with a giant eye roll at Courtney. "They don't have any money and when they do, they spend it on themselves, OK? My mom is down at the boats every weekend, making sure we don't have enough money for breakfast cereal. My dad is—who knows? Forget about college. If I'm going to get out of here, I need to figure it out for myself."

I couldn't argue with any of that, not with Maddy's diamond in my pocket. "Is that why you lasted three hours on the track team? You don't have time for practice, not with all the time being a teen prostitute takes up? And wait—when Mickie said she knew someone who spent a lot of time here, it wasn't me she was talking about, was it? Holy—she called you a whore that morning. She knows about you. How does she know?"

Jessica scoffed. "Probably from her *boyfriend*," she mumbled.

Courtney had had enough listening. "Who is Mickie?"

"Mickie is the star runner on the Midway track team," I said. Jessica sniffed at the word *star*. "You had your chance to take her place," I said to her.

"I sure did," she said, shaking her head at me. "You really have, like, no clue at all." She sat hunched over the corner of the bed, all knees and elbows.

Courtney jumped in. "You're the one having sex with men old enough—"

"Wait," I said. Jessica's rag-doll pose had sent me back to another hotel room, another girl. My palms began a quiet tremble. There was something I wanted more than the diamond in my pocket, more than anything else I could name. I wanted to understand. The answer was just there, on the other side of that memory. "What clue don't I have?"

Jessica looked between us, then shook her head. "All I'm going to say is that I wouldn't take Mickie's place," she said. "Not for a million dollars and really not for some stupid *trophy*."

She tucked herself into an immovable stone.

"You didn't get attacked by just any man when you were here, did you?" I glanced at Courtney. "But a . . . customer."

"A john," Courtney supplied.

"Right," I said. "Looks like filing a false report, right?"

Courtney stared at me. "If she'd *filed a report*, Columbo."

A small twist of a smile played at Jessica's lips. She'd known all along she was faster than I was.

We couldn't get anything more out of Jessica. Courtney took her home—not to jail, but with a set to her uniformed shoulders that made me think she was formulating a story and maybe a scolding for Jessica's mother.

I closed down the Mid-Night again, leaving the front-desk keys in the drop box. Then I went to retrieve my car from the construction site across the road and sat for a while, feeling the roll of tip money against my hip. From here I could watch cars turning onto the interstate, one direction Chicago, the other Louisville.

The tiniest part of me imagined making the same choice, turning not toward home but toward the open road. The cash, in gas money, would get me pretty far.

My job, gone. My mother, now functioning in society better than I ever had. A diamond in my pocket. There was nothing keeping me here, and yet I couldn't make myself turn the key in the car. The diamond that should have meant a new life only felt heavy. An anchor. But I'd always felt that weight—before the diamond, before Maddy's death, before even my father's. I was afraid. I was a real chickenshit, to borrow from Billy. Given every chance in life to prove it, I had: afraid of being left behind, afraid of never catching up, afraid that the person I was supposed to be was someone just like this, someone just like I was.

When my car finally choked to life, I drove to Yvonne's house and returned her keys. "I must have grabbed them by mistake," I said. "I'm really sorry."

"That's weird," she said, shrugging. "I guess I would have noticed at some point."

But there was something in her eyes that I recognized. I'd have to get used to it.

I was a little lighter, but still the diamond pulled all my attention. It was my center of gravity, a black hole into which my entire life might tumble and disappear. That was the decision I'd made. The diamond over everything else.

At home, my mother came out of the kitchen, wiping her hands on a towel. "You should be getting ready. Are you hungry?" she said.

I looked up. I'd heard *angry*, but then realized what she was asking and shook my head.

"Are you sure? I picked up some cold cuts in case anyone wanted to come over after the service."

I stared at her. People in our house again. We were under siege.

"You're not going?"

"Well, no," she said. "I'm not quite ready for that."

For a crowd. For a funeral.

"Most of her mourners are expected to go right into a party, after," I said. "The reunion. Not sure who thought that was a great idea."

"Well, Gretchen won't," she said. "Or Vincent, Fitz, or Mike. Honestly, Juliet, you're not the only one who lost her." She sighed and threw the towel over her shoulder. "You didn't even want to go to that party."

"I still don't," I said.

"Well, you're stuck now," she said, nodding toward the couch where the envelope Shelly had sent home still sat, untouched. "Shelly called to make sure you didn't forget—"

"Six *sharp*," I said, hating myself. I'd picked up some very teenager-like behavior at school these last few days.

My mother gave me a cutting look in response. "Yes, and also your homework assignment. Shelly said not to forget. You'll need scissors. And glue, she said. I got you some."

Great. A kindergarten craft project on top of everything else. Shelly had a knack for revenge.

I flopped down on the sofa and took up the envelope. It was too light for a copy of our *Tracks* yearbook. I pulled out a sheaf of papers. Shelly must have already heard about my light fingers. She hadn't sent the yearbook but instead several pages photocopied from it.

A sticky note on the front, though, gave instructions. This was the project: to cut apart copies of the yearbook's senior photos to create personalized nametags with each attendee's high-school face.

I glanced at the clock. I would never make it anywhere sharp. And for what? We'd only graduated ten years ago. How different could we look?

On the first page, the young faces of Beckwith, then Bell easily caught my attention. Side by side for all eternity. Beck's sideburns were too long, his hair too shaggy. The glower was just about right, though. Maddy, golden and perfect. I sifted through the pages for my own jack-o'-lantern grin and spotted Courtney, too, her hair long but her chin thrust out. A few extra pages had been copied in. Song lyrics, senior quotes, snide comments from the yearbook staff. I'd skipped them the day I'd had my hands on the book, but now I read them through, taking my time. I'd never had the chance to read it all. I found mine easily:

Surely the third wheel on the track team bus.

It had less sting, finally. I'd only stuck so close to Beck and Maddy by her request, after all. I'd been loyal, once. That was nothing to be ashamed of.

I skimmed ahead for Maddy's section. The song I didn't remember, and she didn't have a quote. But the yearbook staff had had their say:

#1 in distance on the track team. All the way, all seasons.

I read it again. This was the thing she hadn't wanted me to read? It was presumptuous, and look where it had gotten them. The season hadn't even started when the yearbook had gone to press. If I'd won state, the *Tracks* staff would have gotten things badly wrong.

As it was, calling Maddy number one in distance had been a safe bet. But to say she went all the way—

I looked back at what they'd printed. Then to mine. Third wheel . . . on the bus?

I flipped through the pages, rereading all the entries. The names, the lyrics, the callouts.

Beck had never been on the bus.

Loose thoughts wanted to come together, but I held them apart, sorted them one by one as I flipped through the pages.

Third wheel on the track team bus. So specific. So detailed.

But these were high-school students scrapbooking their memories and friends, with a few snarky words for anyone they didn't like.

Shadows gathered just at the edge of my mind.

I shook them off and began cutting the pictures apart. My hands worked at Shelly's paper dolls, trying to do a good job, but hurrying, urged on by six *sharp*. Despite the deadline closing in, my mind wandered. Nothing sinister there. It couldn't be. High-school kids weren't capable—

But they were. I knew they were. Hadn't Mickie seen through Jessica? Hadn't she kept score, taken notes, bided her time, and then landed the gut punch at the right moment? Were kids so different today?

I found myself holding the trimmed-out photo of Beck.

He'd never been on the bus, but I was still the third wheel. What was the pay-off for that joke?

What did it mean, if the joke had never been on me? If it had never been a joke at all?

I went back to the stack, turning the pages slowly. There was nothing about Beck. The yearbook staff had liked him—or perhaps, like me, didn't know what to make of him. Or had forgotten him. Or had left him outside, willingly, knowingly.

There was something right and just about that, given how things turned out.

I went back to the paper faces, trimming and glancing furiously at the clock, where time raced away from me, like a nightmare where no matter how fast I ran, I only fell farther behind.

They would want me to speak at the service. I hadn't thought of a thing to say.

All the way, all seasons.

The only way I could have been a third wheel on the track team bus—

I'd held the thoughts apart, but now they slammed together, nothing but wreckage. Shards started flying out.

Sexualized. Beck, saying she wanted away from the team. Courtney's keen eyes as Fitz nursed my twisted ankle.

The scissors fell from my hand.

Fitz stumbling for the door away from the house. I'd guessed then that the puzzle had fallen together for him on who'd gotten Maddy pregnant, but I'd gotten the details wrong.

I stood up. I couldn't believe what I was thinking.

Watch what you say, and who you say it to.

I had no evidence. It was only a terrible feeling, a terrible, sinking realization that I'd been living in a world parallel to the real one. I felt as though I had believed in the Easter bunny for a decade longer than everyone else.

No. It couldn't be true. I walked to the end of the room and back, then again. On the end table, my own heavy-metal smile gleamed up at me, my own narrow shoulders in a Midway High team jersey. I paced past it twice, three times. I wanted to reach in and shake that girl. What did she know that I had forgotten? What had she ignored that I couldn't now know?

"Juliet?" my mother called from the kitchen. "It's almost time to leave, if you're going to get there on time."

I felt again for the wad of money at my hip, the diamond snug inside. I didn't want to get there was the problem. The responsibility of speaking for another human being, of explaining another person's life to a crowd—I didn't want it. I didn't know how to do it. I stopped in front of the photo of myself again. I might as well be that skinny little kid again, running, running—

Running as fast as I could for as long as I could. Wasn't that what I'd said to Maddy that night? To tell her that I'd been doing my best?

But I wasn't doing it now. I turned away from the ridiculous photo of myself.

She'd run the same way, she'd said that night. Only faster because she was being chased. And I'd assumed she meant me.

I'd understood her every move to be about me. My life had been too much about her, hadn't it? Like the photo behind the frame—

The image filled my vision. Maddy and I carried our first- and second-place trophies like infants in our arms, all of us watching Coach accept his due, at last.

She'd been leading me there the whole time. If only I'd been following as closely behind as I should have been.

CHAPTER TWENTY-NINE

In the car, I started practicing a few words, aloud.

"Maddy Bell was my best friend."

This seemed too past tense and yet still not past tense enough for a friendship that had fallen to pieces ten years ago. "Maddy Bell was . . ."

I was late, and I hadn't finished the nametags. Facing Shelly's wrath would not be the most gut-wrenching thing I would do today, I suspected. I pressed harder on the gas pedal. Maybe it was the high heels I was wearing, but I felt as though I was driving through mud. Cars zoomed past me. "Maddy Bell was a winner. She was everything we all wanted to be."

Could I pass it off as true? "Maddy Bell was everything I wanted to be," I said.

What had Maddy been? Fast. But that could mean something else, couldn't it? A word my mother might have used. *Sexualized.* Not the kind of opening you left when saying final words. "Maddy Bell was . . ."

A semi roared past me as though my car was parked in the slow lane. I checked the gauge and stamped my foot on the gas, pedal to the floor, all or nothing.

The car shuddered under me, bucking in a giant forward motion, then immediately nothing, no sound, no power. I pulled the stiff steering wheel as hard as I could to the right and let the car drift, dead, to the side of the road. I tried the key. Nothing.

Cars rushed by, as though I were still standing at the fence at the back of the Mid-Night. That scraggly tree in the courtyard seemed years in the past, like it was someone else's story, someone else's life.

I let the seat back, and something rolled up against my foot. I reached down and pulled up the silver running-man trophy topper from Maddy's room. Here was evidence—evidence against me. What would Gretchen say if I returned him to her?

I tucked the little guy into my purse. It was getting crowded in there. I hadn't trusted any one spot in my room to leave behind the tip cash or the diamond, so I'd brought them both with me, the diamond in a plastic baggie meant for bologna sandwiches.

The door creaked as I emerged high heels first from the car into the dust of a passing tractor-trailer. The driver laid on the horn as he passed, tooting merrily for a mile to let me know his thoughts on my legs. I tugged down the skirt of my dress, checking back toward Midway, then on toward the city. In both directions, only roaring highway, no exits, no fast-food joints, no gas stations with pay phones. Who would I call, anyway? My mother had no way to come pick me up, if she could still drive.

Coach or Fitz—

No one could be trusted. I still couldn't fully believe what simmered just below the surface of what I would allow myself to think.

I started walking back toward town. There would be no ceremony for me, no speeches, no reunion.

This was all fine, though something tugged at me to turn in the other direction.

A car blared its horn on the way past. God, was it the dress? The high heels? Was it being female in public? No one stopped, but I felt ridiculously exposed. I had nothing to arm myself with but the slightly pointy trophy topper. I turned my head resolutely away from the passing cars, toward the horizon. The sun had finally begun to set, but the sky was not yet dark enough for the first stars, or for the cover of darkness. What was I missing, if I skipped the reunion, after all? The chance to compare my messed-up life to everyone else's?

The speech. I would miss the chance to get it right.

"Maddy was—"

Maddy was. Maddy was. I hated the phrase. I hated how quickly a person passed from life, from memory. Could I remember my father's voice? Could I remember what it was like to have him grab me off my feet for a hug? Tears welled in my eyes and I smeared them away.

Maddy had never had that.

Maybe she'd always had her moment with Coach and Fitz, those little gestures that let her know she had someone on her side. That little squeeze on the shoulder to—

Another long horn blast. I realized I'd come to a stop, staring sightless into the cornfields. That little squeeze on the shoulder. I'd seen it a million times. I'd been jealous of it. I'd seethed. Maddy was special. Maddy was *the favorite*. But what did it mean? We're with you? We're proud.

Steady now.

The words came unbidden, and then so did the memory of Coach gripping Mickie by the shoulder.

The cornstalks swayed in a breeze. Maddy was smart. She'd left me that photo not as a gesture of friendship but to make me understand something about her life, to pull me closer. Maybe even to pull me along, because she knew it could be the last act of her life.

"Maddy was brave," I said, starting to walk again, toward Midway, toward home. Maddy was—

Maddy was not the last of them.

I stopped, turned, and started to run.

The shoes were a bad idea. I paused to pull them off and started again, carrying one in each hand. The sun dropped quickly now, its bright pink-orange heat against my cheek. I watched the road. A piece of glass or a nail right now would be the end.

It was already the end, but I didn't let myself think about that. I needed the focus of my youth. I needed Maddy's ponytail jouncing against her shoulder just there ahead of me, so that's what I imagined. I kept my thoughts just there, and the rest of it at bay through sheer will.

That's how the truck crept up on me.

I didn't hear the engine or the crunch of tires pulling up behind me. When the driver decided to let me know he was there with a tap of his horn, I stumbled and fell into the grit and rock at the side of the

road, wrenching the my tender ankle. At my back, I heard a door creak
open. I threw my shoes to the side and hurried to grab the running man
from my purse. He was at least metal.

"You throwing up again?"

Beck. Violent relief washed over me.

"You OK?" he called.

I picked myself up, dusting the gravel from my knee and retrieving
my shoes. He was dangling from the open passenger door of his pickup.
As I approached, he leaned back. He wore a button-up shirt and black
pants instead of jeans. He looked me up and down. "Guess you're going
my way," he said.

I had to hitch the skirt of my dress a little too high to crawl up
into his truck. Beck cleared his throat and busied himself studying the
traffic in the rearview. "That your hunk of junk back there? Were you
planning to run the whole way?"

I closed the door. My breath was labored, loud inside the truck cab.
"If I had to," I said.

He swung the steering wheel and got us moving. "I guess I didn't
want to go to this all that bad. Especially the—first part, whatever
that's going to be. But all of it, really. People talking behind my back
all night . . ."

His profile was lit by the raging sunset over my shoulder. "Only
Courtney knows about that," I said. "And—well, the coaches." I waited
to see what he made of that. Beck was never on the bus. Had he figured
out who had been?

"Can Courtney's exposé be far behind, though?"

"I wouldn't worry about Courtney—"

"Up until the moment she arrests me," he said, "I plan not to think
of her at all."

Watch what you say and who you say it to. I checked the scrape on
my knee, feeling Beck's eyes on me.

"You know something," he said.

"What do you mean?"

"I know you, Townsend. What are you hiding?"

"You don't know me," I said, thinking about the diamond in my purse. Nobody knew me, not really. Not anymore. And even Maddy might have been surprised. Someone had taken her life, but now I was stealing it.

"Better than you think," he said, sitting up in his seat. "Anyway. Something happened, right?"

"You once said Maddy couldn't wait to get away from Coach and Fitz. Why did you think that?"

We both watched a mile tick by. Unlike my car, his truck could handle the speed limit, plus some. "Well," he said slowly. "She used to say things, about getting away, about starting over. I think she felt pressured to be great, to follow in their footsteps. The Olympics, even."

"And she didn't want that?" Hadn't we both wanted that? I wanted to win now, and yet there was no prize, no competition but the obstacles I set for myself. Maybe this was what adulthood was. No more trophies. No more tapes to break through, and all the striving in the world guaranteed nothing.

"Honestly?" he said. "I don't know anymore. It was years ago and I don't know if I ever—"

"Yeah."

He glanced at me and quickly back to the road. "Did the Olympic torch burn brightly in your soul, then? Is that what *you* wanted?"

It was so long ago. I tried to remember what I'd actually wanted back then. All I could come up with was that sweaty hug from my dad at the end of every race, of the silly games and songs on the bus on the way back to school. Of Maddy racing the Coach of the Year trophy toward the front of the bus, laughing. "I think I wanted to be part of something," I said. "And I was."

We rode into the city's edges in silence.

"She did that for me, too," he said at last, so quietly I thought he might not want me to hear it. "People expect something of me, still, because I was with her, did you know that? She created me. Without her, I wouldn't have existed. I didn't mind so much then. Well, I didn't get it, did I? I was just a kid. Now I wonder what I might have been, if she'd just left me alone. I think you might be the only one who—who understands what I mean. Without thinking I'm a monster for saying it."

I didn't think him a monster, but it disappointed me for some reason. Maybe because he was just a guy who still didn't understand the full scope of what we were bumping up against—Maddy's past, but also Jessica being taken home in a police car, and all the girls Billy had pressed into service. The girls at the school, preening and hating each other. Mickie was on my mind. What had that sad, erratic girl with the swagger of a woman twice her age been through already? Who among us had become what we might have been? Who had been giving out the chances, and who had been yanking them away?

As we neared downtown Indianapolis, I caught just the barest glimpse of the university stadium where our state finals had run on without us, lit up for someone else's activity. Beck took the long way to the Luxe, spinning a full turn around the circle monument at the center of the city before arriving at the hotel. We had barely paused in the curved drive before a valet was tugging at my door. I hopped out on bare feet and reached back for my heels and purse.

A clutch of onlookers waiting for their car watched as I slipped into my shoes. A woman among them stared in horror at the streak of dried blood down my shin. I grinned at her. Beck, having finally let the parking guy claim his keys, came around the truck hood, tucking his shirt into the back of his pants. His black boots were dusty. We made a pair, exactly like two kids from Midway High would look walking into a place they didn't belong and didn't want to be. I swept my hair over my shoulders, for a wild moment considered taking Beck's arm.

"What?" he said.

"Nothing."

We turned toward the wide, golden revolving door, turning on its own at the pace suitable for ball gowns and prim old ladies. I entered, then Beck jostled in behind me, close, and then too close, stepping on the back of my heel. "Sorry," he mumbled into my hair.

Inside, the hotel shined as brightly as my memories: the tall, winding stairs to the protruding mezzanine above, the pearl marble floors streaked with silver below. Feasting my eyes all around, I paused at the ornate filigree of the banister spindles on the mezzanine then looked away, but not soon enough.

My child's mind had stored the opulence, the sparkle. Now I saw the decorative detail—all the elaborate and sumptuous features—as things that would need to be cleaned.

A lot of Shinez-All and old toothbrushes had gone into this place.

But the ghosts lived here, too. We had run up that curved staircase and across the slick marble mezzanine to gaze over the glowing lobby below, giggling and daring the coaches to correct us.

"Look at the bald spot on the back of Trenton's head," Maddy had said behind her hand. She'd taken to calling him by his last name, a habit I'd assumed she'd picked up from Beck or his rough friends. "From up here, you can see it shine like the moon. Like the moooooon," she crowed out so that everyone looked our way—other runners, other coaches, some snooty people huffy and put out that they'd booked a nice hotel only to find it overrun by participants in the high-school track meet going on down the street. Fitz guided Coach back to the business of getting us checked in and away from any scolding or correcting. Coach liked Maddy to be the silvered girl on the top of the trophy at all times: fast, stoic, gleaming, a prize. He didn't like her fooling around, especially on stairs. She could get hurt and then where would we be?

"Where'd you go?"

I looked away from the staircase, surprised to find Beck, his side-burns short, instead of a ten-years-gone coach hovering, concerned. "This is where we stayed," I said. He had never been on the bus. "For state."

"I waited in the stands all day for that race," he said, and I might have felt a little sorry that no one had tried to reach him the way they had my parents, except at that moment I caught someone watching us from a doorway on the mezzanine. She turned and fled but I'd already seen her.

Lu—in a Luxe housekeeper's uniform.

"Excuse me for a second," I said, and all the ghosts—former best friend, more recent former best friend—led me up the stairs.

CHAPTER THIRTY

From the mezzanine, I stopped and pondered the lobby below. The Luxe was such a gorgeous hotel, so little of it reminded me of the Mid-Night. But that was where my mind went, looking out over the open expanse, as Maddy had done. I had never been afraid of heights, but now I shivered and pulled back from the railing. Then Shelly was racing across the lobby below toward Beck, and to avoid her I dropped farther back and down the dim hall after Lu.

Lu would be easy to find. The hallways were wide and clear, except for the hulking cleaner's cart parked outside a room down at the end of the hall. I trailed my fingers along the wallpaper. Even the walls at the Luxe felt lush to the touch.

At the cart, I took a quick assessment. Shinez-All, of course, in its big yellow can. There was a talkie unit hanging unobtrusively on one side. Inside, Lu, her back to me, wrestled a pillow into its case. She wore another radio at her waist. I reached over and pressed the button on the radio in the cart. "Come in, Lu," I said. "Over."

She turned, the pillow pressed to her chest by her chin. "Roger," she said. "They don't use all the over-and-outs here." The pillow wouldn't be contained by the case. She let it drop from her chin and held it helplessly. "I miss it."

I crossed the threshold, slow, as though I were easing up on a wild animal. I took the pillow from her—down-filled, only the best at the Luxe—and rammed it into the case one corner at a time, then tossed it in the air to fluff it, caught it, and held it out to Lu. She placed it into the array of pillows waiting on the bed and chopped it, karate-style, with the side of her hand.

"Nice," I said. "You're picking up some luxury skills here. How do they deal with the fleur de whatever up in the railings? That's gotta be a bitch."

273

"Feather duster," Lu said, sneering. "That's what I had to do my first day, all day, all over the whole building. I think to make sure I wouldn't quit so easy. But they give health insurance, Juliet, and the uniform fits. We had to buy another car for me to get here, but—" She shrugged, trying not to look as happy as she sounded. "I didn't think the Mid-Night would ever reopen."

"It wouldn't be the same, if it did," I said.

"What are you going to do? I could talk to someone here, if you want."

I didn't want to say what I thought of that idea. "Yeah, maybe," I said.

She knew what I meant. "So ... you haven't been getting into trouble, right? With the ... killing? Carlos thinks—"

"What?"

She sighed. "He thinks that girl who got beat up there is a liar—"

"She is," I said.

"He also thinks if they can't pin your friend's death on that black man, they'll never pin it on anyone."

Vincent. I tried not to think about the feel of Vincent's lips against my neck. Just more theft. "I think it might have been a white guy, actually," I said.

"You know who? But how—"

"I don't know anything," I said. I didn't know. And I didn't have any way of knowing. Carlos was probably right, in a way. No one in Midway cared enough to solve it. Vincent would go back to the city and grieve. And no one else in the world loved Maddy enough to push for a solution. Except me. I did. And it wasn't just Maddy I loved. I loved Midway. I didn't want this sort of thing to happen in my town, and for everyone to look away. "I should get downstairs. Shelly Anderson has probably put out a missing-person's alert on me already."

"That one is so bossy," Lu said. "She made the catering manager cry."

"Just the one time?"

We smiled at each other, Lu raising her hand to hide her crooked teeth.

"Lu," I said, and then realized I wasn't sure what I wanted to say. Clearly I wasn't one for speeches. "I hope—uh, I just hope this all works out for you. You shouldn't have it this hard."

She slapped at my arm with light fingers. "You're getting so mushy and grown-up."

"Well, you at least deserve a workplace where the hangings can be kept to a minimum," I said.

She crossed her fingers and held them up, grinning.

The walkie-talkie at her waist hissed and crackled. "Luisa," said a curt male voice. "Tonight's event *liaison* is looking for an errant guest. Seen anyone up there in the rooms who shouldn't be?"

The word *liaison* sounded like a swear. We looked at each other, trying not to laugh. Lu shooed me to the door and brought the radio to her mouth. "Roger that," she said. "Sending her down now."

I was out the door before I heard the voice answer. "Did you just call me *roger*? Do we work for NASA, Luisa? Are we in *'Nam*?" Lu's laugh followed me down the hall.

My descent of the mezzanine stairs felt dramatic. I took each slick marble step slowly, clutching the railing and gazing out at the lobby for anyone I knew.

Shelly waited for me at the front desk, red-cheeked and furious. The proper young man over her shoulder shot me a sympathetic look. "Where have you been?" she said, looking me up and down. She sneered at the blood on my leg but didn't ask. "The service is starting any minute, and the setup for the reunion is in a shambles. Where are the nametags?"

But by the look she gave me, I didn't need to answer.

"Two responsibilities, Juliet," she said.

I couldn't remember the second one, and must have looked stricken.

"Being on time," she said, rolling her eyes. "That was the other thing you couldn't manage. Let's get this over with."

She grabbed my elbow and directed me through the lobby to a side room with its door propped open. From the noise, Maddy's service had rustled up a crowd, after all. It sounded like the Mid-Night, the bar, inside.

Once I'd been thrust through the doorway, I realized that was precisely what it was: Yvonne, Gretchen, a few of the regulars who'd been around the night she'd come by, like Mack, his slicked-back hair strange without his red hat. And then a few of the regulars who'd come in the night after, onlookers and gossip hounds, hoping to see something worth the drive and the trouble of putting on their best clothes. I spotted some of the teachers from Midway High, but not the coaches. Courtney nodded at me from across the room. She was clutching a squat glass of brown liquid and talking to a few people I should have recognized but didn't, classmates from Midway who had come early to pay a few respects or have first shot at the open bar.

Shelly still had my arm. She grasped tighter and propelled me through the room, past a set of folding chairs, all of them filled, past everyone, including someone who reached out and missed making a gesture of support or empathy. I couldn't be sure, moving as fast as we were, who it had been.

And then we stood in the front of the room, facing the group.

Shelly pushed me into position and retreated back through the chairs, and the room turned to me, hushing to silence. I spotted Beck in the back of the room, then Fitz. His large frame nearly surrounded a small-boned woman in a necklace of big, plastic pearls.

I was stuck. Not just for the words to begin, but for a single thought beyond the fact that Fitz had brought a date to a memorial service. Was she the real reason why he'd been missing all week, calling in, not doing his regular duty for Coach and the team? It was all the first blush of love?

I searched the room, seeing Coach, finally. He was wearing his Coach of the Year medal on its bright-blue ribbon around his neck.

I imagined what he'd told himself before he'd donned it today: that it was for Maddy, that it honored her memory. He'd probably considered a grand gesture, like placing it in the casket. Or upon her beautiful corpse.

Maddy's silver skin came back to me, and I shuddered. The crowd murmured.

"Maddy was—" I began.

But now I was preoccupied with the Coach of the Year medallion. I remembered Maddy galloping the Coach of the Year trophy up the bus aisle, all of us cheering, the silver runner sprinting toward its new owner. "Why isn't it a girl on the trophy?" rose one of the girls' voices from memory. "That's who's doing all the running."

His Olympic bronze medal was kept in the school case, and yet his award for high-school coaching was too precious to make it there. And now here he was in the matching medallion, a show of honor because Maddy had earned it for him. Not me.

The weight of the purse strap on my shoulder grew heavy.

The trophy Maddy had earned for him, then broken into his office to deface.

The faces in the crowd had gone still and concerned.

I looked around. On a small table, a beautiful silver urn sat amidst a festoon of flowers. I might have made a noise of surprise.

There would be no beautiful corpse. This was Maddy. Maddy's ashes, packaged in a way that she could never be in real life. Contained, at last, and unable to say the things she'd so desperately wanted to say.

And they'd put her in a *trophy*.

My hands shook as I unzipped my purse, drew out the silver running man from Maddy's room, and placed him against the urn. A few gasps in the room cut the silence.

When I gazed out again, the crowd had broken into two camps: those who were worried about me, and those who were worried what I would say.

Courtney stared past me to the runner on the table, then pulled out her phone and began thumbing at it. It wouldn't take her any time to remind herself what might have been missing from Maddy's old room.

But maybe she would let me finish my speech before the handcuffs came out.

"Maddy Bell was my best friend," I said. The room went silent again, so that even those in the back of the room must have heard my voice waver. I took a deep breath to calm myself. "She was my best friend a long time ago, though, at a time that I can barely remember. But she will always mean everything to me, because she was real, she was whole. She was beautiful, and not just on the outside. And she was all these things in the face of a reality that she kept to herself, a reality that most of us couldn't begin to understand, let alone survive." I met eyes with Fitz, then Coach, then Beck. Beck's mouth hung open; he looked nervous. Then Gretchen, who had started to cry. Her eyes darted around, confused. I found Vincent, at last, at the side of the room, watching the crowd. Now I really understood why he'd agreed to this freak-show memorial. He wanted a chance to take a long, hard look at all of us.

"She didn't want us to know what she was going through, or she would have told someone," I said. "She wanted to fix it for herself, once and for all. No—that's not entirely true. She wanted to fix it for everyone. She wanted to—to save them all." I thought of all the girls at Midway High, how insecure, how preyed-upon—not just by men, but by people like Mrs. Haggerty, people who liked to tell other people what was proper. And by each other. That was the worst part. It would take them so many wasted years to know how to be on a team. People in the front rows started to shift in their seats and glance at one another.

"The girls," said a voice in the back.

I raised my head. The woman in the protective curve of Fitz's arm raised her small hand and pulled at her necklace as though she were being strangled.

Teeny. Teeny, all cleaned up and wearing a choker of pretend pearls. "The girls," I said, not quite believing my own eyes. And Teeny, how normal, how young. "I—" Everyone who had turned to see who had spoken up spun back to see what I had to add. What was Teeny doing here, and with Fitz? I looked between them, and then across the room for anyone who might leap in and help me. "Maybe . . . someone?"

They all stared, though some had begun awful signals to each other with their eyes, looking at their watches, shaking the ice in their empty drinks. "Would anyone else like to say a few words?" I pleaded.

The silence dragged.

Finally Gretchen stood and sniffed. "Well, I don't think she'd want me to say much," she said, lifting her chin. "But I loved that awful girl." She put a fist to her mouth, and then talked around it, her voice husky. "I just loved her."

"I did, too," Vincent said, coming forward a step. "It's the only thing I think is true anymore. It's the only thing I know."

Courtney's eyes shifted from one to the other, then to Beck, who had cleared his throat. "I'm with Juliet. It was a long time ago," he said, blushing. "And maybe—we were just kids. But she was important to me."

A few people in the room who hadn't known her had the decency to look embarrassed to be there.

From the corner, Coach stepped forward. "Maddy was a very special person. This has been very difficult to understand . . . I'll just—" He came up the aisle, easing past crossed legs, to stand next to me. He raised the Coach of the Year medal off his chest. In the overhead light, it winked gold to a bright white, sunlit glare.

I cringed away—hot, suddenly, and heavy with memory.

In the split second the medal turned in the light and blinded me, I was no longer standing in front of the silver cup of ashes but standing under a wide, white sky, the sun low over our heads and wicked. A heavy trophy with a ponytailed girl runner at its zenith lay in my arms, burning and sliding against my sweaty skin. Maddy cradled hers. But she was not celebrating. She was shaking and sick, and not sick but mad, and she wouldn't say what was wrong. Fitz put his hand on her shoulder—*steady now*—while the blue ribbon was placed over Coach's bowed head like a priest receiving communion. When he looked up, the coach's medal glinted gold to white into my eyes. And Maddy was crying, but not because the girl from Southtown had called her a slut under her breath, and not because of anything I'd done, I hoped.

Maddy cradled the trophy in her arms like a baby and cried with fury, and then shook Fitz's hand off—

I looked out to find Fitz, but he'd gone, along with Teeny.

"—special runner, special girl," Coach was saying. "Every coach hopes to find a talented athlete in their lineup, and I've had more luck than most." He put his hand on my shoulder and squeezed. Just as he had with Maddy, as he had with his star for as long as I could remember. His stars, and he was finally including me in that list, but I couldn't shake that wonderful, awful day, Fitz's hand on and then flying away from Maddy's shoulder, or the look of pure, rotten hatred in Maddy's eyes as she flung us all off.

But I understood it now, because Coach's hand was leaden, too warm, too much.

"—just want to say what an honor it was to work with such a talent." I took a step backward, forcing Coach's grip loose. "What is it, Jules?"

There was a commotion at the door. "Help," a man's breathless voice said. Fitz bolted into the room, frantic. "Please, someone. Help her."

CHAPTER THIRTY-ONE

Courtney hurried out after Fitz, most of the room at her heels. I was a step toward the door when Coach grabbed my arm. "Are you doing OK, Jules?" he said. "Are you talking to anyone about this? It's a lot to handle."

"Talking . . . ? You mean, like a shrink?" I slid my arm away from him, but then missed the strange warmth of his touch. I probably needed to talk to someone years ago. "No, I—well, no." I didn't want to say that I couldn't afford it. "Shouldn't we—"

"Just take care of yourself, OK?" The hand was back on my shoulder, squeezing. It hurt.

I stumbled away from him and through the chairs, now scattered and empty.

In the lobby, everyone's head had tilted up in the same direction. High above, Teeny clung to the outside of the rail, the pointy, unnatural shoes discarded, and her toes pointing out over the edge of the stairs. Courtney had ascended the first few stairs behind her, slipping up another riser when she thought Teeny wouldn't notice.

Teeny noticed, jerking away and letting one foot slip off the stairs. A collective gasp went up in the crowd. At the same time, the choker at Teeny's throat popped off. It dropped the thirty feet to the marble floor and exploded. The plastic baubles pinged fantastically in all directions against the floor, the wall, the stairs.

A pearl bounced and rolled against my foot. Above, Teeny recovered her purchase, holding a hand out to warn Courtney back.

"Kristina," Fitz said, moving into place below her. "Please let us help you down."

I staggered between classmates to the foot of the stairs and let the cold steel newel post catch me. Kristina.

I'd never thought of Teeny as a person with a past, a person with an age, or with a life she might have imagined for herself. I'd never thought of her as a *person* before.

She wasn't Fitz's date. She was Maddy's friend, somehow, and far from dead. I looked around for Yvonne and then Vincent. *Or are you Kristina?* I was, though, wasn't I? We were the same. Teeny and I had stayed, and nothing we ever stole was enough to make up for what we'd had taken from us. But what did Maddy and Teeny have in common? How had they known each other?

For a moment I wondered if Teeny could have hurt Maddy. But she couldn't have done it, physically. Maddy would have overpowered the smaller woman. Even strangled, she could only have been dragged into place and hanged by someone strong.

Above, Teeny murmured to herself. *The girls, the girls.*

The girls. Like the girl who'd dropped out of school instead of finishing, who'd disappeared into plain sight, disappeared so well that people thought she had died. She was a ghost now, but she'd been a star, Coach and Fitz's first success.

Their first love.

"Teeny," I said. The people nearest me jumped in surprise. "Do you want me to help you pick up your beads? I can fix this for you."

I waved to everyone around me and knelt to pick up the beads at my feet. The others began to join in, uncertainly at first, then with the gusto of a scavenger hunt. Even Shelly dipped to retrieve a bead and appraise it.

Above us, Teeny shifted her weight to watch us.

"Come on down," I said. "Courtney, maybe you could help her."

Courtney inched out toward Teeny and offered her a hand. Teeny accepted the help, stepping down with care. She looked like royalty, except for her bare toes gripping the steps.

Fitz rushed to meet her. He glanced uneasily in my direction, not quite meeting my eyes. "That was impressive. Not everyone is so good with her."

"Are you her caregiver?"

"No," he said, watching the duo approaching. "Nothing like that. She was on the team. A good kid, and someone had to—I took an interest, I guess. Thought I had a plan to get her out of that place she's in now, into a new, nicer facility, someplace with better security, but—I just check in once in a while, that's all, lift her spirits if I can."

"Meet her in the park, that sort of thing," I said.

I didn't need a confirmation and didn't receive one.

"Why did you bring her, if you don't mind me asking?"

"I didn't," he said, leaning in to speak quietly. "I never would have brought her here—that Vincent arranged it. Said she and Maddy were *friends*. They never—How could that be? Anyway, Vincent doesn't understand how delicate she is." He let Courtney hand Teeny down to him, and then escorted her into the crowd where people were scooping pearls into her open hands. She was as happy as I'd ever seen her, as happy as I'd seen anyone in years.

Courtney stood at my elbow. "Well, does Shelly know how to throw a party, or what?"

I searched the crowd for Coach, but he was gone. "I need to talk to you," I said.

"Yeah, I think you might have something to tell me," she said. "About a certain shiny object, probably missing from a certain best friend's room?"

Over Courtney's shoulder, through the broad, rotating door of the hotel, police lights rolled.

"I took it when I went to Gretchen's house the first day," I said. "Someone else broke in, but they might have been looking for what I had already stolen."

Courtney's lips twisted into doubt. "We're still talking about that trophy runner, right? OK, explain it to me. Why does everyone want it? Is it platinum? Is it the Maltese falcon? I don't get it."

"It's a *guy*," I said. "It's not from one of Maddy's trophies. Don't you see? She's the one who stole it first. It's from an award Coach Trenton received our senior year. We didn't get to run our top race, but he did, in a way. He won that award on her back—" I looked away. "Very literally, actually."

Courtney sucked in a breath. "That guy? Are you saying—he's the *dad*? Oh, my God, he's the dad," she said, then looked around and pulled me farther from our classmates. "And then he took her to get—

taken care of? I haven't been able to find the place, but that doesn't mean it wasn't here ten years ago. Oh, wow, this is gross. I mean, maybe not as gross as what we thought before—"

"Courtney, he killed her."

She froze. After a long moment, she surveyed the room, eyes once again keen. "To keep her quiet? But why, after all these years?"

"I think it had something to do with . . . the girls," I said, unable to get Teeny's reedy refrain out of my head. "She wanted to get him out of there, to get him away from the girls on his team now. From Mickie, from—the next girl and the next."

"Mickie's the, uh, young lady from the hotel room?"

"No, Mickie's the *star*." I waved my arm toward the staircase. "And she's cracking up, right on schedule. Teeny was his star, then Maddy, now Mickie, don't you see?"

We stared at each other.

"I'm sorry to say I do. I finally do." She reached for her phone and, checking the room again, thumbed madly at the screen. "I thought all that stuff in yearbook was . . . well, I didn't think it was *true*."

"Did you write it?"

"Some of it, but not all, I swear. Shelly used to stop by, give us funny things to write—but it was a joke. I never thought—I thought it was just kid stuff, you know?"

I thought darkly of Shelly's gossip trade at the bank. If I ever got any money at all, I'd move accounts somewhere else. "Some of us weren't given the choice to think it was kid stuff." I was thinking of what Maddy must have felt when she saw those comments, the photo of her with Coach's hand on her shoulder, forever. It made sense now, how forbidden the book became.

"I'm sorry," Courtney said. "For then, and for now. Are you OK?"

I folded my arms around myself. "I guess so. No."

"I take it he was some kind of father figure to you—"

"I had a father," I said. "A great one."

"Good thing, I'd say," she said, raising her phone to her ear. "Or he might have found you more attractive than he did."

She wheeled and was off. I stood, dismissed, shaking with what she'd said, because I could see the process now, his new crop of girls every spring, his recruits. All the little pretty things dropped in his path, and all he had to do was pluck up what he wanted. Was that the only difference between my life and Maddy's death? A man had already fenced a protective barrier around me?

Shelly and the hotel staff urged the crowd out of the lobby and into the room for the reunion. The party must go on. Meanwhile, the revolving door up front was halted and collapsed to let a significant number of party crashers—the police, led by Courtney, with her gun suddenly strapped against the hip of her dress. Classmates rushed away from me into the safety of the party as the stream of police flooded around me and into the depths of the lobby, up the stairs, to the elevator, and beyond.

Courtney looked back from the stairs. "Juliet," she said. "Get yourself someplace safe. I'm sick of funerals."

I nodded, and then I was left alone in the vast lobby of the Luxe, trembling and cold. A breeze blew through the rigged revolving door, and on it, the sound of more sirens rising. Safe place? I felt as lost as I'd ever been, thinking only of home, and my mother. Now I knew how someone could burrow deep into a place and stay hidden. Was there such a thing as a safe place? A place where you were always welcome, where the lights were always on?

Lu. I was flooded by my need to be near her, to comfort and be comforted, to protect and be protected. To have a friend, to be a friend. I thought I knew, at last, how. I turned and raced up the stairs. Halfway up, I stopped and pulled off my shoes and carried them, to get to her faster.

The cart wasn't where it had been earlier. I stalked the hallway first in one direction and then the other, tripping over a dirty room-service tray left outside a room. Spoons and cups scattered, rattling. The halls were narrower than I remembered, and more complicated. I tried every turn I came to, losing track of where I'd come in along the quiet, plush halls. I passed a set of elevators, then another set, and stopped to decide if I was going in circles. At last I came to a service door and tried the handle. Locked. "Lu," I yelled, pounding the door. "Lu!"

Down the hall, a door cracked open. "Keep it down out there," said a woman's muffled voice.

I tried another hall, coming upon the same room-service tray. Or another one. I looked around. No, the same one but the spoons had been kicked toward the tray.

"Lu?" I said. Lu wouldn't have kicked the spoons. She would have picked them up. I turned and headed back in the direction I thought I'd started, but now I was really turned around. The hallways stretched long ahead of me, the deep carpet stilling all noise, all hints that anyone else might be in the entire building.

I felt chilled, in a different way than I had downstairs. The next elevator I found, I'd take to the lobby and get Beck to drive me home.

Now the halls seemed purposefully long and empty, bloated excess in every detail. I missed the neat symmetry and simplicity of the Mid-Night.

Finally, up a stretch of hallway, I saw light coming through an open door and headed for it.

The cart had been rolled into the room, propping the door open. I squeezed past it. "Lu?" The room was empty of Lu, of guests, of suitcases. I checked the parameters: remote control on the bedside table, water glasses covered with paper doilies and set on a tray. The room had been turned over already, but she'd be back for the cart. The walkie-talkie hung from the side. How much trouble would she get in if I called for her through the system?

I had reached over and grabbed the radio when Coach entered the doorway. We both startled a bit, then he relaxed.

"Juliet, thank goodness it's you," he said, pushing the cart farther into the room.

The door closed behind him.

CHAPTER THIRTY-TWO

"Juliet," he said. "I didn't kill her."

I pushed down the button on the walkie-talkie on the cart and held it. "Who killed Maddy, then, if not you?" My voice sounded thin and quaking to my own ears.

"How should I know?" He paced back and forth in front of the cart, nervously rubbing the Coach of the Year medallion between two fingers like a miser with a gold coin. "I thought they were circling on some guy who beat up a girl there or something."

"That was unrelated," I said. But not really, was it? It was all related. How Coach treated girls—like bon-bons at a party for one—was only a single thread in the fabric of this world in which teen girls were sneaked in and out of the Mid-Night and probably a thousand other places. As long as there were men ordering them as room service. I remembered the song the girls on the team had been listening to, singing along with. As long as we all played along, as long as no one questioned. "I think you know perfectly well who killed her."

"You think I did?" The look on his face was honest hurt. "I loved that girl, just as I've always loved you."

"Not exactly the same way, probably," I said.

Some other emotion flickered over his features. "Ah, OK," he said, looking around the room. "You never thought of yourself as highly as Fitz and I did—"

"Stop it—this isn't about some stupid race," I said. "It's not about running or winning or losing. What you did to her—I will never forgive you, and I will make sure you never touch another girl in your life. With the right jury, maybe your life will be short."

He gave me a look of such disgust that I nearly stepped back. My thumb relaxed on the walkie-talkie. I couldn't keep up eye contact. He edged around the cart slowly. I cowered against it, blocked, and then he was behind me, his breath warm against my neck. I stared into the cart, its contents calming me. Such order. The fresh rolls of toilet paper stacked in a column, the bright-yellow can of Shinez-All ready to take on smears and smells. I concentrated on the smiling cartoon woman on the can.

Coach stood so close I could feel the heat of him. When he pressed against me, the crush I'd harbored came back to me in waves of shame. I couldn't move, couldn't think. The door was closed and so far away. I held fiercely to the radio, hunching over the cart to hide it. "If you think I killed her," he said, "what's stopping me from killing you?"

The floor of my fears dropped away. My mind, blank. Except: My mother. My father. Lu. Beck.

Coach backed off. "I didn't do it," he said. "What is it going to take to make you believe me?"

I swallowed hard. "And what about those girls? Did you do that? Teeny, Maddy, Mickie. Who knows how many girls at all those places you coached before—"

His hands were around my throat in an instant, so fast and so hard that I didn't have time to take a breath. His fingertips met over my windpipe, squeezing until I heard a terrible sound. I dropped the radio and clawed at his hands, then grasped madly for anything. The Mid-Night, the moment Maddy walked in, the appraising look of the young runner finding her zone, all of it rushing at me, through me. The room began to darken, shimmer. The elevator doors I'd been searching for opened, bright inside. I reached—

Static from the walkie-talkie. "Miss? Which room are you in?"

"What the—?" Coach said. His grip loosened. My hand held the can of Shinez-All.

I raised the can over my shoulder and sprayed into his face.

Coach screamed and dropped away from me. The mist caught me, too, eyes, lungs. My throat was on fire, inside and out, and I couldn't see. I leapt away, felt my way around the cart, and to the door, out. My eyes streamed with chemicals and tears. The dark hall, darker yet, and hazy.

I ran.

The halls stretched longer than ever. Corners jumped into place for me to run into them. There were people in the hall now, dark blobs rising out of nothingness. Brought out by the scream, and chattering at me, each other, to call the cops, the cops were already here, do you need help. I pushed through them, around them, through a clattering room-service tray down one hall and around another corner.

"Hey, buddy," said a man's voice behind me. "Leave the girl alone—hey!"

Now I heard under my own booming heartbeat the controlled breath and footfalls of someone coming along behind me. Catching up.

"You're not as fast as you used to be," Coach called.

He closed in, but I could see a little better now and used that to complicate the path. Under my own breath and his, I began to make out the low and heavenly sound of a wide-open space, of voices. I concentrated on that, bouncing off turns and corners with both hands.

I reached the mezzanine just as fingers ripped through my hair and took hold. But our momentum was too great. We entered the high stage of the mezzanine entangled and still moving toward the rail, the stairs. A cry went up below us, but I still couldn't see much except now everything was bright and glaring. I heard something hit the floor, then the marble under my feet was wet and slick, propelling us faster toward the rail and then the nothing beyond.

We hit the railing, hard. For a moment we both teetered at an odd angle against the curved steel.

Voices below cried for help, footsteps on the staircase.

Something cold touched my face. The medal. His Coach of the Year medal, still dangling from his neck, touching my face obscenely. *Sexualized*, he'd said. But he was the one who'd sexualized her. The injustice of this, of that swipe on the wall of a room where she'd struggled for her life—I couldn't stand it.

A wave of black rage welled up within me, and I pushed him, the medallion, everything away.

His arms flew up, and then he was falling backward, reeling on the top step of the staircase, his heels loose and then everything loose and over the railing.

He screamed, but then the medallion around his neck snagged in a bit of filigree, the sturdy ribbon catching just under his jaw.

His head snapped back. The scream cut in half. And then the ribbon gave out, and his body fell to the lobby marble.

Horrified cries rose from below.

I let myself slide to my knees on the wet floor, my fingers laced in the whorls of the railing. All around me, water pooled. It ran off the mezzanine in rivulets, a waterfall.

There was screaming and shouting, voices barking orders. I heard everything and nothing.

At last a hazy figure approached. She holstered her gun and crouched next to me. "We heard it all over the radio," Courtney said. "Smart. And really dumb. What happened in there?"

The trace of him was still all over me, and the Shinez-All coated my skin, my hair. I clung to the railing, water seeping into my dress.

"Cleaning product I swear by." My voice was tight and wheezing. "Cleans up nasty stuff. I got some in my eyes."

She gently pried my hands from the railing and helped me to my feet. "You got that stuff in your eyes? Is everything a blur?" she said. "Oh, wait. I can't believe that just came out of my mouth."

"Things are less blurry than they used to be," I said.

That was true literally, too. My eyesight was indeed coming back. Now I could see the overturned mop bucket nearby. In the dim hall opening at the back of the mezzanine, someone watched from the shadows, the mop still in her hand. I mouthed a "thank you" in her direction.

"Are you hurt?" Courtney said. "Couple of those dance moves looked like they might have knocked the wind out of you." We maneuvered toward the top of the stairs. At the bottom stood an indistinct figure I thought might be Beck.

"Wait, before we go down." I unzipped my purse and pulled out the baggie with the diamond. "I found it in the motel the other night. In the ice machine."

"In the—you know I'm going to want to know more about this, right?" She held the bag to the light. "*Holy* carat size."

"I'll tell you as much as I know." What I still didn't understand was why Maddy had brought the diamond all the way to Midway—and then had hidden it in a place it was unlikely to be found, at least for a while. The imagined scene made me ache for her. She must have known someone else would come looking, that she wouldn't be the one. How brave did you have to be to go through with something you didn't think you would survive?

Like, tomorrow, the next day, and the next.

Courtney escorted me down the stairs as gently as she had Teeny, and at the bottom, Beck took over, turning me away from where Coach lay. "Don't look," he said.

Outside, Fitz stood watching an ambulance pull away from the hotel. When he saw me, his face crumpled. He came to me and pulled me into his arms, tight. His best friend was gone, now, too.

"Was that Teeny?" I said, sniffling against his shoulder. "I promised I would fix her necklace."

"I'm so sorry, Juliet," he said. "Are you OK? They said—I don't know what to make of any of this."

"The important thing is that it's over," I said.

He held on to me, his big shoulders shuddering. I absorbed his grief, and my own. It was time for someone else to take care of Fitz for a change. "It's over," he said. "Poor Maddy."

I didn't bring up the other girls. Things would be out in the open soon enough.

Beck directed me to his truck and helped me into the high seat. "Are you sure you don't want to go to the ER? You hit that railing pretty hard. And your neck—"

"I'll live," I said. As he closed the door and jogged around the truck's hood to join me, I knew it was true. I would, finally.

CHAPTER THIRTY-THREE

I went to the ER anyway, because once my mother saw the finger marks on my neck and the bruise covering my entire right side—you could almost see the filigree imprint—she forced me into Mrs. Schneider's Camry and drove us there, hunched over the wheel.

"If I lost you—" she started.

"I know, Mom," I croaked, wincing as she took a turn too short. She hadn't driven in ten years, but I enjoyed how much she wanted to take care of me.

Much caretaking went into the next few days as I lay in my childhood bed. Vincent stopped by with flowers and awkward silences. "What will you do with her ashes?" I asked.

He hadn't thought it out. "Not sure yet," he said. "Not here."

We agreed on that. Maddy had done enough time here, though I'd stopped thinking of Midway as the problem. "Please don't keep her in that urn on some shelf," I said. I was supposed to be saving my voice, but I had to get this out. "She wouldn't want to be kept in a winner's cup."

Vincent closed his eyes. "Oh no," he moaned. "I never thought of that."

"And the diamond," I whispered. "You'll do something with it?"

"I want to do whatever it was Maddy wanted to do," he said. "I just wish I knew what it was."

"I don't know for sure," I said. "But if you think about that fire she had, you'll think of something."

The girls from the Midway track team brought by grocery-store daisies. "You should be our new coach," Jessica said. Mickie shot her a look but didn't disagree. "You might want to move out of your mom's house first, though," Mickie said, sneering at the wallpaper. She was going to graduate, on time, and was entertaining invitations to run at several schools clamoring over one another to sweeten the deal. Jessica listened to this story without saying anything for a long time.

"I couldn't figure out," she finally said to me, "why you talked that guy up to me."

"He was a good coach," I said. "That was my experience."

"He was a lot of other stuff, too," Jessica said, eyeing Mickie.

Mickie threw her chin out. "Who here isn't a lot of other stuff than what they seem, huh?"

Jessica flashed her a sly smile. They were keeping each other's secrets. "And what about the other one, always fluttering around being helpful and asking if you need anything. It's gross."

"Don't you just hate helpful people?" I said.

"Helpfully pushing me toward a pedophile," she said. The irony of Jessica saying this was lost on everyone but Mickie and me. We shared an embarrassed glance. I had to give her credit, though. She'd sized up the situation on her first day on the team, while I walked around in my own world, letting everything around me stay a blur. "I don't need anyone always fussing around me, you know?" Jessica said. "I'm just there to run."

She had rejoined the team, it seemed. She had time to fill and needed a different way to pay for her escape from Midway.

Lu came by as much as she could, sometimes late, after her kids were in bed. She'd lie next to me and tell me about the terrible things the rich people at the Luxe left behind for her to clean. "I've never seen such filth," she said. "It makes me wish the Mid-Night would open." We didn't think it would. The owners were talking renovations now that Billy was likely to be convicted, but it seemed like an empty promise. Lu and I imagined the building going to seed, the whorls of the balcony rail collecting spiders' webs and birds' nests until someday, far in the future, all of it would be bulldozed. These stories allowed me to drift off to sleep, Lu gone to her early-morning shifts.

Beck brought me a few books to pass the time, then stayed a while. When he caught himself calling me by my last name, teammate style, he corrected himself. I settled on Tom, to make sure I didn't call him what Maddy had.

"She wasn't cheating on me, then," he said one day. "She was . . . that poor kid." And that seemed to tuck her nicely into the past.

When I gained enough strength, I deconstructed my room, tearing down the wallpaper and piling the trophies into a box. Second place, second place. After a while, I got the joke. They couldn't be recycled or donated. Nobody wanted them. They were literally worthless, except that they provided the moment I hadn't yet allowed myself: the moment I finally said good-bye to Maddy.

The box of trophies became trash, but none of it had been wasted.

I kept only the extra copy of my class's yearbook that Shelly had dug up, as a sort of apology, embarrassed to realize the pain she'd caused Maddy.

Everything else from high school, though, went into the garbage: the bulletin board, the wallpaper, the old cross-trainers. After a little hemming and hawing and pro-and-conning, I took the bulging roll of money from Yvonne's tip jar and gave it to my mom for the bills, saving back just enough to buy a new pair of running shoes.

I wore them to the first home meet the girls had, cheering and clapping as Mickie and Jessica tore through the finish line one, two.

This is where Courtney caught up with me. She came up the stands in jeans and a Midway High sweatshirt.

"Brought you something," she said, holding out a paper bag. Inside the bag: the little bits of stuff I'd once treasured. I rifled through them, then stood up, climbed down the risers to the garbage drum and tossed it all.

"You sure?" Courtney said. "There was a pretty cool baby sock in there."

I laughed. "I guess if I took that bag to a shrink, she'd be able to tell me what my problem was—is."

Courtney sat down next to me and stretched back on her elbows on the bench behind us. "Don't need a shrink for this one. What was the lineup? Pretty perfume bottle, romantic postcard, baby sock, little girl's barrette—I mean, that's a trajectory that's fairly clear to me."

It sounded so thin and needy. Maybe I did want those things in my life. Maybe I did want a future, a family. Who would fault that?

But I thought she didn't have the whole story. Maybe the things

I'd collected were the versions of myself I wanted to try on. Test the fit. Could I be this kind of woman? That kind? I wasn't sure I could explain it. "Please don't tell anyone that theory," I said.

"Like Tommy Beckwith, perhaps?"

My face burned. "Exactly like."

"So I have some questions," she said. "The forensics are starting to come in finally, and some of it just doesn't make any sense."

"Like . . . fingerprints and stuff?"

"Yeah, fibers under nails, phone records, all the crime-scene photos. It's just making us go over everything again. Like the photos of her neck," she said, and gestured to mine. The bruises from Coach's hands had finally begun to fade to a smudge of yellow. "It's not like fingerprints or DNA. Not a clinch. But your bruises and hers, well—Like I said, not enough to break the case." A shotgun start made us both look out at the track. Mickie again, fast as hell.

"The thing I never got was the diamond," I said. "Why did she bring it to Midway in the first place?"

"Good instincts." Courtney said, sitting up to watch Mickie's progress. "That girl can fly, can't she? Wow. Well, Maddy's computer from Chicago told us a few things. Her search history turned up a lot of eye-clawing research on what happens to little girls in this world, but there was some repeat activity around some assisted-care facility under construction." Courtney held out a brochure with a shiny new building on the front and photos of happy old people inside. "The theory is that she had plans for her stepmother to live there, but that doesn't seem right to me. You?"

"Vincent's parents, maybe?" I said. "Or grandparents? I don't know anything about his family."

She nodded thoughtfully. "Never thought of Maddy as an adult before now, you know? How she ended up—I mean, not dead. But grown up, making things happen, even with everything she went through, still taking care of everyone else."

Taking care of everyone else. I stood up.

"What's wrong?"

I turned the brochure over in my hand. These had been all over town. "This is the place over by the Mid-Night," I said. "How did Maddy have this?" Thoughts and memories rushed at me.

"She had an application for residence. I guess she sent for information? What am I missing?"

"Could someone younger live there?" I said. The words would hardly form in my mouth. "If they were sick, I mean?"

She looked at me. "How young?"

"Teeny Switzer can't be older than thirty," I said. "Fitz said he was helping her get into some new situation, but—"

Fitz. What would Coach do without Fitz? Nothing. That knock at the door of the Luxe before we knew we wouldn't run state, Coach's airy shoulder shrug that both his assistant coach and star athlete were missing. Fitz had known about Maddy's pregnancy not just because he was an adult and schooled in health and wellness, but because it would have been his job, not Coach's, to make arrangements. Maybe he didn't know the details. That might explain his irrational hatred of Beck.

But those other schools they'd worked, two years here, two years there. How long had Fitz been following behind, sweeping Coach's crimes under any convenient rug?

"But the money fell through," Courtney said. I had to remind myself what she was talking about. The new situation for Teeny that Fitz had mentioned hadn't worked out. "Someone came to town with a lot of money for Teeny's new place," she said in a musing voice. Writing the headline again, this time for the true story.

"In the form of a diamond that wouldn't be missed," I said.

We looked at each other.

"This person with the diamond perhaps made some threats or—or stipulations," Courtney said.

"An ultimatum," I said, imagining it easily. Maddy, fired up, off to meet Fitz somewhere in her little silver car, having slipped the diamond for safekeeping not in her room but in the ice machine. And unplugging it, just in case. And even more just in case—in case of the worst—the photo tucked behind the frame that only I would find.

Not a photo of Maddy being instructed by Coach, though there were a hundred pictures like that. No, this time it was Fitz reaching in. Not to instruct her, but to tame her. To smooth things over. To take care of things.

The deal Maddy wanted to make with Fitz would have been—what? Coach goes to jail? Coach goes into retirement? Maybe she'd allowed herself some hope that Fitz would agree. That he would somehow talk Coach into moving on, at least, as they'd done so many times before. He'd be tired of cleaning up after all Coach's indiscretions, tired of making the apologies, making things right. I remembered watching him pull Teeny out of danger as I drove past the park. He wanted her off his hands, somewhere safe, somewhere with better locks on the doors.

Fitz might have even thought Maddy owed him one. It must have come as a terrible surprise when she didn't consider what he'd done for her a favor. Another surprise: that she'd known about Teeny. I wonder how far her research had taken her, how many girls she'd found among the reports not officially filed, the deals made, the secrets kept?

She hadn't come to help Fitz settle Teeny. She'd come to unsettle the comfortable life he and Coach had built.

With one, beautiful stone, she must have tried to strike a bargain. The diamond, for their retirement. The diamond, for their withdrawal. The diamond, for the girls.

And she lost.

Courtney hadn't said anything for a long time. "The bruises on Maddy's neck were from larger hands than the ones on mine," I said. "Weren't they?"

She pulled out her phone and held it to her ear. To me, she said, "You know, I'm glad no one's keeping score on who's solving this thing," she said. "You're a pretty decent detective. Did you ever think about joining the force?"

"Wait," I said, staring down at the dizzying colors of my new running shoes. Too bright, too clean. I looked like I was trying too hard, but I didn't care. I wanted to try hard. I had already decided what I wanted to be, and now that I wasn't cleaning the Mid-Night Inn anymore, it was time for me to begin. But everything was changing too fast.

Both of them? I would lose both? All?

The desire to deny what I knew was strong. This is how Coach had gotten through so many times. Because the truth of what he'd done and been allowed to do was uncomfortable. I didn't want to face it, or him. I couldn't bear for it to be true, and yet I knew it was.

"Look, Juliet, I don't mind making this quiet, but he's a dangerous guy."

"Just—" I located Fitz in the inner circle of grass. He was noting something on a clipboard and yelling encouragement to the girls racing by. A breeze blew the raw scent of cut grass over the stands, but it didn't smell like spring, like a new start. I only smelled decay, life cut short.

The girls. The girls would need someone to tell them the truth. They would need someone to steady them without a single intimidating gesture.

I had already talked to someone at a college in Indianapolis about part-time school, about scholarships and loans. I would need a job, and I had applications out. It would take years, probably. The plan was hazy. *What could you do different?* my dad had asked me, back when I'd been struggling with my college courses. I could try. Nothing else was up to me, but I could try.

"Just wait by the outside fence," I said to Courtney.

I stepped down from the bleachers and walked the distance to the opening in the fence to the track. Every step was shattering. I felt as though I were leaving pieces of myself behind as I went.

I waited for a lull in the heats, then crossed the red lanes of the track into the grassy field. The girls looked up at my approach, pleased. "Hey, Coach," Jessica said, grinning. She had tied a Midway-red ribbon around her ponytail.

Fitz glanced up from his clipboard, equal parts alarm and hope, then disappointment. His eyes flicked behind me, presumably finding Courtney, maybe a few more officers in uniform by now, a police car or two waiting without sirens or lights. He dropped his arms, the clipboard dangling at his side.

"Fitz," I said.

"I—I knew it would be you," he said. He seemed almost proud. "I thought maybe, if you covered my classes, helped out with the team—maybe . . ."

He'd meant to keep me busy, then, not safe. But he hadn't counted on one thing.

He couldn't have known I would care for the girls more than either of them ever had, not for what they could be, but for what they were, right now.

"I didn't mean to—I never . . . I'm sorry." He gazed over the top of my head.

I didn't check behind me. I had my eyes on the girls. They were all I cared about. They were all I could see. They were starting to look concerned. Jessica took Mickie's arm. I took the clipboard from Fitz and stepped between him and the team, clearing the path for him to leave the field, the track, their lives, and mine. I watched him as far as the fence, then turned to the team.

They waited to see what I would say.

"Young-women Panthers," I started, not sure where it would lead. There were so many things to say. So many things to warn them about. All I could do now was keep them running. They would need to be quick. They would need to run as fast as they could.

ACKNOWLEDGMENTS

My sincerest gratitude goes to the people who made this book possible. Thank you to Sharon Bowers of Miller Bowers Griffin Literary Management and to Dan Mayer and all the good people at Seventh Street Books/Prometheus Books, including Jon Kurtz, Jill Maxick, Cheryl Quimba, Nicole Sommer-Lecht, Jade Zora Scibilia, Bruce Carle, and Melissa Raé Shofner. Thank you to everyone at JKS Communications for their expertise.

I have found support, encouragement, and much more from the Mystery Writers of America Midwest Chapter, especially Clare O'Donohue, Heather E. Ash, Sara Paretsky, Julie Hyzy, Matthew Clemens, Terence Faherty, Susanna Calkins. Thanks also to the Seventh Street Books Bunnies, especially Lynne Raimondo; Catriona McPherson and the Sisters in Crime; Mary Anne Mohanraj; and Christopher Coake.

Thank you once again to all the writing teachers who encouraged me over my lifetime, and a heartfelt thank you to the librarians and booksellers who have taken such an interest in my work. Special thanks to the sweethearts who run Story Studio Chicago and Midwest Writers Workshop for keeping me in school, and all the volunteers who make the mystery-conference world go 'round.

Special thanks to my partners in crime, especially Kim Rader, Kristi Brenock-Leduc, Meghan Eagan, Tricia David, Amanda Lumpkin, and all the readers in my life who couldn't wait to get their hands on my book and tell people about it, especially Beth, Melissa, Scoots, Denise, Doreen, Krista, Sam, and Adam.

Tremendous thanks to my first readers, Yvonne Strumecki and

Lauren Stacks Yamaoka, who gave time, feedback, advice, and exclamation points. Thanks doubly to "Stacks" for her running expertise. Any bad advice Juliet gives is my error, not Lauren's.

The biggest appreciation goes to my family, of course: Paula and Danny Dodson; Mel and Janie Rader; the Bryans; all of the Days; and all of the Raders, including the next generation, who would like very much to be remembered here this time around.

And to Greg, last but most.

ABOUT THE AUTHOR

Lori Rader-Day's debut mystery, *The Black Hour*, received starred reviews from *Publishers Weekly*, *Booklist*, and *Library Journal* and was a finalist for the Mary Higgins Clark Award. Her short fiction has appeared in *Ellery Queen Mystery Magazine*, *Time Out Chicago*, and *Good Housekeeping*. Lori is a member of Mystery Writers of America, Sisters in Crime, and International Thriller Writers. She lives in Chicago with her husband and her dog.